Rose City Free Fall

By DL Barbur

CHAPTER ONE

As soon as James Wendt was done having sex with his girlfriend, I was either going to arrest him or kill him. It would be up to him which happened. I sat there listening to the sounds of creaking bedsprings and slapping flesh coming from cheap speakers.

My partner Mandy and I sat in a dusty storeroom over a Korean market in Northeast Portland. Mounted on a tripod between us was a laser microphone. As long as I kept it aimed at the window of the house across the street, we could hear what was going on inside.

I put my magazine down, checked my watch. They'd been at it for four minutes.

"Soon. He won't last much longer." Mandy nodded, a little pink under her freckles.

She was more than ten years younger than me. I sometimes felt like I was toting a high school kid around, but she was a good partner. I tended to go through partners quickly. It wasn't that we didn't get along, just that I tended to wear them out. They couldn't keep up.

The noises from across the street came to a crescendo. To my ear, Brenda, James's old lady, sounded like she was faking it. She should have plenty of practice. James came by every month like clockwork, made her cash her state checks and give him half the money.

I stood, wincing at the pain in my knees. Who knew that when I jumped out of airplanes more than fifteen years ago, the wet Oregon winters would make me pay for it now? I took a few seconds to limber up. It might be important later.

As we walked down the steps, I made sure my radio earpiece was in place and unzipped my raincoat so I had free access to the Glock on my right hip. I could practically feel the enthusiasm washing off Mandy. She was still young enough to get excited by this sort of thing.

In the store's back room, Mrs. Park was sitting at the desk, pecking away at a computer with one hand, rocking her baby grandson in his little carrier with the other.

"Hello, Detective Miller." She waved at me, not really looking up from her math. "Hello, Detective Mandy." For some reason she refused to call Williams by her last name.

"Hello, Mrs. Park. Might want to stay back here for a little while. Things might get exciting across the street."

She nodded. "We'll be ok." Mr. Park had scavenged some sheet steel and bolted it to the wall between the office and the rest of the store. An SKS rifle leaned in the corner. I had met the Parks one night when I responded to a brief, futile and lethal robbery attempt on their store. They were nice folks.

Mr. Park was cleaning the already spotless counter. The store was empty. I checked my watch.

In half an hour the store would be full of kids coming home from school. If I didn't make my move on Wendt by then, I'd have to wait until after the kids cleared out.

Wendt was a bad man, a meth addict and dealer, in his mid-twenties, young enough to engage in violence for the fun of it, old enough to be good at it. He had a long record, stretching back to when he was a juvie. At fourteen, he'd beat another kid with a bat.

I had two good homicides on him. The first one didn't bother me much. He'd killed a man named Lenny Vaughn over a dope deal. As near as I could reconstruct things, Lenny shorted Wendt, causing Wendt to pull out a 9mm and spray the inside of Lenny's apartment with a full magazine, hitting Lenny almost incidentally in the process. In police work, we called that a "twofer." One criminal dead, another going to jail for a long time, maybe forever.

The problem was that Lenny lived in a duplex. Those fifteen 9mm rounds had gone through the sheetrock common wall without even slowing down. The responding patrol guys hadn't thought to check next door until I got there. I found Mrs. Rosenburg in her living room, lying in a puddle of sticky blood. Her glasses had fallen off her face and her cat had been sitting on her chest. She'd been in her mid seventies, lived alone, liked to take care of the neighborhood children.

Outside of the Parks's store, Mandy stayed in the spot we'd pre-arranged, hanging out in front of the store, right across the street from the apartment building's front door. Brenda lived in a giant old Victorian house converted to apartments. Four apartments upstairs, four down, hallway and stairway down the middle. Front door, back door, both on the first floor. Brenda lived on the second floor. There was a fire escape, but I didn't think Wendt would use it.

I walked around to the apartment building's backyard, a narrow strip of mud with the odd tuft of brown grass scattered here and there. I stood with my back to the wall, right next to the back door.

I'd been looking for Wendt for two months. His fingerprints were all over the shell casings in Lenny's apartment. These days everybody watched CSI and knew to wipe down the outsides of their weapons, but nobody ever remembered to wear gloves when they loaded their magazines. Word on the street was that Wendt had bragged about wasting Lenny. The detective work hadn't taken any startling leaps of deduction. I'd had him pegged as my primary suspect in a few hours. The problem was finding him.

The bastard was sly. He didn't stay in one place for too long, didn't hang with his usual running buddies. But he needed cash from somebody, and I finally found out who he was getting it from.

I knew when November's electronic benefit money would be deposited in Brenda's account. I'd watched him walk up, go in Brenda's place. I'd watched them walk to the corner store and buy a couple of tall Pabst Blue Ribbons before going back to Brenda's. I could have taken him then, but he'd made Brenda carry the beer so his hands were free. I didn't put it past him to screw a gun in her ear if he saw the heat coming. No, I wanted him with a fat roll of twenties in his pocket, with a beer in his belly and still warm and fuzzy from a roll in the hay with Brenda. He would be distracted, making it more likely that I could take him without gunfire.

I didn't care about shooting Wendt, but I knew he liked to spray bullets around. I was worried about who else might get hit, like the Parks and their grandkid.

The back door hung crooked on its hinges. You had to walk up a couple of narrow wooden stairs to get to it. I stood there with my back to the wall, my Danner boots squelching in the mud. When he came out, I would be standing to his right.

I imagined what it would look like if Wendt came running out the door and saw me. He'd reach across his body for his piece, and arc all the way back over to his right before he could bring it to bear. If I stood to his left, he could just pull it out and blast me. Little things like that matter.

If I played my cards right, he would never know what hit him. I checked the hinges of the screen door, it would open out and to Wendt's left, away from me. Marvelous.

Strictly speaking, I was supposed to have all sorts of back up on an apprehension like this. My supervisor would have to be involved, we would most likely use the SWAT team. But stuff like that took time to set up. I'd tried it their way already. Weeks ago, I'd tracked Wendt to an abandoned building. By the time all the ducks were in a row, he was long gone. He must have smelled us or something. This time we were doing it my way.

It was a gray and drizzly day. It wasn't raining currently, but it was November in Portland, so I was sure that would change. It was just cold enough that I wanted a coat when I was sitting around, just warm enough to sweat if I had to exert myself.

"Dent? You there?" Mandy's voice crackled in my earpiece. She had only called me Denton once. I hated my first name, kept threatening to change it. We weren't supposed to use first names on the radio, but I had my own way of doing communications too. Our radios could use almost a hundred channels. Today we were using the Multnomah County Drainage District Levee Flood Patrol tactical channel. Since the river didn't look particularly high today, I figured we'd have it all to ourselves. If the office wanted to get in touch, they could call my cell phone.

"What's up Mandy?"

"I just saw somebody through the window, moving through the second-floor hallway."

"Cool. Stay frosty."

"Damn!" She sounded breathless. "He just stepped out front, looked at me and went back in. I think he made me."

Mandy looked like a cop. She was a fireplug of a woman, with her hair done up in a sensible braid that wouldn't give anybody a handhold in a fight. Today she was wearing tan Royal Robbins "tactical" pants, a polo shirt and a black vest with a bunch of pockets to cover up all her cop crap. She might as well have put a sign around her neck that said "Plan Clothes Cop." There was a reason I wore faded jeans, an untucked Hawaiian shirt and a raincoat that had seen better days. We had talked about this, but like I said, you could only teach somebody so far, then they had to learn for themselves.

"Hold on," I said. "I need you to keep the front locked down for me. Watch those second-floor windows."

Now Wendt would do one of two things. Maybe he would run

upstairs and barricade himself in Brenda's apartment and take her hostage. In which case he would probably end his day with a .308 caliber hole in his head, courtesy of a police sniper.

The second possibility was that Wendt would run out the back. Since running had worked for him before, I was guessing that he would do it now. I pulled my ASP expanding baton out of my back pocket. In its collapsed form it was a metal cylinder, about eight inches long. I knew Wendt would be packing heat, so I was technically bringing a metal pipe to a gun fight. Not too smart under normal circumstances, but I was planning an ambush, so normal rules didn't apply.

I heard him coming, heard the squeak of his sneakered feet on the curling linoleum of the apartment hallway, heard him panting as he ran. Meth is bad for your cardio fitness, I guess. The screen door flew open and I got a flash of a scrawny white dude in a blue satin tracksuit two sizes too big for him, baseball cap backward. Scruffy attempt at a beard. Wendt for sure.

I don't like to brag, but I timed it perfectly. I flicked my wrist out and up, and the ASP went from being eight inches long to twenty-one in an eye blink. The telescoping metal shafts locked into place and the round steel tip landed exactly on the tip of Wendt's elbow with the sweet smack that I associated with a baseball heading for the fence. I heard bones crack. Out of the park baby.

I brought the ASP back for another shot, then yelled, "Portland Police, get down on the ground!" Wendt gave an inarticulate little moan and grabbed his suddenly non-functioning right arm with his left hand. Perfect. He wasn't even thinking about his gun.

"Stop resisting!" I yelled as I unloaded the second blow, lower this time. His knee cap popped with a sound like a coke bottle breaking. He bounced down the steps and onto his face before I could get the ASP back for a third blow. Two shots would have to do. I'd ambush a guy, but hitting him while he was down wasn't right, unless he looked like he was thinking about getting back up.

Wendt showed no sign of going anywhere. He was lying face down in the dirt, making mewling kitten noises.

When I grabbed his right arm and bent it back behind his back, it felt like it was full of broken glass and gravel.

He screamed. I ignored him and cuffed him up, then patted him down real quick, arms, legs, the back of his waistband. I didn't find anything but I could tell the elbow and knee were already swollen.

Looked like we would be stopping at the hospital before we went to jail.

"Oh, man, you broke my arm. My knee," Wendt whined.

"Quit your bitching. You're under arrest." I rolled him over on his back, now his weight was on his broken arm and he screamed again.

There it was, tucked in his waistband, a cheap Brazilian 9mm, bright chrome, fake ass mother-of-pearl grips, fifteen round magazine.

"Dent? Dent?" It was Mandy's voice in my ear again.

"I got him. Come on around."

She popped around the corner a second later. She looked a little annoyed when she saw Wendt trussed up on the ground. I hoped she didn't think I'd cut her out of the action on purpose. I'd talk to her later. The irritation only lasted for a second, then she broke out in a grin.

"We got him," she said.

"Right on. Good work." I handed her the Taurus carefully. I hadn't cleared it. She took it and laid it on the steps.

I had a certain amount of disdain for Mandy's black vest, but I had to hand it to her, she managed somehow to cram the contents of your average police cruiser's trunk in the damn thing. She pulled out two evidence baggies and a pair of nitrile gloves. She donned the gloves, then unloaded the 9mm with precise motions. The gun went in one bag, the magazine and stray round of ammo from the chamber went in another.

I nodded my approval. "Do me a favor and whistle us up a medic and a patrol car for our friend here."

She nodded and pulled out her radio to change the channel. I finished searching Wendt while he cried and moaned. I dumped the contents of his pockets into the dirt beside his head. A roll of twenties, I made a mental note to give those back to Brenda; a crumpled up bus pass; three knives, one in each front pocket, one in his left sock, all of them cheap; then in the bottom of his right front pocket I found a little plastic baggy full of what looked like wet, dirty sugar. Methamphetamine.

Mandy was watching me search as she talked on the radio. She held out a gloved hand and I put the bindle of meth in it. That went in another evidence bag. Compared to the two murder charges, it was like an overdue library book, but we had to be thorough.

Wendt was doing plenty of pleading right now. "Man, you gotta get me a doctor," he whined. "My arm hurts. My leg hurts."

I rolled my eyes. I walked over and pulled him upright, so he was sitting on the dirt on his ass instead of lying on his busted arm.

"Sit still. The medics will be here soon."

I was over in the weeds collecting my baton when the fire truck rolled up out front. I heard the heavy engine come to a halt. I walked around the corner of the house to wave them in, remembering to pull my badge out from under my shirt and let it hang on the chain around my neck. I collapsed the baton and put it back in my jeans pocket.

The patrol car Mandy had asked for rolled up as the firemen were getting their medical gear off the truck. I didn't recognize the kid driving. He was a white guy, tall, blond hair in a high and tight haircut. He wore those wraparound sunglasses I hated so much. I wondered at what point the Bureau quit hiring new cops and just started cloning them up at the research hospital on the hill.

Mr. Park was standing in front of his store, arms across his chest. I saw him speak to the officer, saw the officer nod curtly back in reply and keep walking. Punk. Unless there was shooting going on, you should always stop and talk to the citizens. Part of the salary that kid got paid every year came out of Mr. Park's pocket so the least he could do was shoot the breeze for a few seconds. Besides you never knew when you might need to set up surveillance over a man's convenience store.

The Fire Bureau paramedic that went to work on Wendt was young too, lanky, had a little diamond stud in the side of her nose. When did the hose draggers start allowing stuff like that on duty? She was a little snotty when she asked me to take the cuffs off. She kept looking at Wendt's scrawny little crankster ass, then back at me.

I run about 6'4", two fifty if I've been watching the cheeseburgers and beer. I had about eight inches and probably an easy ninety, hundred pounds on Wendt. After I took the cuffs off, I went over and made a big show of holding Wendt's gun up in its plastic baggie. It must have looked impressive, all big and shiny because she knocked it off. Geez, you go out of your way to keep from shooting a guy and nobody appreciates it. They think you picked on some little guy just because you like it.

The young patrol cop ambled over, his face impassive, his eyes unreadable behind the glasses. He took in the scene: the paramedics working on Wendt; Mandy cataloging evidence; me standing there in my scruffy clothes. I stuck out a hand.

"Dent Miller, Major Crimes." We didn't have a "homicide" division in Portland per se. This would imply that our fair city actually had enough homicides to warrant its own unit. Which it did. But in addition to murders, we handled rapes, robberies, most any violent felonies.

"Officer Bloem," he said, shaking my hand briefly. *Officer* Bloem. Jesus. I had boots with more time on the street than this nugget. I introduce myself with my first name, but he's *Officer* Bloem.

"Soon as they patch him together, we will transport him to the hospital." Mandy and I couldn't transport prisoners in our unmarked car. It lacked a cage dividing the backseat from the front. That was one rule I followed religiously. Bloem just nodded.

The paramedic shook her head. "No can do. This guy can't walk. He has to go by ambulance."

I rolled my eyes. Since Wendt was in custody, the department would have to pick up the ambulance bill, as well as the bill from the hospital. Most of the time, the paramedics patched them up enough so we could carry them to the hospital in the back of a cruiser. We saved the taxpayers some bucks that way.

I took a deep breath, let it out. I did the math in my head: use of force report, reports on the ambulance ride and the hospital visit. I could do some of it at the hospital while we were waiting on Wendt to get fixed up. "Ok. Call him up a limo and let's get this show on the road."

I turned to Bloem. "Guess we won't need you after all." He nodded, turned to go without a word. I watched his back for a few seconds. He walked like he had something up his ass.

I turned, Mandy was behind me.

"Hey, Dent. You go back to the office, do your part of the paperwork. I'll stay with Wendt at the hospital and tuck him in at the jail. If you hurry, you can still take Audrey out for her birthday."

"You sure?" It was Friday night. It didn't seem fair for me to be out having fun while she was stuck with Wendt.

She shrugged. "Sure. I can use the overtime." That was a laugh. My partners usually wound up screaming to work less overtime.

"You rock, Mandy." I headed for the car, not giving Wendt a second glance. When they were running free, suspects were fascinating. Once I bagged them, they were just a statistic.

As I left, she yelled after me. "Don't forget we're catching this weekend!"

I turned, nodded and went on. That meant if a homicide or suspicious death happened over the weekend, it was our turn to catch the call. What she really meant was, "don't show up with beer on your breath like last time." People were picky about stuff like that these days. I had joined the bureau in the middle of a transition. My mentors had all been men with scarred knuckles who figured if you didn't have a drinking problem and a few divorces, you weren't a real cop. Everybody hired since me seemed to be young, educated, and into things like Pilates and yoga.

I retrieved our unmarked car from behind the Park's store, then pulled around front so I could collect my eavesdropping gear from upstairs. They were busy selling Pixie Sticks and Gummi Bears to the after-school crowd. It was like something out of a Norman Rockwell painting, something this neighborhood desperately needed. The kids that weren't inside buying candy milled about out front, ogling the fire truck.

As I was putting the laser thingy in the trunk, I heard a voice. "Excuse me, mister?" I looked around for a second, then looked down. It was a little blonde kid, maybe ten, probably younger, I was bad at telling kids' ages.

"Are you a policeman?" He looked at my dirty jeans, then the badge hanging around my neck.

I nodded, guessing at what was coming.

"Can I have a sticker?"

Every morning, I strapped on two guns, three knives, handcuffs, pepper spray, a baton, a radio and my badge, all of it without the benefit of a black tactical vest. I also always made sure I had stickers for the kids.

I pulled a roll out of my breast pocket. "McGruff the Crime Dog says stay in school." My favorite. I counted the kids on the street, pulled out enough for him to hand out some to his buddies too. Maybe it would earn him some cool points, maybe it wouldn't.

"Here. Some for you, some for your friends."

He smiled. That was pretty cool. Most kids these days didn't seem impressed by something unless it lit up and made noise.

"Thanks."

"Stay out of trouble." I waved and hopped in the car. Ordinarily, I would have stuck around and talked to the kid. Back in my patrol days I always let the kids climb in the front of the car and play with the lights, sometimes the siren.

But today I was in a hurry. Paperwork. Then Audrey's birthday. Driving one handed, I dialed Aud's number. Her voice mail didn't have a message. Just a beep.

"Hey, it's me." I waited for a minute, hoping she would pick up. Nothing. Probably still out. "I'm finishing up. Take me an hour and a half, two hours, tops. Then I'll be over. Bye." I hung up before I realized I should have said "I love you." I always forgot that. Nobody ever said it to me when I was a kid, so I guess I never learned how.

I dialed the shift sergeant, an old dinosaur named Dan Winter, to let him know what went down. It was standard procedure when you arrested somebody. I explained how Wendt had been armed with a handgun and I had to tune him up with an ASP, sent him to the hospital. He grunted and reminded me to do the paperwork before I went home. Dan was going to retire in another year. He already had a place bought out in Sun River.

I bombed west on Burnside, flipped on the radio just in time for a Warren Zevon rock block. Perfect. It was getting dark. The sun was putting on a show behind the west hills. Say what you want about the weather in Portland, we had some good sunsets. I weaved in and out of traffic, compulsively looking at the clock on the dash as I went. I crossed the river, headed straight through downtown instead of turning off to go to Central Precinct.

I really didn't have time for this, but I was doing it anyway.

I cruised up Burnside, gaining altitude and property values as I went. I was cutting through Forest Park, big enough to have a population of black bears. It was hard to believe you were in a major city once you got up here.

The cemetery was on top of the ridge. It started raining as I pulled in, just a light mist. It was quiet and you could see for miles. They called it Skyline Drive for a reason. It was a huge cemetery, but I found the grave quickly. I knew the place well. Sometimes I wondered if I knew more dead people in the graveyard than I did live people in the city down below. I was afraid to do the math.

I parked the Crown Vic, went squelching through the mud, gathering rocks as I went. Mrs. Rosenburg had two daughters and two sons. One of each lived in Seattle, the others in southern California. One was a doctor, I forget which. The others all had the sheen of people who looked good and went to meetings for a living. They seemed to regard settling her estate up like some kind of unpleasant, but necessary task, like homework.

They had buried her up here, over the city where she had lived all her life. I got the feeling this was more because it was easiest than because they put any thought into what she wanted. None of them had seemed particularly interested in finding out who killed their mom.

Her grave was next to her husband's. He'd died ten years ago. Stomach cancer. I stood there for a minute, silently, looking at the Star of David on the headstone. I left the rocks piled on top of the headstone, to show that somebody had come. I'd read on the Internet that was an old Jewish tradition. I'd be back with more after the trial or the guilty plea.

It started raining harder. I slogged back to the car, started thinking about my cases, trying to decide what suspect I would pursue next. I stopped myself and made myself think of where I would take Audrey for dinner tonight.

The graveyard attendant was locking the gate as I pulled out. I waved and headed the car towards downtown and my paperwork.

CHAPTER TWO

Since it was almost four o'clock on a Friday by the time I got back to the office, I thought I had a pretty good chance of finishing my paperwork without having to deal with The Seagull.

The Seagull was my boss, Steve Lubbock. We called him that because of his tendency to swoop in, make a bunch of noise, shit all over everything and then fly away. Lubbock had been working for the Bureau for twenty years, fourteen of them as a Lieutenant. He wasn't ever going to make Captain. I had a hard time thinking of him as a fellow cop. Somebody said the term "Law Enforcement Administrator" around me once, and it stuck in my head. I was a cop. Lubbock was a "Law Enforcement Administrator." That distinction didn't mean much to the outside world, but it made him easier for me to deal with.

As I had hoped, all the cubicles in our office were deserted. I sat down and started typing my reports.

I sidestepped a few issues rather delicately in my use of force report. It wasn't exactly kosher to smack a suspect silly with an ASP baton as they came running out the door. Basically, I had ambushed Wendt, and I would be the first to admit it, at least to myself. It wasn't an approved procedure. Hell, it wasn't even legal. But I knew guys like Wendt. He was just dumb and vicious enough to provoke a standoff on a crowded street or bring on an exchange of gunfire with a bunch of innocent people in the middle. I liked it this way. It was over and done with, with nobody hurt but Wendt.

I flipped on the FM radio, just in time for the blues hour on one of the independent stations. Pinetop Perkins. Outstanding. My office cubicle contained a desk, a computer, a filing cabinet, and a cheap FM radio. Nothing else. Nothing on the walls. The desk was usually bare. My battered leather valise was my real office.

My office was bare for two reasons. For one thing, I never spent any time in it, even before Lubbock became my boss. I preferred to be out on the street. It was also a defense mechanism. I reserved the mental right to quit at any time, to go in and lay my gun and badge on the chief's desk and walk away so I could do something else. I told myself that having nothing in my office to go back for would make that easier.

It was stupid, really. I had never figured out what else I would do, but pretending I had a way out kept me relatively sane. Mentally I had one foot out the door ever since the day I figured out the Bureau didn't give a rat's ass about me. Collectively, it only cared about the Bureau. So I decided I would only care about me, whoever my partner was, and people like Mrs. Rosenburg.

The paperwork wasn't as bad as I had made it out to be in my head. It never was, especially after you developed a knack for it. I was good at paperwork. Early in my career, I'd lost a few cases in court because of a misplaced word here, an unclear sentence there. I hated to lose, especially to some smart ass lawyer, so I'd become a master at paperwork, but I still hated doing it.

A shiver went down my spine and I swiveled in my chair. Damn. There he was: Steve Lubbock, the Seagull, standing in the entrance to my cubicle. Usually, I could feel it when somebody was standing behind me. I'd turn and check them out without even thinking about it. I'd never really figured it out. It was like they gave off vibrations or something. But Lubbock was like some vibrational black hole. The one talent he had seemed to be sneaking up and eavesdropping on people before they knew he was there.

"Why wasn't I notified about the Wendt arrest?" Lubbock asked. When he said it his eyes darted around the room, never landing on my eyes or even my face. Lubbock rarely looked anybody in the eye. When he did, it was usually a sign that he was lying to you and trying to appear earnest.

"I called Winters. I wanted to follow the chain of command." Lubbock was a big fan of the chain of command. I was careful to keep my voice neutral.

Lubbock wrinkled his nose up like he smelled something he didn't like. He was a skinny little dude, short, with a short man's ego. He dressed like a million bucks. I had to give him that. Nice suits, linen, Italian silk, some damn thing like that. I could never tell.

Lubbock's eyes bounced and rolled around in his head like little marbles, never lighting on one thing for long. It was fascinating to watch, although if I wasn't careful I could get seasick. Suddenly they stopped, I could almost hear the tendons straining to keep his eyes still. His beady little eyes focused like laser beams on the knees of my blue jeans. He hated it when I wore blue jeans. Even worse, these particular blue jeans had big muddy spots on them. My boots were covered in mud too.

I might have even tracked some on the carpet. One of Lubbock's first priorities, when he took over Major Crimes was new carpet for the office. He'd fought like a badger for his carpet. At any point in the hundred-step process in the administrative chain, his request for new carpet could have been killed, but finally, he'd won, brought back the signed purchase order for the carpet like a man with a prize deer he'd just shot.

Lubbock took a step forward, bent a little at the waist, I guess so he could see my pants better.

"Miller, you're a Portland Police Bureau Detective, for god's sake. If you aren't willing to dress like it, maybe this job isn't for you."

It wasn't the first time Lubbock had not so discretely mentioned that maybe I should transfer out. I had the highest clearance rate of all the Major Crimes detectives but what the hell did that matter when I had mud on my blue jeans.

I felt myself getting angry. This couldn't end well. I stood up, rather abruptly I guess because Lubbock took a jerky step back. It was the kind of hard-wired reflex that nervous little men with no confidence hated themselves for. He turned red and I suppressed a smile. I hadn't planned it this way, but I'd take it.

"You're right, Steve." He hated it when I called him Steve. He liked to be called "EllTee" by his guys. It made him feel cool. "I should get myself home and change."

I hit the button that would finalize my report. "I just sent the Wendt report to Sgt. Winters."

I pulled my coat off the back of my chair and put it on, picked up my valise. There was an awkward little moment when I took a step forward, waited for him to get out of my way.

Finally, he moved, and I walked away, leaving him standing there in my cubicle.

The halls of Central Precinct were deserted. Friday. It's good to work for the government. I used to stick around on Fridays, make a few phone calls, run down a few leads, look over the occasional cold case. It was quiet on Fridays, I could get a lot of work done. But now

Lubbock was always there, doing what, I don't know, certainly not useful work. A quick poll of twenty cops had shown that none of them could remember Lubbock actually arresting anybody.

Van Halen was on the car radio as I pulled out into traffic. "Little Dreamer," a classic from the first album. It took me back to high school, back to sitting on a hill outside of a Tennessee town, looking at the lights, getting mosquito bit and touching a girl's breasts for the first time.

It was one of the few pleasant memories I had of growing up. I hadn't been back to Tennessee since I was eighteen. My last view of my home town had been in my rear-view mirror as the Army recruiter gave me a ride to the airport.

As I sat there in traffic, watching tail lights and sucking exhaust fumes, I thought about quitting. I did that too much, especially when the bullshit got too deep and I didn't have a good case to work. Lubbock's attitude shouldn't have stung me, but it did. I brought down a grade-A murderer like Wendt without a shootout and instead of an "attaboy" I got static because of my blue jeans.

I knew exactly how much money I needed to walk out the door. I was a cheap bastard, had been even when I was a kid in the Army. I mustered out with enough cash in my pockets to buy a car and live pretty well through college.

I kept my thrifty habits after I graduated and landed at the Bureau. I owned my house outright and, as long as I stayed away from the guitar store and the gun store, I only spent about half of what I made. The rest went into deferred comp, mutual funds, bonds, you name it. I called it my "fuck you" money. I knew someday the Bureau would go too far and I'd say "fuck you" and walk out. Hopefully, it would be after I was eligible to retire, but if it came before, I didn't want those bastards to have a leash on my neck just because of a damn paycheck.

So as I drove, I did a little thing in my head I called "running the numbers." I knew what I had, barring daily market fluctuations, usually down to a couple grand or so. I knew what I needed to walk out the door and not live on cat food for the rest of my life. I still didn't have enough, not yet.

Besides, what would I do anyway? I'd go crazy if I didn't work. I hadn't made the right friends in the Bureau, the ones that could get me cushy corporate security gigs, or find me work as a consultant. I didn't think I would fit into those circles anyway.

Damn. I needed to quit wasting my time with this, needed to just accept the fact that I was in for a while. I constantly felt like the guy in the cartoons with the little angel on one shoulder, a devil on the other. I always had trouble with commitments. I had liked the Army. What the hell could be more fun for a twenty-year-old than getting paid to shoot guns and jump out of airplanes? But after eighteen years of feeling trapped in that dirty ass Tennessee town, the hold the Army had on my life had felt just too stifling.

I had less of a noose around my neck in the Bureau, but it still chafed. Sometimes I wondered what was wrong with me, why I couldn't just be happy with the way things were. Some people are just wired that way, I guess.

CHAPTER THREE

Despite my repeated suggestions that she move in with me, Audrey lived in an apartment off Hawthorne. It was a funky old converted Victorian, painted yellow. I found a space around back and parked.

I didn't see Audrey's Honda in the lot and sighed. She wasn't answering her cell phone, so she was probably working late again. I let myself in with the key she'd given me, tromped up the stairs to her apartment.

Audrey and I had similar tastes in interior decorating: less is more. She was better at it than I was. Her place had an air of Zen-like simplicity, all plain polished wood, low furniture, a few tasteful prints, a single flower vase. My place just looked like I was too cheap to buy much furniture. Which I had to admit was true.

My phone buzzed with an incoming text. "Staying late for a private lesson, back at seven." It gave me time to take a shower and change clothes at least.

Audrey had never said no to moving in with me, but she'd never actually done it either. We each had a closet at the other's place though. Maybe these days that should be counted as a real commitment. Mine held a few changes of clothes and a small lock box.

I opened the box and started putting my gear inside. First came the Glock 9mm off my right hip, then my little .38 revolver out of my right front pocket. Next came the knives, a nice Benchmade folder and a pair of Cold Steel Incorporated push daggers. I finished off with the ASP and my can of pepper spray.

Audrey and I got along pretty well, considering we came from the opposite end of a great many things. The one blow-out fight we'd had was over my tools. She hated them, didn't want them in her apartment, didn't want me to carry them when we were out together. We had finally compromised on the lock box. I put my stuff in there when I came in, put it on when we left. When I was off duty, I usually only carried one gun and a couple of knives. No reason to be paranoid.

I stripped off my clothes and got in the shower. I caught a glimpse of myself in the mirror. Even though it had been there for over twenty years, I still winced sometimes when I saw the tattoo on my chest. It said "Front Towards Enemy," the words molded into the front of an Army issue M18 Claymore antipersonnel mine. I'd gotten the tattoo one evening in Fort Bragg after too many beers. It was still my philosophy towards life, but nonetheless, I regretted the tattoo.

I stood there motionless and let scalding hot water play over my back and shoulders for a long time. I let the warmth seep into my skin and tried to focus on the white noise of the shower, let it fill my mind. I always took ridiculously long showers after work. The deal with Lubbock had bothered me more than I wanted to admit to myself.

I couldn't help it. Sometimes I saw Lubbock, and the past grabbed me with a giant hand by the collar, jerked me back to what was it? Ten years ago now? Yeah, ten years.

James Elroy David. Like many serial killers and mass murderers, he had three first names. He got fired from his job as a security guard at Pioneer Place, the mall downtown. Instead of cooling his jets and collecting unemployment, he came back the next day with an AK-47 and a duffel bag of ammo.

By some cruel twist of fate, Lubbock was the first one there. The rest of us arrived all at once, stared at each other in disbelief as we stood in the middle of the street and watched Lubbock yell orders in a voice a couple of octaves higher than normal. We could barely hear him over the heavy knocking on wood sound of that AK coming through the doors of the mall. He wanted one of us to find a place to park the news media, another to figure out where we were going to park the mobile command post and the rest to set up a perimeter. In that order. Meanwhile, people were running out of the mall with blood all over them.

Some guys actually took off to do what he said. After all, he was a Lieutenant. Four of us just stood there, frozen for a second in disbelief. I didn't know the other three. I was new to day shift. Later I would find out two of them were veterans with some Vietnam trigger time. There was me. I had about five years on the job. The fourth guy was even younger than me, but he knew what was up.

The four of us never spoke, never conferred. We just went for it, while Lubbock stood there screaming at our backs.

I remember walking out of the mall, an hour later, into the bright July sunshine. My feet stuck to the pavement from the tacky blood drying on the soles of my boots. My hands and arms were red up to the elbows from a long, and ultimately futile battle to keep a 16-year-old girl from bleeding out from an AK round to the throat. It was summer, and the mall was packed with teenagers escaping the heat.

Lubbock was standing in the same spot he had been an hour before, still waving his arms, yelling orders and being ignored. When he saw me, he stopped flapping his arms like he was trying to take flight. He balled up his fists and walked towards me. He stuck his scrawny chest out and it reminded me of watching a rooster getting himself psyched up to fight.

"What the hell did you think you were doing?" He was a couple of inches from my face, almost spitting in my eye.

I contemplated shooting him. The two older guys each grabbed one of my arms, hustled me off and stuck me in the back of an ambulance, told me I was having chest pains and feeling faint, told me I didn't have to talk to anybody until I talked to my lawyer and my union rep.

I couldn't get that day at the mall out of my mind sometimes. James Elroy David had fired 120 rounds that day, four full magazines of cheap, steel cased Russian ammo. He'd been in the middle of stuffing the fifth magazine in his rifle when I lined up my gun sights on his right ear and stroked the trigger. Later we'd find fifteen more magazines in the duffel bag dangling from his shoulder.

The mall had almost as many video cameras as a Las Vegas casino. During the inevitable post-shooting recriminations and Monday morning quarterbacking, the tapes were reviewed over and over. A timeline was constructed. Forty-five rounds were fired before Lubbock and the rest of us arrived. The shooter walked through the mall, picking targets carefully. He hit almost as much as he missed, unusual for cases like this.

He fired another forty rounds while we were standing around and watching Lubbock in amazement. From the time it took for us to enter the mall and find him in the food court, standing over the body of one of the maintenance workers, and coolly stuffing another magazine in his rifle, took another 35 rounds. I remembered hearing each one of them as we ran through the mall, dodging bodies and slipping in pools of blood, almost tripping on dull gray shell casings that rolled underfoot. Time had stopped being measured in seconds. Now it was rounds of ammunition that counted, each one another potential dead body, or even more.

The bullets were steel cored, with a thin copper wash over them. A couple had gone through one person and into another.

By the end, it all came down to the numbers. 121 rounds fired, 120 by David, 1 by me. Eighteen dead, forty wounded. Exactly the same number of dead shoppers as the number of soldiers we lost in Mogadishu Somalia, where I'd had my first firefight.

Six of the dead were killed before we got there, in that first rush of firing into the crowd. Nothing I could do about that. People die. It was the other twelve that bothered me. Who owned them more? Lubbock for not being up to the job? Or me for wasting the time to listen to him? I knew where all their graves were. I never left rocks on their tombstones, although maybe I should start.

The water was getting cold. I shook myself to clear my head of one final image from that day. It all ended in the food court and I'd never forget the sundae the girl had been eating. Blood mixed with chocolate ice cream. I hadn't eaten ice cream since.

This was stupid. Here I was, waiting for my girlfriend to get home so I could take her out for a good time on her birthday, and all I could do was chew on the past.

I spun the taps off and stepped out into the steamy bathroom to find a towel. I heard the front door lock click, then the door swung open. I couldn't help it. My first thought was to calculate how many steps it would take to get from the bathroom to my lockbox.

"Hey, that you?" I asked.

"Of course it is. Who else?" I liked Audrey's voice, husky and strong. I felt better just hearing it.

I heard the rattle of her keys as she put them down by the door, then she was standing in the bathroom doorway. She stopped and leaned against the frame with her arms folded, undid her almost waist-length red hair from a ponytail and looked at me with a frank, appreciative gaze that always did more to turn me on than just about anything she could have done with her hands. No other woman had looked at me like that before. I'd never felt particularly attractive before, but she made me feel that way.

I dropped the towel and went over to hug her. She was tall, which meant I was only a head taller than she was. She hugged me back, and I felt her strong fingers on my back and ass.

"How are you?" I asked.

"Tired," she said, and she sounded it.

"The new pills aren't helping?" I asked.

She shrugged against me. "Not really. I'm going to the doctor again on Monday. I think what I really need is some sunlight. They can't put that in a pill. I'm so tempted just to get on a plane and fly to back to New Mexico sometimes."

"I'd miss you if you did that."

Audrey had battled depression off and on her whole life. She'd come to Portland for a new job and a change of scenery but hadn't counted on the winters. Last winter had been tough, I'd watched the vibrant, funny woman I loved spend days where she could barely get out of bed. This winter was looking to be better in some ways, worse in others. She was still miserable at times. The medicine gave her just enough energy to think about leaving.

"Yeah, I know," she said. Much was always left unsaid between us. At times I felt like the only reason she stayed in Portland was because of me, that if we broke up she'd be gone in a heartbeat. I wasn't sure how that made me feel sometimes.

"You're getting my shirt all wet." She slid a hand between us, reached down and gave me a squeeze. "Save that for later. I'm hungry."

She stepped back from me and I saw there was indeed a big wet outline on the front of her silk shirt. It made it stick to her in interesting ways. She saw me staring and smiled before turning to go back to the bedroom.

I finished drying off and followed her into the bedroom where I was rewarded with a nice view of a long muscled back as she pulled her shirt off. Two could play at that game. I was of half a mind to try to find out if dinner could wait awhile but didn't. Things were a little funny when she was feeling down. It was hard not to take it personally sometimes.

I dressed quickly, a fresh pair of jeans, a button-down shirt, the official Dent Miller uniform. I may not be stylish, but I am predictable. I checked myself out in the mirror. Everything was tucked in and buttoned, so I guess I looked ok. Audrey looked a damn sight better in her long flowing skirt and the sweater she was pulling on.

"I'll be ready in just a second as soon as I put my hair up." She stood in front of the mirror fooling with her hair and exposing the fine skin on the back of her long neck. It begged to be kissed. I liked the fact that she could get ready to go somewhere almost as quick as I could.

"Something we have to do first," I said as I stuck my head in my closet. I pushed the clothes aside and pulled out a long flat package. Good. The wrapping paper hadn't gotten torn. I'd paid to have it wrapped. I was awful at wrapping presents.

"What's that?" Audrey was still fussing with her hair, not out of vanity so much as because there was just a lot of it. I walked over and kissed the mole on the side of her neck.

"Happy birthday." I held the package up.

She finally got all her hair contained, turned, and poked me in the chest. "I told you no presents, silly."

I shrugged. "Just something I stumbled into at the flea market." At my house, most of the furniture I owned had come from one flea market or second-hand store or another. I had one ex-girlfriend who refused to come to my place because of it. Auds just thought it was quirky and endearing.

"Let's open it in the living room," she said.

I led the way into the living room and sat down on the couch, casting a glance over by the door as I went. I was relieved to see that her cello was there. Sometimes she left it in her office, which would have made the present I was about to give her no fun. If I had hinted to her to bring her cello home, that would have spoiled the surprise.

"I told you no present," she said again, mock angry.

Or at least I hoped it was mock anger. Money was an issue between us. I made a bunch more than she did and she was determined that I not spend any of it on her. Audrey taught music part-time at local colleges, gave private lessons, played in one of the local orchestras, gigged with trios, stuff like that. She had maybe seven or eight part-time and occasional jobs, usually only three or four of which were paying her at any one time. Somehow, she always made her ends meet, but it was a constant juggle. It would have driven me crazy. I liked my paychecks consistent and as large as possible, a holdover from growing up and not knowing if I'd have anything to eat the next day.

I held out the box and, after a moment she took it from my hands. I was sure the anger was false, mostly. She slid a finger down the wrapping paper and pulled out the long flat cardboard box.

It was interesting to watch her. The look on her face told me that my mention of the flea market had put her on her guard. She was probably expecting something like a rolled up velvet Elvis but steeling herself to pretend to like it anyway. The look changed to one of puzzlement for a few seconds when she opened the box. The sharp intake of breath and widening of her eyes was priceless.

"My God, Dent. Where did you find this?" She was holding a W.E. Hill & Sons cello bow. It dated from 1900, with a silver mounted ebony frog and a silver mounted tip. It had taken me three months to find it. A couple of times Audrey had mentioned that she really liked her cello but was less than happy with the two low-end bows she owned.

"Like I said, I found it at the flea market." I put my hands in my pockets and tried to look innocent.

"Flea market my ass. It must have cost a fortune."

"I got a good deal."

Well, not really. It had cost about six grand, a little over fair market price, but I had gotten caught up in an online bidding war. With only two weeks until Aud's birthday, I had been anxious to seal the deal on a good bow. There were several new empty spots in my gun safe as a result of this little purchase. That wasn't necessarily a bad thing. When I cleaned it out, looking for things to sell, I'd found a Belgian Browning Auto-5 shotgun I hadn't even remembered buying.

Aud had a kind of stunned, almost confused look on her face, like she couldn't believe her good fortune, and didn't want to take the gift, all at the same time. I admired her independent streak but wished she'd just take the gift and enjoy it.

I stood up, reached over and put my hand over hers on the bow. I leaned down and kissed the top of her head. "Just take it, ok? It makes me happy to give it to you."

I realized that it really did make me happy, which was a new idea to get used to. I'd never gotten many presents in my life, so I guess I never got in the habit of giving.

Finally, her face softened, and she smiled. "I don't know what I'm going to do with you."

I had a few ideas of things she could do with me but now wasn't the time. Hopefully later. "What you can do for me now is play your cello with your new bow for me."

"Ok. Sit down." She put the bow down on the low table in front of the couch carefully, almost reverently, then practically hopped over to her cello case. This was getting better and better.

This was the next, in some ways more important test. I'd contacted one of Aud's buddies in the orchestra on the sly. He'd checked the bow out for me and told me it was definitely worth what I'd paid for it, and more importantly, he thought Aud would like it, that it would fit with her playing style. I hoped he was right.

She took a few seconds to tune up, then stroked the bow across the strings. Her cello had a tone that for some reason always reminded me of really good whiskey, warm and a little smoky, hard to put into words. I thought it sounded good, but it wasn't me who mattered.

She was tentative at first, as she got used to the new bow. I couldn't tell the difference between this one and a cheap one that really did come from a flea market, but to somebody with Aud's level of talent, the slightest bit of difference was important. She could tell a difference in the way her instrument sounded and played depending on the temperature of the room and how humid hit had been the night before. Sometimes I was jealous of her talent. I had way more guitars than I needed back home, but could barely bang out "Stairway to Heaven." I sometimes wished I had a talent beyond shooting guns and hunting down dirtbags.

She played snatches of this and that, her warm-up routine changed constantly. Then she settled into Bach. "Cello Suite No. 1." I was proud of myself for recognizing it. I'd never known much about classical music before dating Aud, but I was slowly learning. It was after a minute or two of that piece that I realized I had a winner. She flowed into a long improvisation, at times slow and haunting enough to put a chill down my spine, and at other times something that evoked an otherworldly sensuousness that made me want to stop her and make love to her right there on the floor. As she played her posture changed. She relaxed. Her eyes closed. Her head tilted back, and she got a dreamy smile on her face. Her fingers seemed to float on the neck.

I closed my eyes and let myself relax much more than I usually did. Since the age of sixteen, when I was old enough to whip my dad's ass if he got drunk and mean, I had lived in a constant state of being ready to fight. It had become like breathing to me. If I let my awareness slip for too long, I got antsy, almost panicked.

The more time I spent with Audrey, the easier it became to relax. She was so calm and centered. I felt the pace of things slow down when I was around her and had come to like it. It was like we were in our own little bubble. I sometimes felt like a different person when I was with her.

She played through a series of long, low, sonorous notes and I knew somehow that she was bringing it to a close. I rode along with her, not wanting it to end, but finally she resolved the passage and stopped. I opened my eyes and found her still holding the cello and the bow. She was slightly flushed, with her pupils dilated, and she was breathing a little heavy. I was struck, as I sometimes was, how much the look on her face, right after the playing went well, was like the look right after we made love.

"You know, Dent," she said. "You're pretty good for me sometimes."

I just smiled. If I'd known giving people presents was this much fun, I would have started sooner.

She put the bow and the cello down carefully, came over and straddled me on the couch.

"Thought you wanted dinner?" I asked.

She kissed me in reply, long and hard. I sat back and enjoyed it, all the more because as the days got shorter and darker, the times that she initiated anything physical got fewer and farther between. On their own, my hands went to her waist, found the band of soft skin where her shirt had come untucked from her skirt.

That's when my cell phone started to ring.

"Mmph," I said, our mouths still locked together. Aud kissed me all the harder for a few seconds, then drew back only to bite me on the lower lip. "Ow!" I said.

"Dammit, Dent. I'm tempted to throw that thing out the window." My phone only rang when Audrey called, or work called. I'd tried to trade duty with somebody over the weekend, but everyone either had sick kids or plans. It happened that way sometimes.

Aud looked exasperated. I didn't blame her. I was too. She got up, tucked her shirt back into her skirt and closed the latches on her cello case. I dug the phone out and looked at the number: Central Dispatch. I had hoped that it was just somebody calling in with a question, or maybe Lubbock. I could ignore him. But a call from dispatch usually meant somebody had gotten themselves shot, stabbed, beaten to death or had died in some other unpleasant matter.

I started to dial Central back when the phone rang again. This time it was Mandy.

"Hey! Didja get the call?" She sounded excited. She probably was. She'd been with me for two months and so far we'd spent the whole time working old cases. Random chance had kept me from catching a new homicide since she started. It was an odd job we had. We got excited and developed career opportunities out of homicides.

"Yeah. I was just getting ready to call dispatch."

"I just got off the phone with them." Jesus, did she sit there with the phone in her hand? It hadn't taken me but a minute or two to find my phone.

"What have we got?"

26

Please let it be an easy one, I thought. I very much wanted to spend the night with Audrey, and if was something like Dumbass A shot Dumbass B and was still standing there when the cops arrived, I could be back at her place by midnight. I wasn't up to any Sherlock Holmes action tonight.

"Body of a young female, found dumped in Kelly Point Park. She was bound. The medical examiner hasn't gotten there yet so nobody's touched her."

Damn. The game was afoot, and all I wanted to do was have dinner with my girlfriend.

"Ok. See you there." I hung up. I hoped I hadn't hurt Mandy's feelings, but I really wasn't in the mood to talk right now.

I sighed and started strapping all my gear on. When I was done, I went out to the living room and found Audrey staring out the window at the street below. I stood there, my hands jammed in the pockets of my coat.

"I gotta go. I'm sorry."

"I know. Should I wait for dinner until you to get back?"

I sighed again. "No. Probably shouldn't wait up on me either. This is liable to be a long one."

"Ok." She tried a smile. It didn't quite work.

I walked up and kissed the back of her neck. "I'm really sorry."

She turned and kissed me, not like earlier, but still a good honest kiss. "It's ok. Be careful."

I nodded, and with that, I turned and headed out the door.

CHAPTER FOUR

I didn't waste any time getting to the scene, but I didn't burn up the road either. The victim would still be dead when I got there, and I needed some time to mentally switch gears. Driving to a homicide scene was like the long, slow, up-hill beginning of a roller coaster ride. Once you got to the scene, the ride started in earnest and you never knew how long the drop would last. I would work the case until I had a solid suspect in custody, I had chased every lead, or I keeled over from exhaustion. If a suspect isn't in custody in twenty-four hours, the odds of ever solving the murder went way down.

Part of my brain was humming in anticipation. I was realistic enough about myself to realize that I needed this. I needed this the way a Wall Street Eagle needed a hot trade, the way a Vegas gambler needed a blackjack table. To be even more honest, I needed this the way a junkie needed his fix. My cases were big game hunts. They started with a dead body and ended with another trophy on my wall.

The other part of my brain was still reeling at being torn away from Audrey so quickly. I tried to shut that part off.

The city of Portland had a fondness for parks. We had over two hundred and fifty of them, ranging from the smallest, a whimsy of a park that was only a few square feet, to Forest Park, almost 5,000 acres. It was one of the things that made the city a cool place to live. Most Portlanders had their favorite parks and probably lots of fond memories about them. I tended to put them into two categories: parks where I'd found dead bodies, and parks where I hadn't found a dead body yet.

Kelley Point Park sat at the confluence of the Willamette and Columbia rivers, right smack in the middle of a major industrial area. The wooded acres and picnic tables seemed out of place among the grain elevators, shipping terminals and light industrial outfits that surrounded it. A single patrol car sat at the gate, parked across the entrance. I was glad to see the overhead lights were turned off. I'd found over the years that the best way to keep your crime scene secure was to not draw attention.

Ahead of me, a white van slowed down, saw the police car, and did an abrupt u-turn. The driver stared at me as he drove past, a young guy with one of those goofy shaggy haircuts that were all the rage these days. I could see the outline of another, larger man in the passenger seat. Something seemed off about them. I looked in the rearview mirror as they sped away hoping to get a plate number, but they were gone before I could catch it.

I turned off my lights and flashed my badge to get inside. I drove down a long winding road to a parking lot at the end. The Deputy Medical Examiner's black van was already parked there, along with a couple of marked cars. Mandy's Vic was parked there too, along with a lone Volvo. The Volvo had a sticker on the bumper: "I," a heart, and a picture of one of those little low slung dogs, the kind the queen of England likes.

Mandy was standing next to the Volvo, talking to a guy in his fifties, expensive looking rain jacket, beard, flat-brimmed hat and a halfhearted attempt at a ponytail. The guy probably made six figures a year and still listened to the Grateful Dead. Portland was like that. He had a fat little dog on the end of the leash that kept smelling Mandy's shoes. Corgi. That was what they called them.

Mandy seemed to have that pretty well in hand. I turned to the little knot of people standing at the other end of the lot. A sergeant, I recognized him as Dan Millan, and Rex Fairbairn, the Deputy Medical Examiner. Good, not too many people. I didn't know Millan well, but he had a good reputation and seemed to be doing a good job of making sure my crime scene didn't get trampled to death.

A pair of headlights lit me up, casting my shadow twenty feet ahead of me. Another van squeaked to a stop beside my Vic. These would be the crime scene techs from the ID division.

A short woman with bright red hair got out of the driver's seat. "Evening, Dent," she said, pulling on a pair of latex gloves.

"Hi, Jeannie." A big hulking man with a heavy brow and dark hair that stuck up in all directions got out of the passenger side. "Hey, Roger." Roger grunted back, gave a little wave. I knew better than to take that personally, that was about all anybody ever got out of him.

Roger and Jeannie made an unlikely, Mutt and Jeff pair. But they were both smart as hell and meticulous. If there was anything to be found at this scene, they would find it. If I was ever the victim of a homicide, I would want Roger and Jeannie to work the scene.

"Whatcha got, Dent?" Jeannie asked.

"Dunno. Let's go find out." I turned back to my car for a second and pulled out my shoulder bag, or as Auds called it, my "man-purse." It was almost twenty years old, the brown leather scuffed and worn to softness. I carried around my essentials in there.

Mandy walked up her notebook in one hand.

"Let me guess," I said. "He was out here walking his dog and found the body. He called on his cell phone and there was nobody else in the park."

Mandy's mouth quirked up in a half smile. "Yeah. You want to talk to him before we cut him loose?"

"You got everything you need from him?"

She stopped for a second, considering both the question and the fact that I was leaving it up to her. She nodded slowly.

"Ok," I said. "Cut him loose."

Mandy waved the guy on. He couldn't get into his car and out of there fast enough. I couldn't blame him. Most people only saw dead bodies in caskets at funeral homes. I predicted a few glasses of a nice red or maybe even a bowl or two of Oregon's finest in his future.

There was a strip of grass at the edge of the parking lot, then a steep embankment. I noticed a pair of tire tracks in the grass. It looked like somebody had pulled off the parking lot right to the edge of the embankment. Everybody was standing well away from the tire tracks.

I nodded to Fairbairn and Millman; they both knew me by sight.

I turned to Mandy. "Lead on." I had resolved on the way over to make this Mandy's show.

Mandy led the way down the trail, a camera and a crime scene bag slung over her shoulder. She carefully shined her light on the ground in front of her before setting her foot down. No one in their right might would drag a body across the route we were taking, so the chance of destroying evidence was almost nil. But it paid to be thorough, and we would document our caution in our reports, so no defense attorney could dream up some piece of exculpatory evidence and claim we had destroyed it by trampling around the crime scene. Fairbairn followed us.

Up until now, the victim had been an abstraction. From up above, she was just another shape in the gloom. I'd grown used to dead people, seen them cut in half by trains, seen their heads blown off with shotguns, seen them after they'd sat out in a field under a hot sun for a week. You got used to it, but there was always a feeling of dread as I walked up to a new one. Not so much because I was about to see something unpleasant, but because I was about to crawl into this person's life, get to know everything about them, even things their friends and family might not know. I'd devote myself to figure out who the killer was until I was done. There was an old saying: "homicide detectives get paid by the taxpayers, but they work for God."

She was small. It was hard to tell precisely, with her legs drawn up to her chest, her head bent forward, and her hands bound behind her back, but I could tell from the fine bones in her wrists and the narrow shoulders that she wasn't very big. She was lying on her left side at the bottom of the slope.

"Want to snap a few before I check her?" Fairbairn asked Mandy.

Mandy nodded and took the lens cap off the camera. Her hands shook ever so slightly, but she was cool as she walked around the body in a circle, always conscious of the ground in front of her before putting her feet down. She snapped a photo every few steps, getting a view of the body from all the way around.

In the flash of the camera, I got a better view of the victim. Black hair, dyed and showing blond roots cut almost boy short. She was wearing a black hooded sweatshirt with a "Dropkick Murphys" panel sewn on the back and all sorts of metal studs and safety pins. Her black jeans were dirty and torn, with more patches sewn on at random. A scuffed pair of Doc Martin boots were on her feet. Pieces of dead grass, weeds and, leaves were all over her, consistent with being rolled down the hill. Her hands were bound behind her back by a pair of handcuffs.

I saw dozens of kids dressed like this all the time downtown. Some of them were homeless or semi-homeless. Others lived in nice little suburban homes.

Mandy nodded at Fairbairn and he bent down and put his fingers on the pale white skin of the girl's neck for a few seconds. He liked to tell a story about how he'd put a guy in a bag once, only to have him sit up and start mumbling. Now he always made sure first.

Dead bodies occupied some interesting legal territory in Oregon. The body actually belonged to the Medical Examiner. Cops weren't allowed to touch the body until a Deputy Medical Examiner arrived.

The MX had a duty to figure out how the person died. If it was a homicide, it was our duty to figure out who killed them.

Satisfied that there was no pulse, Fairbairn started rummaging through her pockets, first the sweatshirt, then the jeans. He came up empty-handed.

"No ID?" I asked.

"Nope. Not a thing in her pockets." Damn. The first part of identifying a killer was identifying the victim.

"How long has she been here, you think?" Mandy asked.

"I'm guessing since last night," Fairbairn said. "Her clothes are soaked. The body's still pretty rigid. I'm going to roll her over on her back."

Fairbairn was a big guy. He gently rolled her onto her back with little effort. She had been young. It was hard to tell age on a dead person sometimes, but I had a feeling this girl wasn't even eighteen. Her face looked funny. The right half was pale and white, the left half was blotchy looking in a way I hadn't ever seen before.

"What's up with her face?" I asked.

Fairbairn examined her for a second under the light of his flashlight. "Makeup. Heavy makeup. The rain's washed a bunch of it away. From the way she was lying it all ran down her face and all over her sweatshirt." He pointed to a big smear around the collar of the sweatshirt.

"I'm not seeing any wounds," Mandy said.

"Me neither, at least not yet," Fairbairn said. Sometimes even a gunshot wound wasn't immediately obvious. A bullet or knife could cause surprisingly little bleeding external to the body, but cause somebody to bleed out internally.

Fairbairn ran his fingertips around her head gently, then shined his light on her face and stooped over to where his face was inches from her skin. He rolled first one eyelid open, then the other. From there he tilted her head back as much as he could against the rigor. He shined his light around her neck and felt her throat gently.

"Off the record," he said. "I'm guessing this one's going to be a strangle. Some petechiae in her eyes and cheeks, some bruising on the throat. Her trachea is intact so I'm guessing what killed her was a carotid choke."

Petechiae was the red speckling left over from tiny burst blood vessels, just under the surface of the skin of the face and eyes. They would show up really well against her pale skin. Instead of restricting the flow of air through her trachea, a carotid choke would have killed her by restricting the flow of blood to her brain in the carotid arteries. I knew all too well how quickly that would kill somebody.

Fairbairn pulled up the bottom of the bulky sweatshirt, then the t-shirt underneath, baring her belly. The right half was pale white. The left looked like one giant bruise, blue and red mostly, with some brown and yellow mixed in.

"Yeah, she's been here a while, judging by the lividity."

When somebody died, gravity took over and the blood pooled downward, causing post mortem lividity. Fairbairn ran his gloved hands down her legs, looking for wounds or obvious fractures. He found nothing of interest and stood up. He looked up the embankment.

I turned to Mandy. "So what do you think?"

"I think we don't have a whole hell of a lot yet except a dead girl."

She was right. No identification on the victim. She was most likely killed somewhere else and dumped here. No clue as to a suspect.

I sighed. It was going to be a long night.

"Ok. Let's do a search down here while we wait for Fairbairn"

I realized I was unconsciously referring to our suspect as a he. They almost always were.

We both had compact, powerful flashlights. We started a search of the area, expanding out in a grid surrounding the body. The idea was to walk over each piece of ground twice, from a different direction each time. You might miss something from one angle, only to see it from another.

Bright light flooded the area from above. I squinted and yelled, "Thanks, Jeannie." The techs carried big floodlights in their truck.

"Welcome, Dent," her voice floated down from above. "Want us to start a search up here?"

"Yeah, please," I said. A twinkle of light caught my eye, about halfway up the slope. Something was reflecting light. I made a mental note but continued searching where I was.

The bottom of the embankment was full of scraggly weeds about shin high. There were some scrub bushes in a thin line, then woods, then the river. Mandy and I searched back and forth up to the wood line. Flashlights or no, it was too dark in there to see anything. Later we might decide to bring some more help in and search the wood line, maybe even the whole park.

But I didn't think the evidence would lead us that way.

While we searched, Fairbairn worked on the victim. He knelt over the body and I saw the glint of a pair of EMT shears in his hand. He'd need to get a core body temperature before we put her in the bag. It was a valuable piece of info, but I would just as soon not be there as he got it.

Mandy and I finished our search. Both of us came up empty-handed. I trudged back up the hill to the body, a little disappointed in myself that I was starting to breathe hard. Fairbairn turned to look at us.

"Can I get a hand getting her in the bag?"

I stepped forward but Mandy beat me to it. Together she and Fairbairn lifted the girl into the bag that he had spread out on the ground. I walked past them, looking for the item I'd seen glittering in the light. I shined my light around.

It was an earring, shaped like a small gold butterfly with a diamond in the center. "Hey, is she wearing an earring?" I asked.

Fairbairn was zipping up the body bag. He paused and shined a light inside. "Nope. Both ears are pierced though." I nodded my thanks and he zipped the bag up. I put the earring in an evidence baggie. It might turn out to be hers, it might not. It sure didn't fit the rest of her outfit.

Mandy and I squatted, then picked up the bag. The girl was light, but the term "dead weight" had been coined for a reason. I hated carrying bodies. Fairbairn followed as we huffed and puffed up the hill then across the parking lot to Fairbairn's van. He pulled the gurney out of the back and we put the bag down as gently as we could.

I stood there, stretching the muscles in my back and staring at the bag. I hated it when I had a victim but no name. Somehow a name made them a person to me, and not just a body.

"I'll roll her prints as soon as I get her to the morgue." It was like Fairbairn was reading my mind. Hell, he might have been, we'd worked enough scenes together.

"Thanks. Any chance one of the docs can come in and do an autopsy tomorrow morning?"

So far I had a body with no ID and an earring that might not even be related. I needed information bad and one source was an autopsy. Normally it wouldn't have mattered if the autopsy waited until Monday, but if the girl had indeed been dumped last night, our twenty-four-hour window would be closing soon.

Fairbairn checked his watch. I'd already looked at mine. It was almost nine o'clock. A Friday night. "I'll see what I can do, see who answers the phone."

"Thanks, man."

He rolled the girl into the back of the unmarked, nondescript van and left. Jeannie and Roger were just finishing their sweep of the upper lot and surrounding area. They came walking over to us.

"Find anything?" Mandy asked.

Jeannie shook her head. "Nothing of note. Four pieces of chewing gum. They look old. Two coffee cups and a soda bottle in the trash can. Five cigarette butts."

Jeannie would take these things and catalog them. It would be up to us to have them tested or not. If any of them had been discarded by the killer, there would possibly be DNA evidence, or fingerprints. But most likely they were trash and not evidence. I had hoped for some stroke of luck. Sometimes killers were nervous. They vomited or even defecated at scenes. They left weapons behind with fingerprints or articles of clothing. Once I'd even worked a burglary where the burglar had dropped his own wallet in the middle of the living room. It didn't look like we were going to get lucky tonight.

"We got some good pictures and measurements of the tire tracks," Jeannie said.

Jeannie motioned us to follow. She pointed to the twin tracks in the grass. "As you can tell the grass is really thick, so we have two tracks of depressed vegetation, but no tread imprint. On the sidewalk, we have some rubber transfer as the tires went up over the edge, but again no tread impression. I'll take scrapings of the rubber. We'll also measure the width of the tracks and how far apart they are. We can identify some possible vehicles from that."

I nodded. That was something. I was willing to go out on a limb and guess we were looking for the ever-popular dead body transport vehicle: a van. The way the vehicle had been pulled up over the curb suggested it had been backed up to the edge of the embankment, the rear doors opened, and the girl pushed out like she was garbage. My jaw worked for a minute. Nobody deserved that.

I thought about the white van I'd seen as I pulled in, and cursed myself for not getting a plate.

This was where real life deviated from all the forensics TV shows that had become so popular. On the TV, whenever there was a murder, there was always a mountain of evidence to be found, usually with some cool laser or alternative lighting source. In real life, I never seemed to get that lucky.

We spent the next couple of hours doing a secondary search. It rained harder, so we all put on raincoats and kept looking for anything that could be important.

Despite all my frequent thoughts of quitting, I loved this job because of the people I worked with. For every Steve Lubbock or *Officer* Bloem, there were quiet professionals like Fairbairn, Jeannie and Roger.

I'd just decided it was time to end the search when my phone started vibrating in my pocket.

I answered it. "Miller."

"Dent, hey. It's Alex Pace. Fairbairn tells me you need some help." I could hear the sound of an engine revving up and down in the background. Alexis Pace. Man, she had a nice voice. I grew a little warm picturing the face and especially the body that went with it. But what got me the most excited was the fact that she was a pathologist and I needed an autopsy done.

That was kind of screwed up if I thought about it, so I didn't.

"I'm in a little bit of a jam here, Alex. I've got a body of a young woman, bound and dumped out at Kelley Point Park. That's pretty much all I've got. I've got no ID, no physical evidence at the scene. She's been dead almost twenty-four hours already. It's like she dropped out of the sky. I was wondering what I could do to get one of you guys to do her this weekend. Maybe as early as tomorrow?"

"Hell, Dent, I'll do it tonight."

If I could have reached through the phone and hugged her, I would have.

"I'm just leaving Judo class at the MAC club. I'll meet you at the office."

"You're the best, Alex. What can I do to make it up to you?"

"Grande wet cappuccino, double shot, skim milk. See ya."

She hung up.

I smiled. This would be the cheapest cup of coffee I ever bought.

We reached the front gate of the park and found nothing. Mandy and I stopped there and waited for Roger and Jeannie to catch up.

Mandy was quiet, thoughtful. Normally Mandy wanted to talk about things, a little too much for my tastes, to be honest. But now she was silent. It was interesting to watch cops work their first homicide. For most, it was different than all the other cases they had worked before, even the bad assaults and sex crimes. There was finality to this, a weight that was hard to describe.

"Alex Pace from the ME's office is gonna come in tonight and do our victim."

"Good." She nodded. "I don't think I've ever met him."

"Not a him, a her. Remember Captain Pace? Retired a few years ago, ran North Precinct for a while, and then Special Operations?"

She nodded. "Sure. He retired right after I got off probation."

Jesus. Way to make me feel old.

"Well anyways, this Alex Pace is THAT Alex Pace's daughter."

"Cool." She still looked pensive and distracted. Jeannie and Roger came walking up, looking miserable in their ponchos. The temperature had probably dropped ten degrees since we started this.

"You guys come up empty too?" Mandy asked. Jeannie nodded, shivering with the cold.

"I think," Mandy said, with a glance towards me. "We're about done."

"Ok," Jeannie said. "We'll be around at Central, drying the cigarette butts and stuff. Call us if you need us." Jeannie and Roger still had a couple of hours of work ahead of them: drive back to the precinct, babysit the evidence in the dryer, do the ever popular paperwork.

I watched them walk away, let my mind drift, become unfocused. I could see Mandy staring at me like she wanted to say something but could tell I was thinking and didn't want to interrupt.

Out on the river, a ship horn sounded, echoed off the water.

"Why?" I asked aloud.

"Why what?"

"Why dump her over the embankment?"

"It's a dead body. He had to get rid of her."

"Yeah, but why here? Why Kelly Point Park? This place isn't that big. Why not Forest Park? Why not up in the mountains? Why does he leave her in a place where anybody looking over from the parking lot will see her?"

She stood there, staring. I could all but hear the gears turning. The wind picked up. It was cold and damp down here by the river, felt like dead fingers caressing your face.

"The water," she said. "He was going to dump her in the water."

"Yeah. I think you're right. If you draw a straight line from where we're standing, it's the shortest path to the river. Dumping her down the embankment was just a way to get her down there. She ain't that big, but I'd hate to carry a hundred, hundred and ten pounds of dead weight down that slope. Maybe he's not a big guy, maybe he's just lazy."

"So he was going to dump her in the river. He probably had chains or something. To weigh her down."

"Maybe. Even more weight to carry in that case. So what happened?"

"He dumped her out. She rolls down the hill. Somebody came."

"I think so. He sees headlights, maybe a person. Maybe it's the guy from Parks Bureau, here to check the lot for cars before he locks the gate. But anyway, he's interrupted. And for some reason, he doesn't come back."

She walked over to the tire tracks, shined a light on them. "His wheels didn't slide because the grass was wet. He was excited, scared. He threw the van in drive and stomped on the gas. That's why the divot is there."

"It all fits. So what does that give us?"

"Maybe a witness. Whoever drove in and scared him off."

"Exactly," I said. "But still, why here? Why Kelley Point Park? Nobody comes here. It's in the middle of an industrial wasteland. Only the City of Portland would put a park in a spot like this. I bet the dude who walks his dog here is the only one who uses it all winter. In the summer some people come here to launch their canoes. Hell, there aren't even any hookers out here for guys to bring over for a quickie on their lunch hour."

"My first thought is to say he lives out here," she said, turning in a circle as she looked around the lot. "But nobody *lives* out here. It's gotta be a job. He has to work out here."

I told her about the van I'd seen on the way in.

"Christ," she said. "Do you think that was him? Did you get a plate?"

I shook my head and she looked disappointed.

"Why would he come back?"

"If it was him, he might have been coming back to move her the rest of the way to the river, with help."

"Or it could have been just two dudes coming out here to smoke dope that got scared when they saw the police car."

I nodded. "Could be that too."

"Well, we'll keep it in mind. Can you think of anything else we need to do here?"

I took one last look around the lot. "I think we're done here. You did a good job processing the scene. All the schools you go to, all the books you read, they'll pound all that CSI stuff into your head. That's not a bad thing; we make good cases that way. But remember to take a few minutes and just get inside his head. Think like he does. Put yourself in his shoes."

"Ok."

"Cool. Now let's go to the autopsy."

She nodded again. She was still quiet, but I expected that.

The weight took some getting used to.

CHAPTER FIVE

Led Zeppelin was on the radio when I got in the car. "In My Time of Dying." Not a bad tune, but in many ways, I preferred Bob Dylan's original sparse, acoustic version. Hopefully, it wasn't an omen or anything.

As I drove I kept flipping the case over and over in my head. There still wasn't much to think about. I was hoping if I kept churning the information, I'd get some blinding flash of insight that would open things up.

I really should have known better. In the movies, the detective always had the sudden revelation that solved the whole case, but in real life, cases were solved by grunt work and hard labor.

The new Medical Examiner's office was out east, just past the city limits in Clackamas. The lot was deserted and the building dark. Mandy and I pulled into the lot and parked next to each other.

Apparently, Alex wasn't here yet. I missed the old days when the morgue had been on Knott Street in North Portland. The county used to let a few college students stay in apartments over the building. In return for free rent, they answered the phone at night and let people into the building. Some of them had been fun to BS with. I could usually count on a recommendation for a new band and maybe a free slice of pizza. Now, the new building was locked up overnight and the phones went to an answering service.

I heard Alex coming before I saw her. These days she drove a Mustang that sounded suspiciously like it had a set of straight pipes in place of the mufflers. The engine almost succeeded in drowning out the stereo. Somehow the rumble of the engine and Janis Joplin's "Another Piece of my Heart" seemed to go together perfectly. Cool car, cool music, cool girl. She parked nose to nose to me and both the music and the engine went silent.

I got out as Alex unfolded herself from the car. She was tall, an easy six-footer. Long, lanky, with blond hair that hung almost to her waist, she looked like the archetype of a California surfer girl, with bright blue eyes and a snub nose. I really don't know how that happened. Her dad was an ugly little troll of a man.

"Hey, Dent! Let's get inside." She ran for the door. Oblivious to the rain, she was wearing a pair of shorts and a hooded sweatshirt. I jogged after her, trying very hard not to stare at her ass as she ran in front of me. Working with Alex presented some unique challenges for me.

She let us in the office, the sterile, modern lobby a marked difference from the dungeon-like building the morgue had formerly occupied, and I presented her with her coffee.

"Mmm... You remembered." She blew steam off the top of the cup and took a sip. "Good to see you, Dent." She looked at me over the top of her coffee cup.

"Good to see you too, Alex."

I could never tell if the sexual tension I felt between me and Alex was mutual or all in my head. I was pretty good at getting into the heads of murderers, dope addicts, people like that. But women were a mystery to me.

"Meet Mandy Williams, my new partner."

They shook hands and exchanged pleasantries. Women had a way of sizing each other up that was different than men, but it was still interesting to watch.

"Let me throw on some scrubs and I'll be back in a minute." She vanished into the depths of the office. I hung my raincoat over a chair to let it dry and shook some kinks out of my back.

"So how well do you know her?" Mandy said. She had a slight smile on her face that I wasn't used to.

"What? Why?"

"You might want to make sure she and Audrey never meet, that's all I'm saying."

"What makes you say that?" I felt myself growing red.

"I can just tell. That's all."

Personal lives rarely came up between me and Mandy. She was pretty tight-lipped. Rumor had it around the department that she was gay, but that rumor usually got started about any female officer that didn't look like a Barbie doll or wasn't sleeping with one of the male officers. It was scary sometimes, how much the police department reminded me of high school.

Alex came back in, wearing a pair of blue scrubs. I noticed that they matched her eyes. *Stop it,* I told myself. Her hair was bound up and tucked down the back of her shirt.

She led us through a set of doors marked "Staff Only" and down a long corridor. At the end was a pair of heavy double doors.

She took a quick detour off to the right into a small office. We followed and she waved us into a pair of seats on the other side of the desk.

She turned on the computer and called up the report Fairbairn had already completed.

"Ok, let me get up to speed," Alex said. She read and sipped her coffee for a few minutes. I looked around the office. It had very little of a personal nature. Diplomas, professional books, case files, a few generic art prints. There were only two personal touches that I could see: one was a *bokken,* a wooden Japanese practice sword; the other the picture on the computer desktop. It showed her on a mountain peak, probably Mount Hood, judging by the background, dressed in mountaineering gear. I wondered who had taken the photo. A boyfriend maybe? *Stop it.*

Alex finished her coffee in one last gulp. She stood up and closed the folder. "Let's get you guys some gowns and get started."

We followed her into another room, right outside the double doors. One improvement over the old morgue was that this place didn't stink. At the old morgue, the smell of rot had soaked into the walls. It had been built around the turn of the last century and no amount of updating or new equipment could get the funk out of the walls. At any given time, a sizable portion of the staff had some kind of head cold or raging sinus infection. Nobody had ever caught anything fatal, but the health of the staff had been a major motivator behind finding the money for the new building.

Alex handed us gowns, caps and masks. She rooted through a storage cabinet and pulled out booties that went over our shoes. I gowned up, helped Mandy with tying her mask. She helped me with mine. Mandy looked a little grim.

We followed her through the double doors. Everything was brightly lit and polished stainless steel. Overhead fans constantly sucked air upward and out of the room.

Alex donned a pair of gloves, then wheeled a gurney over to a locker in the wall. She pulled the bag out and onto the gurney, pushed it over to the table. I helped her lift the body bag over to the table. We unzipped it and maneuvered the girl out. She looked very small on the table.

Alex walked over to a bank of switches on the wall and pointed to a circle taped on the floor. "Anything inside the circle will be picked up on the microphone, ok?" Mandy and I nodded. Alex flipped the switch and a red light next to the word "record" came on. Pathologists used voice recorders during their work. It was difficult to keep notes with gloved, bloody hands. The recording would become part of the legal record and could be played in court, so you wanted to be careful what you said.

Alex gave the time and date, then narrated a brief description of the girl's height, weight, and other physical identifiers. She motioned for me to help and we rolled her over on her stomach. The left side of the girl's body was blotchy and bruised looking from the post mortem lividity. The right side was pale white.

"Hands are bound behind the back with handcuffs, Smith and Wesson brand, both shackles are double locked. Handcuffs are removed at this time with a key provided by law enforcement officers in attendance." I pulled off a glove, dug awkwardly under my gown until I came up with a key and dropped it in Alex's hand. I hurried to put a fresh glove on and stuck out an index finger. Alex hooked the cuffs over the finger. The polished metal surface of the cuffs was a prime candidate for prints so I didn't want to touch the outside edges. Mandy was ready with an evidence baggie. I dropped the cuffs inside with a wish that they would show something worthwhile.

Working quickly but carefully, Alex removed the body's outer clothes.

I looked over each piece as we took it. The boots were in rough shape, the leather cracked and gouged, the heels worn down. The pants and shirt were dirty and torn. The dirt was ground in. These clothes hadn't been washed in a long time. All this suggested to me that the girl had been out on the streets for a while.

Socks and a black t-shirt were next. Both were full of holes and dirty. I would have thrown the socks away if they had been mine. They couldn't have been doing her feet any good.

I turned back to where Alex was working on the body. The girl was almost totally undressed, except for her underwear. They were a surprise. They were a matched set, deep blue, all lacy and fancy.

"Undergarments are inconsistent with the outer clothing," Alex was saying. She cut those off and handed them to me. The fabric felt stiff and new like it hadn't even been washed. The printing on the labels inside was crisp and easy to read. Interesting.

There was a camera mounted on a flexible arm over the table. The controls and cable release were covered with disposable plastic covers. Alex took two long shots of the whole body.

Alex started with a top-down examination of the girl. I followed along closely as Alex described the girl from head to toe. There were some scrapes and marks that she paid particular attention to, but no big wounds.

Next came one of my least favorite parts of an autopsy. I had gotten to the point where I could divorce the person from the body, usually. But as Alex arranged the girl's legs and got out her speculum, I turned away a little, pretended to study the clothes some more, as she narrated that part of the exam.

Alex put her tools away, took a minute to stretch out her back muscles. She picked up a hard rubber block, put it under the girl's neck so it would hold her head up.

"I'm going to open up her head before I look at her neck."

Her eyes went from mine to Mandy's. Mandy was silent. She stood there with her arms crossed over her chest. Alex considered for a moment, pointed at one of the two trashcans over in a corner. One was red and had biohazard symbols all over it. I knew better than to grab that one. The other was plain, with a clean liner in it. I picked it up and set it just outside the taped line on the floor. Mandy raised an eyebrow at me.

Alex made three quick, sure cuts with the scalpel, then set it down. I'd learned that this was called "reflecting" the skin, since "scalping" sounded so non-clinical. The skin came loose from the back of the girl's skull with a wet ripping sound. Alex pulled the flaps forward, over the dead girl's face. I looked over at Mandy. She was white and there was a big drop of sweat on her forehead, but so far she was doing ok.

"Hmm…" Alex said. "Pronounced bruising on the back of the head. No fracture to the underlying skull structures." Alex shot a few pictures of the inside of the skin from the girl's head. Then picked up the Stryker saw.

I hated the high pitched whine of that saw, and no matter how good the ventilation in the new room was, I always thought I could smell the hot microscopic chips of bone through my mask. Alex set the saw down, twisted the top of the girl's head back and forth a couple of times. It came off with a pop. I was always surprised at how blindingly white the inside of the skull was. The pinkish white brain underneath always looked unreal, like it was some kind of anatomical display or something. I frequently had that reaction to gruesome images. My brain would check out by saying "gotta be fake man, we can't really be seeing this." It worked for me as long as I was awake. It was when I went to sleep that I stopped believing it.

Mandy had the presence of mind to make it to the trash can before she puked, where she would be out of range of the microphone. She got bonus points for being quiet. I debated going over to pat her on the shoulder, or maybe taking my gloves off and getting her a glass of water or something. I decided against it. She was a little touchy if she felt like she was being patronized, and come to think of it, I had never done it for any of my male partners that puked.

Alex was saying something about "no brain abnormalities" and I looked back in time to see her poking around inside the girl's head. I turned away and looked at the other evidence we'd accumulated.

Mandy came over to stand beside me as I stared at the girl's clothes on the counter.

"What do you make of all this?" I asked, keeping my voice low so there was no chance it would be picked up on the microphone. I tried to sound natural like I hadn't noticed Mandy puking, and like a woman that I was supremely physically attracted to wasn't dissecting a corpse six feet behind me.

Mandy was quiet for a moment. She actually looked green. That was interesting. I'd heard the expression before but had never seen anybody actually turn green, at least not somebody who was still alive.

"Her clothes and her underwear don't match?" Mandy sounded a little tentative.

I frowned. She was right, but the whole puking thing seemed to have sapped some self-confidence. She needed to understand that a cast-iron stomach and an investigative mind didn't have to go together.

"Ok. What else?" I asked.

"Her clothes are dirty, her socks are worn out like she's been living on the streets, but she takes time to shave her legs and her ummm... pubes?" Mandy blushed a little. We were going to have to work on this sort of thing before she had to get on the stand and testify about somebody's private parts. Jesus, how could you be a cop for six, seven years and still get embarrassed by this stuff?

"That doesn't make sense," Mandy continued. "And neither does the makeup."

I agreed. The dirty jeans and sweatshirt on top of lingerie that looked like it came out of a men's magazine, freshly shaved but with dirty fingernails. It didn't match up, unless she'd been killed in the middle of cleaning herself up, then dressed in her old clothes. Stranger things had happened.

I looked back at Alex. She had made the classic "y" shaped incision on the girl's chest, leaving three flaps of skin hanging open. As I watched, she picked up what looked like a pair of pruning shears, opened them up and went to work on the girl's rib. I winced and turned just as the snapping sounds started.

I picked up the bag containing the handcuffs: Smith and Wesson. Professional quality, law enforcement grade restraints, not the cheap pot metal and fur lined crap they sold in the sex toy stores. This was the sort of thing a cop or higher end security employee would carry.

I checked on Alex again. She was holding the girl's detached stomach in one hand over a large beaker. She took a scalpel and made a long cut down the side, so all the contents drained into the beaker. She was humming to herself. I swallowed and looked away again.

I had to get my head right about Alex. First of all, I really was madly in love with Audrey. Second, if something ever did happen between me and Alex, and it ended badly, I knew her dad would kill me. Third, after repeatedly seeing her with human internal organs in her hands, I didn't think I'd be able to be particularly amorous anyway.

When I stepped outside of my life, it seemed pretty messed up sometimes.

"Ok," I said to Mandy. "What else do we have to follow up on?"

"First, we've got the handcuffs to check for prints. The clothes need to go to the lab for whatever we can find, hair fiber, what have you."

I nodded again. "Hopefully AFIS will come back with something from the girl's prints."

AFIS stood for Automated Fingerprint Identification System. Through the system, all fingerprint records were tied together via the FBI. If our victim had ever been arrested or fingerprinted by any government agency before, she would be in the system. I wasn't getting too excited. The girl was young, maybe even still a minor, but if she had been living on the streets, there was a pretty good chance that she had some minor contacts with law enforcement. Maybe there would be a shoplifting arrest or some other minor charge.

"We also need to check missing person reports," Mandy said. "If this girl has been on the streets, it doesn't look like it was for long. She was skinny, but not in that underfed way those kids get. We'll know for sure when the toxicology results come back, but I don't have her pegged for a hardcore junky or meth head either. She still had her teeth and there weren't any needle marks on her."

It sounded like Mandy was coming back from her setback. Her brain was engaged again.

I checked on Alex. She was putting all the organs back, more or less in the same places she found them. On the table beside her was a long row of specimens: vials of urine, blood, intraocular fluid; cross-sections of internal organs; smears and slides. It was a human body reduced to a bunch of samples taken for analysis. As I watched, Alex did a quick check of all her tools and instruments to make sure she wasn't leaving anything inside. Then she picked up the chest plate and settled it into place before smoothing the flaps of skin back down. She was still humming, a James Taylor tune if I wasn't mistaken.

"You know," I said to Mandy. "I never get used to this."

She looked a little relieved.

I walked back over to the autopsy table. Alex was whipping long, wide stitches through the incision. I made a mental note to go to another doctor if I needed a cut stitched up. She paused for a second, pointed at the wall. The red light next to the "record" sign was off.

"We're in the clear if you want to whisper sweet nothings in my ear." She held down a piece of skin that kept wanting to curl up and put a stitch through it.

Damn. Sweet nothings? Where had that come from?

"I dunno, Audrey might get upset."

She gave a theatrical sigh as she tied off the last of the stitches.

I blinked, trying to change gears. It wasn't often that I fumbled for something to say, but when I did I usually locked up tight. As I stood there looking like an idiot, Alex picked up the top of the victim's skull, tried the fit. She didn't like it so she turned it a degree or two, tried it again. She nodded and this time flipped the reflected scalp back into place.

I saw her lips curl up under the mask. She was using finer stitches on the head, in case a family claimed the body and wanted to have an open casket funeral.

I changed the subject. "So what do you think about my victim here?"

Her brows furrowed. Because I was changing the subject or because of my question, I wasn't sure. "I'm still putting everything together in my head. Give me a few minutes to think. I want to make sure I haven't missed anything."

Mandy and I bagged all the clothing in separate brown paper sacks. We gave the room a once over before we left, to make sure we hadn't left anything.

Mandy was a trooper. She walked over to the can she had puked in, pulled the bag out and tied a knot in it. "Where does this go?"

Alex pointed at the biohazard can.

"Drop it in there. It all gets incinerated. Don't ever puke in the biohazard can though. You can get some nasty backsplash if it's already been used."

She was cool about it. I appreciated that. Some people would have taken a shot at Mandy.

Mandy gathered the evidence bags and headed out to her car.

I headed towards Alex's office, trying to make all the evidence fit together in my head. I was also trying to ignore the fact that I was looking forward to being alone with Alex in her office, even just for a few minutes.

CHAPTER SIX

While Mandy stowed the victim's clothing in the trunk of her car, I went in Alex's office. I had to resist the urge to snoop in her stuff. I told myself it was just professional curiosity. I liked to keep my skills sharp and looking through a person's office was a good way to find out about them. From where I was sitting, I couldn't see the front of Alex's computer monitor, but it was reflected in the window. It was open to her email program. Despite myself, I was trying to read the backward words in the reflection.

"Ok," Alex said from behind me. I jumped, looked away from the window. She gave me a puzzled look. "You ok, Dent?"

"Uh, yeah. Just staring out the window. You startled me."

Alex had left her hair undone. It spilled all down her back. She smelled good.

"Want me to email photos of the victim's face to your phone while we're waiting for your partner?"

I nodded and she went to work. In a few seconds, my phone was buzzing with incoming pictures.

"So," I asked. "How's your dad?"

"He's good. Doing consulting work for the Oregon Attorney General and the Feds." Her fingers tapped away at the keyboard. "He was just talking about you the other day. Said it was a shame you were dating somebody and I should ask you out. He said you always seemed like a decent guy."

My mouth hit my chest. Pace had said that? She had to be pulling my leg. He had taken great pains to keep his young, attractive daughter away from anybody with a PPB badge. Alex gave me a cool gaze and smiled. For the second time that night I was speechless.

Mandy walked in and saved me. She sat down next to me, gave me a funny look. I shook my head.

"Ok," Alex said, suddenly all business as she scooted forward on her seat. "Keep in mind all the tox screens aren't in. I don't have any lab work back."

We both nodded.

"I think your victim was manually strangled, and in a somewhat unusual way. Ordinarily, when somebody is strangled, there's damage to the trachea and larynx. It's fifty-fifty whether the victim dies of lack of air to the lungs due to a damaged trachea, or a lack of blood to the brain due to compression of the carotid arteries."

Alex didn't look at me as she said this. I'd once gotten into a fight with a suspect who had nearly killed me with his bare hands. I choked him to death instead and had been lucky to keep my job.

Alex shuffled some papers, cleared her throat. "Anyway. Your victim was choked out by somebody that knew what he was doing. There's only slight bruising to the throat. Trachea and larynx are intact. He knew how to compress the carotids and hold them there long enough to starve her brain of oxygen. On a young, healthy woman like her, it probably took five, six minutes of constant pressure to be sure."

That was a special kind of killer. The guy who could hold that choke for that long to make sure.

"There was a little bit of a struggle," Alex went on, still not meeting my eyes. "There's bruising on the back of her head, consistent with hitting her head on something with a blunt edge, maybe the corner of a table or something. Abrasions on the back and elbow are consistent with squirming around on a floor with coarse carpet. She was dressed, at least from the waist up while this was going on. The bra straps marked her back and there's fiber from the sweatshirt in the wounds."

"Finally, judging by the vaginal abrasions she was raped. I took swabs and I'll have them tested for ejaculate and common spermicides and lubricants."

"So you think time of death was last night?" Mandy asked. Alex nodded, looked at the clock on the wall. Ten o'clock.

"Yes. Right about twenty-four hours ago. Some of the lab tests will help fix it, but I wouldn't guess they will change it within four hours either way."

This was a weird one. A handcuffed dead girl who had been strangled with a carotid choke. I hadn't seen that before.

"What else do you think about her Alex?" It was an open-ended question. I wanted Alex to tell me whatever was on her mind. She was sharp, both about the medical side of things and the psychology.

Alex hesitated, then finally answered. "I think once you find out who ran her porn shoot, you'll have your killer."

That took me aback for a second. I was pretty close to naming a cop as her killer, or maybe a security guard or cop wanna-be. The cuffs, the neck restraint, they were two big pieces to the puzzle I thought. But where was this porn business coming from? This was why I liked to get other opinions, particularly from women if a female victim was involved. They saw stuff I didn't. I realized Mandy was nodding her head.

"Ok," I said, leaning forward. "You left me behind there."

"This girl was living on the streets," Alex said. "Her clothes had dirt ground into them so they hadn't been washed in a long time. Her shoes were shot. Her feet were hamburger from walking with those ratty socks on. Her nails were ragged. But her body was clean, her hair had been shampooed recently."

I nodded. I got that much.

"Her intestines were empty. No food. Nothing. But her stomach was full. Right before she died somebody fed her shrimp, looks like maybe a steak, baked potato, I'm guessing a little red wine. That takes money. Money she didn't have. If she ripped somebody off for say, the thirty to fifty bucks a good dinner would cost, she would have gone to McDonald's, made the money last for a while. She couldn't have gotten into a nice place with those clothes anyway. No, somebody bought that for her. In exchange for what?"

"Why porn? Why not just straight up sex?" I asked. "Maybe he thinks they have an understanding. He feeds her this big meal, she never had that understanding or backs out. He decides it's happening one way or another."

Alex and Mandy both shook their heads.

"Nope," Alex said. "It's gotta be a porn shoot. She's young, good looking. I could believe maybe the guy lets her take a shower, wants her to shave, even that he buys her some new underwear to get her all dolled up. It would be cheaper for him just to hire a professional escort, they already have all that stuff. But it's gotta be porn. It's the make up that tells the tale."

I blinked. I still wasn't getting it.

"The makeup. On her razor burns," Mandy said. "The makeup would be obvious in person. But the shade matched her skin pretty well, so it probably wouldn't be so noticeable on the camera."

"Can't they just take that stuff out with a computer anymore?" I asked.

Alex nodded. "Yeah, but maybe your guy doesn't know how. Maybe she covered them up herself without being prompted, but either way, I'm guessing there were pictures involved. Maybe for publication, maybe for your guy's personal use. But definitely some pictures."

"Ok," I said, trying the idea out in my mind. "He feeds her, lets her shower somewhere, she shaves, he gives her new undies…"

Alex cut me off. "Probably a whole new set of clothes. I'm guessing the photos start with her clothed, end with her naked. He might recycle the clothes, but he's classy enough not to reuse underwear."

How the hell did Alex Pace's little girl get to know so much about how porn shoots were done, and high priced escorts, for that matter? I shoved that out of my mind. It was a question for another time. Like never.

"So he takes pictures. How do we go from there to her dead and dumped in a park?"

"Maybe it's like you thought," Mandy said. "Maybe they had two different understandings. Maybe she thought it was just pictures, but he expected a happy ending."

"Ok." It made a certain amount of sense. "But where do the handcuffs come in?"

Alex swiveled her monitor around. On the screen were the photos she'd taken during the autopsy. "The cuffs were put on way too tight. See how deeply they are in the flesh?" She flipped forward a frame, now the cuffs were off and there was an indentation all the way around the girl's wrist. "The flesh is indented, but there's no bruising. The cuffs were put on after her heart stopped."

"Damn," I said.

"Yeah. My guess is this: they struggle; he puts the carotid choke on her, for a little too long; he thinks she's unconscious so he cuffs her up. He realizes she's dead at some point. He panics, takes her and dumps her."

"Damn," I said again. There it was. The end of a life.

Mandy picked it up from there. "He takes her, puts her in a van. Rolls her out the back at the park and gets interrupted."

"Which explains why he didn't get his handcuffs back," I finished. They both nodded.

I sat there silent for a minute, walking it back and forth in my head.

"It fits together pretty well." I looked at Alex. "You got ideas on where we go from here, I'm happy to hear them."

"Well, there's hair and fiber from her clothes, but you know that." I nodded, that was obvious.

"I scraped her nails, but there was so much crap under them I don't know if we'll get anything good. If you manage to find his place it will be a gold mine of evidence. Her hair in the shower, both head hair and body. Wherever the rape happened you'll have a little blood, most likely. I'm not sure how precisely we can match makeup, but I took swabs just in case you find some at the murder scene. I'm pretty sure he provided the makeup. Most of these little street rat girls don't do the whole cosmetics thing. And you need to find her bag."

I nodded. I had already thought of that. These kids always had a bag. Maybe it would be a hiking style backpack, maybe just a duffel bag, maybe just a really big purse, but they always had a bag. They had to. They had no permanent place to stay so everything they owned had to stay with them.

"Anything else you can think of?" I asked.

"Nope. I'll call you if anything comes up. I'll have tox screens and the full workup done by the end of the week, so you have to remember I'm guessing about the strangle. But I think it's pretty solid."

"Me too," I said, standing up. "Thanks, Alex, you've been a big help." She stood and I shook her hand. I forced myself to keep it brief.

I kept running it back and forth in my mind, looking for holes. A guy cruises, looking for girls he can exploit for a little porn and a maybe a little sex. Our victim fit the bill, hard up enough to be desperate, but not on the streets long enough to lose her attractiveness. Things go south, she winds up dead and dumped in a park. A sad way for a life to end, but it all worked.

As we headed outside, I checked my watch and sighed. I hadn't enjoyed the autopsy, but the worst part of the evening was coming up: I had to call the boss.

CHAPTER SEVEN

I was tempted to make Mandy call Lubbock. She was ostensibly the lead detective on this case. But Mandy was serving a six-month probationary period as a detective. She could be bounced back to patrol during that time, pretty much at Lubbock's whim. No, it was better if I dealt with Lubbock and let Mandy fly under the radar. Mandy was just competent enough for Lubbock to strongly dislike her if he noticed her.

I dialed as I drove. Lubbock answered on the first ring.

"When were you going to inform me that you had a new homicide?" The headache started immediately.

"Right about now," I said, careful to keep my tone neutral.

"From now on, I want to know the second you report to the crime scene," Lubbock said.

"Ok," I said, wondering if I still had a bottle of aspirin in my valise. Again, I bit my tongue to keep from pointing out that obviously somebody had already clued him in on the fact that we had a new homicide. I wondered who his snitch was?

I opened my mouth, intending to give him a rundown of the facts, tell him where I was going with the case. Before I could get a word out, he started talking.

"What are we telling the media?"

"The media?" It took me a second to switch gears.

"You haven't figured out anything for the media? What have you been doing?"

My grip tightened on the phone and the plastic case creaked ominously. "Well Steve, mostly I've been doing detective work, you know, trying to figure out who the victim is, who killed her. Things like that."

"Listen, Miller," Lubbock was almost shouting. "I'm tired of your cowboy attitude. You need to start thinking about what's good for the Portland Police Bureau, not what gets the most glory for Denton Miller. Every homicide case brings a tremendous amount of exposure to the Bureau. There's always somebody who wants to second guess the investigation, say we aren't doing enough. If you aren't taking that into account, you're doing sloppy police work."

Sloppy police work? I had thirty-four homicide investigations under my belt, with an almost perfect clearance rate. I'd checked our records. Lubbock hadn't arrested anybody for five years.

"I'll take care of talking to the Public Information people this time," Lubbock was saying. "But next time I want some media ideas from you when you call from the crime scene. Now give me the details of what we've got."

Mechanically, I rattled off the details. It was hard to hear myself over the hum of anger in my ears, hard to see over the red haze that had settled over my vision. I wanted to hit something.

"So we don't even know if she was killed in our jurisdiction," Lubbock said when I finished. "We just know she was dumped in the city limits, so the murder may have happened somewhere else." He sounded hopeful. If we discovered the actual killing had happened somewhere else, the other jurisdiction would take over as the primary investigators.

"Maybe," I said.

"Well, I want you to keep an open mind to that possibility. If we can put this into somebody else's pocket, the sooner the better. Understood?"

"Yeah," I said. The edges of the phone were pressing into my palm. I wondered if it would actually break if I squeezed hard enough.

"I'll get to work on this media angle. Let me know if anything develops."

"Ok."

He hung up. Not a second too soon. I put the phone on the dash, tried very hard to breathe in and out, slowly and rhythmically.

After the mall shooting, Lubbock had been shuffled around from one harmless assignment to another, community liaison this, coordinator of that, the touchy-feely program of the week, where he just had to go to meetings and "manage perceptions."

No one knew why Lubbock was promoted to head of Major Crimes. I couldn't figure out if it was somebody's idea of a reward or a punishment.

I pulled into the precinct parking garage and sat there stewing for a minute. I found some aspirin in my bag, dry swallowed. I chased them with a couple of antacids, for the heartburn that I knew was going to start any minute now.

I walked up to our office. Mandy had made coffee. Good, old-fashioned cop coffee, from the urn in the squad room that got cleaned out once a year, whether it needed it or not. Black, with an oily sheen floating on top. No cream. No sugar. No foamed milk. No flavored syrups.

I took a cup, inhaled the steam coming off the top. "Ahhhhh..." I said. "Thank you."

"Welcome," she said.

Mandy and I wrote up what we had on the case so far. By the time we reached the end, the words were swimming in front of my eyes like hieroglyphics.

Jeannie came up to the office with a photograph in her hand and sat it on my desk. It was a big fat thumbprint, outlined clear and crisp in black fingerprint powder on the polished metal surface of the handcuffs.

"Hot damn," Mandy said, looking over my shoulder. "You AFIS it yet?"

"Of course. It's in the hands of the Feds now," Jeannie said.

Which meant if we were going to get a match, it could take hours, maybe up to a day. Of course we might not get a match at all, but the print on the cuffs was a good one, detailed and pristine. If our guy had ever been arrested, been in the military, or been fingerprinted under one of a dozen other sets of circumstances, his prints would be in the system and we would get a match. I had a good feeling about this. Guys who murder somebody usually have some kind of run-in with the cops before they escalate that far.

Jeannie stifled a yawn. "Unless you guys need anything else, I'm outta here."

I told her to have a good morning and Mandy and I gave the case file one last glance, looking for something we'd missed.

We hadn't. We were stalled out until we got an identification of either the victim or the suspect.

I looked at my watch. "Let's bag it," I said to Mandy. "If an AFIS hit comes in on the victim, we'll start working the victim. If an AFIS hit comes in on the suspect, we'll start working the suspect. Either way, we'll be going full tilt boogie again. Let's get some rest while the computers do their magic."

She'd agreed, a little reluctantly, I think. Pausing in the middle of an investigation was one of the hardest things to do, but we both needed sleep and there was no sense just sitting here in the office.

I hated this part.

CHAPTER EIGHT

The sky was clear outside, rare for this time of year. I put my sunglasses on and decided to forego more coffee. It would make it all that much harder to sleep if I got the chance. I flipped through the radio as I drove. Nothing but talk shows, nattering on about stupid stuff.

It was hard not to drift off as I drove. It was getting harder to stay up all night chasing a case and just keep going for as long as it took. I remembered when I'd been a nineteen-year-old Ranger and staying up for a week straight, running on a ten-minute cat naps.

I drove to Audrey's on autopilot and was a little surprised when I finally pulled into the lot. I didn't remember the last few minutes of the drive. Yeah, it was hell getting old.

I let myself into Audrey's place and started taking off my gear as quietly as I could. I heard the creak of box springs and a mumble from the bedroom. I debated waking her.

Sometimes, when the depression was hitting her hard, Audrey would spend the whole day in bed if she didn't have a class or a performance. I figured I would take a shower, then, I'd wake her up and see if I could get her to go out with me. I needed sleep, but the sunshine would make Audrey feel better. I could always drink more coffee.

I put the lockbox away in the bottom of the closet and stood in the bedroom doorway for a minute to look in on her. Her red hair was unbound and spread out in a wild spray. She slept on her side with one of my old t-shirts on. For some reason I didn't fully understand, I really liked it when she wore my clothes like that. I was struck by a sudden urge to touch her. It wasn't really sexual, at least not completely. I just wanted to feel that red hair of hers, run my hands along the white skin of her calf. It made me feel a little ashamed of myself for how I'd felt around Alex earlier.

I decided to let Audrey sleep. I padded off to the shower, trying to switch mental gears from work to home. It was tough. I honestly would have just preferred to work my case from beginning to end and stay totally in cop mode the whole time, but I'd learned the hard way that relationships weren't something you could just hang up on a hook and get down again when you wanted to.

I stood there in the shower for a long time, letting the hot water unknot my back. I saw that my right knee had a huge bruise, courtesy of hitting the ground while I was wrestling with Wendt. That seemed like forever ago now.

Over the noise of the shower I heard footsteps, then the shower curtain rattled back on its rod. Audrey stood there with her hair wild and messy and a smile on her face.

"Hey," I said.

By way of answering she stepped into the shower with me, not even bothering to take the shirt off first. I dropped the soap and wrapped her up in my arms. She kissed me hard, her tongue probing between my lips.

"You seem to be feeling ok," I said.

"I've decided I'm going to make myself feel ok," she said. We stood there under the water, kissing and touching, for a long time. I was almost successful in shoving work out of my head. I had a bad second when Audrey stepped back and pulled the shirt over her head. I flashed back to my dead victim, lying white, still, and naked on the autopsy slab. I blinked my eyes, trying to get the image out of my head.

"What?" Audrey asked.

I shook my head and pulled her to me. I bent and kissed the line of freckles that ran between her breasts, losing myself in the feel of warm, living flesh under my lips and hands.

Finally, she pulled my head away and kissed me on the lips. She turned and walked out of the shower, towards the hallway and the bedroom.

The sun shone through the blinds in Audrey's bedroom, leaving lines of light and shadow on her body as she lay back on the bed. She reached over and pulled me down beside her. Between my work and her blues, it had been a while since we had been together. We were in that stage of our relationship where we were comfortable and familiar with each other, but not to the point we were starting to take each other for granted.

As we kissed and touched, I finally let it all go: the case, Lubbock, the tension between me and Mandy. I forgot about all of it and the world narrowed down to just me and Audrey, the feel and smell of her hair wrapped around me and the sweet anticipation of where her roaming mouth was going to kiss me next. I let myself be lost in it.

Later, as we lay in a knot of arms and legs, I reveled in the feeling of dreamy lassitude. It felt good not to think about anything, just to feel. My last thought before I drifted off to sleep was that I'd meant to take Audrey out for breakfast.

"Dent? Dent?"

I opened my eyes. Audrey was standing there, dressed now. I smiled. "Hey."

"It's almost noon. Hungry?"

"Yeah." I flipped the covers back and stretched, partly because I needed to stretch, partly because I liked the way she looked at me.

"What's that from?" She reached out and touched the bruise on my knee. I swore and drew back. Damn. That thing was getting sore. Maybe I was getting too old to be wrestling around on the ground with twenty-year-olds.

"Just a bruise," I said, trying to work some kinks out of my back. I really could have used a few more hours of sleep. But I didn't want to sleep and leave Audrey alone. I had no idea when the phone would ring again, sucking me back into the whirlwind of the investigation.

"I know it's a bruise, silly. Where did you get it?"

Distracted, I looked around for my clothes, then remembered they were in the bathroom.

"I arrested a guy on Friday I'd been looking for. He fought a little," I called over my shoulder.

She followed me. "You got into a fight on Friday?"

I rooted around on the bathroom floor, realized we'd both walked all over my clothes as we got out of the shower. They were soaked.

"Yeah. Remember that guy Wendt? The guy that shot that little old woman? I finally put him in jail on Friday. Well, the hospital first, then Mandy took him to jail."

I gathered up my clothes. "Let me throw my clothes in the dryer for a minute. You want to go get some breakfast?" I asked.

I walked back out into the hall. She was standing there with a funny look on her face.

"You put somebody in the hospital?"

"Yeah. He had a gun. I took him down with my baton." I turned towards the utility room, where the washer and dryer were.

"He had a gun? Jesus, Dent. What happened? Why didn't you tell me this?"

I shrugged, realized the dryer had a load of her clothes in it and put my stuff down so I could unload it. "Not much to tell. I followed him to an apartment building. He came running out the back door. I hit him with my baton, arrested him and he's done."

"But if he had a gun, why did you hit him with a baton? He could have shot you."

We'd had a conversation a few weeks ago, about use of force, about how you always met deadly force with deadly force. About why you never tried to take knives away from people like in the movies. You just shot them. I felt like I'd been speaking Greek. We had these conversations from time to time, but it was beginning to dawn on me that for the most part, they'd been theoretical.

"He had it in his waistband. I hid outside a door and cracked him with my baton the second he walked out the door."

"So you ambushed him?"

"Exactly," I said, pleased that she had gotten it. I turned back to my laundry.

"But how can you do that?" She asked.

I almost explained that it was just a matter of picking the right spot to hide when it dawned on me that we were probably having two different conversations.

"What do you mean?" I asked.

"How can you just ambush somebody when they walk out a door? What did you do to him to put him in the hospital anyway?"

"I, uh… Hit him in the arm and the leg. Look, the guy had a gun. He's already killed two people. The quickest and safest way to do this was to just take his ass out before he knew what hit him."

"You hit him in the arm and the leg. Did you break his arm and leg? Is that why he had to go to the hospital."

"Uh… Yeah." There was no use lying. She'd been curious one night about my stuff and I'd shown her the ASP baton.

She stood there, arms crossed, cheeks flushed. She was mad and I really only had the vaguest idea of why. I stood there naked, my wet clothes in a pile around my feet, holding a double handful of her clean underwear and feeling supremely disadvantaged.

"So you ambushed a guy, broke his arm and leg, then came back here and acted like nothing happened. Jesus."

"It was your birthday," I said. It sounded plaintive to my ears. I started to feel a little angry. For one thing, I didn't like sounding plaintive, and for another, Audrey freely admitted that her sole exposure to violence was movies and the time in fifth grade when another kid pushed her down.

She threw her hands up. "Jesus Christ, Dent!" She turned around and walked towards the living room.

I hated fighting with Audrey. For one thing, I usually wasn't sure what, exactly we were fighting about, just that it usually had to do with my work, and by extension that I was somehow morally bereft for doing it.

I forced myself to take a deep breath, focused on straightening out the laundry. I put on a robe before I headed towards the living room, feeling somehow that I would be at a disadvantage if I fought naked.

She was sitting on the couch, looking out the window, and crying.

I hated when she cried.

"You know," she said. "It's like you're two people sometimes. One is this sweet guy who spent way too much money buying me a birthday gift. You make me feel really good. Then you tell me you put somebody in the hospital, in the same way some guys talk about making a stock trade or something."

"He was a murderer," I said, getting angry all over again. Why the hell did I have to justify what I did to Wendt? Especially after I'd worked so hard to make sure nobody got killed.

"But it's not normal!" It was one of the few times I'd ever heard her raise her voice. "I think that's what bothers me. You don't even see this sort of thing as unusual."

I started to say "it's not," then bit my tongue. I had one of those rare moments of clarity that hit me every so often. I spent most of my time with dead bodies, cops and criminals. The other day I had noticed that I was almost out of Vick's Vapor Rub. I always carried a tub near the top of my valise, under my extra ammo. It was for when I had to go in a house with a body that had been dead for a while. It helped cut the smell. A little.

I opened my mouth, realized I didn't know what I was going to say. She was right. My life wasn't normal.

But I liked it.

My phone started ringing. Audrey picked it up off the coffee table and held it out to me. We both knew it would be work. They were the only ones who ever called.

For a second, I hated my job. I hated it because I was having weird dreams when I should have been lying there asleep with Audrey wrapped around me. I hated it because Audrey was standing there, beautiful but angry at me, and I was going to have to get dressed and leave with the tension still hanging between us.

I sighed and held out my hand. Audrey dropped the phone into my palm.

"Dent," I answered.

It was Mandy. "Hey. We got prints back."

"The victim's or the killer's?"

"Both."

Well, we wouldn't exactly have to be Sherlock Holmes and Doctor Watson to put all the pieces together now. Maybe we could wrap this up soon, and I could try to sort things out with Audrey.

"I'll be right there."

CHAPTER NINE

Central Precinct was unusually empty, even for a Saturday. I wondered how many people were taking a mental health day so they could enjoy the nice weather.

I trudged upstairs to our office, trying to put my head in the game. This was a new experience for me. Usually, when I was working a homicide, it was all I could think about. But right now I was feeling a little cheated and resentful. I hated it when things were tense between me and Audrey.

Maybe after this case, I'd start thinking about a new job in the Bureau. I didn't know how I'd make it happen. I spent way too much time solving crimes and not enough kissing ass.

Maybe it was time to learn some ass-kissing skills. No matter how revolting it might be, Audrey was worth it.

Mandy was the only one in the office. She sat in front of her laptop madly clicking away.

"What's up, super sleuth?"

She gave me a big grin in return and turned the screen so I could see it.

On the screen was a mug shot of our victim. The slate under her chin said "JCPD." I flipped the page and found a report from the Junction City Police Department.

Heather Swanson. Her name was Heather Swanson and she was 17.

She'd been arrested on a minor shoplift, in Junction City, Oregon and taken to the police department to be mugged and printed before being released into the custody of her parents. There was also a missing persons report.

I scanned the second report quickly, three months ago, not long after the shop lifting incident, James and Brenda Swanson had reported

Heather as a missing. She was still technically a minor, hadn't been seen in a couple of weeks. She'd packed a bag and split without so much as a goodbye, pausing only long enough to clean out several hundred bucks from her parents' bank accounts.

Mandy had even researched the parents. They looked like Joe and Suzy Homemaker, good credit, middle class jobs, no arrest records at all, no history of domestic disturbances in the past.

Most murder victims are killed by someone they know. It was certainly plausible that Heather's parents weren't as squeaky clean as they looked. We'd go over them with a microscope later, especially dad. But for right now, they didn't feel like anything other than average suburbanites with an average screwed up teenager to me.

I flipped back to Heather's picture again. Heather Swanson. I rolled the name around in my head, glad to finally have a name to attach to her. She looked like a Heather. She looked like somebody who had no business being dead.

"Good work," I said to Mandy. She nodded. "What about notification?"

"Alex called the JC police. They are on their way to the parents' house."

Good. It was the job of the Medical Examiners to notify families of deceased relatives in circumstances like this or arrange for it to happen. I didn't envy that Junction City cop.

I nodded. Mandy opened another file on the computer screen.

There was another face on top, another booking photo, this time from the Salem Police Department.

It was the guy from the van.

"Dammit!" I said. "It's him. The guy from the van. I should have gotten a plate."

Mandy shook her head. "It doesn't matter now, we've got him."

The photo was six months old. I tried to ignore the slate for a second and just look at the face. Young, but older than Heather, he was maybe twenty-five, twenty-six. Long, limp brown hair, not styled or anything, he just looked like he needed a haircut. Narrow face, brown eyes, hadn't shaved for a day or two in the picture.

I was always struck by how ordinary your average murderer looked. People always expected some kind of mustache twirling villain or at least a set of creepy Charles Manson eyes, but that wasn't how it usually worked. Guys who shot their wives and kids usually looked like any other guy with a wife and kids. I'd never worked a serial killer case, but I knew enough about them to realize there wasn't "a look."

I looked at the name. Gibson Allen Marshall looked like any other twenty something slacker who didn't own a comb or a razor. The only thing remarkable about him in the photo was a busted lip.

There was a report from Oregon's Law Enforcement Data System, which, of course, everybody abbreviated as LEDS. Marshall had a half a dozen arrests, from a couple of different cities, and a sealed juvenile record to boot. Two drunk driving arrests, one from Eugene, one from Salem. Two instances within six months where he got jammed up on multiple charges, there was a reckless driving in both of them, a menacing here, a harassment there, maybe road rage?

There was an arrest for some credit card fraud. Then finally a disorderly conduct, resisting arrest, and assaulting a police officer. I checked the date on that one. It matched the photo Mandy had dug up. That made sense. I'd yet to see anybody go to jail for Assault on a Police Officer without at least one visible injury. We had a certain standard to maintain.

I looked down the page to see if he was on parole or probation and got my first surprise. Marshall had never been convicted of any of it. Nothing. Nada. It was like it had all never happened.

"What the hell?" I said out loud.

"Keep reading," Mandy said.

I scrolled through the report. DMV records. Because of the drunk driving arrests, Marshall's driver's license should have been suspended, and it had been for a short time after each arrest, but in each case, it had been "Administratively Reinstated." I'd never seen that before.

She'd tracked down most of the police reports. I'd been right about the road rage. One report was from Corvallis where Marshall had rear-ended another driver, then wound up punching him out. A second was from the Oregon State police, Salem office. Marshall had gotten angry at another driver about a last second lane change, pointed a gun at him as they sped down the highway and damn near got himself shot by the OSP during the resulting traffic stop. Nice guy. I was glad the DMV had seen fit to give him his license back.

The credit card arrest was from here in Portland. I scrolled through the document looking for a report but I didn't see it.

"Where's the fraud report, the one from here in Portland?" I asked, a little annoyed. That would have been the easiest one to get.

"It doesn't exist," she said.

"What do you mean, it doesn't exist?" I asked. I flipped back to the LEDS screen. There it was, he had been arrested as a suspect in a Portland Police investigation, charged with a bunch of fraud related crimes. Had the case number right there.

"Records doesn't have the report," Mandy said. "It isn't there. They have a record of issuing the case number, they have a record of receiving the report, but it doesn't show up in our database."

I frowned. That wasn't supposed to happen. We'd instituted a document control and case tracking system after an external audit revealed the Bureau had a bad habit of "losing" paper work about incidents that might shine an unfavorable light on the Bureau. Now everything was electronic, and it was supposed to be impossible for a report to just disappear.

"Want to know why the mugshot I gave you is from the State Police and not from where he was booked here in Portland?"

That was a good point, now that she mentioned it. The arrest from here in Portland was more recent, the photo would be more up to date.

"I give, why?"

"Because that doesn't exist either. I got into the mugshots file. His isn't in there. Nor do we have his fingerprint card in ID division. None of it is here. Except for that little notation on the LEDS report, I would have never even known the Portland Police Bureau arrested this guy."

I was beginning to smell something rotten. A lost report I could believe. But the mug and print card too?

"What the hell?" I said.

"I was hoping you could tell me," Mandy said. "My computer kung fu is pretty good, but I've never seen anything like this before."

"Ok," I said. "That has to be some kind of computer screw up." That sounded wrong, even to my own ears. "Any idea of where this guy is now?"

"He's had six different addresses with DMV in the last few years. In Eugene for a while, then Corvallis, up here in Portland, someplace way out in Eastern Oregon. But the piece I find interesting is this..." She moused over to another computer file.

It was another document from DMV, this one a vehicle registration. It was for a Ford Econoline van, registered to a company, "GM Art and Photography."

"GM Art and Photography is solely owned by Gibson Allen Marshall. He filed the paperwork with the state two years ago. I might be able to get his corporate tax returns come Monday," she said.

Mandy looked pretty pleased with herself. She had a right to. She'd run down a tremendous amount of information in the hour since the finger prints had come back.

I looked at the address on the registration. It was a five-minute drive from Kelly Point Park, where the victim had been dumped.

I corrected myself. Heather had been dumped at Kelly Point Park. She had a name now.

It was all starting to fit.

"I know a guy who works out of North Precinct," she said. "I had him drive by the address. I got off the phone with him right before you walked in. It's a light industrial type office complex. The van is parked out front. I just had him drive by instead of sit on the place. If Marshal is our guy, I didn't want to spook him."

"Jesus, Mandy," I said, standing up and grabbing my valise. "Maybe I should just go home. You can call me when you're done with this guy so I can pose in the trophy pictures."

She smiled. She deserved the praise. "What now?" she asked.

"Let's go check it out."

We took my car, but she drove. The sky was cloudless and almost painfully bright, unusual for November.

The streets around Marshall's address were deserted. No traffic, but it meant we stuck out as we drove by in the Vic. I looked at the place out of the corner of my eye as we went by.

I didn't turn my head, tried to give off no sign that I was the least bit interested in the place. It was probably more careful than I needed to be, but you never knew. It was for stuff like this that I wanted a different car than the Crown Vic. I'd been fighting that battle since shortly after I became a detective, would probably keep fighting it to no avail until I retired.

Marshall's building was at the end of a strip of three light industrial offices. The one closest to the road was vacant. The middle one was for a pneumatic drill supply company. The third had a small sign over the door, "GM Art and Photography." There was a big glass window next to the door, with a blind drawn and closed. There was apparently not a big demand for pneumatic drills on a Saturday morning or art and photography for that matter. The only vehicle in the lot was the Ford van.

I gathered all this in the few seconds it took us to pass the place. Mandy banged an immediate right and put some buildings between us and the office. If Marshall was inside, he was liable to be jumpy. I had a gut feeling that if he was our guy, this was his first kill. I imagined him sitting in there, looking out the blinds, waiting. I wondered if he'd seen Mandy's friend in the marked car drive by earlier, wondered if he'd just seen us drive by in the unmarked Vic. Most people wouldn't notice such things, or wouldn't think much about them if they did. But to a guy who'd just killed a girl and dumped her body, it might add up to the heat. I wished I knew enough about Marshall to guess if he was the kind to be sitting there with a rifle in his lap.

Mandy pulled into an empty parking lot and stopped. I closed my eyes and played the drive past the office over again in my head, like a movie. The place was going to be a cast iron bitch to approach. It sat well back from the street, surrounded by open fields of weeds and scrub grass that hadn't been developed yet. Marshall could sit inside the front room with the lights off and the blinds adjusted just right so he could see out, and we would never know if he was there.

Mandy and I got out of the car and walked over to some bushes. We could hide there and see Marshall's office. It was a long way away, but that was why I had a pair of binoculars strapped around my neck.

I focused on the van for a good long while. It was motionless on its springs. There was no sign that anybody was inside. The office was the same. The blinds didn't move. Nobody came in or out. The pavement was still wet from last night's rain but the space under the van was dry. Common sense said Marshall had another car, something we had yet to unearth at DMV, and he just drove the van for work. He was probably either on the run or holed up somewhere, watching the news to see if Heather's body had been found yet.

But as I squatted there in the bushes, my thighs burning from the uncomfortable position, I got the feeling he was in there. I would never be able to say why. I saw nothing. It was just my gut churning the way it would back in Tennessee, when I would go hunting with my uncle before he died. I'd look at a stand of trees and in an instant, I'd be dead certain there was a big buck in there, one big enough to wait for. I'd find a spot and wait, sometimes for hours, sitting there with my back to a tree and gripping the worn stock of an old JC Higgens .30-30.

When I got that feeling I was usually right. It had made the difference between eating venison and eating beans on more than one occasion. I hated beans.

I handed the binos to Mandy and stood, grimacing at the pains that shot down my legs. Christ, I needed to get back into shape.

She found a good spot and looked through the lenses for several minutes. I admired her patience and her stillness. It was rare these days. I bet her mom and dad never bought her a Nintendo.

"Looks empty," she said. Then after a long pause: "But I can't shake the funny feeling that somebody's in there."

Interesting.

"I think it's time to think outside the box for a minute," I said, borrowing one of Lubbock's favorite, tired expressions. I walked over to the Vic and popped the trunk.

While the Vic lacked a certain subtlety, it did have one feature I associated with "real" cars. I defined real as being big, made all of steel, rear wheel drive, and having a trunk big enough to haul a body or two. I kept my trunk full of gear, neatly organized in nylon duffel bags. I figured if I ever needed to haul a body, I could just put some stuff in the backseat.

I found the bag I wanted and pulled out an old black pea coat, followed by a ratty pair of corduroy pants that were big enough to go over my jeans. I put the pea coat on and then a mottled gray stocking cap. The pants were stained and torn. I used them when I worked on my house, cleaning out gutters and such. The pea coat I had picked up at a second hand shop. I completed the ensemble with a big backpack. I looked at myself in the car's mirror. It was a passable attempt at transient chic. It wasn't perfect. Anybody who knew what to look for would probably find the $250 Danner boots I was wearing an odd match for the rest of the outfit.

Transients and street people make great covers. Most people have a tendency to look right past them, either out of fear or guilt, or just general snobbery. I bought a cup of coffee for an old homeless man once and he started crying. He told me he was afraid he'd become invisible or had turned into a ghost, because nobody seemed to notice he was there.

I set out from the parking lot. As I walked, my body language changed. I hunched a little, took shorter steps. Anybody watching would have guessed I was a smaller man than what I was. I lost my direct stare at the world and became more furtive. I also mumbled a little under my breath, not loud enough that somebody a foot or two away could tell what I was saying, but definitely loud enough for someone to hear that I was doing it. It wasn't always mental illness that drove homeless folks to do that, but rather the grinding, constant social isolation. Try living in a city of 800,000 people sometime, where most of them won't even look at you, much less talk to you, and see if you don't start talking to yourself a little bit.

I started trash picking right away. Each of the properties had one of those big commercial Dumpsters with the flip up lids. The good news was that most of the trash was paper and other office trash, so I wasn't digging through bags of week-old rotting food. The bad news, from a homeless guy's perspective, was that I wasn't finding much worth taking. A few cans and bottles was the extent of it. At this rate, it would take me all day to get enough together for a 40 oz. bottle of Steel Reserve.

I fished through the detritus of modern American business, through receipts, invoices, even some personal papers a motivated criminal could have used for some fraud.

I hit a treasure trove of Snapple bottles in the last dumpster before Marshall's. If I ever had to make my living pulling cans, I'd remember that. I stashed them in the backpack.

Finally, I wandered into the parking lot of GM Art and Photography. I made myself keep the same slow, shuffling pace, made myself not look at the windows, not look at the van. Instead, I watched the windows out of the corner of my eye. The blinds didn't move, but I still had a feeling that he was in there, watching me.

I flipped up the lid to the Dumpster and almost blew it. Right there on top, lying on a bundle of shredded paper, right next to an empty ramen noodle container, was Heather's backpack. I knew it was hers the second I saw it: military surplus, dyed black. She'd decorated the edges with metal studs, pushing them through the fabric.

I almost reached out and snatched the bag, almost pulled it out and started rummaging through it right there. But a real homeless guy wouldn't have done that. I shoved the bag aside, gave the rest of the dumpster a desultory rummaging. I hit the jack pot with six Tuborg empties, just the funky kind of beer some guy that owned a photography studio would drink. I made myself pluck each bottle out carefully and put it in my sack. Only then did I pick up the bag.

I slung the backpack over a shoulder and let the dumpster lid slam shut. I shuffled past the studio again, wondering if Marshall was watching. Would he come running out, desperate to get the bag back? Or would there be a sense of relief that one of the biggest pieces of evidence tying him to the murder was walking away with a bum, to wind up scattered and lost?

I walked away from the studio. I made myself keep up the act. Instead of making a bee-line for somewhere out of sight, I kept looking for cans, scoring another half dozen or so.

Finally, I was a couple of buildings away, out of sight of Marshall's place. I sat down beside a dumpster and took a couple of swigs out of a water bottle wrapped in a brown paper bag. The ear piece to my phone was dangling from my shirt collar, under my coat. I pulled it up and pushed it into my ear, trying to make it look like I was scratching my ear. Probably nobody was watching, but you never knew. I reached in my pocket and hit the speed dial for Mandy's number. It barely rang before she picked it up.

"What did you find?"

"I think I've got her backpack," I said, trying to look like I was talking to myself. "Pick me up."

A light rain started to fall, so Mandy drove us to a commercial fueling station a half mile or so away. It had a big awning over the pumps. I didn't want my evidence getting wet.

I put the backpack on the trunk and started pulling stuff out. Most of the top layer was clothes, most of them black. They were the same size as what Heather would have worn. Mandy meticulously bagged and documented each piece as I pulled it out and laid it on the clean plastic sheet I'd pulled out of my trunk.

Finally, I hit pay dirt. I pulled out a black leather wallet with a chain attached and flipped it open. Heather's face stared at me from her driver's license.

Mandy whistled. "And there we have it," she said.

"Yeah," I said. "There we have it."

The bag told me that Marshall probably wasn't an experienced killer. He probably hadn't planned to kill Heather. Throwing the bag in the Dumpster of the studio where he worked was the sort of dumb mistake a hardened pro wouldn't make. That was fine with me. I was catching him early in his killing career, and his mistakes would just make putting him away easier.

I put the license on the trunk and Heather stared at us as we finished going through the bag. There wasn't much, makeup, more clothes. I found a glass pipe and a bag of marijuana, maybe a quarter ounce.

"Are we good with the discovery?" Mandy asked as we finished cataloging everything. "Because if we are, I think it's search warrant time."

I considered carefully before answering. I was a compulsive reader when it came to search and seizure related topics. I was always looking for ways to stretch the envelope when it came to getting evidence. There was plenty of case law saying that items in the trash were fair game, no warrant needed. Hell, one of the cases was even from a former Portland cop who wound up on the wrong side of the line and started taking meth.

"I think we're good to go," I said slowly. "You're right. It's search warrant time."

"Do we want to get somebody to come sit on the place while we get the warrant?"

The wheels started turning in my head. Somebody had to stay here in case Marshall was inside. I ran through the short list of people who I trusted to pull off the surveillance without blowing it. There was one person: me.

But the search warrant affidavit was a critical piece of the case. Most cops sucked at writing them. Mine were a work of art. I wasn't being arrogant when I said that. I was good at it and I knew it, so did many other people at the Bureau. That caused rank jealously among some. It made others seek me out and ask for help. I'd lost track of the times my phone rang in the middle of the night, asking for help writing a search warrant affidavit from another detective, or even a patrol guy. I always helped, writing and re-writing until the damn thing was bulletproof. I never got paid for it. I'd finally stumbled on the solution of having the other cops email me the affidavit at home. That way I could sit there in my boxer shorts and work on the damn thing.

But I couldn't very well sit there doing surveillance in my homeless guy persona and write a legal document at the same time.

Besides, I reminded myself, this was Mandy's case. Sort of. She had good chops. Her paperwork was organized, logical and meticulous. She had to learn how to do this stuff somehow. Might as well start now.

"Let's do this," I said. "I'll stay here and get rained on while you go get our warrant. Round up whoever you can get your hands on. Get some steady guys. Then we'll get inside and see what we find."

She looked a little surprised, then nodded. I came within an ace of telling her to bring the warrant affidavit to me before she took it to the judge, but that would have been tantamount to telling her I didn't think she could cut it. She was too good of a troop for that.

"And don't forget to call Lubbock at home and tell him what's going on." She nodded and took off, not quite squealing the tires. I really had to talk to her about her driving.

I made my way around to the field east of the photo studio. I nestled down in a clump of bushes with my bottle of water in its brown bag. I tried very hard to exude my bum vibe.

From here I was looking at the side of Marshall's building. If he went out the front, I'd see him. If he went out the back, I'd see him. As I settled in, two faces kept coming up in my mind, Marshall's and Heather's. I wondered how long I wanted to live like this, ordering my life around two kinds of people: the dead and the murderers.

I was struck by an urge to call Audrey. I could sit there and talk to her and it would probably look to an observer like I was a crazy old man talking to himself. I shook my head and shoved that thought away. It was out of character. I had no business mixing the personal up with an investigation. That was how people got killed.

I wiggled deeper into the bushes and settled into a long wait, forcing any other thoughts out of my mind. There would be time for all that when it was over.

CHAPTER TEN

Unlike most cops, I liked surveillance work. I could will myself into a relaxed state of watchfulness that was almost addictive. When I was like that, my mind was blank but watchful at the same time. I'd learned to be that way hunting in the woods and fields of Tennessee.

I shifted slightly under my poncho. The cold ground was making my legs stiff and sore. I'd gotten better at waiting, but my body wasn't twelve years old anymore.

Four hours went by. I couldn't remember the last time I'd just sat still for this long. I actually found it relaxing. Most of the time I was either busy working, or trying to squeeze in some time with Audrey. Maybe I should make a habit of this.

My phone vibrated in my pocket. I reached in and hit the button to answer.

"Yeah."

"I just got back from the judge's house in Lake Oswego. We're good to go," Mandy said.

Damn. That was fast. "Ok. I'm going to walk out and meet you in the parking lot of that metal recycling place." I gathered up my bag and staggered off, still remembering to play my homeless guy role, conscious of the fact that somebody might be watching.

The farther I got from the photography studio, the more I let myself be Dent Miller, and the less I was the bum. Still, Dan Millan did a double take when he saw me walk up.

"Jesus, Dent. Your talents are wasted here. You should go be an actor and win an academy award."

"Yeah, but there's very little money in being a bum character actor," I said.

Tasha Jackson, a patrol officer I'd worked with a few times before, stood by her police car, a few feet away from Paul Abbot, one of the other detectives in the Major Crimes unit. Paul was a couple of years older than me, a short, squat man who was running to belly. He bought his suits off the rack at Sears and looked like something out of a Mickey Spillane novel, but he was a good cop. There was a blonde gangly kid standing next to him, dressed in a very nicely cut suit with spit-shined shoes.

Paul stuck out a hand, "Dent. Long time no see." We shook and he gestured at the kid. "My new partner, Tanner Reese."

I shook the kid's hand. "Meetcha."

I turned to Mandy. "Time's wasting. Why don't you brief everybody while I get ready?"

Mandy nodded and gathered everybody around in a semicircle. She laid out photos of Marshall, photos of the front and rear of the building, even a satellite photo of the building from above, all on the hood of her car. I listened as she gave a briefing that was as concise and detailed as any I'd heard before going on a mission in the Rangers. God, it was nice to be around professionals.

As she talked I pulled off my bum coat and opened the trunk of my car. First I put on my soft body armor. Incredible technology, it would stop just about any pistol or shotgun round, and the new stuff only weighed a few pounds. I put on a blue windbreaker with the words "Police" stenciled across the front and back in large, friendly letters.

Next, I pulled out a nylon gun case. The bureau had invested heavily in AR15 style carbines in recent years. They made sense. They were accurate, powerful, and you could teach anybody with normal hand-eye coordination how to shoot one in an afternoon. My favorite long gun though, was an ugly, battered Remington 870 12 gauge shotgun. Most of the finish was worn down to bare metal. The stock bore imprints of what looked suspiciously like a pair of front teeth on the end of the butt. Back in the old days, a good buttstroke to the face had been considered a perfectly acceptable way to subdue a suspect.

Mandy started talking about her plan to enter the building and my ears perked up. This was the part we had to get right.

"Me, Dent and Sergeant Millan are going to the front. We'll knock and announce, but if we don't get an answer, we're going to bust the door and go in. Officer Jackson and detectives Abbot and Reese will cover the back. Dent will have a long gun on the front door team; Officer Jackson will have a rifle at the back. Also, Sergeant Millan and Officer Jackson each have a Taser."

I nodded. Each team had a uniformed officer with a Taser. It was good to have someone in an instantly recognizable police uniform on each team. That way there wasn't any question later about the suspect saying he thought he was the victim of a home invasion or crap like that. The Tasers were good. If Marshall got froggy, we'd just zap him. Each team had a long gun in case this turned into a shootout. We carried pistols because it was convenient and discreet, but if you wanted to stop a fight you needed a shotgun or a rifle.

"Anybody have any questions?" Mandy looked around at the group. "Anybody have any suggestions? Anybody see any holes? Now's the time to speak up if you do."

I liked that. I gave her a big thumbs up. Nobody said anything.

"Ok," she said. "Let's go."

As we were getting in the car, I said "I'm surprised Lubbock didn't want to be here to supervise." I meant it as a joke. Lubbock was notorious for being somewhere else when the guns came out.

Mandy frowned. "I called him three times. He never answered. I left a message."

"Hold on a sec," I said. She stopped, with her hand on the gear selector. Behind us the other cops were lined up in their cars, raring to go. "You mean he doesn't know we're doing this?" By the Bureau's rules, this counted as a high-risk entry. It technically needed Lubbock's approval before we went forward.

"I called him three times. The first time was when I left you here, over four hours ago. I called him right before I got the warrant signed, then again right before we got here. He's never answered."

I thought fast. If we screwed around, the more likely we were to lose evidence. Homicide cases were solved quickly, or they weren't solved at all. Plus, not having Lubbock here was a bonus. There was a good chance he would dick around, holding up the operation while he tried to get the SWAT team to do the entry, or worse yet try to cook up some scheme to hand the case over to the FBI, the State Police or the Boy Scouts, anything to get him off the hook and shove the case into somebody else's lap.

Who had put him in charge of detectives? I wondered again. There were perfectly good community involvement jobs where Lubbock could while away his years until retirement without hurting somebody.

"Hell with him," I said. "If he wants to play with the big boys, he should answer his pages."

Mandy dropped the car into drive and laid ten feet of rubber in the parking lot. I sat in the passenger seat with the shotgun between my legs.

We slid to a stop in front of the studio. I had the car door open and was halfway out before the car even stopped, feeling that familiar calm awareness settle over me. In the next few minutes, I might shoot somebody, might get shot myself, or nothing at all might happen.

Mandy, Millan and I stacked up on the side of the door away from the windows. I carried the shotgun. Mandy and Millan carried the ram between them. It was a three-foot long piece of metal pipe filled with concrete, with handles on either side.

I knocked on the door by kicking on it three times. "Portland Police! We have a search warrant! Open the door! Do it now!" I counted to three under my breath.

"Ok," I said to Millan and Mandy. "Do it."

Mandy looked a little surprised, probably expected me to have waited longer, but I never did this any other way. Doors were cheap. Giving the other guy a chance to react could be expensive. They swung the ram perfectly and the door jamb splintered open. All three hinges let go at once and the door simply fell inward, a perfect score on the door removal chart. They tossed the ram to the ground outside, and we were in.

The trick to something like this was to see everything at once, while focusing on the tiny details. We moved through the door quickly. Doorways were danger zones, called "fatal funnels," because your bad guy could be anywhere in the room, the wide end of the funnel, but you had to come through the opening, the narrow end of the funnel. Cops died in doorways.

But not today. We moved through the room, following the walls, the lights under our guns lit the place up beautifully.

We flowed through the room quickly, moving smoothly, not in the jerky, spasmodic movements they always showed on TV. Every space a person could possibly hide in, behind, or under got a quick look.

The waiting room was small, with a threadbare couch under the front window, facing a short counter with a cash register. I reached down to pull the couch away from the wall with one hand so I could shine my light behind it. I puff of dust came up from the fabric. The magazines on the waiting table were years old. The whole place had an air of disuse.

Millan and Mandy cleared behind the counter. "Clear," Millan said softly.

I nodded. "Clear." Unlike the movies, or a TV show, we kept our voices low instead of screaming. If there was a bad guy inside, he undoubtedly knew we were there, but there was no sense in broadcasting our exact position. Bullets went through walls.

There was a wooden interior door next to the register. We all stacked up beside it, and Dan tried the knob gently. It turned so he pushed it inward, just hard enough so it would have smashed anybody hiding on the other side in the face, but not hard enough that it hit the wall and bounced closed again.

This place was bigger than it looked from the outside. The door opened onto a long narrow hallway, about fifty feet long. There were three doors on the right, two more on the left, not counting the one we'd just come through. At the end of the hall was the back door, where the other cops would be waiting for anybody trying to escape.

The walls were unfinished drywall, taped but not painted. The floor was bare concrete. The walls didn't go all the way up. Obviously the place was designed for a dropped ceiling that hadn't been installed yet. Bare light fixtures hung down from above.

The closest doorway, the one to the right, was closed, but from behind it I heard the hiss of water running, either a shower or a sink. I smiled. Would we get lucky enough to catch the guy in the shower?

Millan turned to me, pointed his fingers at his eyes, then down to the end of the hallway. He pointed at himself and Mandy, then to the doors. I nodded back.

He and Mandy would search the rooms while I covered the hallway with my shotgun. You could only get so many cops in a room pointing guns around before they started pointing them at each other. Even though it was sawed off, the shotgun could be a liability in tight quarters. It was made for the hallway though. By the time a blast of buckshot made it to the end of the hall, the pattern would have expanded to a circle about ten inches across. The exit door was steel, and the back wall of the building was cinder block, so if I had to zap somebody I was confident that the buckshot wouldn't exit the building and endanger the guys standing out back.

I stood in the doorway we'd just moved through, using it as cover. Mandy and Millan stacked up next to the first door on the right. Then they went in, leaving me to cover the hall.

I gave them a couple of seconds to get into the room, then headed towards the doorway they'd just entered. I could stand there and I could cover the hall while still being close enough to help them out if something happened. I felt a drop of water land on the back of my neck. Must be some leaky pipes up there.

Nobody ever looks up. I'd learned that lesson deer hunting in Tennessee, then relearned it in the Rangers.

It was maybe six feet, on a diagonal, from where I was standing to the door Mandy and Millan had just entered. I took my first step and something tugged at my peripheral vision, some flickering of the light.

Then a weight hit my shoulders, sending me crashing to the concrete. I landed on top of the shotgun's receiver. Even though the vest, the impact was enough to drive the breath out of my lungs with a "whuff." I tried to roll over onto my back, but the weight settled on my shoulder blades and I felt an arm slide over my throat like an iron bar.

I tried to drop my chin, so the pressure would be on my jaw and not my windpipe, but it was too late. I heaved and bucked to no avail as little black dots began to swim in my vision.

CHAPTER ELEVEN

As my lungs burned and my vision started to shut down, I gave it one last effort, whipsawing my body back and forth, trying to use my size and weight to my advantage, but my muscles were too oxygen-deprived, my attacker too well balanced, for me to get free. My attacker's forearm was squeezing the carotid arteries in my neck, cutting off the blood supply to my brain.

I remembered being taught to choke people out, remembered the instructor telling us that the onset of unconsciousness was swift, within six seconds or so, remembered him telling us you couldn't apply the choke for too long because brain damage and death were the inevitable outcomes.

I thrashed around, trying to throw the guy off my back, but he was too good. He had his weight centered high up, right under my shoulder blades and his legs were spread wide, so I couldn't roll him off. All I could see was the dirty carpet of the hallway. My vision narrowed and it looked like I was looking through a soda straw. All I could hear was a singing whine in my ears. I tried to yell, tried to warn Mandy and Millan, but my mouth wouldn't move.

Just as my vision was narrowing down to the last pinprick of light, I heard a wet thud and the weight came off my shoulders, just as abruptly as it landed.

I sucked in a breath and rolled onto my side. I got my first look at Marshall. He was on the floor beside me, naked. His long brown hair was wet and plastered to his skull with sudsy water. A rivulet of blood ran from his hairline. Mandy raised her Glock to smack Marshall in the head again.

I still couldn't move my arms and legs. It was a shame. The fear from getting choked out was being replaced by red animal rage. I wanted to get my hands on Marshall and pound his head through the wall until my arms got tired.

Marshall jerked his head aside, so Mandy's blow just glanced off his ear. You couldn't properly pistol whip someone with a gun made out of plastic anyway. She kicked him under the ribs and holstered the gun. Then I heard a peculiar clacking, buzzing sound and Marshall jerked around like a cockroach on a frying pan.

I finally managed to roll over onto my back. The Taser in Dan Millan's hand was connected to the two metal barbs in Marshall's ass by long fine wires. A high, keening wail came out of Marshall's lips. I realized he'd been silent the whole time he'd been choking me.

I fought my way to my knees. The Taser quit shocking Marshall and Millan yelled, "Put your hands behind your back!"

Mandy pulled out her cuffs, but Marshall made a low growl in the back of his throat and tried to rise again. Millan shocked him again and Marshall fell flat.

This time Mandy was ready. When the Taser quit, Mandy grabbed his arms and cuffed them together. Marshall lay on the carpet, panting but not saying anything.

I managed to stand up. Every time I took a breath I felt a hitch of pain in my ribs from where I had fallen on the shotgun. I looked down at Marshall, then at Millan.

"Nice shot," I said, nodding down at the barbs in Marshall's ass.

"Target of opportunity," he said with a shrug.

"You ok?" Mandy asked.

"Yeah," I said. "He was choking me out until you showed up though. Nice job cracking him in the gourd."

It was her turn to shrug. "Seemed like the thing to do at the time. Where the hell did he come from? The shower was still running in the bathroom. We saw wet footprints heading towards the door and figured he ran deeper into the building."

I pointed up. "From up there. Must have been hanging from the pipes. Crazy."

I craned my head back to look up, to see exactly where Marshall had been perched. Bad idea. The singing in my ears came back and my vision narrowed again. I felt myself wavering back and forth and decided to just sit down. I landed hard but it was better than falling over and landing on that damned shotgun again.

I heard Millan get on the radio, calling up an ambulance.

I didn't quite go all the way out, but I wavered on the verge of unconsciousness for what felt like a long time before things finally started to come back into focus.

I tried to get up again.

"Sit down, Dent," Millan said. He pulled the shotgun off me and handed it to Mandy. "You're going to the hospital."

I wanted to argue with him, but I felt so weak and exhausted that I just sat there instead. Marshall lay there without saying a word the whole time, just stared at me with heavy-lidded eyes.

The ambulance crew always seems to get there faster when they know it's a cop that is hurt.

It turned out to not be so bad. After a few minutes of arguing, I managed to convince the ambulance crew to wrap an elastic bandage around my ribs and turn me loose. After a final admonition to go to the emergency room if I felt light-headed, dizzy or had trouble concentrating.

Millan looked surprised when I stepped out of the back of the ambulance. "That didn't take long. Aren't you supposed to go home and get some rest?"

"I'll rest when I'm dead. Let's go."

Marshall's studio was bustling. While I'd been in the back of the ambulance getting poked and prodded, Mandy had called in the cavalry.

Evidence techs were working in every room, searching, photographing and cataloging. If there was a remote possibility that something would be of evidentiary value, we would take it. I believed firmly that it was better to take two truckloads worth of stuff and not use most of it than figure out that we had to go back, get another warrant and seize something we'd left behind on the first visit. A good defense attorney would tear you up on stuff like that in court.

Mandy was in the waiting room. Paperwork and a laptop computer were spread out on the counter in front of her. I hovered over her shoulder for a minute before she recognized me. She turned and jumped. She'd been wrapped up in the screen in front of her.

"Dent! Hey. Are you ok?"

I grunted an affirmative. "Where's Marshall?"

"Downtown. We'll go interview him as soon as we're done here."

"Did he get Mirandized?"

Her mouth compressed into a line. I was being a jerk and I knew it the second it came out of my mouth. Even rookies didn't forget to Mirandize suspects these days, or at least if they did, they didn't last long.

"Yeah, Dent. He got Mirandized." She turned back to the computer screen and went back to work on her evidence log.

I sighed. "Look, I'm sorry. I'm being an asshole. You're doing a great job. I'm just a little bent out of shape over getting my head handed to me."

She kept pecking at the keys for a minute, ignoring me. Finally, she stopped.

"Yeah. You're right. You are being an asshole. But there's something you should see."

She turned and walked back towards the hallway without another word, leaving me to follow or not as I liked. I shrugged and fell in after her. My stomach did a little flip flop as we walked past the spot where Marshall had ambushed me. She led me to the first door on the left and stopped, making a little "after you" gesture.

I stepped into the room. It had been turned into a miniature gym. The floors were covered with mats. A punching bag hung from one corner. Weights were scattered here and there. I walked over to a big bookcase along one wall. It was full of books on combatives and martial arts. One book on Brazilian Jujitsu fell open to a section on chokes when I opened it. I found a copy of *Championship Fighting* by Jack Dempsey, a personal favorite of mine, out of print and easily worth a few hundred bucks. There was some crazy stuff too, a book of ninja secrets of invisibility.

Damn. A martial arts guy. I'd lost count of the number of guys I'd pounded into the ground who claimed to be martial arts experts. They claimed to have all sorts of exotic techniques, which I dealt with by hitting them really hard. Jack Dempsey really did have the right ideas.

Still, I felt a little better. At least Marshall had been trained. I still wished I'd been able to pound on him a little bit. Intellectually, I knew Tasers were a good idea, but when a guy dropped out of the rafters and tried to choke you, it always felt good to leave the guy spitting out some teeth.

"Any sign of a second guy? The other guy I saw in the van?"

Mandy shook her head. "No sign. Marshall lives here alone. Only one toothbrush, the only clothes are his, no sign of anybody else."

"Huh," I said.

"That's not all," Mandy said from the doorway. "Come check this out."

I followed her to the next room down the hall. Half of it was set up as a photography studio. A half-dozen lights on stands were set up around a bed in the center. Cameras on tripods were lined up on one wall. A couple of clothes racks stood in one corner, holding all sorts of lingerie in all different sizes.

On the back wall, there were banks of computers. I counted three monitors and six computer towers. A young woman sat hunched in front of them, a laptop balanced on her lap with cords running from it to one of the computers in front of her.

"How's it going, Casey?" Mandy asked.

"We're almost there," she said, pushing a stray lock of blond hair out of her eye. It looked like somebody had trimmed her hair with a pair of dull pruning shears. I couldn't tell if it was from neglect or one of those haircuts people spend a bunch of money on.

Casey was in her late twenties, but she looked even younger. She was wearing a shapeless gray sweatshirt and jeans and looked like any one of the hipster kids I saw hanging out when I went downtown. It was hard to believe but she was a consultant for the bureau. She had helped us put half a dozen assholes in jail, mostly guys who were into kiddie porn. She was a little weird, in that way that hyper-intelligent people can sometimes seem to be on their own planet, but she had demonstrated a willingness to go after evidence like a rabid pit bull. She would stay awake for days at a time so she could help put some perv in jail. That made her a good troop in my book.

I walked up and looked over her shoulder. The screen of the laptop was an incomprehensible mess of menus and command line boxes. I wasn't stupid and could puzzle my way through just about any piece of technology I put my mind to, but Casey was on a whole other level. This stuff changed incomprehensibly fast. Keeping up with it was a fulltime job that none of us had the time for. I hoped maybe someday the mayor would give her a medal, or at least a gift certificate to a decent hair stylist.

She gave a little shake of her head and I heard bones pop and crackle in her neck. She shut down all the windows with a few keystrokes.

"Ok," Casey said. "I've got all the hard drives locked down so nothing can write to them. I'll take them back to the shop and start imaging them tonight. Is there anything you want right now?"

"Are there any pictures?" I asked.

She turned to look at me. Casey had big blue eyes that looked way too old for her face sometimes.

"Dent, there's almost nothing but pictures on here. Thousands of them. He's serving them up on the Internet."

This was going to be big. "Ok. Can you just show us the most recent ones?"

She nodded, flipped on one of the monitors. It was huge, probably cost half a week of my salary. I watched as Casey opened up some folders. Lists of digital photographs spilled down the screen. She sorted them by date, opened the first few.

There she was. Heather.

"That's her," Mandy said. "Our victim."

Casey opened about fifty photos, all of them timestamped from the night Heather was killed. She was clothed at first, then slowly undressed, never looking comfortable with what she was doing. I failed to see how anybody could find the pictures titillating. Maybe I was biased because I'd seen Heather dead and discarded like a worn out pair of shoes, but as I looked at the pictures I saw fear and vulnerability that removed any sexiness. To me, she looked like a scared young girl with her clothes off. But then again maybe that was the attraction for these guys.

"Click on some more, just at random," Mandy said. More pictures popped up. Maybe a dozen other girls.

"Jesus. They all look pretty young," Mandy said.

"Yeah," I said. "Real young." I could feel the can of worms getting bigger. We'd have to do our best to identify each one of the girls, figure out how old they had been when the pictures were taken. I wondered how many of these girls would turn out to be dead. Then there were all the guys who had bought or downloaded the pictures. Certainly, they would be all over the country, probably all over the world. This would probably wind up going Federal.

"We need to talk to Marshall," I said. "Soon. While he's still off balance from being arrested."

Mandy nodded. "Yeah. Casey has the computer end sewn down. Paul and Tanner are helping with the evidence. What do you say we go sit down with Mr. Marshall and chat him up?"

"Let's do it."

I fidgeted in silence during the whole drive back to Central Precinct, forcing myself not to tell Mandy how I thought she should do the interrogation. It was her deal, and she would probably do fine. An ex-girlfriend had once called me a control freak.

In the old days, our interview rooms used to have big one-way glass windows that looked like mirrors from the inside so we could stand there and observe interrogations. But all the TV cop shows ruined that for us. I'd always been amazed how much your average criminal was into TV cops shows. Some of them got angry when we didn't act like the guys on TV did. It was a weird world.

Now we did interrogations in a plain square room with the walls painted an unnatural color somewhere between beige and pink that was calculated to put people into a warm, fuzzy cooperative mood. Bland, abstract art prints hung on the walls. It looked like a dentist office waiting room. The chairs for the interviewer and interviewee looked the same, but the one for the interviewer was slightly taller and infinitely more comfortable. Instead of the one-way mirror, we had hidden video cameras that covered the subject from three different angles and the place was wired for professional quality digital sound. Progress marches on.

Mandy and I were in the next room over, watching Marshall on the monitors. He sat impassively still, dressed in disposable paper clothes.

"What do you think?" I asked Mandy.

She was quiet for a minute, standing there with her arms folded across her chest. "I'm wondering if we should have somebody else interview him. He tried to choke you to death and I'm the one who cracked him in the head with a pistol butt."

I sat down in the hard plastic seat in front of all the recording gear, suddenly feeling very tired and very sore. She had a point. "It's up to you."

She watched Marshall on the monitor for a moment. "I'll give it a shot. I think he's going to invoke anyway."

"What makes you say that?" The smartest thing you could do if you got arrested was to invoke your Miranda rights. You didn't have to talk to anybody. Most of the people I'd put in jail had wound up there, directly or indirectly, because of things they said to me.

The Supreme Court said we had to tell people about their right to remain silent, but most suspects were too stupid to shut their mouths. They all thought they could talk their way out of the jam they were in, even ones that should have known better. After all, everybody was smarter than the cops. I could count on the fingers of one hand the number of people I'd arrested for major crimes who had been smart enough to invoke their Miranda rights.

"I dunno," Mandy said. "He just seems like the kind of guy that would invoke."

"It's up to you," I said again.

Mandy nodded and walked out. I watched on the video screen as she walked in the interview room. She didn't say anything to Marshall at first. Instead, she busied herself with arranging her props: a thick file folder full of mostly blank paper, a videotape with "security footage" written on it and all sorts of evidence stickers, a couple of fingerprint cards sealed in a plastic bag. It was all fake. We never took real evidence into an interview with a suspect if we could help it. But it made them sit there and wonder what the hell you had on them.

Finally, Mandy stopped futzing around and sat back in the chair. "Gibson, I'm Detective Williams. How are you?"

Marshall was silent for a moment, then, instead of looking at Mandy, he looked directly into the lens of one of the video cameras, the one that was concealed in a big swirl of black in one of the paintings on the walls. He spoke very clearly and distinctly.

"Detective Williams, I would like to exercise my rights not to speak with you until I have spoken with an attorney." It was the first time I'd heard him speak. His voice was soft, almost girlish.

Damn. He'd invoked. And we'd obligingly recorded it from three different views and in high definition sound. The interview had to stop. We couldn't interview him without his attorney present, which meant there wouldn't be an interview. Anybody with a pulse and a legal degree wouldn't agree to have their client interviewed by the cops.

I watched as Mandy gathered up her stuff and left the room silently. Marshall sat there quietly, still unmoving as a patrol officer came in and collected him. He would go to the Multnomah County jail on the hourly shuttle we ran out there.

Mandy came back in, slammed her stuff down on the table before sitting down and crossing her arms. "Damn. I knew it."

"Listen," I said. "That wasn't your fault. It couldn't be. You never had a chance to even start the interview for crying out loud. The guy had his response planned before you even went in the door."

"I know," she said, putting her feet up on the desk. "But it would have been nice to wind up with a confession on my first case out of the chute."

That was her ego talking, but I would be the last person in the world who could give her a hard time about ego. I had wanted a confession on my first murder case too. I'd gotten one, but my suspect had been the product of fetal alcohol syndrome and had probably grown up chewing the lead paint off windowsills.

"I don't think we need it. We've got the victim's stuff in his dumpster, pictures of her in his studio right before she died, and the fact that he obviously likes to choke people." I rubbed my throat. "And that's just for starters. Who the hell knows what Casey is going to find on those hard drives. I'm betting we'll get hair and fiber matches, DNA, stuff like that. We've got this guy nailed down."

She frowned then nodded. "Yeah. But it would still be nice to have a confession."

She had a point. Even though everybody watched forensic police shows on TV these days and loved to hear about fingerprints and DNA and Ninhydrin steaming and god knows what else, there was still nothing quite like watching the guy confess to the crime on video, preferably while he shared some details only the murderer would know.

"Well," I said. "We aren't going to get one. So let's put it aside and move on. It's easy to get sidetracked and bang your head against the wall over something you don't have, instead of working what you've got. So what's left to do?"

Ever organized, she pulled out her phone and started going down the list. "Casey has the computer servers at her office. The crime scene team is finished out at the studio. Jeannie and Roger stripped the place down to the bare walls. We pulled hairs and a saliva sample from Marshall down in booking, so we're good to go there. It will be a while before all the forensics stuff comes back. I've got the probable cause affidavit ready to go with Marshall to jail, so we don't have to worry about him going anywhere until Monday at the earliest. We have a meeting with the DA on Monday morning to review the case."

She wasn't missing anything.

"So where does that leave us?" I asked.

She went back over the list again. "I think that leaves us with nothing else to do until we get some forensics back and have a chance to talk to the DA. Which means it's time to get some sleep." She put her phone away and stood.

Sleep sounded like an excellent idea. My chest hurt. My throat hurt. My back hurt. The burnt adrenaline from the fight earlier in the day left me feeling cranky and rough around the edges. I followed Mandy out to the parking lot. We were both tired and didn't say much. But there was one last thing I had to take care of before we both went home.

"Hey," I said as she slipped her key into the ignition. She turned to look at me.

"Thanks for pulling Marshall off my ass. I would have been done if you hadn't tuned him up."

She shrugged. "You would have done the same for me."

"Yeah, but what's important is that you did it for me today." I shuffled my feet. I was never very good at this kind of stuff. "Look, I'm a difficult partner sometimes. I don't do things the way most people do. I'm not the most diplomatic person in the world. But good police work is important to me. Most of the cops in this Bureau aren't worth a damn, but you've got what it takes. You've done a great job on this case. You haven't missed a trick and you've actually taught me a thing or two. I'm glad you're my partner."

That got me a real smile and I was glad to see it. The Bureau needed kids like her. Somebody had to catch the criminals when I retired to go sit on a couch and watch Matlock all day.

"Thanks, Dent. You are a jerk sometimes, but I've learned a bunch from you too."

"Thanks. I think. Look, we've had our little emotional moment here, so now let's go home and get some sleep."

She laughed and nodded. She laid twenty feet of rubber peeling out of the parking lot in front of me. I was tempted to chase her and teach her a thing or two about handling a car, but I was just too tired.

CHAPTER TWELVE

I drove home, too tired to even listen to the radio. The sun went down as I drove, and it started raining, which did nothing to improve my mood. By the time I got home, I was in a funk. I didn't even feel like calling Audrey.

I couldn't talk to Audrey about certain things. That was an uncomfortable realization, considering I'd more than once asked her to move in with me, was constantly on the verge of asking her to marry me. My job was like a foreign language to her. She had been brought up in a loving, middle-class home. She'd never been in a fight. Hell, she'd never even *seen* a fight except on television. When we talked about the uglier parts of my job, she treated me almost as if I had some kind of disease. I don't think it was intentional on her part. I think there was a side of me that she had no frame of reference for dealing with. When we tried to talk about it, we more often than not just wound up arguing. So I just didn't talk about it much anymore.

I couldn't sleep, so I drank. I sat there in my chair, my phone on my lap and a tumbler full of Bushmills in my hand. I wanted to talk to Audrey, wanted to talk to somebody. But I knew that if I tried to explain how my day went, how I'd almost been choked out, somehow we'd wind up in an argument. Her questions always seemed to imply that if I'd tried hard enough, if I had just tried things a different way, the violence wouldn't have been necessary. I don't think she meant to do it. I certainly don't think she meant to attack me personally. I just think she wanted to live in a world where stuff like that didn't happen.

Audrey might as well have been from a different planet, as far as I was concerned. She'd come from this gentle, bright existence where her mom and dad loved her, loved each other. I'd grown up in a single wide trailer with fist-shaped holes in the walls. Instead of wading through blood and shit, she made her way through life creating music and teaching people. She was like the promised land to me, someplace I could visit, but I wondered if I was fooling myself when I thought I could live there.

The whiskey didn't even burn on the way down. It had a rich, almost caramel flavor. It was still early. Saturday night. I wondered what Alex was up to.

Dangerous ground. I took my tumbler with me and wandered around the house, feeling antsy and restless, all thoughts of sleep somehow gone.

I opened up a closet and pulled out my favorite guitar, a 1965 Fender Stratocaster, made right before CBS bought, and ruined, the company. The body was Candy Apple Red. The maple neck had that broken in feel that only comes from decades of playing. The wood on the edges was just slightly rolled over like it had molded itself to my hand over the years. I sat down on my stool and struck a g-chord. The damn thing sounded like magic and sex and thunder, all rolled into one. It was louder than any un-amplified electric guitar had any right to be. The tone was bell-like on top, woody on the bottom. The strings were brand new, but the tuners and other hardware were all original, fifty some years old, yet they still held perfect tune.

I shuffled my way through some blues licks, then made a pass at the first solo to Hendrix's version of "All Along the Watchtower." I'd been working on that one for a couple of years now. Sooner or later I'd get it down, all the way through.

I looked at my watch and realized I'd been sitting there for almost twenty minutes. I had no musical talent at all, but a fine guitar could transport me just by its sound and looks alone. I stopped playing and looked at the Strat. Most of the designs that originally dated from the Fifties hadn't aged well,unless your tastes ran to kitsch, but that Strat still looked as fresh and sleek as it had back then. The shape somehow made me think of rocket ships and women both at once.

The paint was a little checked and crazed from the years, but it still looked cool. There was no other word for it. It wasn't "beautiful," it didn't have a "good aesthetic." It was cool. Cool in the way that hot rods, Harleys, and fighter planes were cool. To my blue-collar eye, it was so cool it was art.

I'd spent whole summers in my teens, reading Rolling Stone and Guitar Player magazines over and over again, looking at pictures of Strats. The magazines came from money I scrounged mowing lawns, hauling scrap. I kept them hidden from my dad the way other kids hid their porn. He hated all those long-haired, dope smoking hippies.

He'd thrown my Hendrix albums out twice when he was drunk, and I always scraped the scratch together to buy them again. The only guitar I'd had back then was a no-name Taiwan import. I'd left it in the trailer when I left for basic training, and since I never went back, I had no idea what happened to it.

Months later, I walked out the gates of Fort Benning, right after graduating airborne school, my wallet flush with payday cash. I was passing the row of bars, and tattoo parlors, intent on getting a little drunk, when I saw my Strat, sitting in the window of a pawn shop. I looked at the price tag, on a card woven between the strings, and turned to go. I got halfway down the block before it occurred to me that I had enough money in my pocket to just walk in and buy it. That was a new thought for me. I had never spent that much money on any single thing before, had, in all honesty, gotten used to my dreams being just that: dreams that would probably never come true.

I walked out fifteen minutes later with a guitar case in my hand and a nagging suspicion that I might be hallucinating. Despite having graduated basic, having gotten my airborne wings after jumping out of an airplane, buying that guitar made me finally feel like a man. This was something I'd dreamed about, lusted after, and I finally had it in my hands. It was a new idea, one I definitely hadn't learned from my old man. As I walked back to the base with my Strat, it occurred to me that I didn't know if my father had any dreams, or if any of them had ever come true. It was the first time I ever felt sorry for him, and the start of maybe learning to forgive him.

I didn't get drunk that weekend, didn't get laid. I also didn't get a bad tattoo or a case of the clap. What I got was a bad set of blistered fingers. By Sunday night, the night before I'd leave for Ranger school, I could play "Sunshine of Your Love" all the way through, and most of "Hey Joe."

Sixty-eight days later, I had a handful of brand new Ranger tabs to sew on my uniforms, and a little more swagger, but secretly my biggest relief was that I could get that Strat out of storage. I'd reconciled myself to the fact that I would always be better by far at shooting a rifle than playing guitar, that I was probably never going to make it big in a rock band, but the guitar was mine. It took me away from the oppressiveness of the Army, the sad desperation of the kids around me who needed to prove that they were men.

Many nights during Ranger school, as I sat up to my neck in swamp water, or froze my ass off on the side of a mountain, I dreamed about having that Strat in my hands, the way other guys dreamed about their girlfriends. I knew it would probably never take me anywhere except in my own mind, but that was enough.

I sat in my living room twenty years later, with the guitar in my hands, trying to remember the kid who had bought it. That was a long time ago: a handful of girlfriends, a combat tour, at least two dead men at my hands. That kid from Tennessee didn't even seem real to me anymore. I hadn't been back to Tennessee since the day I got on the bus to join the Army.

My eyelids fluttered and I realized I was in danger of falling asleep right there on the stool. I cased up the guitar and locked the closet, shoving my reverie to the back of my mind.

I finally wound up sitting on my ratty old easy chair with my whiskey glass in one hand and a book in the other. I had hundreds of books. I'd been collecting them ever since I was a kid when my secret vice was reading. They were stacked haphazardly on shelves all around the house. But there was a handful that I never bothered to shelve. They always sat on the end table next to my chair.

I jerked awake at the sound of a phone ringing. "Yeah," I croaked.

"Dent. How're tricks?" That gravelly voice brought back some memories, some of them good, some of them bad. It was Al Pace. My former boss at Major Crimes, and Alex's father.

"Jesus, Al. How are you?"

"I've got enough money to keep me in scotch and cigars and I'm married to a woman half my age. What more could I want? I need to see you, Dent."

"What for?" I felt like I was several seconds behind the curve, I was still half asleep and trying to remember that Al wasn't my boss anymore, wasn't even a cop anymore.

"I think you're about to stick your dick in a hornet's nest if you haven't already. We can't talk about it on the phone. We need to talk face to face. Tonight."

I was quiet for a minute, processing. If I couldn't trust Al, I had nothing left. "Ok. Your place?"

"Yeah. My place. Gina's having one of her parties, but I'm barricaded upstairs in the study, so you'll have to run the gauntlet."

Great.

"I'll be there in a few."

Al grunted in reply and hung up. I took a few minutes to drag a toothbrush around in my mouth and headed for the door.

I wondered if Alex would be there, and shoved the thought out of my mind.

CHAPTER THIRTEEN

The gray November drizzle had set in. I threw on my raincoat, but still got a good pelting on the way to the car.

I crossed the river and wound my way up into the west hills. Al had one of those modern looking houses perched on the side of the hill. If we ever had that big earthquake they were predicting, he was screwed. The streets here were narrow and choked with cars. His neighbors were doctors, lawyers, software developers, that sort of thing.

There were cars parked all along the street on Al's block. All the cars were expensive, BMWs, Audis, Mercedes, that sort of thing. I squeezed my plebeian Crown Vic into a spot.

The rain had stopped by the time I got out of the car, but it was still damp and cold. I started walking towards Al's house when I felt that little tickle at the back of my neck. Over the years, I'd learned to pay attention to that feeling. It was hard to explain, but sometimes I could feel it when somebody was watching me.

I looked up and down the rows of cars, still walking nonchalantly, my fingers curling around the grip of my little Smith and Wesson in my coat pocket.

Finally, I saw him.

There was a gray Mercedes parked at the curb directly across from Al's house. The rear windows were blacked out with heavy tint, but the windshield was clear, letting the light from a streetlight shine inside. The guy in the driver's seat was massive. His shoulders took up half the front seat and strained the seams of his suit coat. Meat hook hands rested on the steering wheel. The guy looked Samoan, maybe Hawaiian and he was easily 350, maybe even 400 pounds.

He was no chauffeur. I took in the flat, affect-free stare and recognized the type: a thug in a suit. I'd learned to recognize other cops, soldiers, really professional security people, types like that. We all had a certain look that was hard to describe and even harder to disguise. He was a thug, just like me. I could practically smell it on him.

He inclined his head slightly. A little nod to say, *I see you, you see me, we know what we are and it doesn't have to be a big deal. At least not tonight.* I nodded back. No reason to be rude. He was probably some socialite's idea of a pet bodyguard, one step up from a Rottweiler. Some of them were titillated by that sort of thing.

I felt his eyes on me as I walked up onto the porch and rang the bell. It was all I could do not to turn around and stare back.

A college kid in a tuxedo that didn't quite fit him opened the door. At first, I had no idea who he was, then I realized Gina must have rented a doorman for a party. Jesus. How the hell did Al wind up like this? I remember when he shared an apartment with four other cops and I had to help him haul his couch to the dump because one of the other guys had come back from a trip to Tijuana infested with crabs.

The kid in the monkey suit looked at me top to bottom, took in the scuffed boots, jeans and raincoat.

I pushed my way past him. "I'm expected." He didn't offer any resistance. I hadn't really expected him to.

A babble of voices came from my right. I peeked into the living room and saw a gaggle of tan, fit women with collagen and silicon in all the right places, but no sign of Al. None of them noticed me so I scooted right past, towards the stairs. The kid in the suit eyed me suspiciously.

"Dent?" The voice came from deeper in the house. I craned my neck around the corner and saw Alex looking at me from the kitchen. She was sitting on a counter, her honey hair loose and spilling around her. She wore a strapless dress that showed off several square feet of perfect skin and held a wine glass in one hand.

"Dent!" she said, almost squealing. "Cool! Come on back here."

I told myself I didn't have any choice and headed back to the kitchen. The expensive-looking stainless steel counters were covered with chafing dishes and appetizer trays, undoubtedly the product of one caterer or another. I doubted that Gina actually *cooked* anything.

Alex grabbed my hand and pulled me into the kitchen, pausing to give me a peck on the cheek that felt electric. God, she smelled good.

"Dent! Please tell me you've come to rescue me from this vapid party! If it wasn't for Manuel and Regan here, I'd already be out of my mind."

I realized two things, in roughly this order: first, that Alex was about half in the bag, her breath smelled of too much wine and her speech was slurred; second that there were two other people in the room. An older Latino man and a young woman, both dressed in the same kind of threads as the doorman, were staring at us, looking distinctly uncomfortable.

"I was about to scream, in there listening to Gina and her friends talk about counting carbs and getting the fat sucked out of their asses, so I wandered back here. It turns out Manuel is from Guatemala and is saving money to bring his brother and sister into the country. Regan is taking a semester off from Lewis and Clark to study transactional analysis among immigrant populations. Isn't that cool? I thought it was much more interesting than fad diets and liposuction. I tried to tell one of those shriveled up little bitches out there what a bad idea liposuction is but she blew me off. I mean hey, it's not like I'm a doctor or anything, right?"

Alex downed the last of her wine in one gulp.

Manuel was standing there with an appetizer tray in his hands. His eyes kept darting towards the door. Regan kept picking a tray up, then setting it back down again.

I opened my mouth to speak, not quite sure what I was going to say when I was interrupted.

"THERE you are! Get those trays out in the living room! My guests are starving."

I turned to find Gina Pace, famous around Portland for, well, being Gina. Daughter of a famous developer, she had cut a wide swath through the city's social scene for years, remaining perpetually unmarried but constantly linked to one famous figure after another. She'd gone through a rock musician phase, then a local politician phase, before finally settling into a string of relationships with local cops, which some wags had called the "Badge Bunny" years. She'd somehow wound up married to Al in a surprise ceremony on top of Mt. Helens, which had left many a head scratched and many tongues wagging, not least of which was Alex's. She'd been horrified to find out that her "stepmother" was only about five years older than she was.

Gina was short, about thirty-five, and had glossy black hair. Like Alex, she wore a strapless black dress. But where Alex looked wonderful, in that girl next door sort of way, Gina just looked underdressed, not quite trashy, but almost.

"Hello... Dent." I saw Gina searching for my name for a second, her eyes darted up and to the left, a neuro-linguistic sign of searching her memory. Then her eyes flicked over me from head to toe, taking in my clothes the same way her doorman had. "Are you here to see Al?"

"Yeah, we have some business. Didn't mean to crash your party. I'll just run up..."

"Oh! But you have to meet everyone!" For the second time in a couple of minutes, I found myself being pulled along by my wrist. Gina dragged me into the living room. All eyes swiveled towards us as we entered. I felt like a particularly toothsome piece of road kill being sized up by a bunch of vultures wearing Prada. Gina unleashed a flurry of introductions, barraging me with each woman's name, the name of her husband (if she had one), name of ex-husband(s) (if she had any of those), occupation and etc. It was dizzying.

They were all lean, with that pinched face underfed look that spoke of too much Pilates and not enough cheeseburgers.

Most of them had tans that were too perfect to be anything other than artificial. Apparently, they had all mutually agreed to dye their hair the same shade of not quite blonde. 21st Century Stepford Wives.

"Dent used to work with Al, catching murderers and rapists. His most famous case was when he shot that whacko who was shooting up the mall."

A titter went through the crowd. Half of them grimaced in distaste, no doubt perfectly happy to sleep at night knowing people like me were out there to do their killing for them but non-plussed at actually having to *talk* to me. The other half bothered me more, they all moved in half a step, their eyes shining with anticipation at latching on to a real-life bad man, a real killer. I must have made corporate raiders and hostile takeover specialists seem lame by comparison.

"What did you feel when you shot that man?" A voice from the back asked.

The word "recoil" was on my lips when I was interrupted.

"I don't think Dent wants to talk about that right now."

I turned and there was Al, all five-foot-six of him, dressed in a natty black sweater and gray slacks, an unlit cigar in one hand and a half-empty glass of scotch in the other. His ugly little troll head looked a little balder and the hair growing out of his ears seemed a little longer than the last time I saw him, but it was still good old Al.

He turned to Gina. "Sorry honey, I need to hijack my guest back from you."

Now Al grabbed me by the arm. This was getting old. He led me back through the house to the stairwell. Behind us, the conversation picked right back up without missing a beat. We passed Alex in the hallway. She had refilled her wine glass from somewhere.

"Careful, Dent. They'll eat you alive." She seemed even tipsier than before. I opened my mouth to reply, but she giggled and headed for the bathroom.

As I followed Al up the stairs, he shook his head. "You know, Dent, for years I kept a dozen alcoholic detectives on task and solving homicides, but I'll be damned if I can make my wife and my daughter tolerate each other."

I didn't have a reply to that one, so I just followed him. Al's study was impressive, all wood and brass. He favored a nautical motif, but as far as I knew, the only time Al had spent on a boat was the time he and I both fell out of a skiff trying to haul a dead body out of one of the city's reservoirs in Washington Park. It sure looked masculine as hell though.

There was another man sitting in one of the stuffed leather chairs in front of Al's desk. Even though he was sitting down, I could tell he was tall and lean. He had short blond hair in an old fashioned butch cut and wore a suit that, to my untrained eye, looked expensive. I couldn't quite tell how old he was, at first I thought about fifty, from the fine lines around his eyes, but then he turned his head to face me and he looked much younger, maybe mid-thirties.

"Dent, this is Sebastian Bolle from the FBI." As Al spoke, the man stood. Good grief, he was taller than me. Had to be at least 6'6", maybe even 6'7". When he stuck his hand out to shake, his cuff slid back, revealing a wristwatch that looked heavy and expensive. Interesting, a Fed with money.

"Nice to meet you," I said. He had one of those neutral handshakes, not a limp wrist but not one of those guys that try to turn every handshake into a dominance game either. On impulse, I said, "Your guy out front seems to be doing a good job of keeping watch."

That earned me a thin smile. "Edward is a professional."

Interesting. Edward was apparently not a Fed. They always called each other by "Agent So and So" with strangers. You had to be accepted into the club before they would use first names around you. I wondered what Bolle was doing with a thug for a driver.

We sat. Al offered me a cigar, which I declined, and a tumbler full of single malt, which I accepted.

"You've been a busy boy. How are your ribs?" Al said as I let my first sip of the single malt roll around in my mouth. I tried to imagine what adjectives they would use in one of those magazines. Peaty? Iodine? Fruity finish? Hell with it. It tasted great. I swallowed it.

"News travels fast," I said. "I'd hoped to keep that little fiasco quiet."

Al shrugged. "You know how word gets around in the Bureau." He unlocked a desk drawer in front of him and pulled out a couple of file folders. "Do you have any idea who you just arrested?"

"Gibson Marshall? Punk-ass kid with a taste for porn and an attitude problem. He seems to have a talent for getting out of things but I don't think he's getting out of this one."

Al slid the first folder over to me. I opened it and scanned quickly. It was all about Gibson Marshall, most of it stuff that Mandy had already uncovered. Nothing new here.

"And?" I asked.

Al slid the second folder over. The first thing inside was a color 8x10" glossy of a fit-looking man in his late fifties, maybe early sixties posing in front of an American flag. I turned past the photo of and found myself looking at a dossier on one Henderson Marshall, owner of Cascade Aviation, a small private air force that contracted almost solely with the United States government and was rumored to be a CIA front company. He was also co-owner of Transnational Resolutions, a large private security firm that worked almost solely for the US government. They employed hundreds of former Special Operations guys, Green Berets, SEALS, Delta Force, guys like that and set them up with bodyguard and "protective detail" work all over the world. Essentially, Marshall had his own private army.

I flipped through the rest of the dossier. Gibson had ties to dozens of other companies, real estate, import-export, shipping, you name it. There was also a detailed list of political contributions. According to the list, Marshall the Elder had never met a politician too conservative for a donation.

"He must be so proud of his son," I said.

"I don't know about proud," Al said. "But he sure has spent a bundle getting the kid out of trouble. On some of the minor arrests, once it became obvious that the old man was willing to spend a bottomless amount of money to defend and appeal, the charges were just dropped. No DA or city attorney in their right mind will spend hundreds of thousands of dollars in their budget to get a misdemeanor conviction, particularly if the case isn't airtight. You and I both know most cases aren't airtight."

"The best defense money can buy. I thought justice was blind," I said.

"It is blind," Bolle said. "Justice doesn't see most of the crimes the rich commit."

That was strange to hear from a Fed, even stranger coming out of the mouth of someone like Bolle, who just exuded a certain aura that I'd come to associate with the upper crust. The accent was eastern. Boston, maybe?

It put me in mind of the Kennedys, touch football on Martha's Vineyard, that sort of thing.

"The old man made the misdemeanor charges go away by throwing money at it," Al said. "We all hate that but we know it happens. It gets worse. The State Trooper who arrested the younger Marshall for the gun and road rage incident isn't a State Trooper anymore."

I felt a sinking feeling starting in the pit of my stomach. "Do tell."

"A week after the trooper arrested Marshall, a sixteen-year-old police explorer claimed the Trooper had molested her in his squad car on numerous occasions. He was investigated and fired."

"Was it true?" I asked.

Al shrugged. "All I can tell you is that the girl is being raised by a single mother, who worked as a waitress. Mom quit her job. They are both driving brand new cars and an educational trust fund has been set up in the girl's name. They haven't even had time to sue the State Police yet, so you tell me where the money came from."

I felt like a giant rug was being pulled out from underneath me.

"What I'm saying," Al said, "is that you need to be careful. At the very best, every aspect of this case is going to get scrutinized. If you forgot to put a period at the end of a sentence, this guy's lawyers are going to try to spin it into a conspiracy to frame him. Everything you've ever done will be examined, reexamined and cast in a way to make you look like you aren't credible."

I felt cold all over. "Jesus, Al. This is horrible timing. This wouldn't bother me so much if you were still the boss at Major Crimes, but Lubbock, man."

Al nodded. "Yeah, I know."

Bolle shifted in his seat. I'd all but forgotten the man as Al's words kept sinking in deeper. I turned to the Fed.

"So what's your angle on all this?"

Bolle cleared his throat. "I work for a specialized unit in the Bureau.

We focus on crimes of national, or even international importance. We've long suspected Mr. Marshall of using his businesses, and his contacts at CIA to engage in various illegal activities. His companies support operations in Afghanistan, Iraq, Uzbekistan, all over the world. There have been reports of stolen money being taken out of those countries, looted artworks, weapons dealings, perhaps even narcotics smuggling."

Bolle took a sip of his scotch before he continued.

"We had an informant inside Cascade Air, a disgruntled employee who told us he had evidence. The night he was supposed to meet with me, he was called in to work a last minute flight to Pakistan. I wasn't too worried. This isn't an unusual event. Cascade Air's operation tempo is incredible. They frequently are short-handed and call crews in at the last minute. My guy got on the plane in Albany, but he never got off in Pakistan."

"Jesus." There was a lot of space between Oregon and Pakistan, much of it the Pacific Ocean.

"We've been working this thing together for almost nine months now, Dent," Al said. "This informant was the closest we've ever gotten to anything solid and bam! He's gone."

"You figure the son's working with dad?" I frowned. That didn't seem to fit.

"Actually, no," Bolle said. "Henderson all but disowned his son. He appears to have lost all hope of Gibson inheriting the business, has even cut off all contact with him other than to provide him with lawyers."

"So Junior decided to go into the internet porn business. I guess entrepreneurship runs in the family."

"Indeed. Gibson doesn't have contact with his father, but he still has contacts with some of his father's employees. He's been photographed on several occasions driving his van to the Cascade Aviation facility here in Oregon. We've intercepted phone calls from him making references to 'making a delivery' but we haven't had the resources to follow up on it."

"One thing doesn't make sense," I said. "You said the son was talking about taking something *to* the guys at Cascade Aviation?"

Al and Bolle both nodded.

"What could it be? These guys are flying to Iraq, Afghanistan, Pakistan, places like that? Those places have all the dope and guns and money in the world. We grow a bunch of pot here but taking that over there would be like selling snow to the Eskimos. What the hell is worth smuggling *in* to those countries?"

"That's what we would very much like to know," Bolle said.

I sat there for a minute, thinking, trying to put all the angles together. "Jesus. This thing just gets deeper."

Al nodded. "I called you over here tonight for two reasons. One was to warn you. I think you are in for a hell of a ride. The other was to offer you a job. Would you like to be a Fed?"

That took a second to sink in. "Start over again as an agent? No offense," I said, looking sidelong at Bolle. "It's just that I'm a little old to be a rookie again."

"Actually," Bolle said. "You'd be brought in as a special consultant. You'd be given a Federal commission, Special Agent status, able to carry a firearm, but you'd only work some of the more sensitive cases. We've no intention of making you go to the Academy at Quantico and run obstacle courses and all that."

"Huh." Not exactly the most articulate response, but the offer had come out of nowhere. I found the prospect of going back to work for Al intriguing.

Al looked me in the eye. "I don't expect an answer right now, but I need you to think about it, Dent. Somehow the bad guys discovered our informant and threw him out of an airplane. It had to be a leak. You're a man I can trust and there aren't too many of those around right now."

I felt a flush starting to creep up my neck. I was saved from having to respond by a commotion from downstairs. I heard two female voices yelling at each other. I couldn't quite make out the words other than one, which was certainly "bitch."

There was the tinkle of glass breaking.

It was Al's turn to blush. He stood straight up and with an "excuse me" went out the door. Bolle and I sat there in embarrassed silence, trying to pretend we couldn't hear Al speaking loudly downstairs. After a few minutes, he came huffing back up the stairs and appeared in the doorway, chomping on his cigar furiously.

"Dent, could I get your help with something downstairs?" I popped out of my seat like a jack in the box, almost tipping it over. I remembered to turn and shake hands with Bolle. His face was a perfectly polished impenetrable mask. I envied people who were able to do that.

"Please think about our offer, Detective Miller," he said.

I promised I would and followed Al back downstairs. Out of the corner, of my eye I saw Gina standing in the center of the living room, using a napkin to dab at a trickle of blood coming from the corner of her mouth. She seemed to be spreading it around on her face more than she seemed to be wiping it off.

She was surrounded by her friends, all of them talking in low voices.

Al bypassed all of that and led me straight into the kitchen, where Alex sat on a stool holding a bag of ice over the knuckles of her right hand.

"Hi, Dent. I just punched my stepmother," she slurred. "But she deserved it."

Al closed his eyes. I could see him counting to three. He opened his eyes and handed me Alex's handbag, a little black thing only a little bigger than my palm.

"Dent. Would you do me a favor and take my daughter home, she's had way too much to drink."

"Ummm. Ok." There was no way in hell I was going to say no. It was Al. I would do anything for Al. Alex's drinking had been a problem before. Two years ago she'd been arrested for driving under the influence. It had caused a big stink but ultimately hadn't cost her job. If she tried to drive right now, there was a pretty good chance she'd wind up in a ditch, not just the back of a police car.

"Cool!" Alex said. She got to her feet, not as shakily as I would have expected and interlaced her arm in mine. She all but skipped to the foyer, dragging me along as we went.

Alex skidded to a stop outside the living room, almost sending us to the marble floor in a tangle. She pointed at Gina.

"If I feel sorry for slugging you in the morning, I'll call and apologize."

She frowned. "But I don't think I will."

"Just leave," Gina said. From her tone of voice, I expected her eyes to turn red and her head to start spinning around on her shoulders.

Alex waved expansively. "Good night, ladies. It's been fun. Arianna, try not to fall when you're playing tennis. Those cheap implants you got in Mexico might break and your boobs and ass will deflate."

There was a collective hiss from the crowd in the living room and I all but dragged a giggling Alex out the front door. She leaned against me and put an arm around my waist as we went down the stairs. It was probably forty degrees out and she wasn't wearing a coat. I debated giving her mine or going back for hers and decided just to keep walking her to the car. It wasn't far and the cold might help sober her up. Besides, I was acutely aware of the heat of her body, even through the layers of my shirt and coat.

Edward, Bolle's bodyguard and driver, regarded us impassively. He might have tilted an eyebrow up the barest millimeter, but that might have been my imagination.

CHAPTER FOURTEEN

Getting a giggling, uncoordinated Alex into the passenger seat of my car turned out to be an adventure. I learned something in the process: Alex had very definite tan lines. Once she finally got in the seat, she settled her dress back down to her knees. She either didn't notice that I'd noticed, or didn't care. I shut the door gently and looked out at the lights of the city for a few seconds, trying to concentrate on the view and not what I'd just seen in the dome light of my car.

"This is Al's daughter," I reminded myself under my breath. "And she is very drunk."

I took a deep breath and got in. The ride, mercifully, was short. Alex only lived a few miles away, out Skyline Road. She sat snuggled up against me the whole way, her head on my shoulder and her hand on my thigh. I was very conscious of her breast brushing my upper arm.

I was treated to a long, rambling monologue on the evils of her stepmother. I heard how Gina had snookered poor innocent Al into marrying her while Al had still been mourning the death of Alex's mother. I heard how Gina only wanted Al for his money, and would probably dump him as soon as she had her hooks into him deep enough to take him for all he was worth.

I had a slightly different take on things. I remembered Al going after Gina with gusto, and I really doubted Gina was after Al's money, considering she had more than he did. But I'd learned a long time ago not to argue with drunk people.

What shone through all this was how much Alex idolized her father, probably more than he deserved. Alex had been a teenager when I'd first met her, all those years ago, and even then her life had revolved around making her dad happy.

We rolled up to Alex's little bungalow. She futzed around trying to get her car door open and I realized that bracing night air or not, she wasn't going to make it to the door unassisted. I got out and walked with her.

She bumped her hip into mine and said, "So tell me, Dent, what do you like for breakfast?"

"Huh? Why" I was concentrating very much on putting one foot in front of the other, and not on the sway of her hip against mine. Promise.

"So I can go look in my fridge and see if I can feed you in the morning, or see if I have to make a grocery run."

We stopped in front of the door. "I just need to get you inside, Alex, then I'll be on my way. I don't think you should do a grocery run."

I was digging through her purse, trying to sort through the odds and ends for her house key by feel when she leaned over and licked me on the ear. I dropped the purse.

"Alex!"

She giggled as I bent over, wincing at the pain from my busted ribs. I gathered up everything I could find and stood up.

"Alex. Knock it off." This was getting ridiculous. It was also getting harder to find her keys.

She giggled again. "Oh, come on."

I finally found her key ring. I slid it in the lock and the door popped open.

She headed in past me, pulling on my arm. "Come on inside."

"Alex. No. I need to go."

"Why?"

"You're very drunk."

"I'm not going to puke and make you hold my hair or anything. I'm not THAT drunk."

"That's not what I mean. I..."

She leaned forward and kissed me, full on the mouth this time. Her tongue darted between my lips and I realized I was kissing her back. My hands just sort of fell naturally to her hips and I stopped thinking, just enjoyed the pure animal sensation of her lips on mine. She started backing farther into the house and I followed.

She ran a hand down my belly and with a deftness that belied her earlier clumsiness, unzipped my pants. She slid a finger inside and stroked me. I jumped at the electric touch.

Somehow that brought me to my senses. I stepped back away from her, almost moaning as the connection between her finger and my skin was broken. I fumbled with my zipper.

"Alex. I'm sorry. I can't."

"You can't? What do you mean you can't? I finally have you in my house. I just had my hand in your pants, and you're telling me you can't? Why the hell not?"

For a second my brain locked up on that one. Why not, indeed? Everything had felt pretty good so far. Why not? Oh yeah.

"Audrey," I managed to choke out. "I'm with Audrey. It wouldn't be right."

Plus there was Al. Al had sent his drunk daughter home in my car because he trusted me.

"Oh yeah. Audrey," Alex said. "I forgot about her."

I almost said "me too" but managed to choke it off in time.

"Look, Alex. I really have to go. I'm sorry…"

Sorry for what? Not sleeping with her when she was drunk? That didn't sound right.

"Anyway," I continued. "Get some sleep."

"Ok," she said. And started crying.

I can handle gunfire. I can't handle tears. I needed to get out. Besides, the memory of that kiss, and the touch wouldn't go away. The animal part of my brain was telling me I was stupid to walk out that door.

I fled. There was no other word for it. I fled into the night, got in my car and went home, where I faced a sleepless night.

CHAPTER FIFTEEN

I was late for work the next morning, but for the safety of myself and others, I stopped for coffee. My only concession to Portland coffee culture was I usually bought from Starbucks, mainly because you couldn't go more than a couple of blocks without tripping over one. None of that foamed milk, cinnamon, chocolate stuff for me though. I just drank coffee, plain black coffee, preferably so strong that there was a nice oily sheen floating on the top.

I juggled my coffee, the steering wheel, and my phone so I could call Mandy.

Mandy didn't answer. Usually, she'd pick the phone up during the first or second ring like she was waiting for somebody to call her up with details of where to find Jimmy Hoffa or something. Maybe she was sleeping in too.

Traffic didn't get any better as I entered downtown. People were blocking the street, protesting some damn thing or another. That happened so much in downtown Portland that nobody even bothered to find out what the protest was about. We just tuned in the news to find out how much it snarled traffic.

I parked in the garage next to Central precinct, keeping an eye out for Mandy's work car as I went. I finally found it and parked next to it. Good, she was here, maybe she had just forgotten to turn her phone on.

I wound my way up the back stairs and into the lobby. I felt grateful for the caffeine molecules soaking into my brain. Planning my day and getting through it now seemed like a real possibility, as opposed to just sitting around like a lump.

I popped out of the stairwell on my floor, right next to the bank of elevators, and stopped in my tracks. There was a guy standing there, waiting for an elevator, tall, shaved head, maybe my height, maybe a little taller. Under the expensive-looking charcoal suit he was wearing, I could tell he had the long lean build of a runner. He was one of those people who looked perfectly poised and centered when they stood like they were rooted to the ground and immovable.

I was looking at him in profile. The face tickled something in the back of my mind, some memory.

He turned his head and our eyes locked. I felt something I hadn't felt in a long time: real fear. It shocked me. After a while, my fear had been replaced by a kind of anticipation, almost a longing for a good adrenaline rush. But this was different. I literally felt a tingle run down my spine, like somebody had hooked me up to a low current battery. It was like I'd come around a corner on a jungle trail and locked eyes with the biggest snake in the jungle. His face was flat, expressionless. I saw his eyes measure me up and down like a butcher who was thinking about how to best carve up a side of beef.

The elevator dinged and the door opened. He gave me the slightest of smiles, or did I imagine it? Then the doors slid shut behind him and he was gone. My paralysis broke and I stepped forward out of the stairwell.

I stopped again, replaying what had just happened. I chased murderers for a living. Why was I rooted to the spot like a kid at a haunted house over a bald guy in a business suit?

I started moving again, striding deliberately towards my office. This was ridiculous. I really did need a vacation.

The detective office was quiet. I didn't see Mandy anywhere, or that many other people for that matter. Since Lubbock took over, most of the guys stayed out of the office as much as they could, preferring to do their work from coffee shops or an empty office at one of the other precincts.

I didn't see Lubbock, a good sign, but I did see his flunky Dan Winter. Winter was standing outside my cube, a very bad sign.

"Sergeant Winter." I nodded, hoping the fact that he was standing in the doorway to my cubicle was just a coincidence, but feeling a sinking feeling that it probably wasn't.

Winter put on his serious, authoritative face. He tried to play mentor to all the guys under him, despite the fact that he really wasn't much older than most of us, and had skated his way from one make-work assignment to another in the bureau. Mostly he had followed Lubbock around, acting as his Aide De Camp and toady in whatever assignment Lubbock happened to be working.

"Dent, I need you to come with me." Without another word he turned and started walking towards the conference room. I shrugged and followed him. This should be interesting.

He led me to the conference room and shut the door behind us. Lubbock sat on one side of the table, with a guy I vaguely recognized as a civilian employee from Human Resources. Lubbock was nervous. I could tell from the way his eyes kept darting around the room.

"Have a seat Miller." Lubbock attempted a commanding voice and failed miserably. His voice broke on my name, heading upwards an octave.

I thought about saying I preferred to stand, just to be a jerk, but decided against it. I pulled a chair out well away from the table and sat down across from Lubbock with my legs crossed. I tried to relax. Winter remained standing, his hands hooked together under his paunch, guarding the door I guess.

Lubbock opened his mouth to speak and I cut him off, timing it perfectly. "What can I do for you, Steve?" Sometimes I couldn't resist being just a little bit of an asshole.

He frowned in irritation and it took him a couple of seconds to get back on track. "We are here to discuss a very serious matter."

We didn't usually meet in a conference room with one of the toads from Human Resources to talk about the weather. Lubbock paused, staring at me. I sat there keeping my face neutral, staring back. I wasn't going to make this easy.

He swallowed. "You're being suspended, pending an investigation into the arrest of Ian Wendt. Mr. Wendt has made some very serious allegations of excessive force against you and Detective Williams. These are allegations I have a duty to take seriously."

Every time a suspect got banged around by the cops, he would make an excessive force complaint. We had to investigate them, but unless somebody died, or the allegations were substantiated by another cop, nobody ever got suspended while the investigation was taking place.

"What's this really about, Steve?" I tried to lock eyes with Lubbock, but he refused. His eyes would settle down for a fraction of a second, then slide away. The HR guy wrote my question down on a pad.

Lubbock blushed. "This is about doing the best thing for the City of Portland. Wendt has a broken knee and a broken elbow. This is a very serious situation. I have to act."

It was like a speech he'd memorized by rote. I felt a vein begin to throb in my temple. I almost started arguing with him, almost started to tell him Wendt was a violent psychopath, that I'd saved Wendt's life by taking him down the way I had, saved some other cop the trouble of shooting him. But the HR geek was sitting there with his pen poised over his legal pad, waiting for me to say something. It occurred to me that I should have my union representative here.

"Also, it has come to my attention you failed in your duty as a police officer last night. You witnessed an episode of domestic violence, and instead of making a mandatory arrest, you drove the perpetrator home."

I blinked, for a moment not understanding what he was talking about. Then I realized he was talking about Alex. Most people thought of domestic violence as a husband beating up his wife. But strictly speaking, the law covered "family or household members," which technically included Gina and Alex. The law made it mandatory for police to arrest the primary aggressor in a case of domestic violence, so strictly speaking, I should have arrested Alex last night, or called somebody else to do it.

I realized Lubbock had spoken only in generalities, hoping to get me to blurt out my account of what happened. It was an old investigator's trick.

So I kept my mouth shut, playing an old investigator's trick of my own, letting the silence build. Lubbock broke first.

"We'll need your badge, your bureau-issued weapon, and your bureau car. You are to take no police action while you are suspended. You will call and check in with Sergeant Winter twice a day and make yourself available for interviews."

"What about the Marshall investigation?" I asked. The HR guy wrote that down. The initial hot flush of anger was receding, replaced by a cold fury that I hadn't felt in a long time, since the last time I'd left my father's trailer up that hollow in Tennessee.

"Sergeant Winter will take over the Marshall investigation. I also have some concerns about that case. I feel like there was a rush to judgment in making that arrest. You exposed the Bureau to some real risk with that."

I suppressed a snort. Now I knew what this was about. Now I knew how Marshall had gotten out of all those other deals: because of people like Lubbock.

I dug into my valise, pulled out my notes on the Marshall case. It struck me as funny right then, we had been calling it the "Marshall case," but it wasn't really. We should have been calling it the "Heather Swanson" case.

Heather was the one who was dead. I wondered if her family had claimed her body, or if she was still sitting in a meat locker out at the ME's office. I slapped the notepad down on the table. The HR guy jumped at the sound.

"There you go, Sarge. I'm sure your superior detection skills will do the victim justice." HR Guy recovered quickly and started scribbling away.

Lubbock pulled a face. "You are to have no contact with Detective Williams. I'm going to remind you that collusion between two members of the Bureau who are under investigation is an offense that is punishable by termination."

That pissed me off even more. If they wanted to mess with me, that was one thing. But Mandy was a good kid, a great cop. This wasn't right.

I pulled my badge from around my neck and put it on the table, followed by the car keys. I reached down and popped the magazine out of the Glock on my hip and added it to the pile. I stood, made a half turn and drew the gun, pointing it away from everybody at the wall.

The HR guy squeaked when he saw the gun. He didn't scream, didn't yell, didn't exclaim. He squeaked. Like a mouse.

"Relax," I said, standing there with my gun in my hand. "I just need to unload it." I stood there staring at him. He stared back.

"Well," I said. "Go ahead. Aren't you going to write that down? I said 'relax. I just need to unload it.' You've written everything else down, you should write down that too."

He hesitated for a second, then started scribbling again.

I jerked the slide back and the round popped out of the chamber. It rolled under the table and I didn't even bother to pick it up. I just put the gun down on the table. I brushed past Winters and was on my way out the door. Winter followed at a discrete distance but didn't try to talk to me, which was a good thing. I wasn't exactly in a conversational mood.

I walked down the stairs on autopilot, hearing Winters huffing along behind me. I felt like I was in some kind of a daze. I managed to make it out of the building without seeing anybody I knew. I was glad for that.

I stepped out of the building. The city was loud today. Car horns echoed up and down the canyons formed by the buildings. People bustled by, ignoring me standing there on the sidewalk. It was like watching some kind of movie going by in front of me. I felt like I was in my own little bubble, insulated from what was going on.

I realized I had no way home. My bureau car was now suddenly off limits. My pickup was parked at home. I didn't really feel like taking the bus. The last thing I wanted was to be around people. I sat down on a park bench, suddenly exhausted, unable to move.

I saw a homeless guy across the street, picking through a trash can, and I wondered how easy it would be to just sit there on that bench, letting the world pass by until I became like him. Living life second by second seemed incredibly attractive to me just then.

My phone rang, jolting me out of my reverie. My hand grabbed it by instinct, but I couldn't make my mouth work. I just sat there, mute, holding the phone to my ear.

"Dent?" For a second I thought it was Alex. Then I realized it was Audrey. I hadn't realized how similar their voices were.

"Hey," I mumbled. On top of everything else, I now felt a hot flash of guilt over the vivid memory of the image of Alex's skirt riding up over her hips, over the feeling of her breast pressed against my arm.

"You ok? You sound weird."

I looked at the bum across the street. He'd finished digging through one can and was moving on.

"I'm fine." I lied reflexively, without thinking about it, pathologically unable to admit something might be bothering me.

"You don't sound fine. What are you doing? I'm downtown and I wondered if by some miracle you might have time for lunch."

I almost laughed. "Yeah. I have time. I've got plenty of time all of a sudden."

"What do you mean?"

I squeezed my eyes shut, suppressed a giggle that came up from nowhere. "It's hard to explain. Where are you?"

"Just leaving school."

"I'm out here in the park blocks. Can you pick me up?"

"Sure. Be there in a few." She sounded puzzled.

"Ok. See you then." I hung up without saying goodbye. A bus hissed to a stop down the street and I felt a sudden urge to go get on it. Somehow just then being on a bus full of strangers seemed more attractive than getting into a car with the woman I'd all but begged to move in with me just a week ago.

But I didn't get up. It would have taken more energy than I had at the moment. Instead, I sat there with my valise in my lap, staring a hole in the pavement. I didn't know how much time passed, just that I jerked when I heard a horn honk, and there was Audrey in her little red Honda, waving me over.

I folded myself into the car and she pulled away from the curb. I sat there staring straight ahead, knowing I should say something, but I was struck as dumb as when I had answered the phone. I felt an urge to speak, but I couldn't force my brain to come up with any words to say.

"Dent, what is it? You look horrible."

It was easier, somehow, with her prompting me.

"I just got suspended from work." Did I really say that?

"Suspended? What for? For that Wendt guy you told me about?"

No, I wanted to say. Not at all. That's the reason they're giving, but you see it's actually because I ran into the wrong people, people that can apparently kill a young girl, dump her body, and then get the cop doing the investigation suspended from his job. Apparently, you really can get away with murder.

But that didn't make sense to me in my head. The idea of speaking it out loud made even less sense.

"Yeah," I said. "Over Wendt." It just seemed easier.

She drove for a while in silence, shifting through the gears. I realized she was headed towards the bridge that would take us across the river and towards her place.

"I'm sorry to hear that, Dent." But I could almost hear her thinking *but I'm not surprised.* That little Honda was so small that our hips practically touched when we sat in it, but she felt very far away from me just then.

I didn't know what to say to that. I'd always known there were people like Lubbock in the Bureau, far too many people who would roll over and play dead if it was in their political best interest. But I'd never guessed that even Lubbock would intentionally screw up a homicide investigation.

We crossed over the bridge and I found myself looking at the gray water below, remembering a case I'd had a few years back. A doctor, of some kind, endocrinologist? Gastroenterologist? It didn't matter. He'd parked his Jaguar on the bridge and jumped. He finally turned up a week later caught on a snag way the hell downstream. Rich guy. Pretty wife. Nice kids. I never had figured out what made him jump.

The hum of the tires changed as we crossed from the bridge back onto the street. Audrey looked at me, her eyes big and liquid. She brushed a stray strand of hair out of the way.

"Let's go to my place. I wonder if it would do you some good to call Betty."

I blinked, trying to understand that. Betty was one of Audrey's friends. She was a therapist. She was into all sorts of holistic mental health care stuff. Integrating your personality, finding your inner child, stupid stuff like that.

"Why should I call Betty?" I asked, still not understanding. I replayed the last few seconds of our conversation over in my mind, trying to figure out what I had missed.

"I thought she might, you know, help you deal with things."

"Deal with things?"

"The stress. Maybe try to help you handle things better next time."

"What do you mean, handle things better next time?" I felt like I was having a completely different conversation than the one she was having.

I saw Audrey's fingers tighten on the steering wheel. She rarely got angry, or at least rarely showed it.

"I mean maybe you need to figure something out so the next time you arrest somebody you don't break his arm and leg, Dent."

I sat there for a minute staring straight ahead, not seeing the road or traffic in front of us, but wondering if the plastic dashboard of the Honda would break if I punched it. It had never crossed my mind that Audrey wouldn't share my sense of outrage at being suspended for arresting Wendt.

My phone rang, saving me from having to reply. I picked it up and saw that it was Mandy on the display. I let it ring a couple more times while I decided what to do. Hell with Lubbock. I'd talk to whomever I wanted. I answered it.

"Hey," I said. I heard an odd shuffling noise on the other end, a couple of seconds of silence, and then the line went dead.

I frowned. I hung up the phone and put it back in my pocket.

"Who was that?" Audrey asked.

"That's not really important," I said.

I was so angry I was cold. The little voice in the back of my head said I should just keep my mouth shut, that I was probably going to say things I regretted if I kept talking. I kept talking anyway.

"I think what is important is that I'm trying to figure out what the hell gives you the right to tell me how I should arrest people. I'm trying to recall the last time you arrested some guy with a gun stuffed in his pants and I'm drawing a blank here. Think you can help me out with that?"

"I'm not the one who is doing the judging, Dent," she said softly. "Your boss is. Your own police department." Her voice was so calm, so rational, that it pissed me off more than if she'd been screaming at me.

I sat back in my seat and closed my eyes. "Look. I'm sorry. This whole thing is really... complicated. It's not what it looks like on the outside."

Because you see, this is all a conspiracy to help keep a murder quiet. I'm being framed, just like OJ Simpson. I decided to keep that to myself.

"The thing is, Dent, all I've got to go on is what you show on the outside, because I never get to see what's on the inside."

Even shut, my eyes felt like somebody had dragged sandpaper across them. What I really needed was a decent night's sleep, unfilled with memories of past violence, and empty of visions of friends' daughters trying to drag me into bed. I felt the car lurch as we went over a bump and realized we were pulling into the parking lot of Audrey's building. We stopped in Audrey's parking spot and sat there in silence.

Audrey put her hand on my arm. "I'm sorry we're fighting. Let's go inside. You look like you need some rest. You can sleep. I'll get us some lunch. We can talk after that."

Food and sleep. She had a point. I felt fuzzy, worn around the edges, disconnected from what was going on around me. The idea of filling my belly and falling into a nice, dreamless sleep was plenty attractive.

My phone rang again. I snatched it out of the pocket and saw Mandy's name on the display again.

I heard the same odd shuffle I heard last time like the phone was being scooted around on the floor or something, then a snippet of what sounded like a muffled curse in a man's voice, then silence as the phone went dead again. I sat there looking at the phone. What the hell was going on? We were forbidden from talking to each other. Was she trying to signal me somehow? If so, it was a dumb way to do it. Phone records were easy to subpoena.

Something tickled at the back of my mind, something I didn't like. Sleep and rest were fine, but the more I sat there with my phone in my hand, the more I realized I was being stupid. Sitting in Audrey's house and moping wasn't going to get me anywhere. I needed to act, to get out there on the offense. I'd need some help, and as much as I loved Audrey, this wasn't her field. I needed to talk to Mandy, Bureau policy be damned, and I needed to talk to Al. Al would know what to do.

Audrey was standing outside the car, looking at me. "Come inside."

I put the phone away carefully.

"Not yet, Audrey. I've got some things I need to do. Can I borrow your car? Just until I can figure out a way to pick up my truck?"

"Things to do? Do what? You're suspended."

"I know there's some stuff I have to do, people I need to talk to. People who can help."

"You can talk to me, Dent. I can help."

She stood there with her keys in her hand and I realized she was almost crying. I wasn't sure if it was from anger or fear. Maybe it was both. The voice in the back of my head told me that should bother me more than it did, but I shoved it away. An icy purpose had settled over me. I had a mission now, and everything else was secondary.

"I know you can, Auds. But right now, I need to do some other stuff. I just need to borrow your car for a little while." All the color drained out of her face.

"Fuck it," she said, and I jumped. I never heard her swear. She threw the car key in. It bounced off my shoulder and landed on the floor. "Go do what you have to do, Dent. If you feel like coming back, do it. If not, that's ok too."

I sat there watching her ponytail swing across her back as she walked away.

I almost got out and followed her, told her I was sorry, told her I'd spill the whole story of what was going on and do my best to help her understand.

Instead, I unfolded myself from the Honda's passenger seat, fished around on the floor until I found the key. I squeezed myself in behind the steering wheel and started the car.

CHAPTER SIXTEEN

I tried Al's number as I drove, but got no answer. I very much wanted to talk to Al just then. He would know what to do. I didn't leave a message. I didn't want any recordings out there floating around. I was taking enough of a risk just using a cell phone as it was. The damn things were way too easy to monitor. I considered calling Alex to see if she knew where to find her dad, but I thought that would cause more problems than it would solve. Someday Alex and I were going to have to sit down and have a long talk, but today wasn't the day.

Mandy lived in an apartment complex in south-east Portland. One of those anonymous places that I hated so much. I threaded my way through traffic on Division Avenue, turning the problem over in my head as I went.

I needed to be careful. I wondered if the other side was done screwing with me. It sounded like they'd found Wendt, got him a lawyer and had created some kind of leverage on Lubbock. I wondered what that was. Lubbock seemed so squeaky clean it was hard to imagine anyone having leverage on him. I wondered if Al would be able to tell me.

Right now this stank of an attempt to discredit me as a cop, to taint my investigation against Marshall. It might very well wind up that everybody "knew" Marshall had killed Heather, but there would be no conviction because enough doubt got slung all over the cops. Hey, it worked for OJ.

I wondered if I would receive an offer: tell the story we want and all the trouble with Wendt will go away. Hell, maybe they'd make Wendt go away. If Wendt was locked up, you could make a lot happen inside a jail for a few cartons of cigarettes. If Wendt was out walking around, it would be easy enough to arrange for a drug overdose.

What would I do with an offer like that? More than once in my police career, I'd been wrong. But I'd never been dirty. I'd never even taken a free cup of coffee the whole fifteen years and I sure as hell wasn't going to help somebody cover up a murder.

I needed a wire. If the offer came I'd want to record it. It would be inadmissible as evidence, but it would still be useful.

Al would be able to get me a wire. If I couldn't get a hold of him in time, Casey probably knew somebody.

I felt the edges of reality slipping yet again. If someone had told me a week ago that I'd be jacked up and suspended, that a powerful businessman would be trying to cover up a murder committed by his son, I would have laughed.

Things like that didn't really happen in real life, just in TV shows.

I thought about all the cops I'd known over the years, ones who had been disgraced and turned in their badges, or in a couple of cases, gone to prison. Most of the time I hadn't been surprised. But there were a few that had shocked me, guys that wound up getting kicked out of the Bureau for stealing money, or diddling some teenager, stuff like that.

I wondered if they'd really done it or if maybe they'd tried to arrest the wrong person too.

Memories of jumping out of airplanes in the Army came back to me. I would always remember that time between jumping out of the door of the plane and the chute snapping open.

I would always remember that feeling of disconnection from everything, no feeling of falling, that feeling of having no ties to anything.

I had that feeling now, like I was in freefall like somebody had kicked me out of an airplane and I was waiting to see if the chute would open.

Driving one handed, I fished out my phone and dialed Casey's number.

"Dent!" She answered. "I was just getting ready to call you. I imaged the hard drives from Marshall's apartment. There are dozens of girls on there. I ran the images through facial recognition software and I got six hits. They are all girls or young women who have disappeared on the west coast in the last two years. None of them have been found."

"Oh no," I said. My head was full of stuff I needed to tell Casey, but my thoughts derailed.

"Do you think he's a serial killer?" I'd never heard Casey sound uncertain, tentative before.

"Maybe," I said, then shoved it out of my mind. "But we've got a bigger problem."

Then I spilled it all out. About how Marshall's previous arrests had been swept under the rug, about how Mandy and I were suspended, and probably Alex too. It sounded crazy, but it still felt good to say it out loud.

"Wow," she said, then there was silence on the line for a minute. I could tell she was trying to decide if I'd gone crazy.

"That's pretty crazy," she said finally.

I pulled into Mandy's apartment complex. "Whether you believe me or not, be careful. Get yourself to a safe place where nobody will look for you."

There was silence again. "Ok," she said finally. "I'll hide an image of the data too."

"Perfect," I said as I parked the Honda. I hung up.

I knocked on the door a few times. No answer. Mandy's car was here, but where was she? Maybe she went for a walk, or out with a friend.

I gave it one last half-hearted knock and turned to go. Something felt wrong, but I was under orders not to talk to Mandy during the investigation. Standing in front of her door in broad daylight felt like handing my enemies a favor.

I folded myself back into the Honda, cursing the little car. I had to figure out a way to pick up my truck, soon.

I pulled out onto Division Street and kept one eye on traffic while I dialed my phone. Al didn't pick up this time either. I sat there and listened to his answering machine, wondering if I should leave a message.

In my rearview mirror, I saw a marked police car pull in behind me, then the overhead lights came on. Muttering under my breath, I pulled over, and kept my hands on the steering wheel.

Office Bloem stepped out and strutted up to the door.

"Step out of the vehicle. Do it now."

"What's wrong, Bloem?" This was weird.

"Get out of the car." He put his hand on his gun.

I decided to comply, figured we'd sort it all out later. He stepped back to make room for the door to open.

"What's going on?" I asked after I unfolded myself from the car. I realized he had his Taser in his hand.

"Get back!" he yelled.

"Huh?" I said. Then he pulled the trigger on the Taser.

I dropped to my knees as every muscle in my body seemed to tighten then release randomly. I heard myself scream. It seemed to last forever.

The current cut off and I leaned forward on my hands, panting.

"Stop resisting!" Bloem yelled. I tried to tell him I wasn't resisting, but he just zapped me again. Somehow this time it was worse. I hit the ground hard and lay there flopping around. I wondered if I was going to wet myself.

I don't know if I blacked out for a little while or what, but when I came to my senses again I was looking at a bunch of polished cop boots standing around me in a circle and I was being handcuffed.

"He charged me when I pulled him over," I heard Bloem say.

Reflexively I tried to jerk away from my hand being put in the cuffs. This was wrong. My reward was a good shot to the kidneys from somebody's balled up fist.

"Stop resisting!"

I tried to jackknife away. I didn't succeed but I did feel one of the Taser barbs rip out of my skin. *How about that? Your toy isn't going to work anymore.*

I was in a frenzy. No rational thought, just pure fight or flight reflex. Since flight wasn't an option, it was all fight.

I actually don't remember it very well. It's just a blur of head butting, elbows, knees and blows to the back of my head.

It ended predictably. I lay slumped over in the back of a Crown Vic panting, my hands cuffed behind me and my legs hogtied together. My ears were ringing and I felt woozy from more shots to the head. Through the divider, I could see Bloem standing on the curb with his head leaned back, his nose gushing blood.

Part of me was gibbering that I was in deep trouble, that I had just fought with a bunch of cops from my own department. The other part said something rotten was going on and Bloem deserved it. In retrospect, both voices were right.

All I saw was a sea of cops. Police cars were scattered haphazardly all over the street, lights flashing. As I watched a handful of them jumped into cars and took off down the street, I guess for another call.

As I watched Winter rolled up in his unmarked car, conferred with Bloem, then walked over to the car I was in. He opened the door and stood in the opening.

"Miller, you're under arrest." He read me my Miranda rights off the little card he kept in his shirt pocket, just like good little newbie cop straight out of the academy. I just sat there and stared straight ahead, not even acknowledging his presence. It was all starting to sink in by then and I couldn't figure out how I'd gotten here, couldn't understand the chain of events that took me from investigating a homicide one day to being read my rights in the back of a police car the next.

Winter stepped away and a young cop I didn't know slid in behind the wheel. He kept his mouth shut and so did I.

It was interesting to watch the process from the other side. I was taken to East precinct, mugged, printed, stripped of my belt and shoelaces. I'd done it to people a thousand times. Once I got to the station everybody was dryly professional. There were too many eyes around to be otherwise. The precinct seemed busier than usual like everyone had found some reason to just happen to pass through the area where I was. I felt like some kind of caged animal on display.

I overheard them talking. Portland's prisoners usually went to the Multnomah County jail, but I was going to Clackamas County, standard procedure when we arrested one of our own cops.

The same young, silent cop drove me down to the jail. I sat in the back of the car, sweating and smelling the funk of hundreds of prisoners that had taken similar trips.

Of all the things I had to worry about, the one that preyed on my mind the most was Audrey's car. I knew it would get towed off the street, and she'd have to pay the impound fees. She depended on it to get around to her gigs and lessons.

We pulled up to the sally port at the jail. They were apparently expecting us. Two deputies came out and met us. The booking room was deserted of other inmates. I was stripped, searched, and given a pair of faded orange coveralls. Everyone was curt and professional, but like East Precinct, a lot of people were standing around watching, watching another cop get treated like just another prisoner. I felt like I should be selling tickets.

They put me in segregation, the place for all the prisoners who couldn't quite get with the program and for people who might be in danger from other prisoners. That suited me just fine. I was solitary by nature and the last thing I wanted to do was hang out with a bunch of inmates.

The cell was small. Just long enough for me to lie down, just wide enough for my fingertips to brush either wall. The walls were featureless cinder block and high up was a single light fixture behind a grill. There were no pipes, conduits or anything else a person could use to hang himself. The only thing in the room was a mattress that smelled strongly of disinfectant and faintly of piss.

The door was heavy and metal, with an observation slit cut into it. Other than the hum of the light overhead, it was silent inside.

I flipped the mattress up against the wall and lay down on the floor. I ached all over from the beating I'd taken.

I crossed my hands behind my head and lay there, staring at the light up above.

CHAPTER SEVENTEEN

I don't know how long I was there. There was no way to keep track of time in the windowless, featureless cell.

At times I heard footsteps in the hallway outside and low, murmured voices, but that was it. Every now and then a face would pass by the slot in my door, a pair of eyes checking to make sure I wasn't trying to kill myself in some creative manner.

I passed the time by thinking about music. I used to do that in the Army, crammed in the nylon web seats of an Air Force transport plane waiting to jump out the back.

The door slid open and I raised my head blinking. I must have fallen asleep. A big deputy stood there, hands as big as canned hams hanging by his side. His ponderous gut spilled over his old-school leather duty belt.

"Up."

I stood without arguing. He cuffed me quickly and professionally, manipulating me into positions where I was always off balance, right on the verge of toppling over but not quite. I knew if I made a move against him, he would have put me on my face and started having a boot party on the back of my head. I guess you learn a thing or two doing this for a living.

Winter was waiting for me in an interview room. He had his uniform on. I'd only seen him in it a couple of times. His badge was nice and shiny.

I sat down across from him. My chair was bolted to the floor. He had a folder full of papers and a fresh legal pad in front of him. I wondered what was in the folder. Surely he didn't think I was stupid enough to fall for the blank papers in a folder trick.

Winter looked at me, letting the silence build, waiting for me to say something. I felt a prickle of irritation. Sitting there silently was a technique you used on dumb street maggots.

Finally, he said something. "Well Dent, I guess the good news is that she's not dead."

"Who?"

He measured me for a minute and I had two thoughts. One was that there might be more going on here than I thought. The second was that there might be more to Winter than I gave him credit for.

"I'm talking about Mandy, Dent," he said softly.

That took me back for a second. "Mandy? What about her?" He leaned forward, and I saw some steel in Winter. It had been buried under years of bureaucratic ass kissing, softened by desk jobs and admin postings, but it was there.

"How about if you cut the shit, Dent? You caved in the back of your partner's head. We have you at the crime scene because you passed a delivery truck driver on your way up to her apartment. What were you doing, Dent? Were you going to try to talk her into your side of the story?"

Somewhere behind me, I heard the jaws of the trap snapping closed.

"Then," Winter continued. "Bloem sees you fleeing at a high rate of speed, and you tried to take him out."

He looked at me for a second, his nostrils flaring. It was either a hell of an act or he believed it.

"The only chance you've got to save your ass is to come clean with me right now and hope your partner's brain doesn't swell up so much she dies. So how about you tell the truth, Dent?"

Nice. Floor me with the accusation, then try to get me to admit to it. There was an art to getting people to do things against their own self-interest, like confess to crimes, whether they'd done them or not.

I leaned forward across the table, lowered my voice to a conspiratorial whisper.

"Ok, Dan. Here's what I've got to say."

He leaned forward.

"I refuse to answer any questions without an attorney present." I leaned back in my chair.

His face turned red and for a second I thought he was going to come across the table at me. That was when I knew he wasn't in on it, that he was a true believer. He really thought I had tried to kill Mandy. I wasn't sure if that worked for me or against me.

Winter got control again, set his face into a mask. He got up without saying another word, just took his folder and his legal pad and walked out. After a minute or two, the same deputy took me to a deserted cafeteria, put a tray down in front of me. He sat across the room with his arms folded as I consumed a sandwich with gray mystery meat on it, chips, a few carrot sticks. I wasn't hungry, but I made myself eat anyway.

When I was done he took me back down to my cell.

I lay back down on the floor, shoving the thought of Mandy being hurt out of my head.

I don't know how much time passed. Eventually, it must have gotten dark outside. I couldn't tell because the light in my cell never stopped burning. I lay there thinking about guitars and amps and tones, endlessly flipping different combinations around in my head, steadfastly pushing any thoughts of Mandy, Audrey, my job out of my head. The walls of the cell were heavy cinder block, just the thing to break your fists on, or maybe your head, if you got too wound up.

At some point it was morning. This time another deputy came, younger, leaner, but no less competent. Some guys liked to talk trash about corrections officers, considered them inferior to "real" cops. I have to admit that I'd done it myself because I'd run into some real dirtbags working in jails, but the guys I was seeing now were impressive. Maybe they'd called out the A-team for me.

The young guy cuffed me up, then led me to the cafeteria. The food line was almost empty and the trash cans almost full, so I figured they were letting me eat after all the other inmates. Five minutes after I was done I couldn't even remember what I ate but my burps tasted like bacon.

Back in the cell, I resumed my position on the floor. The food churned in my stomach and I lay there, smelling my own gas and looking at the ceiling.

A face kept coming to mind: the big bald guy I'd seen at Central Precinct.

The more I thought about it, the more I was sure he had been in the van with Marshall when I passed him outside Kelly Point Park.

The door to my cell rattled open. It was the young guy again. He motioned me up and I cooperated, standing passively while he cuffed me, careful not to do anything he would interpret as hostile. I wanted nothing more than to break somebody right now, but this guy was just doing his job.

He marched me back to the interview room. I was a little surprised to find Bolle and Al sitting there. I remained silent as the deputy sat me down and un-cuffed me. Al's face was impassive the whole time. I ignored Bolle.

The deputy left and I took a deep breath.

"I didn't do it," I said to Al. "I didn't hurt Mandy."

He gave me a small tight smile. "I know," he said softly.

For a second I couldn't talk. My throat felt almost swollen shut and my eyes blurred with tears. For the first time since I'd put my gun and badge down on that conference table, I felt like things might be alright. Al believed me. I had a short list of people that mattered, and Al was near the top of it.

I almost didn't care if I went to prison just then, didn't care if the world thought I was a dirty cop. Al believed me.

Al looked down, pretended to read the papers he was shuffling while I put myself back together. Bolle brushed some imaginary lint off the lapel of his suit. I pushed the lump in my throat back down, swallowed the tears. There would be time for this later.

Bolle looked up. "But it may not matter what we believe. You have a big problem and I'm wondering what you are planning to do about it?"

Bolle was good. He had a reserved, almost effete air about him, but when he fixed me with those eyes, I could tell there were some layers to this guy.

I stumbled for an answer. What was I going to tell him? That I'd spent the time since I'd been arrested fantasizing about different electric guitars? Ask him if he thought Sea Foam Green was a better custom color for a Stratocaster than Fiesta Red? I could be a real dumbass sometimes.

"Mandy," I managed to croak. "How is she?"

Al looked up at me. "Unconscious. Her brain is still swollen and she's in intensive care. She could still die, Dent."

I squeezed my eyes shut, opened them again. God. Mandy was such a nice kid, would be such an incredible detective some day.

"She can't die." I refused to accept that outcome. I couldn't accept it.

Bolle shrugged. "Well, she is certainly the key. If she wakes up, and if she's capable of speech and normal brain function, she can testify that you didn't attack her. I'd be very interested in knowing what she has to say."

I fixed Al with a look. "Who is the big guy, bald, looks like a shark in a suit. I saw him at Central Precinct, right before Lubbock suspended me."

Bolle nodded, looked long and hard at me as if appraising me anew. He shuffled through the folder in front of him, pulled out a stack of 8x10" photographs. They had the flattened look of shots taken through a long lens.

It showed Gibson Marshall, sitting at an outdoor café. Across from him sat the big bald guy, in a different suit than the one he'd been wearing when I saw him, but definitely the same guy.

I shuffled through the photos. They looked like they'd been taken a few seconds apart. The two men looked like they were arguing. Gibson's hands were animated, his mouth open wide. The other guy looked more restrained. His hands were folded in front of him.

"Those were taken just a couple of hours ago," Bolle said.

"Gibson Marshall is out of jail already?"

Bolle sneered. "Gibson Marshall was being let out of jail while Lubbock was suspending you and your partner. A judge heard his petition for bail at five that morning and released him into the custody of this man." Bolle's finger tapped the bald guy in the photo.

"His name is Rickson Todd. He's a business associate of Gibson Marshall's father. He's got an impressive background, former Army Special Forces, a stint in Delta Force before he got sent over to CIA. After a couple of years of that, he supposedly went private. He dropped out of sight for a few years before he reappeared as Cascade Aviation's director of operations."

I looked at the surveillance photos again. "Where was he yesterday when Mandy was attacked?" I felt cold all over. I was imagining a sight picture, first on Todd's chest, then on Marshall's.

Bolle and Al both shifted uncomfortably, and for a long moment, neither one of them spoke. Finally, Al cleared his throat.

"We had them under surveillance yesterday. Todd and Marshall were together. They broke our surveillance right before Mandy was attacked. That was about half a mile from her apartment."

The room was silent for a minute.

"I'm sorry, Dent," Al continued. "We didn't put it all together until later. We assumed you would be the primary target. We didn't even know Mandy lived in the area until later."

I closed my eyes again, trying to force it out of my mind. That's how it happened sometimes. The facts were staring you right in the face, but you didn't put them together until it was too late. It had happened to me more than once.

"These bastards are slick," I said, trying to sound more forgiving then I felt. "They work quick."

Al and Bolle both nodded. "You have to remember something," Bolle said. "We are working against a very potent combination. Todd has incredible skills and experience. He also has access to a fortune. He could blow several million dollars on an operation like this and Gibson Marshall's father would barely even blink."

I was silent for a minute, processing all that.

"But I think we may be able to help you," Bolle said.

"How?"

Bolle leaned forward across the table. "You do realize that Todd will be looking to kill you now? He'll make it look like another inmate did it, someone with a grudge against the police, or perhaps a suicide. It will stink to high heaven to anyone with any common sense, but all Todd cares about is what people can prove, not what they know. As long as he muddies the waters enough so that the younger Marshall doesn't go on trial for murder, he's a success."

I felt a chill down my back. I suddenly realized that my isolation at the jail not only protected me from a random shank in the ribs from a passing inmate but also set me up for a more organized, more professional hit. If I was found hanging in my cell, a victim of my own despair, heads would roll. Prisoners weren't supposed to be able to kill themselves. But maybe that vast fortune of the Marshall family could smooth some of that over.

I had that feeling of being in freefall again, like everything I'd always taken for granted was gone and I'd been shoved out the door of the plane, unable to even look over my shoulder and see if there was a parachute strapped there or not.

"I need to know something else, Al. Is it all just a joke? Being a cop? Do people really get away with this? Murdering a girl and framing the cop that's investigating it? I know we've always had a few bad eggs at the Bureau, but is it all just a front? Is the place just rotten?"

Al didn't answer for a long time. He looked older, deflated somehow, like a man who'd had seen a little too much, been disappointed a time too many.

"I know if I wanted to go bust black kids for selling crack on street corners, I'd get funding and support all day long."

His eyes took a far-away look that I recognized as a man looking into his past and maybe not liking what he saw.

"When Alex first started college, I got a hint, the barest whisper, that a guy I'd busted for fraud, an accountant at a big developing firm here in town, had maybe been innocent, that maybe he'd been set up by his boss because he knew where the dirt was on certain projects involving big chunks of city money. The accountant hadn't gone to jail, you basically can't go to jail on white collar stuff these days, but he was ruined professionally. I started snooping just a little, very quietly."

Al fidgeted in his seat, not meeting my eyes. Then he continued.

"I couldn't bear the thought that I'd put an innocent man through the justice system, got him labeled a criminal, but I knew I had to be careful."

He was silent for a minute, rubbed the side of his chest like it hurt.

"Anyway, one day I opened my mail. There was a big envelope. Inside was a copy of the case file on the accountant. There were some pictures of Alex outside her dorm at the college. Copies of her enrollment paperwork from the college, floor plans of the dorm room. And a bunch of newspaper clippings about young women being attacked on college campuses. Date rapes, abductions, homicides, that sort of thing."

He was quiet again for a few seconds, rubbing his chest.

I remembered Alex when she was in college. I went to Al's house frequently in those days for card games, barbecues, the occasional mentoring session when I was stuck on a case. She'd breeze in and out of the house on summer vacation, spring break. She'd been pretty then, in a slightly awkward, post-adolescent way. But back then, I'd thought of her as a kid. It wasn't until later I started thinking of her in other ways.

"What did you do?" I asked softly.

"I took the envelope I got in the mail and locked it in a safety deposit box," Al said. "Just in case. Then I forgot about the accountant and went back to planning operations where we busted black kids for selling crack on street corners."

The ground was coming up fast, and there was still no sign of a parachute opening. I looked at Al anew. He'd always seemed untouchable to me, a square-jawed hero like something out of a legend.

Bolle leaned forward. There was a strange fire in his eyes, a light that I'd come to associate with true believers, guys who would give everything they owned to one church or another, or maybe even strap a bomb to themselves and blow themselves up for the greater cause. I hadn't seen that light in the eyes of too many cops. Maybe that was why we were losing.

"I need men like you, Dent, people I can trust. Most cops never even see the bigger picture, they just keep busting those kids on street corners selling crack and telling themselves that's what matters, or they just coast their way to retirement, doing as little as possible, or they become dirty, become part of the problem."

That light in his eyes was a little scary, a little too much for me right now. He fixed me with that stare and wouldn't let me go.

"Join my team, Dent. We can take the gloves off, the way you've always wanted to."

"Maybe," I said. "But right now I'm in jail. If I get convicted of what they're saying I did, I'll be in prison. I'm not much help to you there."

Bolle sat back, that smirk on his face again. "If Todd can get Gibson Marshall out, I'll get you out. You're going to be transferred into Federal custody. I can make that happen."

"You know," I said. "All the people I've arrested get to have arraignments and lawyers and such. Seems like I've been here a while without any of that."

Bolle waved that away. "I've got a lawyer for you if you need one. Your arraignment keeps getting pushed back. With luck, none of this is ever going to see a courtroom anyway."

Interesting. He was waving away the justice system as easily as Todd and the Marshalls appeared to. I wondered if Marshall's trial for killing Heather Swanson would ever see a court room. Somehow she had gotten lost in the shuffle.

Al and Bolle were packing their stuff, getting ready to go. Al looked troubled.

"Someone will be here for you tonight," Bolle said. "Stay safe until then."

I wanted to ask him questions, but the deputy was coming in and they were going out. I didn't want to discuss anything with the deputy present. I just stood there like a piece of meat while he cuffed me up. I wondered if he was taking me to my death, if I'd get shanked by a passing inmate on the way back to the cell, or if I'd suddenly get depressed and figure out a way to hang myself in the cell. It would all be unfortunate. The deputy might even lose his job, but that was nothing a little bit of the Marshall family fortune couldn't make all better.

As we walked, me always three steps ahead of the Corrections officer and to his left, on the other side of the red line painted on the floor, I was far more alert than I had been. I saw the hallways of the jail anew, eying each potential opening and hiding place, where before I'd been in a dazed funk. If somebody had wanted to slip a knife in me then, they would have done it. Now, handcuffed or not, they'd get a fight.

Soon we were back at the cell, and I actually breathed a sigh of relief when the door slammed shut and locked behind me. I still chose the floor over the stained mattress. I lay back down on the concrete, put my hands behind my head and focused on the ceiling.

Guitars were the furthest thing from my mind now. Now it was all strategy.

CHAPTER EIGHTEEN

I trusted Al.

I came to that conclusion after lying there, staring at the ceiling for maybe an hour, maybe a little longer. If someone had told me the week before that it would take me an hour to decide whether I trusted Al, I would have cheerfully broken their jaw.

But now, all bets were off.

Everything I thought I could count on was gone. I'd always known there were corrupt cops at my department, but I'd always figured it was small time, individual stuff. Maybe we had the occasional guy who would skim some cash from a drug dealer, maybe take a freebie here and there, but I'd never even suspected widespread corruption.

I'd never done it myself. You find yourself taking a freebie, maybe a cup of coffee, then a whole meal and before you know it, you're in a back room somewhere being handed a greasy bag full of $20 bills.

Now I questioned everybody. I questioned the whole damn department. A couple of times I started to add up the number of people that had to be complicit in setting me up, but my mind just skidded away from that.

But I didn't question Al. I'd seen him make the right choices too many times.

Besides, if Al wasn't being straight with me, I truly had no hope. There was nothing left that could save me.

That left Bolle. He wasn't like any Fed I'd ever known, and the more I thought about him, the less I realized I knew about him. He didn't appear to be attached to the Portland FBI Field office. I was familiar with most of the Special Agents that worked there. He could have been part of some anti-corruption task force. That's the sort of thing the Feds probably wouldn't advertise.

All I knew is that I was heading for the ground way too fast and I needed to find a way to pop my chute before I hit. I lay there, coming up with one plan, then discarding it as unworkable, only to work on another one for a while, only to run into yet another dead end.

Even if I somehow "proved" my innocence, what was to stop the evidence from disappearing? Or more "evidence" from being generated that I was guilty? Before, I'd operated on the assumption that if I just got to the truth, everything would be ok. Now I wasn't sure the truth mattered.

The cell door rattled open and the older guard stood there, still fat, and still looking mean as hell. We must have had a shift change while I was lying there.

He chained me, and led me through the corridors, twisting and turning until I was thoroughly lost, although I had the impression we must be working our way towards the outside. He popped me down at a desk, put down the clear plastic baggie with my personal effects in it, minus my guns and knives of course.

I looked up and got a surprise. I'd expected Al, or maybe Bolle, but instead it was Eddie, Bolle's driver. There were FBI credentials hanging around his neck, he was straining the seams of a suit, he even had the regulation Fed haircut, but he didn't look like a Fed, didn't walk like a Fed, didn't stand there waiting like a Fed. He looked like a thug in a suit. There was no way anybody was going to mistake him for a Fed.

A guy with a handlebar mustache and Captain's bars on his collars was standing in the corner, his arms crossed over his chest and a sour expression on his face. As Eddie signed the paperwork, I kept expecting the Captain to see through this charade for what it was, to put a halt to things and send me back to my cell.

But he didn't. I watched in disbelief as Eddie and the captain signed the paperwork. Eddie walked over to me, and without a word pulled me up out of the chair by my biceps, with about as much effort as I would expend opening a jar of peanut butter. Christ, he was huge. I didn't have a real appreciation for how big he was until he was standing right next to me. He was remarkably light on his feet for such a big guy.

He pulled out a pair of cuffs and put them on me, almost laughably loose, then the deputy removed his own cuffs. Eddie steered me towards the door, pausing only to collect my bag of personal effects between a thumb and a forefinger.

The corrections guys just stood there, stony-faced and silent, as we headed out to the sally port. From there Eddie deposited me in the backseat of an unmarked car. I got to ride on a real upholstered seat this time instead of hard plastic.

I was silent until we pulled out of the garage and were out on the street, then I breathed a sigh of relief.

Eddie heard me, looked back in the rearview mirror. "What's the matter?"

"I didn't think we were going to make it out of there. No offense, but you aren't the world's most convincing FBI agent."

"I don't have to be convincing, man. I had official paperwork."

I guess he had a point there. A few blocks from the jail he pulled into the parking lot of a fried chicken joint and drove around to the back. He got out, came around and opened my door.

"What, are we going in for a snack?"

"Funny," Eddie said. "Look, you're the one in the back of the car in handcuffs, so no fat guy jokes, understand? Or you can just stay that way." He dangled a handcuff key from one finger.

I nodded and turned in my seat so he could get to the cuffs. He unshackled me and dropped my plastic baggie of stuff in my lap.

"There. I thought you might feel better with your belt and shoelaces back."

It was a small kindness, but an important one. I did indeed feel better with my belt and shoelaces back. I sorted through the pocket clutter in the bag, putting everything back where it belonged. I missed my weapons.

Eddie drove silently. I stared out the window and planned. We glided on to I-205 South, then at the interchange got on the I-5 headed back North, but before we got to Portland he took one of the Tigard exits and we dropped off into the middle of bland suburbia on Highway 99. We passed fast food restaurants and strip malls before he took another turn onto Bull Mountain Road. We ran out of suburb fast and into farm country. Our tires crunched up a long gravel driveway and we stopped.

The house probably hadn't been designed as a fortress, but it could pass for one. Low, squat and rambling, it had a slate roof and heavy stucco walls, not quite bulletproof, but close. It sat at the crest of the hill with no trees for a hundred yards around it. It was all open fields. They were fenced off, presumably for livestock, but they were all empty. The nearest house was almost a half a mile away. There was a big barn behind the house. One door was half open and I saw several cars and sport utility vehicles lined up inside.

Eddie came and let me out. When he slammed the door behind me it seemed very loud. It was quiet out here. He motioned for me to follow, walked to the front door and punched in a code on the numeric keypad on the front door. I noticed a small video camera half hidden behind the light sconce next to the door. The door clicked and he pulled it opened. As we passed through, I noticed that the door seemed unusually thick.

The inside was barely furnished. It was all functional, couches scattered haphazardly in the vast living room, a large-screen TV parked in one corner, but no decorations, no sense of any one person living here. I followed Eddie through a kitchen that could have served a medium-sized restaurant. He led me to another door with a keypad. He punched in another code, turning his body ever so slightly so I couldn't see, and it too clicked open revealing a set of stairs. The camera here was a little more obvious, mounted right on the ceiling with a big "x" of duct tape, the wire trailing down the wall.

I followed him down towards the sounds of people talking. The basement had been finished as one big room running the length of the house, with only structural pillars breaking the line of sight. There were desks, computer displays, and workbenches scattered everywhere. Bolle sat in the center of the room at a long conference table strewn with papers. Al was over in a corner, standing with his arms folded next to a youngish-looking man that needed a haircut and a shave. They were both looking at a computer monitor that showed a map display of the Portland metro area. A blinking red dot was moving up I-5 towards North Portland. When Al saw me he reached up and flicked the screen off abruptly. He forced a smile and started walking towards me.

I didn't smile back. Instead, I stood there taking in the room one slice at a time. It looked a combination office, conference room, high school science lab ,and storage room. An Asian woman sat on a chair in a portable office cubicle, staring at a computer screen. Two men were cleaning guns. As I watched they field stripped a pair of rifles with the ease born of long familiarity and started scrubbing. One, a Latino guy had long hair in a ponytail and some blurry tattoos on his forearm. The white guy sported a buzz cut and a lack of a neck.

I looked back to Al as he walked up. His companion was so skinny I could count his ribs through his Foo Fighters T-shirt.

The guy was young, couldn't even be thirty yet and had the pallor of somebody who spent too much time indoors.

Al stuck out his hand. "It's good to see you, Dent."

I didn't take the hand.

"We need to talk. Alone," I said, staring at Al.

Bolle stood from where he'd been looking at a flat screen display. "But I'd hoped to introduce you to the other members of the team," he said, walking over to us. He had his suit coat off and now I saw a long flat automatic pistol of a type I didn't recognize strapped to his hip in a fancy looking holster. It didn't look like Bureau issue.

"We need to talk. Alone," I said again to Al.

"Ok," Al said softly. He grabbed his suit coat, put it on so it covered his own gun, a plain old Smith and Wesson, and started up the stairs. I followed. Bolle also put on a coat and fell in behind me. I hadn't really wanted to talk with him, but I didn't say anything.

Al walked through the kitchen and out to the back porch. It was covered with dust and the pool was murky and green. Al folded his arms across his chest.

"What can I do for you, Dent?"

"Who are these people?"

Bolle answered for him. "Members of my team."

"Bullshit," I said, still staring at Al.

"What do you mean?" Al said, still soft, but I could see the vein starting to throb on his temple. Al rarely got mad, but when he did you weren't likely to survive the explosion if you were standing too close.

"Those people aren't Feds. The woman and the nerd in the T-shirt are civilians. They aren't in the game." I turned to Bolle for the first time.

"Your 'driver' is a thug in a suit. He doesn't make a very convincing FBI agent, by the way. The two hard cases you've got down there are street muscle. If we strip them down, we're liable to find at least one 'born to lose' tattoo between the two of them."

Bolle withdrew inside of himself. It was strange to watch. He became still. His facial expression became bland and fixed. His eyes unfocused and his body posture changed slightly. His weight settled lower, towards his hips. It was subtle. You wouldn't see it if you weren't attuned to things like that.

I felt the hair on the back of my neck stand up. I'd known one other guy who acted like that when he got pissed. His name had been Arthur Anthony Levy and he'd been a serial rapist I worked almost nine months to catch. I also suspected that Arthur had buried some bodies somewhere along the line, but I'd never been able to prove it. I'd worked on Arthur in the interrogation room for hours, playing cat and mouse with him as he indulged his ego. Finally, I'd suggested that the reason he raped women was because he didn't have the skills to pick them up in a bar, and Arthur had gone flat just like Bolle had just done. At the time I had wondered if this was the face Arthur's victims had seen.

Bolle was quiet for a second. "You're absolutely right, Dent. They are criminals. Eddie has felony convictions in three states. Mickey should go to jail just for touching that AR15 he's cleaning. Felons can't have guns you know. And Fredrico is a convicted sex offender." His voice was slow and smooth and oily.

That sank in for a minute. "Why?" was all I could think of to ask.

"Because I have a soft spot for unfortunates, Dent. You see, the thing all three of those men have in common is that they all went to prison for things they didn't do. They were all framed at one time or another."

I remembered where I had just come from, remembered being led through the halls of the Clackamas County jail in handcuffs, wondering if the guard had been paid off to let somebody stick a sharpened toothbrush smeared with human feces in between my ribs. I remembered all that and I shut my mouth. The ground was still coming, and I was starting to feel like I wasn't even wearing clothes, much less a parachute.

"What, Dent?" Bolle asked. "No protestation that every con has a story about how he's been framed? No affirmation that our criminal justice system only punishes the guilty and protects the innocent? Where is your sense of outrage?"

I kept my mouth shut for a minute, looking off in the distance. On a clear day, the view from here would be incredible. Even with the November sky, I could see halfway across the valley. Off in the distance, a heavy black cloud was drifting towards us, rain on the way.

I looked at Bolle, hard. He didn't shrink away. I had to give him credit for that.

"I can't figure you out," I said.

"You're not supposed to. The only reason you're here is because Al says you're useful. That got you in the door. If you want to know more about me, I'm going to have to see you work. If you don't like it, Eddie can come get you and drive you back to your cell."

I was tempted to tell him to whistle Eddie up and tell him to take me for a ride. Something stank about this. I had the feeling I was making a bargain when I didn't have a clue what my end was supposed to be.

"Just go with it, Dent," Al said softly. I looked at him, seeing a balding guy with a little too much paunch, a guy who could easily be somebody's grandfather, but I was remembering the Al of years ago, the guy who had all but held my hand when I was a young detective, the guy who had taken a chance on making me a detective in the first place.

"Ok," I said, feeling tremendous relief.

I was doing what I'd always done, trusting in Al.

CHAPTER NINETEEN

Everyone was sitting around the big table and pretending everything was fine when we went back downstairs. Bolle made introductions all around. Mickey and Frederico each shook my hand with a grunt, their faces flat, hard and expressionless.

The kid in the Foo Fighters T-shirt was Henry. He was Bolle's computer expert and had a handshake like a limp fish. Eddie I already knew.

The woman was May. Bolle said she was a psychologist. Her face was that perfect mask, polite but impenetrable. She sat down next to Eddie and put a hand on his arm with an easy familiarity.

Bolle cleared his throat and everybody fell quiet. "For Dent's benefit, here's where we are. After his meeting with Todd, Marshall holed up in his studio and hasn't moved since. Dent impounded his van, but this morning a couple of employees of Cascade Aviation dropped a rental off, another full-size Ford Econoline, white."

He took a sip of water before continuing. Everyone around the table was quiet.

"The Cascade Aviation compound in Albany has tightened up security considerably since Gibson got arrested. Todd appears to have brought the boy in line. As soon as he got out of jail he went straight to the studio, none of his usual partying. He's even dumped his cell phone, unknown if he'll acquire a new one. He hasn't made any landline calls from the studio, nor has he accessed the internet, as far as we can tell."

Interesting. Bolle and his people had this kid wired in tight. It was a shame they hadn't been on him the night he killed Heather.

"So right now we're in a holding pattern. We're waiting for Todd or Marshall to make a move. Hopefully, the pressure of the arrest will force a move and we'll be able to figure out what they are doing."

I found it interesting that nowhere in there did Bolle mention any concerns about Marshall getting away with killing a teenage girl.

"Where are we at from a technical perspective Henry?"

Henry cleared his throat and gave a nervous glance around the room.

"We're waiting. Marshall's landline phones are covered, his internet connection is covered. If he gets a new cell phone, we'll pick up on it pretty quick. If he drives off in the new van, we've found good spots to 'poon him, no matter what way he goes."

Bolle nodded his head, satisfied.

I spoke up. "What do you mean 'poon him?"

I had a long list of things I wanted to do to Marshall, but that wasn't on it, at least not until I figured out what it was.

Henry looked pleased that I had asked. From the cargo pocket of his pants, he pulled out an electronic gadget. It was two black boxes stuck together, each about the size of a pack of cigarettes.

"This is an electro harpoon, or 'poon for short. You hide it on the likely path of travel of your target vehicle. We like using the back side of a speed bump, but just about anywhere will do. When he drives over it, you pull out your remote." From another of many, many pockets, he pulled out what looked like a garage door opener.

"And pull the trigger." There was a hiss of compressed air and the top box shot off the bottom. It almost made it to the ceiling before coming down and putting a scratch on the table.

"The top box is a GPS receiver and a cellular transmitter with a very strong electromagnet to stick it to the bottom of the car. It actually uses the car body as its antenna. The GPS unit reads the car's position. The cell transmitter feeds me the info. As long as he's within range of a cell tower, we can track him."

I had a passing familiarity with surveillance gear, but I'd never heard of that one, much less seen one. "Who's there watching him, waiting to activate this thing?"

Henry started to open his mouth, but Bolle cut him off.

"We have other assets in place. May, do you have any insights into Marshall's behavior?"

May's voice was dry, professional. "The inactivity is chafing on him. All his drugs were confiscated and he hasn't had a chance to purchase more. He's had no sexual contact, so all of his preferred methods of mood regulation are closed to him. His ego will make him want to

143

retaliate, against Mr. Miller in particular if given the chance. Marshall can't tolerate the slightest insult without overreacting, and he sees his arrest as the ultimate insult. I'm frankly surprised Todd has kept him stationary for this long. I expect some kind of action from him in the next twenty-four hours. He won't be able to contain himself much longer."

Bolle nodded. "Thank you, May. So that leaves us waiting, which frankly I'm not satisfied with. All of our intelligence up until now indicated that Todd and the people at Cascade Aviation were planning something big. Does anybody have any ideas?"

"Yeah," I said. "I do." All eyes turned towards me. "I might be able to get a full picture of what Marshall was doing before he killed that girl. I'm not sure if it is related to this Cascade Aviation thing, but it might help."

"How?" Bolle asked.

"I need to meet with a contact. It needs to be face to face. And I need to be alone."

"Dent, you're supposed to be in jail, for Christ's sake," Al protested. "We can't let you go run around the city."

I shrugged. "My source isn't going to meet with you. And the meeting has to be face to face."

Bolle put a hand on Al's arm. "It's ok. If he can help us let him go."

I almost smiled. I'm sure the fact that his staff could track me with GPS transmitters had something to do with his easy acquiescence.

Bolle stood, looked at Eddie. "Get Dent set up with a package. We need to get this thing rolling."

Apparently, one of Bolle's "packages" consisted of a new ID, a car, a cell phone and a gun. Henry took a couple of digital photos of me against a grey background. Twenty minutes later he handed me a driver's license, a concealed handgun license, and a Visa gold card, all with the name "Harlan Stephenson." The address on the licenses was the house we were standing in.

I rubbed my thumb over both IDs. They were excellent. I'd seen my share of fake documents and I saw no way of telling that these weren't real.

"Are these backstopped?" I asked Henry.

He looked wounded that I would suggest otherwise. "Of course, all the way through an NCIC check. You have a driving history, excellent credit, the works. The gold card has a five thousand dollar credit limit."

Outstanding. A cheap fake ID will only hold up to cursory

inspection. If a police officer ran the ID number through a Department of Motor Vehicles or criminal history check, it would be quickly revealed as a fake. Henry had told me these documents would hold up to close scrutiny. I had no way of testing it, of course, but I hoped that he was being straight with me and that the data quality of the documents matched the physical quality.

Henry handed me a cell phone. There was one number programmed into memory.

"That's the duty phone here," he said, pointing to a phone on the table. "There's somebody here to answer it all the time."

And no doubt Henry could track me to within a few blocks by the pings the cell phone transmitted. Most people don't realize that even when you aren't talking on your phone, it periodically communicates with cell towers in your immediate vicinity. Anybody who has access to the cell system's computers can triangulate and locate your position to within a few dozen feet. I was willing to bet Henry had access.

Eddie led me over to the storage shelves. "Let's get you a gun," he said.

"Got any .45's?" I asked.

"I got anything you want, as long as it's a Glock and it's 9mm."

He had a couple of different sizes. I chose the model 19, the medium frame. It would conceal pretty well under the un-tucked shirt I was wearing. I made sure the piece was unloaded and did a couple of practice draws.

I walked over to a mirror and checked myself out, making sure the gun didn't cause a noticeable bulge.

Eddie followed me over. "You look smashing 007." He did a surprisingly good British accent. He handed me two loaded magazines for the Glock. I loaded the gun up with one and stowed the other one in a carrier on my left hip.

"Now you need a car." Eddie opened a lockbox and started hunting around inside. "I'll go get one ready."

He headed up the stairs and Al walked over.

"Look, Dent, I wish you'd reconsider this and at least tell me where you're going."

"It'll be ok, Al. I meant it when I said my source would get spooked if anybody but me showed up."

For all I knew, Casey did contract work for the Feds too, but Al didn't need to know that, at least not right now.

Al looked pained. "Look, Bolle doesn't know how far to trust you.

He put both your name and the Harlan Stephenson identity on the Feds No-Fly list. He's afraid you're going to hop a plane and take off on him."

"I'm not planning on running, I just need to meet my source."

He shrugged. "I just thought I should tell you."

I walked upstairs without another word. Eddie was standing in the driveway next to a Dodge Charger. He'd pulled it out of the barn for me. He tossed me the keys and I caught them.

"Thanks."

"No problem. Don't scratch it and bring it back with a full tank."

I nodded and slid behind the wheel. There was something about Eddie I liked. I drove through the streets of Tigard at exactly the speed limit, signaling each turn and stopping fully at each stop sign. I felt like there was a big sign attached to the back of the car: "escaped prisoner inside." Although I guess I wasn't technically escaped. After all, the Feds had sprung me, gotten me a fake id and given me a gun.

It was getting dark and traffic was picking up. Soon the evening rush hour would begin. I'd have no choice but to sit through it.

I rolled up I-5 North, keeping an eye out for cars behind me. Traffic wasn't as bad as I'd feared, just heavy enough to actually work to my advantage. As I rolled across the Marquam bridge, I sped up, weaving in and out of traffic. It was a calculated risk, I was attracting attention and breaking the law, but I knew traffic cops hated stopping people on the bridge, and I wanted anybody following me to have to speed up and show themselves.

The cell phone Henry gave me sat on the seat next to me, its little green light blinking. As the exit for Interstate 84 eastbound came up, I shut the phone off. For all I knew the car might be wired for sound and equipped with one of Henry's electro harpoons, so I resolved to pull out the battery and lock the phone in the trunk, first chance I got.

I took the exit for I-84 at the very last second. I waved an apology at the driver behind me and floored the accelerator. I kept the ponies running until I got to the Hollywood exit, then darted off the freeway.

I was counting on Bolle having limited resources. He couldn't use any of the people I'd met to follow me. I knew what they looked like. He'd indicated that he had more people working, keeping Marshall and the Cascade Aviation people under surveillance. One of the reasons I'd wanted to get out of the house so fast after announcing my intention to go alone, was that I didn't want to give Bolle enough time to set up an effective surveillance team.

Each time I made a crazy maneuver, it made it harder to keep a good overwatch. Just because you're paranoid, doesn't mean they're not after you.

Casey lived in Gresham, a town east of Portland. But before I stopped at her place, I had shopping to do. I pulled into a Wal-Mart parking lot, in a dark corner of the lot where the video cameras wouldn't pick up my plate. I put my ball cap on, held my head down and tried to slouch for the sake of the video cameras at the front door.

Inside, I bought a prepaid cellular phone with cash, and a few sundry other items I thought might come in handy. I was in and out in a matter of minutes. I'd used an automated checkout so there would have been no clerk to remember me. It seemed like sometimes our goal in society was to eliminate human interaction. I wasn't sure exactly how I felt about that. It would probably cut down on the number of homicides, I guess.

After driving around randomly for a few minutes, I tried Casey's number. There was no answer, and no message on her voice mail, just like always. Just a beep.

I drove around for a few more minutes, hoping for a callback. Then I decided to go straight to her place.

I'd been to Casey's once before, to drop off a laptop I'd seized as evidence in a homicide. Her combination of business headquarters and crash pad was in a light industrial area. I'd never found out the full extent of what she did. I knew she did contract work for computer investigations and forensics for a variety of clients: police departments, private business, it was rumored even some alphabet agencies.

I did know she specialized in Internet kiddie porn cases, would stay up for a week at a time living on herbal tea and vegan stir fry to roll up a ring that might stretch over three or four continents. She was probably responsible for putting more truly bad guys in jail than half the detectives in my office put together. It was a wonder to see her in court. She could explain the most complicated web of computer geek knowledge in a way that a Neanderthal could understand. I'd thought about asking her out more than once. She was cool, and I thought I could get over the nose ring and tattoo thing. But she had a tendency to keep the world at arm's distance. Besides, there was Audrey now.

I found a dark parking spot a couple of blocks away from her place, got out, and shut my door quietly. I stood there for a minute, just soaking in the surroundings and listening. It was just after nine, and this part of town was quiet. All the businesses were shut down for the night. There was no traffic, a good thing, and a bad thing. Anybody coming would be easy to hear, but I'd stick out like a sore thumb. I hoped no eager beaver cop would decide to cruise by while I was walking around.

I kept mostly to the shadows. Luckily, I was wearing my usual dark, earth-toned clothes. They would blend into the shadows and half-light of a night time urban environment better than solid black and had the added bonus of not making me look like a wannabe ninja. I paused at the corner of the building next to Casey's. Her car was parked in the lot, everything looked quiet and normal.

I walked across the parking lot quickly, then up to the heavy steel door. There was a speaker grill next to the door and the fisheye of a surveillance camera. I frowned. The front door was ajar, open just an inch or two. This wasn't right. One of the reasons Casey had picked this place was so she could turn it into a miniature fortress. There was no way in hell she would just leave the door open.

I drew my Glock almost without thinking about it, held it down behind my leg. I paused for a second, feeling an unfamiliar pang of indecisiveness. Casey had a fondness for shotguns, and I'd feel awful silly if she blew me in half because I walked in unannounced through a door she'd forgotten to lock.

But the hair on the back of my neck was standing up. I knew something was wrong.

Ordinarily, I would have waited for some backup before charging in, but now I was on my own. It was time to either go through the door or get back in my car and drive away.

I took a deep breath and moved through the door. I knew I'd been right when the rich, meaty smell of blood filled my nostrils.

CHAPTER TWENTY

My foot slipped in a puddle of blood by the front door and I almost fell down.

In the light from my flashlight, I saw Rolf, Casey's dog, lying in a bloody heap, his head misshapen. I stepped over him and kept moving, following the walls and trying to move fast. I only used my light when I had to, turning it on for a quick flash to orient myself and then moving away from the spot where I'd been standing. My guts kept twisting tighter and tighter. I was waiting to see a muzzle flash and hit the floor before I even heard the boom.

Casey's place was a warren of rooms, full of computers, monitors, oscilloscopes, stereo equipment, more stuff I didn't even recognize. The three rooms in front were business, the three in the back were personal. I moved through them all, not finding anybody.

In the back I found a heavy steel door leaning drunkenly against the wall, held up by only one twisted hinge. On the floor were four blue spent shotgun shells. They were from special "lockbuster" rounds. The projectile inside was made out of powdered metal bound together with epoxy. It would blow the hell out of a metal or wood door frame, or a set of hinges, then disintegrate into powder.

The room inside was empty, but I could see that the walls, ceiling and floor were reinforced with heavy marine grade plywood. Part of our contract with Casey had specified that she maintain a secure room to store evidence. Apparently, this was it.

I found the rest of the story in the bedroom. A pistol gripped shotgun lay on the floor, an empty shell half ejected from the action. The floor in front of the door was chewed up by a blast of double-ought buck, but I didn't see any blood on the floor or the walls. Two probes from a Taser lay on the floor, the thin wires trailing out behind them.

Satisfied that I was alone, I walked back through the building, putting the pieces together. Somehow they'd gotten in the front door. I wasn't sure how, as the door showed no sign of being forced. Then they shot the dog. When I went through the front room again, I found a fat .45 ACP shell casing I'd missed before. The dog's body was still warm. This hadn't happened too long ago.

Maybe Casey had been asleep, maybe not. She kept odd hours. But anyway she had just enough time to fire one round from the shotgun. I wondered if they had Tased her at about the same time she had pulled the trigger. That would explain the shot being jerked low and into the floor. Then they'd blown the doors off the hinges and cleaned out the evidence locker.

It spoke of desperation. They were willing to attract more attention, up the ante of violence to make the evidence on the servers disappear. I wondered what was on them. I was willing to bet it was more than a simple Internet porn scheme.

Casey was gone. So was the evidence. I stood there for a minute, trying to figure out what to do.

I realized I was technically an escaped felony suspect, standing in the middle of the scene of a kidnapping that was a possible homicide. That got me moving. I'd had one thing pinned on me, I wouldn't have another.

There was a duffel bag at the base of Casey's bed. I dumped the mess of smelly gym clothes on the floor and put her shotgun inside. It wouldn't have been my first choice of a weapon, but it wasn't bad. I pulled a washcloth out of the bathroom and wiped off everything I'd touched.

I left the front door open, and as I walked across the parking lot in the direction of my car, I dialed the number Bolle had given me.

Al answered.

"Al, do you remember Casey? The computer contractor?"

Al had viewed Casey's association with the Police Bureau with a jaundiced eye. He'd always been a little conservative about certain things.

"Yeah. Little blond gal, blond some of the time anyway?"

"That's her. She had the servers from Marshall's place. Somebody just killed her dog, Tased her and took the servers. They took her too, I think."

"Why didn't you tell me you had evidence there? We could have protected her."

"I'm still not ready to put all my cards down in front of Bolle. The question is, what do we do now?"

"They're getting desperate. Whatever fallout this kind of behavior will cause, it must be worth it to tie up loose ends, get any witnesses out of the way."

When he said "witnesses" and "loose ends" my stomach went cold. It was obvious. Why hadn't I thought of it right away?

"Dent," Al said. It was hard to hear him through the buzzing in my ears. I started running towards my car. "You need to come in. If Todd or Marshall find you, they'll kill you. We've stirred up some kind of hornet's nest here that is bigger than we imagined."

I threw the bag with the shotgun in the passenger seat, slid behind the wheel, and nearly broke the key getting the car started.

"Al. You need to listen to me." I tried to keep my voice level.

"Ok."

"Mandy. Where is she?"

"In the hospital, at OHSU. Why?"

And then it occurred to him. "Oh, no...."

"She's the other loose end. If she wakes up, she can tell people I didn't attack her. What room is she in?"

He told me and I wrote it down on my hand as I pushed the car through the side streets. I was going too fast to keep a low profile.

"Al, how fast can you get some of Bolle's hard cases over there to sit on her room?"

There was silence on the line for a minute.

"I'm working on it."

"Work harder. Do it yourself if you have to." I hung up as I swung onto the interstate and started zigzagging through cars much faster than I should have on the rain-slick interstate. The pavement was grooved and the water pooled, deep in places. I forced myself to slow down a little. I wouldn't do Mandy any good if I wrapped myself around an abutment on the way there.

I wondered if Audrey was another "loose end," a way to get to me. I wasn't dumb enough to assume that Todd and his boys didn't know about Audrey. They probably knew my favorite breakfast and the size of my underwear by now. Money had a way of opening doors.

I hit the I-84 to I-5 interchange at about eighty, way too fast, but I made it. I leaned way over to fetch the phone out of the passenger seat, nearly putting the car into the guard rail.

I dialed Audrey's number, waited impatiently as it rang.

"Audrey, I need you to call me. I need to know you're ok" I said, as soon as her voice mail beeped.

I put the phone down, blew through a red light at the end of the exit ramp that would take me to the hospital. I left a trail of blaring horns in my wake, but so far I saw no red and blue lights in the rearview mirror.

CHAPTER TWENTY-ONE

OHSU sat on top of a giant hill. The road up was narrow and twisted. I got flipped off by two joggers and a bicyclist on the way up, but who jogs dressed all in black anyway?

I slowed down as I entered the parking lot. OHSU security were notorious for being both bored and overzealous.

I parked the car and forced myself to walk and not run. Fortunately, I knew my way around the hospital from all the times I'd come here to interview a victim of an attempted homicide or serious assault. I went in a pair of sliding glass doors near the Emergency Room.

My mind raced, trying to come up with a plan. Visiting hours were technically over. I didn't know if my newly minted Federal credentials would get me past the nurse, but even if they didn't, my presence would hopefully deter any plans Todd and Marshal had to harm Mandy.

I needed to see Mandy, make sure she was still alive, make sure I hadn't screwed this up so comprehensively that my partner was already dead.

I cleared my mind, saw an unattended clipboard lying at an empty nurse's station and snagged it. Forget wearing a ninja outfit and creeping around in air conditioning ducts. The best way to sneak into any building was to look the part and carry a clipboard.

I forced myself to breathe, and think of nothing on the elevator ride up. First things first. Make sure Mandy was still breathing and go from there.

The doors slid open, all too soon. In front of me was a nurse's station. A tired looking woman sat there talking on the phone. I stepped out, gave her a professional, distant smile. She looked at me, distracted, and nodded. Perfect.

The hallway stretched out to my right. I knew Mandy's room would be all the way on the end, to the left. I started that way.

A door at the far end of the hall swung open and a guy wearing nurse's scrubs stepped out. He took a look to the right and left and then looked at me. Our eyes locked.

He recognized me. I could tell because when we made eye contact, he froze and his eyes got a little wider, his mouth opened just a little bit. He was no nurse, not any more than I was. He was a young guy, mid-twenties, with a crew cut and the bullet head and squat neck of somebody who spent hours in the gym.

Unconsciously, his hand went down to pat something tucked in his waistband. He leaned forward towards me.

Weapon! My brain screamed. I dropped the clipboard, leaned forward myself. We were maybe thirty feet apart, separated by the narrow hallway. If he pulled a gun he couldn't miss.

Out of the corner of my eye, I saw the nurse behind the desk frown, start to put the phone down. Damn. We were attracting attention.

Down at the end of the hall, the guy spun on his heel and went back through the doorway.

I was moving by the time it swung closed behind him. I charged down the hallway, pausing for a second at the door to Mandy's room. I caught a glimpse of her there on the bed. It was hard to tell which was whiter, her skin or the mass of bandages wrapped around her head. Her hair was unbound, the first time I'd ever seen it that way. I would have never guessed it was that long. She was breathing.

I closed my eyes in relief for a second then ran back out into the hall. I pushed the door open, determined to catch the guy and make him tell me what was going on. The door had one of those signs that showed a stick person walking down a flight of stairs.

My brain caught up with my body right as I moved through the door frame. I caught a flash of the fist coming at me from the corner of my eye and lowered my head just enough to catch it on the skull instead of square on the jaw. Still, it was like a flashbulb had gone off right in front of me when it landed. If he'd connected with my jaw he would have knocked me out.

I spun, throwing my own right, which he slipped easily. It went sailing over his head as he charged in low, trying to take my balance. I had just enough time to squat as he wrapped me up, but he still drove me backwards into the wall. I managed a half-ass punch into his abdomen. The kid's belly was like a rock. I probably hurt my hand as much as I hurt him.

He was smaller than me, by six inches or so, but his muscles were rock-hard. We clinched like a pair of boxers, throwing knees and elbows. He kept trying to take my balance and throw me to the ground, or worse, over the railway of the narrow stairwell landing. He was silent except for the occasional grunt.

I swallowed panic. The kid was better than me, faster. I was keeping up with him, barely, countering each move he made, absorbing a glancing elbow or knee here, barely dodging a head-butt there, but I was playing a defensive game, I wasn't getting any shots in. This couldn't last for long.

I put all my energy in a desperate attempt to throw him, he countered easily, threw a knee that narrowly missed my groin. It exploded against the inside of my thigh and I staggered backwards, throwing him off balance for half a second as the resistance went away.

I heard something clatter to the floor and we both looked down involuntarily. A big fat syringe was lying by his foot, where it had fallen out of his pants. It was full of amber colored fluid.

I bet that was for Mandy, I thought, and that was what made me stop being scared. I got angry instead.

We both recovered at the same time. He tore his eyes away from the syringe and launched himself at me, grabbing me around the waist and slamming me against the wall again. I absorbed the attack, nearly blacking out when the door handle dug into my kidney.

He left an opening and I took it. I took my right hand, grabbed his ear, and pulled. I'd pulled taffy once or twice as a kid and oddly, that was what came to mind now. At first, there was resistance, although not as much as I would have expected, and then, with a wet ripping sound, the top three-quarters of his ear came off in my hand.

He staggered. His mouth came open and his hand flew up to his ear. His eyes went to the bloody chunk of cartilage in my fist. They were full of disbelief.

I dropped the ear and hit him. I don't know much when it comes to "martial arts," but I know how to hit people. I blasted a right cross into his open mouth. I put every bit of my weight into it and there was a satisfying crack as his jaw gave. Blood and bits of teeth pelted the wall beside him. He staggered against the guard rail, his head lolling on his shoulders.

All I could see was red. I moved in, wanting to pound his face into a pulp, then maybe I would pick up that syringe and jam it into him and see how he liked it. I blasted a left jab in that flattened his nose, then another right into his already broken jaw. I felt pieces of bone turn into powder when that one landed.

I hauled back to hit him again but it was too late. I watched in sick disbelief as he stumbled once on rubber legs, then tumbled sideways over the rail of the stairway landing and out of sight. I had enough time to take half a breath before I heard a heavy thump from down below.

I stood there for a second, not believing. The scene of him going over the rail kept playing over and over again in my head. I kept hoping the ending would change and I'd see him lying there at my feet.

It didn't change though. I finally forced myself to step forward, to look over the railing.

He was lying on the stairs below, face down. It looked like he'd landed on the top of his head, as it was folded under his body in an impossible looking position. A thick trail of blood oozed slowly out from under him and started dripping down the first stair until it pooled up enough to drip down to the one below it. I stepped forward, trying to see if he was breathing, and heard a crunch under my right foot. I looked down, at first afraid I'd stepped on the syringe, but I realized it was his ear. I kicked the thing away from me in disgust. It sailed between the guard rails and fluttered down to land on his body.

I tore myself away, looked for the syringe. I found it and stuffed in my waistband after making sure there was a cap on the needle.

The stairwell was silent. The door behind me was still shut. I realized the whole fight had taken fifteen, twenty seconds at most. I needed to get moving.

I walked down the stairs, made myself touch him. My stomach felt like it was going to turn inside out at the grinding of the bones in his neck as I moved his head ever so slightly to take a pulse.

He was dead. No doubt about it.

I stood there over his body. A voice in the back of my head said *that's number three.*

I pulled the ID off of him. The face on the card was his, but I would bet the name was fake. Whoever gave him the card had the ability to fake OHSU ID cards. Interesting. Maybe it would have fingerprints on it.

Fingerprints got me thinking about evidence. Belatedly, I looked around for cameras, was relieved when I didn't see any. I was sure I would be on video coming in the building, but there would be no footage of the actual fight.

That gave me pause. I was thinking like a suspect. Not a cop. I'd just killed a guy, arguably in justified self-defense, and I was trying to figure out how to get away from the scene.

I heard voices from behind the door up top. That spurred me to action. I stepped gingerly over the body, careful not to step in the blood.

I started moving down the stairs, checking myself for blood as I went. I had less on my right hand than I would have expected. As much of it was from my busted knuckles as it was from ripping his ear off. I had to pause, swallow a sour rush of vomit in my mouth as I remembered the feeling of his ear coming off in my hand. I leaned against the cool wall for a second, feeling beads of sweat pop out on my forehead.

Fuck it, and drive on, I thought, as I wiped my bloody hand on my jeans.

I came out of the stairwell and tried to look cool as I made my way back to the parking lot. There were a few people walking around, but nobody paid me any mind. I kept checking the phone. Still no signal.

I shivered in the wet cold outside. I hadn't realized how hot I'd been.

I sat down in the car, started the engine and sat with the phone in my hand, watching the windshield wipers go back and forth.

I'd just killed somebody, and so far, had gotten away with it. I should call 911, explain how I'd been attacked, let the facts sort themselves out. Surely everybody would understand: It was a conspiracy to kill me and my partner because we'd discovered a plot involving the psychotic son of a prominent businessman, oh and don't forget the secret CIA Air Force that was up to something. We didn't know what, but we were sure it was bad.

I almost laughed.

I picked up the phone and dialed Bolle's number.

CHAPTER TWENTY-TWO

Bolle answered himself this time. "Miller. Where the hell are you?"

I almost spilled the whole story. I'd found there was a powerful need to confess after you killed somebody, a need to explain it all, convince everybody around you that you'd done the right thing, that you had no choice. The person you were really trying to convince was yourself and that was a process that never ended.

It occurred to me just in time that I was talking on an unsecured cell phone and Bolle was probably recording it.

"They tried for Mandy at the hospital."

He was silent for a second.

"Is she safe?" When he spoke it sounded like he had some genuine concern in his voice. It was enough to keep me from hanging up.

"Yeah."

He breathed a sigh of relief. "Good. I've got a material witness warrant for her on the car seat beside me. I've made arrangements with a private ambulance company I trust to move her to a secure private care facility. It's a step we should have taken earlier when we moved you out of the jail. I'm sorry."

I chewed on that for a minute. As the adrenaline left my body, it was getting easier to think.

"Ok. There were some complications at the hospital."

"We're hearing traffic on the police scanner. A trip and fall?"

"I heard one of the nurses mention something like that," I said.

"We need to meet."

He was right. We needed to meet. But I wanted the initiative. I'd just killed a man and I trusted exactly one person in the world right then, myself.

"I'll call you back in ten minutes and tell you where."

I hung up the phone before he had a chance to speak and pulled off into a parking lot. It took me a second to realize where I was. I'd been driving in a daze down Barbur Boulevard, towards Tigard, towards Bolle's safe house, in fact. I didn't remember the last few minutes of driving. I didn't know if I'd done something stupid like run a red light. I swallowed hard. I needed to pull it together.

I was in the parking lot for the Tri-Met bus station. The lot was only half full. I found a spot near the back and parked nose out.

I liked it. There were only two ways in and out. I could see both of them from where I was sitting. The lot was dark. Behind me was a narrow stretch of scrubby woods and a steep drop to the interstate below. I'd actually recovered a body down there once, and knew the lay of the land. Might as well make it here.

I dialed Bolle back and told him where to meet me, hanging up again before we could talk about anything of substance. I just sat there for a few minutes, listening to the radio. Rush. Damn. I hate Rush.

I put the Glock in my lap, covered it with my folded raincoat. I sat Casey's duffel bag on the seat behind me, where I could reach back and grab it. Pistol grip shotguns looked cool in movies, but they sucked for hitting things more than a few feet away. Inside the car, the lack of a stock made it much handier to move around, and across the width of a parking space, I could just point the thing.

Bolle's car glided into the lot with a hiss of tires on wet pavement. I started my car, pulled forward a couple of feet, then flashed my headlights. I kept the car in gear, with my right foot hovering over the gas and my left on the brake. Big Eddie pulled the Mercedes into the parking spot next to me, nose first. He nodded as he went past, then stopped the car so the back window was even with mine. It motored down and there was Al, with Bolle sitting beside him.

I looked at Al. He looked tired, older than I'd ever seen him.

"Get in," I said, ignoring Bolle. Bolle frowned but stayed silent. Al, God bless him, didn't hesitate. He stepped out of the Mercedes, came around and got into the car beside me.

I looked at Bolle. "Don't follow us. We'll call when we're done." I didn't wait for a reply, just rolled up the window and pulled away.

I drove in silence for a while, turning onto Capitol Highway and then winding my way through the residential neighborhoods, watching for headlights behind me.

"You wearing a wire?" I asked Al.

"No," Al said. "He wanted me to."

"Why?"

"May predicted there was a better than even chance you would want to talk to me alone."

"She pretty good?" I asked.

"Yeah. She's pretty good, one of the best profilers I've ever worked with."

"What else did she predict about me?"

Al didn't even hesitate. "That there's a good chance you'll work yourself into a state where you trust no one, could even potentially become violent towards anyone you perceive as a threat. She says you're in an extremely emotionally labile state because your schema of how the world works has been shattered and you feel betrayed."

"What do you think about that?" I'd driven in circles long enough. I popped back out on to Capitol Highway in a different place than where I'd left it and accelerated.

"I think I'm a lot more scared of that Glock you've got in your lap falling on the floorboards and going off accidentally than I am of you shooting me with it on purpose."

I twisted in my seat to stick the Glock back in the holster.

"Thanks. Those plastic guns make me nervous." Al said.

I nodded. "Al?"

"Yeah?"

"What the hell does 'labile' mean?"

"I dunno. I was going to ask Alex. She studied that stuff in medical school."

I snickered and he did too. Before I knew it, we were both laughing so hard I had to pull over to the side of the road. It was ridiculous, but the release felt really good. I was laughing at the image of Al, all studious and professional looking, listening to a psych briefing he didn't understand. But mostly I was laughing because I had to do something to release the pressure building in the back of my mind. It was either that or break my hands pounding my fists on the steering wheel in front of me. My schema, or whatever the hell it was, had indeed been broken, and it made me want to do some breaking of my own.

After a minute or two, I dried my eyes and pulled away from the curb again. Good thing there was no traffic out, I was liable to get pulled over acting like this. I took a deep breath, focused on my driving again for a little while.

"I killed a guy back at the hospital," I said.

Al nodded. "I know. We were listening to the Bureau's radio traffic on the way over. What happened?"

I told him. I tried to keep my voice level and clinical like I was talking about a stock market deal or something.

Al sat in silence while I explained. When I finished he sat in silence for a second, turning the syringe I'd taken from the dead guy over in his hands.

"Bolle says he thinks he can run interference on this one. It shouldn't be hard. You're supposed to be in Federal custody so even if by some freak chance your name comes up as a suspect, nobody will take it seriously. Henry and Casey managed to get into the server that stores the security camera footage."

I was winding my way up the west hills. I needed some fresh air and had a spot in mind. I turned to look at Al.

"Al, you're talking to me about covering up a murder. What is this? What's Bolle's game?"

Al sighed. "The rules are different once you reach a certain level, Dent. Without even realizing it you've landed on a chess board where everybody has more money and power than you ever dreamed of. When that happens to most people, they wind up dead, or in jail, or nobody ever hears from them again. Bolle's been playing this game for a long time. He's good at it. You can tell because he's not dead or in jail. There's no going back now. I suggest you just go along with him."

"Does he do any good?"

Al was quiet for a long time. I pulled into the park at Council Crest. It was empty tonight. The wind was bitter cold and lashed with rain up here, but despite the clouds, there was still a decent view of the city spread out in front of us.

"You've got to measure good in different ways sometimes, Dent. The FBI ten most wanted list is a joke. If I were to arrest ten people in this country, the ten who do the most harm every day, half of them would be names you read about in the newspaper, the other half would be people you've never heard of. But those people are untouchable, Dent. The best we can do sometimes is stymie their plans, embarrass them. We can't really make things better, but if we just sit and watch, they'll get worse."

I sat there for a minute, watching the rain hit the windshield. I just wanted to sleep for a couple of days. Maybe when I woke up all of this would have gone away, but even if it didn't, I would at least feel better.

"What do you think I should do, Al?"

He sat the syringe on the dash, folded his hands in his lap and took a deep breath. "I think you should stick with me and Bolle. I think we're your best chance of coming out of this alive, and out of jail. I also think you can help us. You may feel like you're making a deal with the devil, but I think it's the right thing. It's a good fight. It's dirty and ugly and sometimes I feel like I can't even see the moral lines anymore, much less tell if I've crossed them, but in the end, it's always the right fight."

I sat there as the rain poured down harder, all thoughts of getting out of the car and walking around gone. In the end, I did what I always did: I trusted Al. It surprised me a little, how easy it was to kiss it all goodbye: my badge, my career, my pride at being a cop.

"Ok," I said. I put the car back in gear, started driving back down the twisting road.

"Good," Al said. "I've been trying to figure out a way to approach you for the last year or so. It's funny how things work out sometimes."

"Yeah. Was it hard? Leaving it all behind?"

"You mean giving up a badge, and respect, to become almost a criminal? Because that's what we are Dent, don't make any mistake. Bolle may have FBI credentials, but those aren't going to help any of us if we lose. We'll wind up dead, or in jail, or just disappearing just like those other people."

I nodded my head.

"Yeah, it bothers me sometimes, but you need to remember something," Al continued. "It's the same fight we were supposed to be fighting before, the real fight. It's what I'm here on this planet to do and I think you are too. The rest is just window dressing."

I thought about that for a while. In a way it was intoxicating. How many times as a cop had I ranted and raved that to really do our job, the kid gloves had to come off, that all the sheep just needed to mind their own business and let us do our jobs? To finally have a chance to fight with no rules, to be able to take the battle to the enemy by any means necessary, the thought was exhilarating.

But that little voice in the back of my mind pointed out that Al was talking about my new boss covering up a homicide I'd committed as casually as some guys talked about their golf dates.

I had a feeling that the free fall was over, that my parachute had finally opened, it was just that now I had no idea where I was going to land, or what would be waiting for me when I got there.

While I was thinking, Al picked up the syringe again. "I'll have Alex analyze this, see if she can tell us what this is."

It took a second for what he said to sink in. When it did, I jerked a little in my seat. "Alex? She's in on this too?"

"A little. I've used her skills a time or two. Bolle is eager to bring her in further, but I just don't know. At any rate, Alex isn't stupid. I think she's figured out more than I've told her."

"No," I murmured. "Alex isn't stupid." Memories of that night when I took her home rose up, and I pushed them back down just as quickly. It made me think of something else though; I swore and started digging for my phone.

"What?" Al asked.

"Audrey. I haven't been able to get a hold of her since all this started." I dialed her number again. Still no answer. I picked up speed, heading back to the bus station.

"Look," I said. "I'm in. I want to work with you and Bolle. I don't know whether I trust Bolle yet, but I trust you, so I guess I have to trust him. But I've got to go check on Audrey. They got Casey, they made a play for Mandy. I know Audrey wasn't directly involved in the investigation, but I have to know they aren't making a play for her too."

Al nodded. "I can't fault you for that."

We pulled in to the transit center lot. The Mercedes was still there. Eddie had turned it around so it was facing out in its parking spot. I pulled in beside it. Al collected the syringe, clapped me on the shoulder and stepped out of the car. Bolle's window rolled down. He looked non-plussed, staring at me until Al got in next to him. Al gave him a nod and Bolle sighed.

"Mandy is being loaded into a guarded, private ambulance as we speak," Bolle said.

"Thank you," I said. It was good to know Mandy was safe. My worries about Audrey still gnawed at me though.

"Dent has agreed to join us," Al said. "He's got one loose end to tie up, though. We haven't been able to get a hold of Audrey. He's going to go check."

Bolle nodded. "Understandable. She wasn't directly involved and Todd likes to limit the collateral damage of his operations, not out of any moral conscience but to limit the attention they draw. I doubt she was a target, but I appreciate your need to feel that she is safe. Loved ones are important."

Bolle sounded like a man talking about how global warming was important like he understood it in the abstract, but it didn't have any personal meaning to him. I itched to know a little more about him.

"Thanks," I said again. "Let me tie this up and I'll get straight to work."

Bolle nodded and said, "Take care of it, then get in touch. I wish I had enough people to spare to send with you, but right now we are desperately trying to re-acquire Todd, and I have another team sitting on Marshall."

"That's ok," I said. "I don't mind working alone."

His mouth almost quirked in a smile. "Indeed. Good luck." He rolled up the window without another word and the Mercedes pulled away.

CHAPTER TWENTY-THREE

I parked a couple of blocks from Audrey's and walked in. It was a calculated risk. It limited my mobility and made me more vulnerable to ambush, but I was betting that if somebody was watching Audrey's house, they would be focused on someone driving. In the darkness, if I walked in, I'd have a decent chance of spotting the surveillance before they spotted me. I'd gotten great mileage in the past out of not doing what people expected.

All was quiet. Over the year we'd been dating, I'd made a mental note of all the vehicles that tended to park around Audrey's building. All the cars parked outside right now looked familiar.

Audrey's car wasn't there. I wondered if it was still in impound. I let myself in the building and walked up to her door. I put my hand on my gun and let myself in, ready for a fight but knowing as I stepped through the door the place was empty. It just felt that way.

Still, I pulled out my gun and light and cleared the place. It didn't take long because it was so small, but I did a thorough job of it. I was sick of getting ambushed.

Audrey's cello was gone, as was the bow I'd given her. I checked and her suitcases weren't stacked in the back of her closet where they were supposed to be. I pulled open drawers, didn't see the amount of underwear and stuff like that I expected to see. I checked the dirty clothes hamper next. Empty.

Her toothbrush was gone from the bathroom.

She clearly hadn't been kidnapped. She'd left of her own accord.

I stood in the middle of the living room, feeling like the last piece of my life had been jerked away from me. I couldn't think about anything for a minute. There was just a mounting sense of suffocation.

I tamped it down before it reached critical mass, reached that tipping point where I'd just sit down on the couch and refuse to get up again, or just put the Glock in my mouth and pull the trigger.

I dialed Audrey's cell. It went straight to voice mail.

It beeped and I just sat there with the phone pressed to my ear, letting the voice mail record silence. I didn't know what to say. The only thing that occurred to me was to scream "where are you!" but that didn't seem like it would help. I finally put the phone down without a word.

A wave of fatigue washed over me. Despite the coffee, I felt like I was asleep on my feet. I looked at my watch. Almost midnight.

Mandy was safe. Casey was gone, but there was nothing I could do about it. Audrey was gone. Presumably she was safe, but there didn't seem to be anything I could do about that either.

I swayed a little on my feet, tried to remember when the last time I'd gotten some decent rest.

"Hell with it," I said. I took my coat and boots off, put my Glock and phone on the coffee table, and lay down on the couch.

CHAPTER TWENTY-FOUR

The phone jolted me awake. I was groggy, but had the presence of mind to make sure I was picking up the phone, and not the gun before I pressed it to my face.

"Miller," I said. It came out as a croak. My breath tasted like a large animal had been using my mouth for a toilet.

It was Al.

"It's Marshall. He's moving. Some Cascade Aviation employees dropped off a new van at his place. He's in it and driving south on Interstate Five."

I was on my feet and moving, gathering my stuff.

"Ok. I'll get on the five and head south. How much of a lead does he have?"

"He's just over the Marquam bridge."

I did some fast math. By the time I got on the freeway, he'd have a substantial lead. Well, I'd always liked to drive fast.

It was just after three in the morning. Audrey's neighborhood was silent. Even the dog that usually barked at me when I walked by was quiet. I could hear the cars hissing down the freeway almost a mile and a half away. It was dry and cold and clear. I could see the stars through the haze of the city's lights, unusual for this time of year.

Once I hit the interstate, I dialed Bolle's number.

Big Eddy answered with a grunt.

"Where is he?" I asked.

"Hang on. I'm transferring you to Henry."

There was a burst of static, then Henry said, "Dent?"

"Yeah, it's me. Where is he?"

"I'm about a mile behind him," Henry said. "I'm in a van on the interstate. We just left the city limits of Portland. We've got Eddie, Bolle and Al in a Mercedes, right behind us. We 'pooned him when he pulled out of his place and fell in behind him. I was hoping you'd pull up with us and we'll take turns staying in visual contact."

Strictly speaking, we didn't need to keep Marshall in visual range. We could let all the electronic toys work their magic. But following a dot on a screen wasn't the same thing as keeping eyes on your target. Marshall could dump all sorts of things along the way, and we'd never know it.

It wouldn't take that long to roll a body out of a back of the van. He'd done it before.

I sped up a little more. "Have you got me on your tracking screen?"

Henry was quiet again. I got to listen to his heavy breathing for almost a full thirty seconds before I lost my patience.

"Listen, bud," I said. "It's three o'clock in the morning and I don't have time for this. I know you're tracking my cell phone. Am I gaining on him or not?"

"Yeah," Henry finally said. "You're gaining. Slowly, but you're gaining."

"Fine. Let me know if anything changes." I snapped the phone shut and tossed it on the seat beside me.

I needed to sleep. Everything had a far away, dream-like quality. I would have killed for a good cup of strong black coffee.

There was little traffic on the road. Most of it was heavy eighteen wheelers making the long haul down to southern Oregon and California. I wondered what it was like to be one of those guys. Just you and a truck, some Johnny Cash on the CD player, singing about murderous women and the coming apocalypse. It didn't sound so bad. Maybe something I would keep in mind for a future career.

I caught a late night blues show on the Community College radio station out in Troutdale. Robert Johnson, "Hellhound on My Trail." Maybe there was a God. If there was, he had a sense of humor.

The miles rolled by easy, we were out of Portland and heading south before I knew it. I always liked road trips, they gave me plenty of time to think, which was usually a good thing.

Now I wasn't sure it was so good. The weight of everything was crashing down. I fingered my chest, where usually I would feel my badge through my shirt, but tonight nothing was there.

In my mind, I kept seeing those empty drawers in Audrey's apartment.

I pulled out the other phone, the clean one I'd bought. I dialed

Audrey.

She wouldn't be up, but at least I could leave a message, give her a number where she could contact me. It rang and I started thinking about what I was going to say.

"Hello?"

I jumped in my seat when she answered, almost swerved into the other lane.

She sounded sleepy, confused. I could see her in my mind's eye, sitting up in bed. What bed I wasn't sure, but I could see that long red hair tousled and flowing down her shoulders, beautiful in spite of being woken up in the middle of the night. I felt a jab of almost physical pain, a mixture of lust and loneliness that was so sharp it almost took my breath away.

"Auds, it's me. Dent."

"Dent." It was a statement, almost, not quite a question.

"Where are you?"

It took her a long time to answer, so long I thought the connection had been broken. But then she answered. "Home."

I wanted to tell myself that she went back in her apartment, that by some cosmic joke we had just missed each other at the apartment, that she had walked in the door only minutes after I had walked out. But I knew better.

"New Mexico." I knew the answer, but I had to say it anyway.

"Yeah, Dent. New Mexico. Home."

There was static on the line. The asphalt hissed under the tires of the car and I stared straight ahead, concentrating on that broken white line between the lanes, counting the dashes as they went past.

When I got to fifty, I said, "I didn't do it, Auds. That stuff they said, it wasn't true."

The inside of the car felt hot and close all of a sudden. I turned off the heater, but that wasn't enough, so I rolled down the window.

"I want to believe that," she said. Over the phone line, I heard a muffled voice, rising inflection like a question was asked. Where was she? Things hadn't been going well with her parents for a long time. A friend's house? Who would that be? It bothered me that I didn't know.

"But you don't," I said past the lump in my throat.

She put her hand over the phone, muttered something to somebody that sounded like "It's ok," and then she was back. "I want to believe that, Dent, but it's hard."

"Why?" I asked.

"You come home and tell me matter of factly about ambushing a man and breaking his knee and arm like some guys come home and talk about a stock trade. Then you're in jail for beating up your partner. I have to wonder if after a while, the violence... the violence just doesn't stop with you."

She stopped but I didn't say anything, just waited to see if she would continue.

"I'd like to think I'm wrong, but they arrested you, Dent. Weren't you the one always telling me that all the conspiracy theories were wrong, that if somebody went to jail they deserved it?"

I saw two sets of tail lights up ahead. If my guess was correct, it was Henry's surveillance van and Bolle's Mercedes. Part of my mind was tracking details like that, the other part wanted to put my fist through the windshield in front of me.

"Dent?" Her voice sounded far away.

I realized I was just driving along, staring ahead, with the phone at my ear. My mouth felt paralyzed like I'd been struck dumb.

The last time I'd cried was at my mother's funeral when I was twelve. I'd held it together through the service, through the graveside, rode back silently to the trailer. Then I watched my dad plant himself in an old lawn chair in the back yard, twist the cap off a bottle of Jim Beam and throw it out into the grass. I'd walked out of the trailer then, still in my new suit, and just started walking.

Somehow I wound up sitting on a rock overlooking the valley, a place I used to spot deer. I sat down there and the hot, bitter silent tears came. For how long I didn't know, but when I walked away from that spot I knew I was going to leave Tennessee one day and never come back.

Now, I felt the twin tracks of tears on my cheeks and almost couldn't believe it. It had been so long.

"Dent?" She said, a little louder, sounding both irritated and worried.

That's when the anger hit. Bolle, Al, Big Eddy, a bunch of people that were criminals, they all believed that I had been set up, that it was all a lie, but Audrey didn't. Al had seen through the lies immediately, but the best Audrey could do was tell me she wasn't sure.

"Dent? Are you still there?"

All sorts of things came to mind, ugly, mean spirited things, but I couldn't bring myself to say them, because I could see her in my mind's eye, in better times, laughing, making love, playing the cello. I couldn't square those things with what I wanted to say.

I took the phone from my ear, and without even thinking about it, flicked it out the open window. In the side mirror, I watched the ghostly green of the display arc through the black, then wink out when it hit the pavement.

I rolled the window up, drug my sleeve across my face to wipe away the tears. From nowhere, a saying from my military days came to mind.

"Fuck it. Drive on." I'm not sure if I said it out loud or not, although I probably did.

I shoved Audrey into a little room in my mind and firmly shut the door. I had a bunch of little rooms like that. My mother was in one, my father in another. James Ellroy David and the other men I'd killed were right down the hall. Sometimes you just had to put things aside so you could go on with business. We had an acronym in the Army, FIDO: Fuck It. Drive On.

The phone Al had given me rang. It was Henry. He sounded harried.

"I just locked on to Marshall's cell phone. Listen." There was a click and I was hearing a different conversation.

"...deliver the package?" The voice was deep, measured, controlled. I figured it was probably Todd.

"Yeah, I'm delivering the package." A different voice this time, younger, higher. I realized it was Marshall. He giggled and the hair stood up on the back of my neck. "I might unwrap this package before I deliver it though."

"Look," Todd said. "We need to stay professional here. Just deliver the package, we assemble it with the others and send them off on the next flight."

"Yeah," Marshall said. "But the little bitch bit me when I went to the back of the van to check on her. She's not going to work out very well for our clients if she keeps that up. Maybe I should start the break-in process myself."

"You're on a cell phone." Todd's voice was icy, controlled. I wondered if maybe he wasn't above arranging an accident for the boss's son. I started running what Marshall had just said through my mind, trying to catch up.

"Oh yeah," Marshall said, then giggled again. "It's a nice package, but it's got some problems."

"Well, sometimes packages fall off the truck, and that might be what needs to happen here, but don't blow it by doing anything yourself. There's too much heat right now. This is going to be our last shipment for a while. Get the package to the airport, we'll put them all on the plane and we'll make decisions about delivery while we're en route."

I passed Henry's surveillance van. Up ahead I could see more taillights, another van maybe, it was hard to tell in the darkness.

"That's a shame..." Marshall trailed off. The vehicle ahead of me swerved.

"Knock it off, you little cunt!" I heard Marshall yell.

"What?" Todd asked.

"She, errr... the package was sliding towards the back door. I'll fix it when I get a chance to pull off. Fix it good."

"Take it easy," Todd said. "I can't fix another shipping error like the last one. We almost lost everything on that one."

"I know." Marshall sounded like a petulant child denied a toy.

"I'll see you at the airport," Todd said.

"Ok. I'll be there in an hour."

One of them hung up, probably Todd. There was a buzz on the line and Henry came back on. "Get that?"

"Yeah," I said.

I got that. And more. It was so obvious. Why hadn't I seen it before?

"Patch me through to Al," I said.

The phone clicked again. "Dent?"

"Yeah, Al. Did you hear that?"

"We did. We're processing it now."

"I can process it for you right now. I know what they're shipping to the Middle East. It isn't dope, or guns or even money."

"What is it?" Al asked.

"Women."

I stomped on the accelerator.

CHAPTER TWENTY-FIVE

I closed to about fifty yards, my mind racing. I needed to stop that van. I was tempted to just ram the damn thing off the road. But I knew Casey was probably lying in the back of it and didn't want her to get hurt.

"Dent? Dent?" I'd set the phone down on the seat beside me. Al's voice sounded tinny through the speaker. I picked it up and put it to my ear.

"Women, Al. That's what they are sending to the Middle East. Marshall isn't just in the porn business. He isn't a serial killer. He's finding girls to ship overseas."

"What?"

"There are no records, no immigration checks, no security checks because these guys are the air courier for the CIA. What do you think a nineteen-year-old blond is worth to some people?"

"That's crazy, Dent."

"Yeah. Doesn't sound very twenty-first century does it? Look. You heard that conversation he had with Todd. He's got somebody in the van. I think it's Casey."

He was silent for a minute, then Bolle came on. "We've got you on speaker phone Dent. What you're saying makes sense. What makes you sure it's Casey in the back?"

"Because she's being such a pain in the ass. They're talking about throwing her out of the plane Al, just like they did with your informant. We gotta stop that van. Where are you?"

"We're about two miles behind you, Dent. I'm not sure about stopping the van. Henry and his boys aren't shooters. We've got Eddie with us, and could catch up with you, but the rest of my team is even farther back. If we try something it will have to be once he gets off the freeway. It could turn into a hostage situation."

"We gotta do something. What about the State Cops, can't you get them to do a traffic stop?"

"This is a sensitive investigation, Dent. We need to consider our security needs," Bolle said.

"Funny. That's the sort of thing my old boss would have said."

I shut the phone off but elected to put it on the seat instead of sending it out the window after the last one. I looked at a passing mile marker and consulted my mental map of the interstate. An idea presented itself.

When you know your enemy, you know his strengths and his weaknesses. I pulled right behind Marshall's van, a bland white job like any one of a thousand others. He was cruising in the left lane, despite the fact he was going maybe five over and the highway was deserted.

I put my high beams on for a few seconds, then flipped them on and off. Predictably, he gave me a brake check. If I hadn't been expecting it, I would have rear-ended him. I could just hear him talking to himself, "if you want to go faster, you can pass me."

So I did. I noted the "Rest Area 1 mile" sign as I whipped around the van on the right-hand side, then cut back in right in front of him to give him his own brake check. I did it a little more gradually than him. The last thing I wanted was to get rear-ended by a vehicle that weighed twice what mine did, particularly when I thought Casey was rolling around on the floor in the back. I made him slow down plenty, and when he pulled right to pass me I moved over to block him. When he flipped on his own bright lights, I rolled down the window, stuck out my hand and flipped him the bird. He responded by closing the distance between my rear bumper to his front to a few inches.

Perfect. Classic road-rager behavior. I saw the exit for the rest area coming up and floored the accelerator, leaving the heavier van behind, but not too far. I wanted some distance to get set up but I wanted to make sure he saw where I was going. Thankfully, the rest area was deserted. I laid thirty feet of rubber getting the car stopped. The front tires bumped into the curb, but not hard enough to flatten them, I hoped.

I left the car sitting there, across three parking spots with the door open. I paused on the sidewalk just long enough to make sure Marshall was following me. He was.

Dumbass.

I pulled my hat down low and the collar of my jacket up high. I drew the Glock and held it against my thigh.

His headlights swept over me as I stepped into the bathroom. It smelled of urine and cigarettes. I checked each stall. Empty. Good. I stood at the far end from the door with my back to the wall. One bank of the fluorescent tubes overhead was burnt out. I palmed my little Surefire flashlight with my other hand.

I heard the van screech to a stop outside, then a door slam. Something smacked the walls of the bathroom from the outside.

"I don't know who you are, but you fucked up bad!" Marshall screamed. He sounded like he was enjoying himself. He probably was. After all, Daddy had gotten him out of everything so far. Not this time.

He was quick coming through the door, an ASP baton in his hand. I was a little surprised by that, not that he had a weapon, just the type. I'd expected either a gun or maybe some kind of martial arts weapon, nunchucks or something stupid like that.

I lit him up with the light and pointed the Glock at him. The flashlight was bright. He flinched and brought a hand up over his face.

"Hello, Gibson."

He was surprised to see me, but he recovered quickly.

"Officer Miller. Or should I say, Dent? That's what your partner was screaming when I visited her. I think she's sweet on you."

I almost shot him then. But I knew once I pulled the trigger, I couldn't take it back. I wasn't sure what would change, but something would.

"Your daddy must be so proud. Does he know you're selling girls on the side or is this something you're running under his radar?"

Marshall sneered and I hated him. For a second he reminded me of every rich kid I'd ever had to deal with.

First, there had been the kids at high school, sons and daughters of the middle management at the coal mines. Their parents hadn't been rich enough to send them to private school, but they still liked to look down on us trailer trash.

Then it had been the frat boys in college. I'd been older and blooded in the Army. The fights had seemed inevitable back then. I had put more than one on his ass, had even relished the opportunity. Then I'd dealt with them as a cop.

"Daddy's definitely into a higher class of pussy," Gibson said. "It blinds him to the business opportunities inherent in the classic American street trash split tail. I'm telling you, Miller, they're the commodity of the future. There are millions to be made. We could let bygones be bygones and I could cut you in."

"You're a piece of shit, Marshall."

He rolled his eyes. "And you're a dumb cop. I've wrecked cars worth more than you make in a year. What the hell are you doing out of jail anyway?"

"Pointing a gun at you. Drop the baton."

He took a step forward. "What? Are you going to arrest me again? Last time I checked they weren't even letting you write parking tickets. People like me do what we want. People like you and that silly cunt in the van are disposable, like the paper I wipe my ass with."

"Put the baton down, Marshall."

"What are you going to do? Shoot me?" He took another step forward, sure of himself. All his life Gibson Marshall had done whatever he wanted, with no consequences. He didn't see any reason why this should be any different.

"Yes," I said softly.

He looked surprised when I shot him twice in the chest. He stood there, dumbfounded for the split second it took for me to get a sight picture on the bridge of his nose. Then I stroked the trigger again, careful not to jerk it, and a palm-sized piece of skull and hair leaped off the back of his head and stuck to the wall. He tumbled to the ground like a puppet with its strings cut.

It always surprised me how my ears didn't ring after a gunfight. As I stood there in the bathroom, the gun dangling at my side, I could hear whatever was in Marshall rustling as it left, then there was the hum of an engine outside, the soft click of a car door. I just stood there, looking at Marshall, not feeling much of anything.

There was the slightest, barely audible, the scuff of shoe leather and Big Eddie peeked through the doorway, his gun muzzle not quite pointed at me. He saw me and grunted, holstered the gun. He regarded Marshall clinically.

"What happened here, man?"

I pointed at the ASP baton. "He made a sudden furtive movement."

Speaking seemed to break the spell, and I remembered the point of this. I holstered the Glock and walked up to Marshall's body. Bolle and Al were stacked up behind Eddie in the doorway. I bent over Marshall's body and, careful to avoid the spreading stain in the crotch of his jeans, fished out the keys to the van. I shoved past Al and Bolle.

"Miller, what the hell happened here?" Bolle all but shouted.

"I told you. He made a sudden furtive movement." I repeated it mechanically. I found the button for the door locks on the van. The lights flashed once when I pressed it. I walked around to the back and pulled open one of the double doors.

I almost got a pair of Doc Martins in the face for my trouble. Casey launched a kick at my face as soon as I opened the door. I recoiled out of the way just in time so that it just took a little skin off my ear. If I hadn't been on the ball it would have knocked my teeth down my throat.

Casey was lying on her back in the van. Her hands were cuffed underneath her, duct tape covered her mouth and bound her ankles together. She looked dirty, cold and royally pissed.

"Casey, it's Dent." I stayed out of leg range until I saw some recognition in her eyes. When she nodded at me I reached in, helped her to a sitting position. I grasped one end of the duct tape on her mouth. "This is going to hurt like hell."

She nodded again, so I pulled, grimacing at the feel of it coming off her skin and the big angry welt it left behind on her skin and lips.

"Ahhh! That hurt." She took a deep breath. She sounded congested and I wondered how well she had been able to breathe with the tape on her mouth. She looked around.

"Where's Marshall?"

"Dead," I said as I pulled open my knife so I could cut the tape on her legs. "I shot him in the bathroom."

Bolle, Al and Eddy walked up. They were all looking around the parking lot, for witnesses. It was four in the morning, but we were pushing our luck staying at the rest stop. Sooner or later some freeway traveler, even a State Trooper, would roll up.

Her legs free, Casey hopped out of the back of the van and almost collapsed. I reached out to steady her. Somehow her personality always made her seem bigger than she really was, but as I stood there holding her up, I realized she couldn't weigh much more than a hundred pounds. That made me get angry at Marshall all over again. I wished I could shoot him again.

After a second she got her feet under her and I let go, keeping an eye on her in case she needed help again. I saw that there was a handcuff key on Marshall's ring. Cute. But it did come in handy to unlock Casey.

Rubbing her wrists and walking stiff-legged, she headed over the sidewalk and towards the men's room. Eddy raised an eyebrow. I shrugged and followed.

Inside the door, Casey stopped and looked at Marshall's body. She spat on his face, then started kicking the body. She almost slipped in the blood on the floor, then kicked him again, slinging droplets off her bloody boot all over the wall.

"You know," Eddie said conversationally from behind me, "She's really getting covered in evidence."

He was right. I put a hand on Casey's shoulder and finally she stopped, just stood there with her fists balled up and her nostrils flaring.

"He was gonna throw me out of an airplane, Dent. He and his buddies shot my dog, kidnapped me and then he told me all about how he was going to rape me then throw me out of an airplane into the Pacific Ocean from twenty thousand feet."

"Yeah. I know. He uh… won't do that again."

That sounded lame even to me. I'd never been good at this sort of thing.

I'd never seen somebody so close to crying without actually doing it before. I'd seen plenty of thousand-mile stares in my time, on the faces of soldiers in combat for too long, on the faces of victims of the nastiest things you can imagine, stuff that they won't put in horror movies, but Casey had one of the worst ones I've ever seen.

"He and his buddies took girls off the streets and sold them. It was all there on the servers we took, not in so many words, but once you figured out what was going on, you could read between the lines and see it."

"Hey," Big Eddy said softly. "We gotta go before there are witnesses and stuff."

Casey looked from Eddie to me curiously. "Witnesses? You're a cop, Dent. You're supposed to shoot guys like him."

"Well," I said. "Things are a little complicated right now. It would be best if we got out of here, and sort of kept things quiet."

The bathroom had one of those cotton hand towels on a continuous loop that. Eddie pulled a butterfly knife from a pocket, flipped it open and used it to cut a big chunk of the fabric out of the loop. He laid it on the ground and pointed to Casey's foot.

"Hey," he said softly. "Let's get that wiped off." His voice was soft, soothing, something I wouldn't have expected from him. He helped her steady herself as she wiped the blood off her foot onto the towel.

She finished and headed outside. "Which one is your car?" she asked over her shoulder.

I pointed to the Charger. Bolle's Mercedes was parked a couple of feet behind.

Al was watching the parking lot. He looked pale and had an odd expression on his face like maybe he was reconsidering whether this whole thing was a good idea.

Bolle was talking into a cell phone. He looked pissed.

I let Casey into the passenger side of the car. She reached over to buckle her seatbelt and I realized she was shaking and shivering. She was wearing jeans and a tank top but I figured there was more to it than the temperature. I fished my trench coat out of the back of the van. I was about to shut it when I saw the duffel bag holding the shotgun sitting there. I snagged that too.

I handed her the coat. She wrapped herself up in it and nodded her thanks. I sat the duffel in her lap.

"Here. I took that from your apartment because I thought I might need it. I thought you might like to have it back."

She unzipped the bag, saw what was inside, and curled her hand around the pistol grip, all without saying a word. Her finger was off the trigger and the safety was on, so I figured what the hell.

Eddie cocked an eyebrow at me when I walked back over. "What's in the bag?"

"Her sawed-off shotgun."

"Sure that's a good idea? She seems upset."

"If you think she shouldn't have it, you're welcome to try and take it away from her."

"Good point."

Eddie walked over to the van, looked inside for a minute, then fished his butterfly knife out again. He started cutting around the edges of the carpet in the back.

Bolle snapped his phone shut and walked over to me.

"You want to explain to me what the hell you were thinking?"

"No." I let the word hang there in the air. I just stared at him, offering no other explanation.

He waited for a second, then got tired of the game. "What do you mean 'no'?"

"I mean, no, I don't want to explain it. If you don't understand why it was important to get Casey out of that van in a hurry, there's no amount of explaining I can do that will make you understand it."

Pissing off the new boss right after he got me out of jail probably wasn't the wisest thing in the world, but truth be told, I resented Bolle. He'd gotten me out of jail for his own purposes. I still didn't know what his game was, or what he expected in return.

The debt I owed Bolle scared me, and I always get angry when I'm scared. I owed Al my life, many times over, but that was different. I trusted Al. He'd had more than ample opportunities to screw me over, to use me for his own ends, and he'd never done it. Bolle was different. I didn't know if I could trust him, and that usually meant I couldn't.

"Look," Al said. "We need to get out of here. There's a dead man in that bathroom in there. Let's settle this somewhere else."

Bolle seemed to relax a little when Al got him focused on the immediate problem. It would be interesting to see how this played out in the long run. In the end, I didn't much care. My job was gone. My girlfriend was gone. What else were they going to do to me? Take away my birthday? At least Casey and Mandy were safe.

I heard a ripping sound and we all turned to look at Eddie. He had cut the carpet out of the back of the cargo van in one big piece, maybe five feet by six. He folded it in half, tucked it under one arm and dug in a pocket. He came out with a pair of latex gloves and extended them to me. He was already wearing a pair.

"Here you go, Wyatt Earp. Let's get our friend wrapped up and in the back of the van."

I accepted the gloves and followed him into the bathroom. We got Marshall onto the piece of carpet. Eddie plucked the wad of blood, bone and hair off the wall and dropped it on Marshall's chest. He pulled out the knife again, pried something out of the wall. I saw that it was the slug, its nose mushroomed from the trip through Marshall's head. It had hit a stud in the wall and, most of its energy spent had lodged itself close enough to the surface for Eddie to dig it out. The two bullets I'd put in Marshall's chest hadn't exited.

"Find your casings, bro."

I hadn't thought of that. I spent a few minutes shining my light around before I found the spent 9mm casings on the floor. I put them in my pocket.

Eddie wiped what he could of the blood and brain matter off the wall and floor with more of the towel roll. He pulled the rest of it out of the dispenser and wadded it up behind Marshall's head, where it would catch the worst of the blood still leaking out. Then with a mutual grunt, we rolled Marshall up in the carpet, hauled him outside and deposited him in the van.

Bolle and Al had broken into the maintenance shed and pulled out the "bathroom closed" signs and set them up on the sidewalk. Our luck was still holding, but I didn't think we could count on that for long.

Eddie slammed the rear doors of the van, brushed his hands off, and checked the sleeves of his suit coat for stains. He grunted in satisfaction when he saw that they were clean. I got the idea that he'd done this sort of thing before. Bolle was on the phone again.

I looked at Al. "I'm taking Casey with me. We'll see you at the safe house."

He nodded, still a little pale-faced. I tossed the van keys to Eddie, who caught them with a wink.

I got in the car, started it and drove off, trying not to look at the van as we drove past. The guy in the hospital stairwell had been one thing, at least I'd left him there for somebody to find, at least I could say that was self-defense.

But Marshall was different. All the "sudden furtive movement" stuff aside, I'd shot him down in cold blood, and now I was helping hide the body. I started adding up the potential prison time and just decided to stop. The hell with it. I was supposed to be in jail right now. What was I worried about?

Casey was staring straight ahead. Her hand was still on the grip of the shotgun. Maybe Eddie was right. Maybe that wasn't such a good idea, but I didn't say anything. I just decided to drive extra careful and not get pulled over.

I drove south on the interstate, then got off and got back on going north at the first chance I got.

"I'm going to take us to a safe place. We can get you some clean clothes and you can figure out your next move."

She nodded, still staring straight ahead. "Ok. But I gotta go bury my dog soon."

I grimaced. "I hear you. But we need to lay low for a while. After we get a chance to settle in somewhere, I need you to tell me what you know about Marshall and his buddies, about what they were doing with the girls."

"Yeah," she said softly. "But it's all gone."

"What's gone?" I asked. But I had a sinking feeling that I already knew what she meant.

"The evidence. It's gone. I had it all, Dent. I decrypted email conversations between Marshall and addresses in Saudi Arabia, Bahrain, Uzbekistan, you name it. They never came right out and said what they did, but they talked about picking out the right package and had pictures of different girls attached. It wasn't too hard to figure out what was going on. It was like they weren't even all that worried about getting caught."

"How many?" I asked.

"At least a dozen. They got about a million for each. But it's all gone. I imaged the hard drives onto a different machine. That's what I was using to work from. It took a while to get it figured out but it was there. Emails, pictures, Cascade Aviation flight schedules, I managed to put together a dozen transactions when the news came out about you being in jail."

"None of that is true," I said hurriedly.

"I know. Do you think I'd be sitting in a car with you if I believed it? I figured they set you up somehow. I was sitting on the servers and the images, trying to figure out who to go to with it when they came in and took everything, the images, the servers, everything. And they shot my dog."

Dammit. I was hoping she was going to tell me she'd cleverly made a second copy, uploaded it to some site in the Bahamas or burned a copy disguised as a Buckaroo Banzai DVD or some cool computer hacker trick like that. I didn't understand this stuff very well.

"I'm sorry about your dog. But, ummm… you're sure you didn't have another copy?"

She shook her head and she looked like she was on the verge of crying again.

"No. They kept asking me the same thing, over and over, 'where's the other copy?' 'who else did you tell?' I think that's one of the reasons they didn't kill me right away. They thought there might be other copies out there and they wanted to make me talk. That and Marshall had constructed a nice little fantasy for himself. I'm sorry the evidence is gone, Dent."

Damn. No evidence. But maybe it wouldn't matter. I guess we were about to find out just how far on the outside Bolle really operated.

"It's ok. We may be able to get them anyway."

"Who's we, Dent? You're supposed to be in jail. Who the hell were those guys back there? I recognized Al Pace. I met him a few times before he retired. But what about the other two?"

"They're Feds." Well, that was true in Bolle's case, and sort of in Eddie's.

"They're on a special task force," I said. "I'm hoping you'll sit down with them and explain what you just told me. There still may be a way to get to these guys."

She broke her straight-ahead stare for the first time in twenty miles. "Do you trust them?"

I took longer to answer than I would have liked. "I think so. I trust Al. Implicitly. And he works for them, so that's going to have to do."

She seemed to accept that, went back to staring straight ahead. I hoped I hadn't sealed her death warrant by sucking her into this. Maybe I should just drive her to the airport and tell her to disappear. Knowing Casey, she could probably create a new identity for herself, book a plane ticket and transfer a million dollars into an offshore bank account with a laptop computer while she was sipping a latte at the airport coffee shop.

I didn't know Casey well, nobody did, but I knew her well enough that she probably wanted in on the fight, probably wouldn't walk away even if I tried to get her to.

The most important thing was Casey believed me. She knew I hadn't beat up Mandy. I needed people like that around me right now.

CHAPTER TWENTY-SIX

The mood in the safehouse was hushed and tense when we arrived. Henry sat in his corner, pecking away at three different keyboards and watching a half a dozen different computer screens. He was wearing a t-shirt that said, "I see the Fnords!"

Bolle and Al were both talking into telephone headsets. Bolle was animated, gesturing as he spoke. There were two empty coffee cups on the table in front of him and he was drinking out of a third. Al just looked tired and rumpled.

Casey wandered over to stand behind Henry and look over his shoulder. Even after all she had been through, she couldn't resist the warm glow of a computer screen.

"Kind of an interesting crowd, huh?" A voice said in my ear, a voice I recognized.

I jumped and turned. Alex stood there, dressed in a sweater and jeans. Her hair was loose and spilled over her shoulders. I swallowed hard. Down boy.

"Alex! What are you doing here?"

She turned bright red, opened her mouth to say something, then apparently thought better of it.

She held up a plastic evidence bag. Inside was the syringe I'd taken off the dead guy in the hospital stairway, was it just last night? It seemed like forever since I'd done that.

"Dad called me in the other night for a little off the books work. The syringe is full of potassium chloride. It's the same stuff they use in lethal injections."

I shivered. That had been close. Another thirty seconds and I would have walked in Mandy's hospital room just as he was injecting it into her IV line.

"Mandy's doing fine," Alex said. "She's showing some signs of improvement. May and I have been sitting with her at the care facility. Mostly we've been getting in the way and annoying the nurses. They don't need the help of a pathologist and a psychiatrist, but Bolle wanted one of us to be with her all the time."

A wave of relief washed over me, competing with the confusion I felt at seeing Alex here. "I'm glad to hear that. What are her chances of getting better?"

She shrugged. "It's too early to tell. All we can do right now is wait."

Now that I was over my initial surprise at seeing Alex here, I took a closer look at her. She looked tired. There were dark circles under her eyes.

"How did you wind up here? I didn't know you were a part of this."

She smiled. "Dad likes to think he can keep things from me. He tried to tell me he was working some cushy investigator job for the Attorney General's office. When he called last night asking me to look after Mandy and identify the contents of a syringe, I made him level with me."

"Thanks for your help," I said. I meant it. I'd never lost a partner before, never come as close to losing one as I had the night before.

"You're welcome."

Over at the table, Bolle took off his headset and put it on the table.

"Listen up, everybody. Time to have a briefing." The chatter died down and everyone started drifting towards the table.

"Thanks," I said. She reached over and squeezed my hand for a minute. What was that in her eyes? Just pity for a messed up cop or was it something else? And if it was something else, what was I going to do about it? I wondered if she regretted the pass she made at me and was here just out of a sense of obligation to her father.

Everybody sat down around three sides of the table, so we could see the huge flat screen monitor hung on the wall. This place reminded me of a cross between some kind of science fiction movie war room and a frat party. Bolle touched a button on a big remote control and the lights dimmed as the screen came on. Very theatrical. I bet it was Henry's doing.

"First up, Henry is going to bring everybody up to speed on communications intercepts."

Henry cleared his throat, took a quick, nervous look around the room, and started talking.

"Since the younger Marshall's... disappearance, there has been a tremendous amount of traffic on cell phones and landlines that we know belong to the Cascade Aviation people."

It was his turn to press a button. A bunch of line graphs with dates popped up on the screen. They didn't make any sense to me at all. I wondered if I should sit there and look dumb or nod my head sagely like I knew what I was looking at.

"They use decent encryption, so we can't tell what they are saying. We could maybe have them brute force decrypted by next summer if we can get the NSA to give us enough computer time."

He paused to take a drink out of a giant coffee cup. "But even if we can't tell what they are talking about, the increased volume of traffic certainly does tell us that we've stirred up a hornet's nest."

Another button press and another picture came up on the screen. This one was a grainy video of the side of a black SUV. I recognized Todd inside, with a telephone handset held up to his ear.

"Our opposition has a few blind spots. For example, this gentleman is making sure he's talking on an encrypted phone, but he sits and yaks on it in a location where we can bounce a laser off his window and use it to listen to his side of a conversation."

A recording started playing on the speakers in the room.

It was scratchy, at times distorted, but I recognized the voice. It was the same man Marshall had been talking to on the way south with Casey. Todd.

"… your son. I've got my best men out looking for him."

The laser microphone could only pick up one side of the conversation.

"Yes, sir. Yes sir," Todd's voice boomed out of the speakers again. He sounded nonplussed. "I'll put the next flight on hold if that's what you want. But I'm not sure this problem with Gibson is at all linked to our operations."

Todd was quiet again for a minute, listening.

"Yes, you are right. I can hold the Company off for twenty-four hours, maybe forty-eight, but after that, it is going to be difficult."

A few more seconds of silence.

"Yes, sir. I'll keep you updated. Yes, sir. Goodbye."

Todd hung up the phone. "Damn," he said softly, almost too quiet for the laser to pick up. He sat there for almost three full minutes, I knew because I watched the timer at the bottom of the screen. Then he picked up his phone and dialed a number

"We're not sure exactly where this call went," Henry said.

"Somewhere in the Portland metro area. He wasn't on long enough for us to track it down any closer than that."

"It's me," Todd said curtly. "The old man has got cold feet about Gibson disappearing and he's put all special flights on hold. You're going to have to sit on the packages for a little longer."

There was a long pause and Todd rubbed his bald head. "I know. I know. I'll have somebody deliver more dope later today. But keep them in good shape. This is going to be the last shipment for a long time. Gibson is no longer reliable. That little bitch he has with him needs to go sky diving. I hope to Christ he doesn't screw up and let her get away."

Beside me, I felt Casey stiffen. She looked really small sitting there in the dim light of the screen. I admired her for how she'd held up so far. Part of me wanted to reach over and squeeze her hand, or chuck her on the shoulder or something, but with Casey, you never knew how you were going to be received.

"Yeah, I know," Todd was saying. "Keep your act wired tight for a few more days and we'll have it made." He hung up the phone and did a deliberate scan of the area around him, starting with his right side view mirror, and continuing all the way around. I recognized it for what it was because I did it all the time myself, particularly after my attention had been taken away from my surroundings by a phone call.

I leaned forward. Did Todd stop for just a fraction of a second and look directly into the camera? He betrayed no sign of concern, and it was so brief I almost convinced myself I was imagining things. Something nagged at my subconscious, but I couldn't quite get it to come forward.

"This is where we stand right now," Bolle said. "Todd doesn't know Gibson is dead and that we have Casey. The elder Marshall just knows his son is missing. So right now we're on hold, waiting for them to make a move. Todd keeps referring to 'packages.' It sounds like he's got a group of girls that he wants to ship to the Middle East but he has no way to get them out of the country until Marshall gives the go-ahead for this special flight to come into the country."

Bolle stood. All eyes were on him.

"This is our chance. Todd will be waiting at the airport with the girls to send them out. We're going to hit them and hit them hard. That will be our chance to find out what's coming into our country on those planes."

"Let's not forget we might just want to rescue those girls that are about to get shipped to someplace very dry and sandy," I heard myself saying it before I realized it. Oh well. I never was very good at keeping my mouth shut at meetings. Beside me, I saw Casey nodding.

Bolle had one hell of a stare, I'll give him that. Those burning, believer's eyes fixed me like twin searchlights. I think most people would have been intimidated by him, but in the last few days, I'd had the shit kicked out of me twice, been framed for a murder, and found out my girlfriend split for the bottom half of the country.

"I'm going to be very honest with you Miller. If my sources are correct, what is on that plane is a matter of the gravest national security. I feel for those girls, but I don't want you to misunderstand me, the cargo that is coming into this country is much more important than what is going out."

That hung in the air for a minute like a bad smell that nobody wanted to comment on.

"Let's keep one thing in mind," Al said in that easygoing, conciliatory way that I'd seen him use countless times before when two detectives were arguing over a case. "Bolle isn't saying the girls aren't important. They are. They're just a very close second to what's on that plane. And on a pragmatic level, if we're going to get to that plane, we're going to have to get those girls. One is the key to the other."

His tone said "trust me," the way it always had in the past.

I nodded, feeling somehow like I'd made an ass out of myself, but not quite sure how.

"What we all need to do now," Al continued smoothly. "Is get some rest. We've all been burning at both ends for a long time now. We finally got a relief team in to take over the surveillance, so I want everybody to get some sack time. I've got enough cots, sleeping bags and couches upstairs for everybody to have a spot to rack out. I've got catered food coming, so you don't have to worry about that."

That was Al at his best, taking care of the troops.

"Anybody have anything to add?" Al looked around the table. Nobody said anything. "Ok. Get some rest." Everybody started to stand and stretch. A look around the table revealed a lot of bags under eyes and rumpled clothing.

My stomach rumbled and I rubbed my eyes. Some food and a bed sounded like an excellent idea, but I had something I had to do first.

Alex was standing by the stairs, hesitating and looking over her shoulder at me. She smiled when I walked over.

"Hey," she said.

"Hey. I need a favor."

"What?"

"This place they're keeping Mandy, where is it?"

Something passed her face, something I couldn't quite read. It almost looked like disappointment. Christ, I was too tired for this stuff.

She named an address over in Southeast Portland. Damn. More driving.

"Thanks," I said, not sure if I should just go, or what.

She took a step closer to me.

"We should probably talk, about, you know…"

"We should," I said. "But first I gotta go see my partner. I almost got her killed."

A flicker of something passed across her face. Annoyance? Disappointment? Maybe both.

"Ok," she said softly.

"Let's talk when I get back though," I said. "I, uh, I really want to."

I was halfway across the room when I realized she was still standing there, looking at me. Jesus. I wasn't the most socially graceful person under the best of circumstance, but throw in a few days without sleep and killing two guys and I turned into a real tool. I'd make it up to her somehow.

CHAPTER TWENTY-SEVEN

I drove around in circles until I was sure I was clean of surveillance, then I drove to the clinic. It was in a cul-de-sac not far from Powell Boulevard, inside an old converted Victorian house. There was a discreet sign on the porch that would have been easy to miss.

I took a minute to scope out the neighborhood. Parking was mostly on the street here. Among the Hyundais and Toyotas and Lexi were two pickup trucks I found interesting.

I was a long time aficionado of the American pickup truck. I found it offensive that they were increasingly becoming a favorite suburbanite vehicle. I had seen dozens of giant trucks that would be put to no better use than occasionally hauling a set of golf clubs. That was wrong. Pickups were for work, not for some kind of rugged fantasy image you indulged in between your office job and taking the kids to soccer practice.

These two trucks didn't fit that mold. They were a few years old and well maintained. They'd been washed, but not waxed or detailed. There were work gloves in the cab of one truck. An atlas open to Portland sat on the bench seat of another. The beds of both trucks were clean, but they'd obviously been used for more than golf clubs and hauling furniture home from Ikea. They had deep gouges all the way down to the metal. They'd been used to haul feed, gravel, wood, machine parts, you name it.

The clincher was the gun racks. Over half the homes in America had a gun in them, but in Portland, it was déclassé to admit it. If you hunted or shot skeet, or just wanted to blow away the occasional burglar you kept your mouth shut about it. Mentioning that you owned firearms was somewhat akin to farting in public.

Not so out in Eastern Oregon. Out there guns weren't totems. They weren't a hobby. They weren't a political statement. They were just a tool, like a shovel or a good cultivator. You never knew when you might need to pop a coyote or put down a sickly animal. You put a gun rack in your truck, not because you wanted to show off, but because it was the handiest way to tote the damn thing around.

Well, in the back of my mind I had always been curious to meet Mandy's family. I just hoped they'd gotten the message that I was one of the good guys.

I walked up to the porch. At second glance, the house was more than it appeared. The door was steel, not wood. The windows had that greenish, distorted look that came from heavy polycarbonate, shatter resistant, maybe bullet resistant. The fisheye of a video camera was mounted at eye level on the door. I pushed a button on a metal box with a grill mounted next to the door.

"Can I help you?"

"It's Dent Miller. For Mandy Williams."

There was a long pause. I started getting itchy between my shoulder blades. I didn't like standing out in the open. I was reasonably sure I hadn't been followed, but not certain. Finally, there was a buzz from the door and when I pushed, it gave.

I was in a small foyer, with another metal door directly across from me. The only furniture in the room was a metal desk with "receptionist" on one of those little placards. Receptionist my ass. The guy standing behind the waist-high desk had a crew cut and no neck. He was a thug in a suit. The suit fit him ok, but not well enough to disguise the bulge on his hip. He looked halfway competent, unusual in the security world. You had to pay well to attract decent people and most security outfits wouldn't do that.

"Shut the door please, sir." He said, flat and mechanical. I pulled the front door shut and he buzzed the inner door open with a switch on the desk. Interesting. The inner door apparently wouldn't open while the outer one was open. What the hell kind of clinic was this?

Mandy's family was waiting on the other side of the door. Between the five of them, they probably added up to half a ton. They stood there in a semi-circle, blocking the hallway, in almost identical postures, arms folded, faces dour. They all wore jeans, faded but washed; denim or checked shirts; work boots scuffed and broken in, but clean.

They were all big enough to strain the seams of their shirts and had heavy plain features and short hair. But they weren't stupid. Your average urbanite would probably look down on them, but dumb ranchers didn't last long. You had to be able to do a little of everything, be your own veterinarian, your own mechanic, your own doctor sometimes even. And you had to be a financial genius to make any money at it. No, these men were used to relying on themselves and nobody else, thank you very much.

I couldn't tell which brother was the oldest or the youngest, they all looked so damn much alike. But dad was easy to pick out. He stood in the center, an older version of all the rest. On one thick, veiny forearm that was threatening to split the seam of his shirt, was an eagle and globe tattoo, with "USMC" inked below it. It was a little blurry and faded, like the sort of thing a young Marine might get before shipping off to some exciting little place called Vietnam.

I stepped forward, held my hand out to him. "I'm Dent Miller. And I don't care what anybody says, I didn't hurt your daughter."

He measured me for a minute, up and down, looked me in the eye. I bet he was an NCO, I thought. He reminded me of any one of a dozen men who had kept my dumb ass alive while I was in the Army.

He too reached out and took my hand in a grip that was like an arbor press. "I'm Dale Williams and I believe you. If I thought you'd hurt my daughter, you'd already be a dead man."

I figured we'd get along fine.

Mr. Williams made introductions all around. The brothers all looked the same, but I managed to sort out the two older ones. I would have bet they'd done a little military time themselves. The two youngest just weren't old enough yet. They looked like grown men at first glance, but I realized they were maybe fifteen and seventeen.

I shook hands and nodded with each. There were no smiles. After introductions, each one stepped away and took a strategic seat where they could see down a hallway or keep an eye on a door. Interesting. They weren't just here for a visit. It looked like Mandy had her own personal protective detail.

I was left standing in the middle of the hall with Mr. Williams. The place was decorated like a nice hotel, all carpet, and artwork, mahogany furniture. But it smelled like a hospital, and in the background, I could hear the beeping of machines. Nurses walked through in scrubs, giving us a wide berth.

"I'd like to see her, if that's alright with you," I said. He nodded, jerked his head down a hall. I followed behind him.

"I always worried something would happen to her," he said as we walked. "I worried about her just like I worried about Robert when he was in Afghanistan, and Danny when he was in Iraq. Young David there is making noise about joining up as soon as he graduates, and I reckon I'll worry about him too."

We stopped by a closed door. A vein throbbed on Dale's forehead and I realized I was dealing with a man who felt that the natural order of things had been undone, that everything he believed in couldn't be trusted. I was looking at another man in free fall.

"I've prepared for the day I might bury one of my children in the service of this country. But I never figured on this. First, they told me her own partner put her in a coma, damn near killed her. Then I get down here and she tells me with her own mouth that you didn't do it, that it's all a lie."

He put a hand on the doorknob but didn't open it yet.

"I don't know who to trust," he continued. "Mandy says I should trust you."

"You're right," I said. "Don't trust anybody. It's spook stuff. We stumbled into something big. I'm not sure how big, but we crossed some people that swat people like you and me like flies."

"Christ. I thought I'd never have to deal with this again." Unconsciously, he fingered a long jagged scar that ran the length of his jaw line on one side of his face.

"Soon, I hope you won't have to," I said.

He stopped rubbing and looked at me intently. "Any luck finding the men that did this?"

I hesitated. What I was about to do was phenomenally stupid. I'd just met the man two minutes ago. But he deserved the truth.

"The one that's most directly responsible is a step on. I need that kept quiet."

'Step On' was an old Vietnam term for an enemy casualty that you had actually seen lying on the ground dead. You could step on him if you wanted to. I'd heard some did.

I had a feeling Mr. Williams probably had a step on or two in his past and would know what I meant.

He looked at me. His nostrils flared unconsciously as if he were trying to detect the slightest scent of a lie.

"I appreciate that," he said finally. "But it sounds like there might be more to it than just the one man."

"There is," I said. "Much more. But I don't know how much. But do me a favor?"

"What's that?"

"You just worry about taking care of that daughter of yours. She's a special one and you should be proud. You leave the rest of this business to me. I've got nothing to lose anymore. You do." I jerked my head down the hall towards his sons and looked at the door to his daughter's room.

That rankled him a little, I could tell. But wisdom has a way of keeping pride in check.

"I'll agree to that for now." He reached into a shirt pocket, pulled out a card. He pressed it into my hand. "But if you need some cover son, you get in touch."

I looked at the card: Dale Williams and Sons. Fine Oregon Beef. A home number, cell phone, fax number, address. I put the card in my wallet.

"I'll do that," I said.

He nodded, satisfied, and stepped aside.

I took a deep breath and walked into Mandy's hospital room. The light was dim inside, and at first, I thought I was in the wrong room. The figure on the bed had to be somebody older, somebody heavier. I stood there, sick to my stomach, for a second or two before her features finally resolved themselves under the swelling and bruises. Her face looked twice as broad as it was supposed to be.

She seemed to be asleep, but right as I was turning to go she opened her eyes. They were bloodshot. The blue of her iris contrasted strangely with the bright red.

"Dent," she mumbled. When she opened her mouth I could see one of her front teeth was broken in half. "Hey."

"Hey yourself." It sounded stupid but it was all I could think of to say.

"Winter was here," she said. Her speech was low and slow, hard to hear. "Tried to tell me you beat me up. Dumbass."

"Yeah," I said. "Things got a little confused for a while."

"I set him straight..." Her voice trailed off and her eyelids fluttered. I thought for a second she'd gone back to sleep, then her eyes snapped back open again. "It was that Marshall kid. And some big bald dude. Scary looking."

"Yeah. I know."

"Winter said they'd find them. I wanna be there. Gimme a coupla days."

"Yeah. Ok." My eyes were tearing up and it was a little hard to talk.

"This stuff hurts though." She lifted one splinted arm and grimaced. "I feel pretty dopey."

"Yeah. You get some rest ok?" I hated myself for it, but I just wanted out of the room. I'd always hated hospitals. They could put all the Martha Stewart decorations up they wanted, but this place was still a hospital. It sounded like one, smelled like one and there was somebody important to me lying in a bed. That was a hospital.

"Yeah. Coupla days. Then you come get me and we'll find that Marshall and his buddy."

Her eyelids drifted closed again and I was relieved, hating myself for it. I swallowed the lump in my throat. I looked down at her. I wanted to reach out and touch her, squeeze her hand or give her a pat on the arm, something. But everywhere I looked I saw either a bandage or a bruise.

I stood there while her breathing became slow, deep and regular.

Finally I turned and walked into the hall.

Mr. Williams and Mandy's brothers were all standing down the hall, in a semi-circle around a small balding man in a white coat with a stethoscope around his neck. They were talking in hushed tones and the doctor looked a little nervous surrounded by the Williams brothers. Oh well. Maybe it would be an incentive. Mandy's father must have seen me in the corner of his eye.

He turned, gave me a slow steady nod. I returned it. There was a flat expression on his face I recognized. I probably had it on mine too. He turned back to the doctor and I walked down the hall and out the front door.

Anger is a funny thing. I get pissed too frequently. I'll be the first person to tell you that. It isn't healthy, for me or for people I run across. In my younger years, right after I got out of the Army and my first little bit of time on the Police Bureau, I beat up some people who probably didn't deserve it: frat boys, penny ante thugs I arrested who resisted more with their mouths than their fists.

I probably should have gotten fired from the Bureau for a couple of them. These days I probably would get fired, but those had been different times. A couple of busted up dirtbags was an expected price to pay in developing a good cop. Al had brought me along, helped me channel things into productive things.

As I walked over to my car, I felt it settle over me, that ice cold, deliberate anger. Anger wasn't even a good word for it. I don't think there's a word for it in English. Maybe German has a word for it. They're good at that. On second thought, maybe the Japanese would be the place to look. Those Samurai guys would probably understand this.

As I slid into the car, my actions were calm, deliberate. My mind was linear, focused and rational. But if Todd had appeared in front of me, I would have killed him without the slightest hesitation. If he'd been surrounded by an army, I'd just kill them too. I had no thought of myself, of any kind of future. I just wanted Todd in my gun sights or, better yet, in my bare hands.

I'd kept it all buried until now. I'd been treating this like another law enforcement exercise, albeit with some strange twists. I'd been viewing Marshall and Todd the same way I viewed anybody else I hunted, as one more head to put up on my trophy wall. It had snapped to the surface when I shot Marshall, but I'd buried it just as quick.

Now I let myself feel it all. My job was gone. There was no use fooling myself. I'd killed two people and covered it up. There was no way I was going to work at the Police Bureau again.

Audrey was gone. I wondered if I'd just been fooling myself all along, trying to force things to be something they really weren't. I wanted a woman, wanted a wife in my life very badly. But that was probably a pipe dream. Guys like me weren't cut out to have relationships.

And then there was Mandy. I'd only seen people beaten that badly a handful of times, and most of those people were dead. I didn't know what else they'd done to her, had gone out of my way not to ask. Things like that were only supposed to happen to the vast majority of the population I put into the "victim or potential victim" category. It wasn't supposed to happen to people on my team.

I could feel it coming, like some kind of storm just over the horizon. I was going to run into Todd, the elder Marshall's Cascade Aviation, the CIA, whoever wanted to come to the party, and I was going to destroy them all. Hopefully, it would be a good day to die, because I didn't much feel like coming back.

CHAPTER TWENTY-EIGHT

Eddie was sitting on a bench outside the safehouse when I pulled up, meditatively eating a sandwich.

I parked my ride and walked over to him. He was wearing different clothes than the last time I saw him. His hair was wet and he smelled of soap.

Eddie swallowed.

"He's in a bag with about a hundred pounds of logging chain, in the Willamette."

"You put any holes in him?" If Marshall's body slipped out of the chains, decomposition gases could make his body float to the surface.

Eddie looked offended like I'd asked him a stupid question. "You mean other than the ones you put in him? Of course, I did."

I got the feeling that maybe this wasn't the first time Eddie had made a body go away.

"Thanks," I said. I wasn't sure what else to say to a guy who had helped me cover up a murder.

"No problem," he said as he stood and brushed crumbs off his shirt. He clapped me on the shoulder.

"Look, I think it was a good idea to waste that guy, but all I'm gonna say is, next time let's have a plan, ok?"

With that, he walked into the house.

There was a tense quiet in the basement of the safe house that I recognized. It was the quiet that fell over people who realized all their training, all their preparations, all their planning, was about to get tested. They realized that very soon, a few short minutes of chaos were going to decide whether they could cut it or not.

I'd felt it before, before that fateful raid in Mogadishu, before any one of a dozen police raids. You would think after a while it got routine, but it didn't. The human animal never gets used to volunteering for the risk of imminent death. You either get so sensitive to it you can't do it anymore, or you get addicted to it. In one fashion or another, I'd been doing it for twenty years, so I'm not sure where that put me.

Everyone was sitting around a table, waiting for me and Eddie, apparently, as there were two empty chairs and Bolle had an impatient look on his face. I recognized most of the crowd: Henry; Casey, still looking pale and tired; Al; Bolle; Frederico; Micky; and not least of all, Alex. There were a couple of guys sitting by Frederico and Micky. I hadn't seen them before but it wasn't hard to recognize them for the thugs they were.

Alex seemed to be intentionally not looking at me. Great. One more thing to worry about.

As soon as Eddie and I took our seats, Henry killed the lights and turned on the big briefing screen. Once again it filled with a picture of Todd sitting in his black SUV. The picture had that grainy, flat quality of something shot through too much magnification.

"We got lucky and nailed Todd talking on his cell again with our laser. We missed the first few seconds. Our hide is several hundred meters away, on top of an empty industrial building and it takes our guys a little time to get the laser on his window. But we got most of it."

He hit a button and the video and audio started rolling. "… wait much longer." Todd's voice had a tinny, metallic quality on the recording. He held the phone up to his ear, listening for several seconds before speaking again.

"I'm proposing that we honor our commitments to people on both sides. These relationships have taken years to develop, but can be destroyed in a heartbeat. I think we need to make one more flight. This incoming cargo is vital to our plans. The outgoing cargo will take care of our immediate obligations. It will leave a few customers unsatisfied, but they were near the bottom of the waiting list and we've always made it clear that we can't be held to a firm delivery time. We can solve several different problems with this one flight and then take some time to regroup and rethink our operations."

The focus tightened even further. Todd was holding the phone to his left ear and I realized the operator was hoping to pick up some sound from the phone's speaker. The image jittered wildly for a second. The problem with using magnification that high was the slightest movement made the picture swing wildly.

When Todd started speaking again, all we heard was a garbled mess. The operator jerked the magnification back a notch or two, recentered on the window and we were able to hear again.

"... no sign of him or the last package. I've got my best people looking for him. I think we have to face the possibility that your son has decided to go off on his own. He can compromise too many parts of our operations to take that lightly. That's why I think we should get one more flight in, then roll up our operations for a while. Hopefully, we'll find your son after that, but at the very least I think we need to reconstitute our operations in a manner that will limit the amount of damage he can do."

Interesting. The "your son" bit made it clear Todd was talking to the elder Marshall. Of course, taking any of this to court would bring up some embarrassing questions about what, exactly had happened to the younger Marshall. Involuntarily, my eyes flicked to Bolle. I wondered what plans he had to cover that contingency. I wondered if they involved letting me hang.

On the screen, Todd was talking again. "No. If he was in custody, or if the woman had escaped, I would have heard about it. The Bureau's operational security is slightly better than the Boy Scouts'."

Bolle pulled a face at that one.

"I'm glad you agree," Todd said. "They are taking care of a few odds and ends on the other end. I expect the plane to land at about 0400 this morning. It will take maybe a half an hour to fuel and make the transfer. They should be wheels up and on the way back by 0430, taking a great many of our problems with us. By dawn, we'll have our entire operation packed up and moved."

Todd was silent, listening. He stared straight ahead, sitting rigidly with the phone pressed to his ear. Something tickled at the back of my mind, something that seemed wrong that I couldn't quite put my finger on.

"Very good, sir," Todd said. "I'll call you when we are mission complete and we'll start working on the next phase." He nodded once, then closed the phone and put it inside his jacket. The sound of the SUV's engine blared out of the speakers for a few seconds before Henry silenced it. He hit a button and the lights came on.

"There it is," Bolle said. "Our window of opportunity opens at 0400 and closes at 0430. We're going to take Cascade Aviation down. I want what's coming in on that plane."

Bolle stood up and paced around the room.

"Todd was right, the Bureau's operational security is only a little better than the Boy Scouts. The local police are even worse. Todd has some of their key people in his back pocket. This operation will be limited to the people in this room. Once we've taken the Cascade facility down and secured it, then I'll present it to the Bureau and local law enforcement as a fait accompli, but not before."

He fell silent, looked around the table, looked everyone in the eye.

That sense of the ground rushing up to meet me was the strongest yet. I'd done operations like this plenty of times in the past. Those had always been sanctioned law enforcement raids.

Something stunk about this. I wondered if Bolle had any official sanction for what he was doing at all. Al trusted him, but maybe Al was wrong. I wasn't terribly well connected with the Feds, but there were people I knew. Within a few days, a week maybe, I could have a discreet report on who Bolle really was.

I didn't have a week or even a few days. By dawn tomorrow it was going to be all over. I needed to decide whether I was in or out.

Al stood up, cleared his throat and all eyes were on him. I felt a wave of nostalgia wash over me. How many times had I watched Al give briefings just like this one?

I couldn't count the number of homicide suspects, sex offenders and robbery crews we'd taken down together. Al was like magic. Every operation he attached himself to seemed to run better.

"Listen up," he said softly, and every eye was on him.

That was a trick Al had, he could walk into a room where there were fifteen conversations all going on at once, with nobody paying attention, and within thirty seconds he'd have everybody listening to him. Most people would start yelling to get everyone's attention. Not Al, he always did the opposite. It seemed like the softer he talked, the more people listened to him.

"We're going to keep this simple," Al said. He clicked a computer mouse and a satellite photo popped up on the screen behind him.

"This is the Albany airport. Cascade's complex is here, south of the main East/West runway."

The view zoomed in and we were looking at a large square of tarmac with planes parked on it, surrounded by hangars on three sides. There were a couple of other buildings, probably office scattered around a road leading out to a gate in the airport fence. I didn't have a good sense of scale until I realized the plane parked in the center of the tarmac was a C-130 Hercules. It wasn't the biggest plane in the world, but it was still almost 100 feet long.

The complex was huge. I looked around the room at the dozen or so people sitting there. We didn't have enough shooters. I'd want the better part of a SWAT team just to clear one of the hangars, much less the outlying buildings.

You'd need even more people to maintain even a semblance of perimeter control. I started doing the math. I wouldn't want to pull this off with less than 75 people. I'd feel better with a hundred. I'd want entry teams, snipers, staged medical assets, prisoner handling teams, perimeter control, hell, for something this big you'd need one person in charge of bringing in water, soda and pizzas. After the initial excitement was over, it would take hours to search a complex that big and people needed rest and something to eat.

Al must have been reading my mind. Come to think of it, he probably was. He taught me everything about this sort of thing the Rangers hadn't.

"We're going to have to limit our objectives on this operation, at least initially. We don't have enough people to establish total scene dominance the way we'd want. This means some suspects will probably escape; some evidence will probably get destroyed. We're willing to accept that. Our focus will be on that airplane, its cargo and the van that will be driving out to the tarmac to meet it."

My stomach did a slow roll. Yeah, Al was right. Some evidence might get destroyed, some suspects might escape. What he was leaving out was that the suspects might very well outnumber us and decide to stick it out and fight.

"We going to have two teams make a simultaneous assault on the airplane, with the third team in reserve. Team One is going to go right in the front gate."

I looked at the photo and felt my stomach flutter again. We would be barreling down a straight road with multistory buildings and hangars on each side. Nice place for an ambush.

"Team two is going to be in charge of blocking the plane's escape," Al said. "As soon as we get word the plane is ten minutes out. Frederico is going to borrow one of the airport fire department's engines. They're going to block the taxiway back on the runway, and move in on the plane. As soon as they are close enough they will use the water cannon on top to blast high-pressure water into the C-130's air intakes. Ideally, you'll get all the engines, but if you can shut down just one side, that should be enough."

Frederico nodded. At least somebody had done some thinking there. All this was going to go to hell if the plane just took off again while we were all standing there with dumb looks on our faces.

"Team three will be in vehicles back at our hide sight. Henry will be handling communications and surveillance. He'll have the plane's transponder and will be able to let us know when the plane is due to arrive. May and Alex will be our medical element. They will take charge of any hostages we recover."

He looked around the room. Everyone was silent. I looked around and saw a bunch of expressionless faces. I replayed Al's plan in my mind. I almost couldn't believe I'd just heard it come out of his mouth. There were a million places where this thing could fall apart, a million ways where somebody could get killed, hell, we could all get killed.

I almost stood up, walked out and left the house, leaving them all to carry out their little suicide mission. This was crazy. Al could tell me to trust Bolle all he wanted, but if this was all the resources he had for an operation like this, I wasn't interested. I'd take my chances with prison.

"Listen," Al said. "I need you all to realize something. This operation may not go the way many of you are used to." He looked at me as he said this. "We don't have many of the resources I wish we had. We haven't had the luxury of training together. We're doing this thing on a shoestring. But I want you to remember something."

He flipped a switch on the remote and there she was. It was a picture of Heather Swanson. I realized who she was with a start. It had only been a few days since I'd found her dead in the weeds, dumped like so much garbage.

It was her driver's license photo, and it took me a few seconds to recognize her. For a brief moment, I was ashamed of myself. The second I stepped onto the ground where she lay dead, she'd become my responsibility. Somewhere along the way, I'd forgotten that. Marshall was dead, but he was just the beginning.

Al, you bastard, I thought. He knew me better than anybody. He knew I'd never been interested in promotions, better carpet for my office, any of that. I just lived to catch the truly bad guys.

"I want you all to look at this picture," Al said. "These guys may not be the ones that strangled her, but they had a hand in it, and we think there's another van full of girls just like her ready to get shipped off to God knows where. So, this operation may not be perfect. But it's worth it."

Nobody said anything but you could feel the atmosphere change, feel the resolve come together.

"Ok," Al said. "I want everybody to stay here, get some rest. We're going to get back together at midnight for a final mission briefing and movement to staging areas. There's food upstairs and enough beds, couches and cots laying around for everybody."

Papers rustled, chairs scraped as everybody got up at once.

I looked up at the screen. Heather's face still hung there, I'm sure not by accident.

I felt a hand on my shoulder and almost jumped, I'd been so deep in thought. It was Al.

"You ok, man?"

I turned to look up at him, struck anew at how old he looked. "Yeah, Al. I'm ok."

"You up for this? You look tired. You've been through a lot lately." We both knew what he was really asking. He wanted to know if I was willing to follow him again, only this time with a bad plan, not enough resources and a greater than usual chance of dying.

"Yeah, I'm up for it, Al," I said. "I just need some rest."

"Good." He clapped me on the shoulder again. "Find a place to crash upstairs."

I opened my mouth to say something, what, I'm not sure, but Henry walked up with a big stack of maps and computer printouts and soon he and Al were deep in conversation.

I got up and walked upstairs, feeling Al's eyes on me the whole way. There was a big glass sliding door at the back of the house, looking off the West, the directions the storms came from. I stood there a long time, turning things over in my mind.

The question in my mind was this one: if I followed Al, and everything went to hell and I died, would it matter?

Everything I had was gone. Audrey was gone, although even then I was honest enough with myself to realize I could go on without her.

What I really missed was the weight of my badge hanging on a chain around my neck, under my shirt. In the Army, my Ranger tab had kept me from being one more white trash redneck from Tennessee. Later it had been that badge. It made me special, a little apart from other men, to be honest, made me feel a little better than them. I lived to catch criminals. Everything else in my life could be messed up, but it was all ok as long as I was taking care of guys like Wendt and Marshall.

Life as something other than a cop seemed unthinkable.

The wind blew and rattled the glass in its frame. It was cold in the house like nobody had thought to turn on the heat. I rubbed my eyes and yawned. I could only handle so much heavy thinking at once. I needed a sandwich and a nap. Sometimes if you focused on where your next meal and bed were coming from, the big stuff took care of itself.

I had one more thing to do first. It was an idea I'd had rattling around in my head for the last few minutes. I'd finally decided it couldn't hurt.

I stepped through the big sliding glass door to the porch behind the house. I dug the business card out of my wallet and dialed the number. Mandy's father picked up on the second ring.

"It's Dent Miller. I need a favor."

CHAPTER TWENTY-NINE

It was time to get ready. I think I managed to sleep for an hour or two, but I wasn't sure.

My gear was in a big pile. I took my time sorting it out, checking each piece before putting it on. First came the soft body armor. It was new stuff, very light and flexible, a far cry from the vests we'd worn back when I first started as a cop. Then came a set of black Nomex coveralls. They were cut generously enough to go on over my jeans and t-shirt. I didn't even have to take my boots off to get them on and off. Outstanding.

I buckled on the pistol belt next. The holster hung down and had a strap that went around my thigh. I didn't care for it too much, but it was what all the cool tactical kids were wearing these days. I snapped a flashlight onto the grooves molded into the frame of my Glock and slid the gun into place. Spare pistol magazines and a regular flashlight went on the belt, along with a Leatherman multi-tool and a first aid pouch with two gunshot bandages inside. If I had to dump my shotgun and tactical vest, I still had enough stuff around my waist to keep any bad guys entertained for a little while.

Next came the outer tactical vest. I grunted as I lifted it. The panels inside were ceramic, much lighter than the old steel ones, but it wasn't something I'd want to wear out dancing. The plates would stop assault rifle rounds though, so they were worth toting around.

The outside of the vest was covered with pouches. I filled them up with flex-cuffs, chem-lights, a couple of door wedges, a small mirror with a collapsible handle. All of your basic supplies for a gunfight in a confined space.

I went over to a crate by the wall and grabbed a pair of flash-bang grenades. Made by the Def-Tec corporation, they had machined steel bodies with a cardboard cap at one end and a conventional hand grenade pin and spoon at the other. Unlike a military hand grenade, the bodies of the flash bangs didn't burst into fragments. Rather they blew out the cardboard end, unleashing one hell of a roar and a blinding flash, but no fragments. They were technically non-lethal, designed to distract and disorient, but if one landed in your lap you were bound to have a bad day.

I examined them carefully, bending the pins just right and then taping them down with some electrical tape. I was making sure the pins wouldn't come out if they snagged on something, but I could still pull them out if I wanted.

Somebody, probably Eddie, had thoughtfully attached a panel of shotgun shell loops on the front of the vest. I filled the top row with buckshot, the bottom with slugs. That way I would be able to tell which kind of ammo was which, even in the dark.

Next came the shotgun itself, a Benelli semi-automatic. I worked the action a few times with it unloaded. It was nice and smooth. The gun looked like it had been fired just enough to break it in, no more.

I practiced shouldering the gun, found the sweet spot where the glowing tritium dot in the front sight would land right on the target each time. I threaded seven rounds of buckshot into the magazine. The side saddle attached to the receiver held six more. I put four slugs in ammunition holders in the stock. I put my radio into a pouch on the vest, ran the wires for my earpiece and throat mike through the channels built into the vest. Then came a black Nomex balaclava, and last a helmet.

I pulled on goggles and thin Nomex aviators gloves. I had no exposed skin, and most of what I was wearing was fire resistant. SWAT operators had gotten heavily into fire-resistant materials because drug labs had a bad tendency to blow up when you threw things like gunfire and flash-bang grenades into the mix.

I jumped up and down a few times, tried a few deep knee bends. Considering the weight I was carrying, I had pretty good mobility. I found a few pieces of gear that rattled when I moved. I adjusted them so they were quiet, then jumped up and down again. Perfect. I was as silent as a 250-pound man wearing 40 pounds of gear could get.

I set my helmet and gloves next to the shotgun, then pulled the balaclava down off my face. There was no sense in wearing all that stuff until the show was about to start.

"You look like you've done this before." It was Big Eddie. He was standing there looking like a black tactical version of the Pillsbury Doughboy. The M-4 rifle slung around his neck looked like a scale model next to his bulk. The ceramic plate on his chest covered a pitifully small area. I wondered if it was worth his while to even wear it.

I smiled. "Yeah. A couple of times. At least I'm not jumping out of an airplane this time."

Eddie gave me a long look, up and down. Then he nodded, apparently satisfied by what he saw. Part of me bristled at that. Who the hell was he to look my gear over like I was some kind of rank newbie? I relaxed when I realized I'd been doing the same exact thing to him. I had to smile.

Eddie reached over and smacked me on the back with a blow that would have knocked over your average ox. "Looks like you're good to go, man. We'll be home in time for lunch."

"Sounds good."

Eddie nodded and walked off.

I did one last check of my gear, making sure my hands knew right where to go for everything: shotgun ammo, pistol magazines, flash bangs, extra flashlight. I was satisfied that everything was good to go, then shoved it out of my mind.

Gear was a funny thing. If you didn't have the right stuff, didn't take care of it the right way, or have it in the right place, you could die. Professionals always took a keen interest in gear. But you could take it too far.

I'd known guys, both in the military and in law enforcement who obsessed over gear. A half a dozen glossy gun magazines came out every month, their pages full of gun porn. The latest pistols were spread out in living color, bigger than life-size, just like the playmate of the month with a staple in her belly button. It was easy to spend thousands of dollars and all your time chasing the latest perceived edge you thought you were getting with a custom pistol, a new knife or a brighter flashlight.

All those guys were trying to buy control. They knew sooner or later, on an airfield in some third world country, or in some dark alley that was covered with broken glass and used needles, they were going to have to fight to live. The thing nobody wanted to talk about was that you could have all the right gear, be trained like a Delta Force ninja, make all the right moves, and still die from a bullet out of a $50 pistol fired by some street punk who shut his eyes when he jerked the trigger.

I think that was what made some guys lose it. Not the thought of going up against a trained adversary, or even going up against somebody better armed. It was just sheer random chance. Some guys just couldn't get over the fact that the universe wasn't fair. They thought if they bought the right stuff, did enough work, they deserved to be invincible.

My life had been a long exercise in learning that life wasn't fair. I guess I started learning it at my mother's graveside, learned it some more when the jail cell door slammed shut and learned it well and truly when Audrey's voice sounded so far away on the phone and I knew she'd left.

I squeezed my eyes shut and for a second I could smell Audrey's skin, feel her hips under my hands, hear her playing her cello. I shivered. I'd been trying very hard not to think about Audrey. Part of me couldn't believe she was gone. The other part wondered why I'd ever expected anything different. I could count the number of girlfriends I'd had on one hand. I'd never been very good at that sort of thing.

"Hey, stranger." In my disconnected state, I mistook her voice for Audrey's for a second, but when I opened my eyes, Alex was standing there, in jeans in a gray turtleneck. Her hair was tied up in a loose ponytail and she had an H&K pistol holstered on her hip. A medical bag was slung over one shoulder.

"Hey yourself," I said. "You're going to be part of this dog and pony show too, huh?"

She shrugged. "I'll be sitting a half a mile away while you guys do your thing. Hopefully, you won't need me."

"Yeah. Hopefully."

We stood there for a second in uncomfortable silence. I nodded at the bag she was carrying.

"It's good to know you've got me covered."

She frowned. "Is it? I don't know much about this sort of thing, but isn't this a half-assed plan? If it wasn't for you and my dad, I'd get away from this place as fast as I could."

I hesitated. She probably knew more than she let on, and she was right.

"I dunno, Alex. I just feel like I need to see this thing through to the end."

I hesitated again, debating, then I told her about my plan B, about the arrangement I'd worked out with Mandy's dad, stepping close to her and lowering my voice as I talked, so we wouldn't be overheard.

She nodded as I talked, stepping closer herself. When I was done she didn't step away, she reached out, took my hand.

"Dent..."

Eddie interrupted, yelling down from the top of the stairs. "Alright, let's saddle up. Everybody in the vehicles."

She leaned forward and kissed me, then wrapped her arms around me. I was surprised at first, but I found myself kissing her back and liking it. I wondered why the hell I'd been waiting for so long. I felt cheated by the vest I was wearing, it kept me from feeling her pressed against me.

"That means you too, Miller," Eddie said from the top of the stairs.

I didn't want to, but I pulled away, fumbling for something to say. There was a brief distraction when I realized my shotgun sling had somehow gotten tangled up in the strap to her medic's bag and we both laughed, grateful I think for something else to focus on.

I finally got untangled. "I gotta go." It was all I could think of to say.

"I know. Good luck."

I turned and walked up the stairs, trying hard to shove what just happened out of my mind.

CHAPTER THIRTY

I managed to sleep on the drive down. I could write a book about the weird places I've slept: in the back of a C130 before we all jumped out, in police cars, under my desk in my office.

You'd think it would be impossible to sleep with two ceramic plates strapped to your body and thirty pounds of other stuff hanging off, but I leaned my head back against the cold metal inside the van and dozed off before we even hit the freeway.

I dreamed about Alex and I was glad. I'd been a little afraid to dream, the way things had been lately. I dreamed about kissing her for a good long while, then, right as things were getting interesting, I woke up, partially due to the dual discomforts of an erection and a full bladder, partially because we were getting off the freeway. Maybe my subconscious knew where the dream was heading and just couldn't do that with Al sitting in the passenger seat.

I shifted, tried to get more comfortable, and had to settle for less uncomfortable. I took a look around the van. Eddie looked like a mountain in the darkness, fast asleep with his back against the driver's seat.

I didn't know the driver, some guy in his early thirties with a much older man's eyes. Bolle and Al were betting that in the darkness, the guard at the gate would confuse the driver for Gibson Marshall long enough for us to get inside the perimeter.

Mickey sat across from me on the floor of the van. He looked keyed up and nervous. His eyes were a little wild, and he had a death grip on the forestock of the AR-15 planted muzzle up between his knees.

He noticed that I was awake and looking at him. He looked at his watch.

"Not long now."

I nodded, not really wanting to talk.

"Why the shotgun and not a rifle?" He asked, nodding at the Benelli hanging on its sling.

"Just like 'em I guess."

"Buckshot or slugs?"

"Both," I said.

"Neither one will go through body armor."

"Nope," I said.

He patted the receiver of his rifle. "I'll stick with my rifle. I'm glad we managed to get the 77-grain ammo instead of the 62."

At that, I shut my eyes and gave up any pretense of participating in the conversation. If Mickey was worried about a 15-grain difference in the weight of his ammo, his priorities were all wrong.

That was the main thing that was bugging me about this. Always before when I went into action, it had been with guys I knew. When you hung out with a group of guys and trained together, you knew who was good to go and who wasn't. Some guys were screw ups and there was nothing you could do about it, but at least you knew.

Mickey, the kid driving, even Big Eddie, I didn't know much about them. I didn't know if they would fold up under pressure. I didn't know who would shoot wildly at a sound in the dark, who would refuse to shoot at all.

I opened one eye half-way. Mickey was messing with the rear sight on his rifle, muttering to himself.

It didn't look good for the home team.

The road noise under the tires changed and I perked up. We were pulling off the freeway and onto surface streets. The back of the van had no windows, so I had to open my eyes and risk another conversation with Mickey to see out the front windshield past Al and the driver's head. We were winding our way around some side streets in the light industrial area by the airport.

I was hoping to catch a glimpse of some street signs. Another thing that was bugging me about this operation was that I didn't know the area. I'd memorized a map of the streets around the airport but that wasn't the same as having a good working knowledge of the geography.

The van rocked to a stop. Bolle's voice crackled over the molded rubber plug in my ear.

"We're going to hold here for ten minutes. Then it's show time."

We were parked in a dark alley, about half a mile from the airport, if

I'd gotten the street names and landmarks correct. I opened the back door of the van and slid out, almost falling down when I discovered that my right leg had fallen asleep. I limped over to the gutter and started the laborious process of getting to my fly under all the layers of gear. The two Suburbans were parked behind the van, their headlights dark.

"Miller, what are you doing?" It was Bolle's voice in my ear again.

Between holding my body armor and shotgun out of the way, I had my hands full, but I managed to key my radio.

"Pissing. And stretching. I'm not going to go into action with a full bladder and my legs asleep."

There was silence on the radio for a moment, then the sound of doors opening, as men piled out onto the street to line up on the gutter like some kind of firing squad. Too much coffee and too much sitting were taking its toll. I think the cold was good for us too. Sitting in a nice warm vehicle in the wee hours of the morning had left us sleepy and sluggish.

I zipped up and did a few jumping jacks to get my blood flowing. When I was done I felt much better.

"Alright, let's load up and go," I couldn't tell if Bolle sounded faintly amused or faintly irritated. Maybe it was a little bit of both.

Mickey piled back into the van with me, still mumbling to himself. At least he wouldn't be able to wet himself if things went bad. Al climbed in the back too. For this next stage, it would be important that only our driver was in the front of the van. Bolle and the others in the Suburbans would wait here until we took care of the gate guard.

"Thirty seconds." Our driver may have been young, but he sounded cool.

Eddie and I slid around so we were sitting at the rear of the van, with him facing one door, me the other. I put a hand on the door release. Eddie had a Taser in one hand.

I pushed all my thoughts of bailing out on the operation out of my mind.

There was no turning back now.

CHAPTER THIRTY-ONE

I eased the door open and slid out with Eddie close behind.

The security guard was an old guy, maybe seventy, too damn old to be standing out here in the cold and the rain.

I turned on the light attached to my shotgun, and he stood there in stark relief, his nose red and runny over his little doughnut duster mustache. The uniform was cheap polyester khaki under an even cheaper blue nylon windbreaker. His piece was some kind of revolver in an ancient clamshell holster.

"Federal Agents! Don't move!" I gave him my best yell, put the glowing dot of the shotgun's front sight on his chest, watched his hands, and hoped for the best.

We'd glossed over this moment, back in the briefing. Todd and the rest of his cronies were bad dudes, criminals, armed and dangerous. I had no problems smoking one of them, but this security guard presented a problem for me. He was armed, and therefore a potential threat, but he was also probably somebody's grandpa, working for maybe ten bucks an hour and no benefits.

So I pointed the twelve gauge at him and hoped he would give up.

He pulled a hand out of his windbreaker. My jaw clenched and I felt my finger move off the frame of the shotgun. But the hand went up to his face, to shield his eyes from the light mounted under my Benelli.

"Ehh?" was all he got out. Then I saw a little red pinpoint of a laser sight dancing around on his chest like a firefly, just before Eddie pulled the trigger on the Taser.

The guard hit the ground and I breathed a sigh of relief. I let the shotgun hang on its sling and moved in, grabbing one of the guard's wrists and flex-cuffing it to the other. I gave the slightest tug on the butt of his gun and it popped into my hand. Maybe I'd make it up to the guy and buy him a decent holster.

I slid the revolver into a pouch on my vest and sat the guard on his skinny haunches.

"What the hell's going on?"

I ignored him and busied myself with pulling the Motorola radio out of the holder on his cracked leather duty belt.

"We're the FBI, pops," Eddie said. The old man winced as Eddie plucked the Taser barbs out of his skin. "We got no beef with you. We're here to raid your employer."

The two Suburbans slid to a stop behind the van, their headlights dark as Eddie and I each grabbed one of the guard's arms and started marching him towards the guard shack.

"What the hell for?" the old man asked.

"Overdue library books and cutting the tags off mattresses," Eddie said, straight-faced as he lowered the man to the floor of the guard shack. There was a phone inside. I unplugged the handset and tossed it out into the weeds.

Eddie positioned the man so he would be by the heater. "Now you just sit tight here and keep your head down. This will all be over soon."

As Eddie and I ran back to the van, I finally noticed the low-pitched buzzing drone that had been in my ears. It was a plane coming in for a landing and to me it sure as hell sounded like a C-130. God knows I'd jumped out of enough of them to know.

"The plane's coming in right on schedule," Henry's voice came over the plug in my ear. "Touching down right... now."

The engine note changed as the pilot started braking. Eddie and I jumped in the back of the van with our legs hanging out. We didn't bother shutting the doors. Al and Mickey were hunched by the open sliding door on the side of the van. We took off with a jerk that nearly sent me tumbling out and under the wheels of the Suburban behind us.

We barreled west down the access road. I saw glimpses of an office building and dark silent hangars rushing by on either side. We hung a hard right onto the apron and the two Suburbans overtook us on either side, the red and blue lights mounted under their grills flashing. I craned my neck around to see through the windshield.

The concrete apron was huge, easily big enough for five or six of the C-130's, but it was empty, apparently, all the other aircraft were either in the hangars or deployed somewhere. The C-130 was just finishing a slow, ponderous turn back towards the taxiway as we sped across the apron. It jerked to a stop and there was a bloom of white light as the rear ramp started to lower. I saw figures seated inside, but it was too far away to make out detail. A fuel truck was speeding across the apron towards the plane.

There was an eighteen passenger van parked on the apron. It was too dark to see inside.

The folks by the van finally saw us charging across the apron. Somebody opened the back door of the van, saw us and abruptly shut it again. He started gesturing wildly to the crew chief standing inside the ramp of the plane.

I realized the four huge props were still turning and that there was no sign of the fire truck. I got a sinking feeling in my stomach.

"Go!" Bolle screamed over the radio. "Faster! Faster! Frederico where are you with the fire truck?"

Our driver floored it. I hung on to keep from tumbling out of the back of the van.

I watched the scene ahead of us unfold like a slow motion car wreck. Our van and the two trucks with the rest of Bolle's team, and the fuel truck were all converging on one spot, where the passenger van with "Cascade Aviation" painted on the side was parked. Meanwhile, the C-130 was wallowing away from us, the light coming out of its back getting smaller as the rear ramp slid upwards on its hydraulics.

It reminded me of one of those stupid word problems they made us do in math class. Instead of one train leaving Memphis westbound and another leaving St. Louis eastbound, it was three carloads full of a half-ass SWAT team headed north and a giant airplane also heading north. We were gaining slowly on the plane, but I knew that would change soon.

Besides I was a little unclear exactly what we were supposed to do even if we pulled alongside while the plane was still moving. I wasn't exactly keen on the idea of sticking a knife in my teeth and jumping from the van to the plane like some kind of modern-day pirate.

Now the Cascade Aviation van fired up and started following the plane. I wasn't sure I understood the logic behind that, but it made our job easier. If the van had taken off the other way, headed right towards us, it would have made us split our forces to catch it.

Off in the distance on the taxiway, I saw a pair of red and blue flashing lights.

"We're coming." It took me a second to place the voice that crackled over my radio. It was Frederico. His voice was low and slurred, not like he was drunk, more like he was hurt.

He coughed and his open microphone picked it up. "Ran into a couple of security guards outside the fire station. Be right there."

As it grew closer, I realized the vehicle was a fire truck, one of the low slung rigs you see at airports, designed for fast attacks on airplane fires. I wasn't sure if was Frederico driving or if he was the figure hanging on to the water cannon for dear life, but whoever was behind the wheel, he was doing a hell of a job.

The fire truck rounded a corner damn near on two wheels and went into a long skid, the rear end sliding around and threatening to swap ends with the front, a sure precursor to a nasty, rolling pile up. Most people would have a tendency to jerk the wheel hard, over-correcting and signing their own death warrant, but the driver let it ride with a smooth touch. The rear end of the fire truck gave a final little wiggle and then it was back on track and accelerating, barreling down the taxiway at the C-130.

Again, physics wasn't on our side. The guys in the fire truck were going to get one chance at this. By the time they passed the plane and got the fire truck turned around, the plane would be long gone, onto the runway and probably into the sky.

The water cannon kicked on when the plane was still out of range, the long arc of foam and water just splashed down on the taxiway. But they were closing fast.

I craned my neck to see under the wing of the plane as the water splashed down the side of the fuselage and along the wing. The cannoneer was flicking the stream of water back and forth along the left wing, hoping to get enough water into both engines to drown them out.

We had to shut down two engines on the same side to keep the plane from taking off. It had seemed reasonable in the planning room. The cannon put out hundreds of gallons of water in just a few seconds, plenty to drown out the plane's engines, but we'd counted on the plane being stationary.

It looked like it wasn't going to work. The closing speed was just too fast. Then, right as the truck and the plane were about to pass, the engines on the left side quit, both at once, as if someone had thrown a switch.

The Hercules gave a drunken lurch to the left as all the power on that side suddenly went away. The driver of the fire truck had just enough time to twitch the wheel before the top of the cab kissed the bottom of the plane's nose cone, sending the truck sliding off the runway into the mud.

This time it was too much for the driver. The truck flipped and rolled twice like a Tonka toy thrown by an angry three-year-old before it started a long slide on its side, plowing up a wall of mud in front of it.

The plane's nosed slewed back over to the right at the impact and I heard the scream of tortured rubber and a rapid series of pops as the Hercules' tires gave way under the sideways force. In slow motion, the plane slid 90 degrees to its direction of travel. The wing closest to us pitched up towards the sky and I heard a long succession of rattling smashing sounds as the wing on the other side dug into the ground. The plane ground to a halt in a shower of sparks and flying pieces of aluminum.

Well, I guess we stopped it, I thought.

The Cascade Aviation van hit its brakes and slid on the foam on the taxiway, sliding sideways and almost tipping on its side before it stopped just short of the Hercules. Eddie and I looked at each other wide-eyed.

"This is like a Dukes of Hazard episode!" he said, and inexplicably, laughed. Even more inexplicably, I found myself laughing too. It was crazy sometimes, what you would find funny, but I'd done it before. Just when things were going sideways, my funny bone would get tickled.

Mickey, his eyes rolling like a spooked horse, looked at us like we were crazy. Al just looked irritated as Eddie and I sat there cackling at each other as we hung halfway out of the back of a van barreling towards a wrecked airplane.

"Get ready." Bolle's voice brought me back to my senses. We were coming up on the van and the plane.

Our driver had apparently been paying attention to the wild, panicked slide of the other van. He started braking early before we hit the sudsy firefighting foam all over the taxiway. Ahead of us, I could see figures milling around inside the van. The plane was still. Steam or smoke was roiling up from the far side, and the odor of aviation fuel was heavy in the air. Not good.

It's funny how you can get shot at and not even realize it for a few seconds. Our driver did a great job of getting us slowed down before we hit the foam. I heard a heavy hammering sound against the sheet metal body of the van, one, two, three, in rapid succession and frowned, trying to figure out what it was. Then our driver's throat exploded. His hands flew up in the air and blood fountained out of his carotid like it was coming from a garden hose. It sprayed a heavy coat all over the inside of the windshield and then he slumped forward with a gurgling gasp.

The van careened over to the left, and Eddie, Al and I all scrambled for the wheel at once. Al got there first. He leaned over the driver, whose head was lolling around as he sprayed even more blood, and managed to both grab the wheel and push the gear selector into neutral.

We slid off the taxiway into the soft mud. The van swayed drunkenly from side to side.

I thought for a second we would just coast to a stop in the field, but then the van started to lean farther and farther to the left. Through the blood-streaked windshield, I saw the world tilt at a crazy angle, then the van slammed down on the driver's side. I had just enough time to think how lucky I was to land on Big Eddie instead of the other way around when Mickey landed on me, driving all the air out of my lungs and my helmeted head into the side of the van.

CHAPTER THIRTY-TWO

I didn't get knocked all the way out, but things were a little fuzzy for a few seconds. I came around to the taste of blood in my mouth and a remarkable quiet. Somebody's boot was grinding into my ear.

I tried to talk, but "ack," was all that came out.

The quiet was ruined by the smack of a bullet against the roof of the van. Now that I was paying attention, I could hear the muffled crump of the rifle shot.

"Incoming fire," Eddie said. "We need to get off the X here." As if to accentuate his point, I heard another round hit the van. Something plucked at my pant leg and I felt a sting in my calf. It wasn't hard enough to be solid hit from a gunshot. It might have been a piece of bullet jacket or a piece of the van knocked loose.

Eddie was right. The van was a big conspicuous target sitting on its side in the middle of the field, and we obviously had the attention of somebody with a rifle. I fought to my knees. I felt my ribs settling back into something resembling their original configuration. Body armor or no, I was very, very sore. Between the fight with Marshall, the fight in the hospital stairway, and now this, it was a wonder I didn't have a collapsed lung. Every time I took a breath I felt a hot stitch of pain in my side.

Al was already up, tending to the driver, who hung from his seat belt, gurgling and thrashing. Despite his own advice, Eddie moved to help him. Mickey was crouched by the back door, hunched over his rifle. He didn't look like he was going anywhere soon.

Rangers lead the way, I thought. I headed out the back of the van, grabbing Mickey as I went.

"Go! Go! Go!" If nothing else, I'd learned how to yell when I was in the Army.

It worked. Mickey popped up and was practically glued to me as I burst out of the van. The fact that I had my hand twisted up in the webbing on the back of his vest probably didn't hurt.

The van was lying on the left side. The back door on the bottom was open, but I had to duck low to miss the one hanging down from the top. As soon as I stepped out, I heard the whip crack of a bullet passing right over my head.

Whoever our shooter was, he'd probably been waiting for somebody to come piling out of the back of the van.

I broke left and headed around the van, half dragging Mickey. I almost scorched my cheek on the muffler as I went by. I ran until we were behind the engine block and took a second to take stock.

There was a lot of shooting. The two Suburbans with the rest of Bolle's team were stopped by the Cascade Aviation van and the wrecked airplane. I saw a confusing knot of running figures and muzzle flashes, but nobody over there seemed to be paying attention to us. I leaned around the front of the van, just enough to get an eyeball out from behind cover.

I saw nothing, just an open expanse of torn up dirt, tarmac, and about two hundred and fifty yards away, a dark hangar. I leaned out a little farther and a bullet smacked into the van, not far from my head. I flinched back, but not before I caught a glimpse of a muzzle flash.

Our boy was on the roof of the hangar. I fixed a mental image of where I'd seen the star-shaped flicker of the muzzle flash.

Another round hit the hood of the van. I looked around.

We were screwed. The sniper had obviously held his fire during our high-speed charge across the tarmac, but he'd been good enough to plug our driver as soon as we slowed down to a manageable speed.

There's not much cover on an airfield. We were a good hundred and fifty yards from the Suburbans and the plane. I'd bet even money he could hit most or maybe all of us if we just took off running. The rifle shots were a sharp crack, not a heavy boom. They sounded to me like something light and fast shooting, maybe an M-16 or something like that. He could dump a whole thirty round magazine at us while we were running and be well into another before we hit any kind of cover.

Another round hit the van and I heard somebody inside swear. We were running out of time here. He could just keep firing blindly into the van. Vehicle sheet metal doesn't stop even light rifle rounds very well, and we couldn't all fit behind the engine block.

"Dent! Make the sniper go away!" Al yelled from inside. He sounded more stressed than I'd ever heard him.

"Working on it."

I looked at my shotgun. It was totally the wrong tool for the job unless I wanted to just make noise and hope I scared the sniper away. The buckshot would fall to the ground before it even got across the tarmac. The slugs would probably fly that far but they weren't accurate at that range. I could probably count on hitting the hangar, and that was about it.

Mickey was sitting there, his back hunched against the bottom of the van, looking out at the field, in the direction nobody was shooting at us from, at least not yet. I looked at his rifle. It had an awfully short barrel, but it was better than the shotgun.

I reached down and grabbed Mickey's rifle. He snapped back to reality and snarled at me, no words, just a deep animal sound from the back of his throat. He was pale and I realized there was blood coming from his hairline.

"Hey, dude, relax. I just need to borrow your piece for a second to take care of that sniper. I'll give it back."

Mickey stared at me, mute, like a chicken watching a card trick. Another round slammed into the van and the driver made a very final sounding rattling noise from inside.

"Goddammit, Dent!" Al bellowed from inside. "Kill that sniper!"

I don't know what made me do it, but I pulled the security guard's battered old Rossi revolver out of my chest pouch, handed it to Mickey butt first.

"Here. Trade me. You take this. I'll borrow the rifle." He took it, wrapped his hands around the chipped wood grips of that old wheel gun and let me disconnect the sling of the rifle and take it.

I was surprised, but it beat the hell out of my other idea which was to pound him over the head with the butt of my shotgun until he was unconscious and take the rifle from him. I pulled an extra magazine out of his chest rig and stuffed it in a pocket.

The M-16 in my hands was a kissing cousin to the one I'd carried in the Army. I flipped the selector lever to "auto" as I leaned out around the front of the van.

A bullet made a geyser of mud a foot away from me and I saw the muzzle flash again. The guy was either supremely confident or stupid. He wasn't changing positions between shots.

The trick to shooting full auto is to fight the urge to jam the trigger back and let all your ammo go in one long burst. After a few rounds, you were shooting into the stratosphere and hitting nothing. Before you knew it you'd be sitting there with an empty rifle and a dumb look on your face.

I settled the glowing red dot of optical sight just below the spot where the muzzle flash had come from and started stroking the trigger, I held it back for a few rounds and as the recoil made the rounds rise up over my target, I let up.

I was only off the trigger for a fraction of a second, just long enough to settle the muzzle back down and hammer away again. I'd fire five, maybe six rounds at a time. It only took a second or so longer to empty the gun this way, but you had much better control.

Guns always run out of ammo much quicker than you think they will, but I was ready for it. The bolt on an M-16 locks back on the last shot, giving it a different feel. As soon as it happened I pushed the magazine release button with my trigger finger, sweeping the empty magazine out of the well with my left hand on the way to retrieve the new one. I slapped the new magazine home and hit the bolt release with the palm of my left hand, then I was back on the trigger, rocking and rolling.

Back in my Ranger days, I'd practiced mag changes until my fingers bled. I'd won many beers betting nobody could beat my time of just over two seconds. It didn't feel like I'd slowed down much.

When the gun clicked dry again, I just stood there for a second, looking through the heat shimmer coming off the barrel of the rifle, at the spot where I'd seen the muzzle flash.

After a few seconds of nothing, I figured if the guy wasn't hit, he was at the very least suppressed.

Dumping sixty rounds of rifle ammo in about thirty seconds isn't very good for your hearing. My ears were ringing and everything sounded like it was underwater. I jerked another magazine out of Mickey's chest rig and reloaded the rifle. He didn't seem real keen on trading back so I flipped my shotgun around behind my back on its sling and decided to keep the rifle. Mickey just sat there, diligently watching the big empty field for bad guys.

Al and Eddie came out of the van. Both of them were soaked with blood.

"You get him?" Al asked. It was hard to hear him.

I shrugged. "Not sure. He quit shooting. How's the driver?"

"Dead. I tried to save him, but he bled out."

There was a long burst of gunfire from over by the plane and somebody screamed. Al looked at me and Eddie, caught sight of the shotgun slung over my back and the rifle in my arms, looked at Mickey staring off into space with the cheap Brazilian revolver in his hands.

I shrugged.

"We need to get over there," Al said, and took off running towards the Suburbans without waiting to see if anybody followed.

Eddie and I took off behind him, forming a wedge with our guns pointed out. I spared Mickey one last glance. He was still staring off into space.

We passed the two Suburbans first. They were sitting with their engines running and the doors open. There were a couple of bullet holes in the windshields and plenty of shell casings underfoot.

Then we passed a body lying on the tarmac. It was one of Bolle's guys. He was lying face down, arms outspread, with a long fan of blood and brain matter on the ground behind him and on his back. Nobody's come up with a way to bulletproof your face yet.

There was a knot of huddled figures behind the Cascade Aviation van. We passed more bodies on the way, a couple of Cascade Aviation thugs, one more of Bolle's team. The C-130 was turned broadside to us, still tilted to starboard at a crazy angle. Whoever was inside had managed to crank the rear ramp halfway down and somebody was lying on it, firing quick bursts with what sounded like a submachine gun.

Bolle was hunched behind the van's engine block, shooting over the hood. His face looked drawn and pale. Another one of his guys was kneeling by the front bumper, gun out.

Also huddled behind the van was a bunch of young women, five, maybe six, I couldn't tell because they were all huddled together in a pile. They were dressed in disposable coveralls like you give to prison inmates, and had their hands bound in front of them with zip ties. Todd's shipment.

They were all young, mostly blond, and scared as hell.

One lay curled in a ball, screaming every time a gun would fire. One had a spreading stain on the chest of her coveralls and bloody froth on her lips. Another clutched at blood oozing out of her ankle.

I grabbed Bolle's arm and spun him toward me. My hand came away wet. He was bleeding from somewhere.

"We need to get them out of here," I said, pointing at the girls.

"I need to get on that plane," he screamed back. There was that holy fire in his eyes again. I didn't like it much.

Off in the distance, I heard sirens, not close, but they were coming. You couldn't have a full auto gunfight near a medium-sized city without somebody calling the cops.

"Look," I said. "The local cops are coming. Let's get the girls out of here and just hold a perimeter. The plane's not going anywhere."

He shook his head. "We can't let the locals get in that plane. They'll screw up everything." He turned and squeezed off another burst.

Dammit. I needed to know what his agenda was, but now wasn't the time to sort it out. One of the last remaining windows in the van blew out, scattering broken glass all over the girls. Big Eddie moved over, squeezed between the girls and the van and knelt so he could shoot through the interior. A couple of the girls were sheltered by his bulk. It was a noble gesture, but it wasn't going to last for very long.

The guy in the ramp kept firing short bursts. He didn't seem to be that good of a shot, but he didn't seem to be running out of ammo.

I opened the driver's door to the van and leaned in, ignoring the pool of blood all over the driver's seat. The engine was running and it even sounded healthy, considering the amount of lead that had been pumped into it.

I grabbed Bolle again.

"Look," I said, and pointed at the guy shooting around the front of the van. "We put him in the driver's seat, load the girls back in the van. When they're ready, I'll throw a flashbang under the plane's ramp. That will distract the gunner long enough for us to smoke him. The van takes off and we rush the plane."

Bolle was silent for a second, then nodded. I'm not sure who was the most stupid: me for suggesting the plan or him for agreeing to it. Al heard the plan and just looked at me, his face unreadable.

Bolle's other shooter practically leaped into the driver's seat. He seemed pretty steady, but I couldn't blame him for wanting to leave. That left the girls.

I jerked the closest one to her feet and aimed her at the sliding door on the side of the van. Thankfully it had doors on both sides.

"Get in!" I yelled. "You are all leaving."

She started to get in, then screamed. Her hands flew to her cheeks and she just stood there. What now?

I looked in the van. Lying on the floor was a young woman, her curly hair matted black with blood. She was dead. I grabbed an ankle and pulled her out of the van, feeling my gorge rise at the limp boneless feel of her as she slid along the floor. I pulled her to the tarmac and left her there.

I all but picked up the other girl and threw her in the van. Eddie was ushering the others along, his voice oddly gentle coming from a guy the size of a refrigerator and dressed in a commando outfit. They climbed over the blood and broken glass and then they were all inside.

I pulled a flashbang out of my vest. There was no time to ask if everybody was ready. I was afraid the guy in the plane would put a burst into the back of the van.

I pulled the pin, let the spoon fly. I really had no idea if I could throw the damn thing far enough to get it to the plane. It looked a long way away. I hurled it as hard as I could and yelled "Banging!" as soon as it left my hand, just like they taught us in the Rangers.

The driver didn't even wait for the grenade to go off. As soon as I yelled, he stomped on the gas, damn near running over Eddie's foot as he peeled away. There was a long, stomach curdling moment when we were standing there with nothing between us and incoming fire. I watched the flashbang sail through the air in slow motion, remembering just in time to avert my eyes before it went off.

My throw was pretty good. Just before I closed my eyes, the grenade looked like it was going to land right by the ramp. When it went off, I saw the hot white flash even through my closed eyes. The bang was like an ice pick to the ear. After a while, your ears got numb to the sound of the gunfire, but the flashbang cut through.

It was my turn to lead the way. As soon as the bang detonated, I took off running for the ramp. I emptied the M-16 as I ran. It was a lousy way to hit anything, but I wanted to give the guy on the ramp every incentive not to shoot back. I figured if the guy could hit me after being flash banged and while I was emptying my rifle at him, it was just my day to die.

The carbine clicked empty a dozen feet from the ramp and I let it drop. I hadn't grabbed another extra magazine from Mickey. Besides, for close work, I really liked shotguns.

The ramp was down to almost waist level and tilted at a crazy angle. I pulled the shotgun up and turned on the light mounted on the forearm. The gunner was dressed in a flight suit and helmet. He was sitting there pawing at his eyes. There was a little German submachine gun slung around his neck.

He dropped a hand away from his eyes and grabbed for the grip of the sub gun. I put the dot on the shotgun's front sight over his face and pulled the trigger.

I stood there for a second, taking a breath and making a point of not looking down at what I'd done. I needed a few seconds to let my brain catch up to events.

I couldn't see much inside the plane and was unwilling to stick my head in the opening. I turned to Big Eddie.

"Bang it."

He nodded, plucked a flashbang out of his harness. The rest of us moved up the fuselage of the plane so we were forward of the ramp and stacked up in a line.

Eddie pulled the pin and flicked the grenade through the opening. We waited a long, breathless couple of seconds. Someone inside the plane yelled, loud enough for us to hear through the skin and then the grenade detonated. It wasn't as loud since it was inside, but the ramp opening was outlined in the bright actinic light for a fraction of a second, then we were moving and scrambling inside.

I had to press myself up over the edge of the ramp. It only took a second or two, but I felt incredibly vulnerable scrambling up with the shotgun slung over my back. Then I was up. The inside of the plane was chaos.

There were a few red lights on, but no other illumination, other than the lights under our gun barrels. Two guys in flight suits were pawing at their eyes over by a door on the starboard side of the plane. One had a crash ax in his hands.

I slid and nearly fell. The stink of hydraulic fluid was heavy in the air, and I realized there was a big puddle of it all over the back half of the plane.

I started wondering if the flash bang grenade had been a good idea after all. There was a big scorch mark along one side of the plane where the grenade had detonated, and the nylon webbing of the seats was starting to smolder and burn.

I saw a bunch of dark-skinned men on the deck, dressed in the same disposable coveralls the girls had been wearing. They were all in a pile where the floor and the starboard side of the plane met. It looked like they had slid there when the plane leaned over. Their hands were zip-tied in front of them. It took me a second to realize there was a third man in a flight suit underneath them and they were beating him. He must have been the crew chief. He was wearing a headset with a microphone, and a pistol in a holster strapped to his thigh. He wasn't fighting back, just holding on to the butt of the pistol for dear life, to keep it from being snatched away from him.

Bolle, Eddie, Al and I all started screaming at once, telling everyone to put their hands up. The two men in flight suits by the door complied at once, putting their hands up. The guys on the floor looked at us for a second and went back to beating the other aircrewman.

We all moved forward towards the pile on the floor. There was a hollow boom from the front of the plane and I felt a bullet whiz over my head, couldn't have been more than a couple of inches away.

I jerked my shotgun up and in the light from under the barrel, I saw a man standing in the stairwell leading up to the flight deck. He was wearing a flight suit and had a big shiny pistol shoved out in front of him in a perfect Weaver stance. All four of us fired at the same time. Under the fire from a shotgun and three rifles, the guy just about came apart.

"Bolle, Eddie. Get those two." I jerked my head towards the other two flight crew members. They both had pistols strapped to their thighs but showed little inclination to use them. That might not last forever.

"Al, cover the flight deck." Somehow I'd become the de facto leader of this little dog and pony show. I wasn't sure how that had happened, but for now, I was happy to go along with it.

I moved forward, towards the pile of men fighting on the floor. I was beginning to feel like we could pull this off. If we could just get the men on the floor of under control, we'd have everyone at gunpoint.

You can do a dozen things right in a fight, but it's the one thing you do wrong that always bites you.

CHAPTER THIRTY-THREE

I moved forward towards the knot of men on the floor with no clear plan, and I got too close. I don't know what I was thinking, maybe that if they didn't knock it the hell off, I'd just empty the shotgun in the whole mess and sort it out from there.

I never saw the knife before I got cut, but I heard the click of the blade snapping into place, even over the noise of the other guys screaming.

The guy on top of the crew chief, a little wiry guy with an olive complexion and a nose like a ski slope, stood up, grabbed the muzzle of my shotgun with his left hand and shoved it to my right. I jerked the trigger instinctively, succeeding only in blowing a hole in the side of the plane. His right hand was a blur, whipping out and back, and suddenly my left forearm felt very cold.

Then I saw the knife, a little thing, maybe a three or four-inch blade. He must have pulled it out of the pocket of the crew chief on the ground. In that peculiar clarity of imminent death, I saw that he had the remnants of a zip tie on each wrist and his left hand was bleeding. He must have cut himself when he severed the zip tie.

I swung the shotgun around with my right hand. It was awkward and had little power, but it deflected his knife jab away from my throat. The blade glanced off the barrel of the shotgun and raked along the front of my body armor instead. The blade got fouled up on something, maybe some ammo, or maybe the body of one of the flash bangs I still had, and it delayed him from whipping back for another strike. That probably saved my life.

I was much bigger than the guy, a foot taller, and probably twice his weight. I put the receiver of the shotgun against his chest and just drove forward, using my legs and mass. He went ass over tea kettle over the knot of guys still fighting on the floor. I gained a few feet of distance with that move. I fought to bring the shotgun back around to point it at him.

The back of his head exploded in a big inky cloud and he hit the ground in a boneless heap. Al was standing only a couple of feet from me when he triggered his rifle.

I finally got the shotgun under control and pointed it at the guys on the floor.

"Put your hands up!" I figured even if they didn't speak English, having a gun pointed at you was sort of a universal language.

In reply one of them screamed something I didn't understand. He finally succeeded in jerking the gun out of the crew chief's holster and started to raise it. Al squeezed down on his trigger, letting half a magazine go at once, blowing the guy with the gun away, putting rounds into the men on either side of him. Having their buddies' insides splashed all over them seemed to calm down the guys that were left.

"You ok?" I heard Al ask over the ringing in my ears. I held my left arm up in front of me. A big droplet of blood fell off the end of my pinky. It was hard to make my fingers move, they felt like they were far away, like my arm had somehow grown longer. My hand felt weak. It still didn't hurt. It just felt cold.

"I think so," I said and coughed. I realized it was getting hard to breathe. I looked over Al's shoulder. The fire had spread. Now half a dozen seats were burning. The flames were several inches high and giving off thick greasy smoke. As I watched, a big flaming gobbet of molten nylon dropped off the frame, right into a puddle of hydraulic fluid.

"Oh, shit," was all I had time to say. Then the puddle caught fire.

The floor in the whole back third of the plane was on fire in seconds. It started creeping up the starboard side of the plane, where the fluid had soaked the insulation. More seats started catching.

It wasn't as bad as I thought it would be, at least at first. The coveralls I was wearing were Nomex and the boots were heavy leather. The guys on the floor screamed. The disposable coveralls were no protection. I turned away, there was nothing I could do other than shooting them.

I looked towards the rear of the plane. Eddie and Bolle each pulled one of the handcuffed crewmen up off the floor. They were screaming, but they were wearing Nomex just like we were. The coveralls weren't supposed to keep you alive for sustained periods in a fire, just keep you from burning to death, long enough to escape, which was what we needed to do now.

The fire was worse back near the ramp. Other stuff was catching and burning as I watched, wiring, more seats. I ran up to the door on the starboard side and tried to throw the handle with my right hand. It moved a little then stopped. I guessed the fuselage of the plane had warped a little when it tipped over. I could see shiny marks on the locking bar where the crew had been going at it with the crash ax.

I had something better. I pulled a slug out of the stock of the shotgun and promptly dropped it. I realized my hands were shaking. The heat on the back of my neck was getting unbearable. I took a deep breath, tried not to think about the fact that I'd dropped a live shotgun round into the flames at my feet, and pulled another round off my vest.

I fed it into the magazine, managed to make my left hand rack the bolt handle, bringing the slug up to the chamber.

"Watch your eyes," I yelled. I put the muzzle of the shotgun against the bar and pulled the trigger. It blew the bar almost in two. I backed up, aimed a leg and threw a kick. I figured I'd either open the door or break my foot.

When it popped open, I almost fell out. I grabbed the door frame with both hands, stepped out, and hit the ground rolling in a perfect parachute landing fall. It's amazing what you don't forget.

I scrambled to all fours, wanting to get out of the way before Eddie and the others came piling out. The ground underneath was wet. At first, I thought it was just from the rain, then I realized my nose was full of the smell of aviation fuel. I looked towards the front of the plane. When the wing had struck the ground, it had bent upwards at a crazy angle. Aviation fuel was pouring out of rent in the aluminum skin.

I took off running, hoping the others would have the good sense to follow me. I could see the airport fence. I lowered my head and charged. The soles of my boots felt oddly soft under my feet and I realized they must have partially melted back on the plane.

I made it fifty yards or so, just out of the puddle of fuel, when everything blew up. There was a surprisingly gentle push at my back, just enough to knock me forward, and then a hot wind blew over me that stank of burnt hydrocarbons. Then the air was surprisingly still for a fraction of a second before I felt a cool wind blowing back the other way. It was air being sucked into the fire.

I stood and my shadow in front of me was as long and well-defined as if it had been cast by the setting sun. I turned and looked. The outline of the C-130 was lost in the giant fireball. It had to be several stories tall. I had to look away. If it hadn't been for the balaclava and the goggles over my face, I probably would have lost my eyebrows, even at that distance.

I looked around for Al and the others and saw nothing but fire and burning pieces of airplane. I heard sirens in the distance.

It was time to leave.

I pulled the shotgun sling loose, let it fall to the ground and ran for the fence.

CHAPTER THIRTY-FOUR

I hit the fence line and stopped to catch my breath. The Albany airport didn't have an extremely secure perimeter. The weeds had been allowed to grow knee high up to the fence on both sides and there was no lighting. I sat down in the shadows and tried to think like a cop for a couple of seconds.

The Albany police department was medium-sized. They had maybe five or six people on at this hour. More could be drafted to help from the county and state police. A sergeant, or at best a lieutenant, would be running the show, responding to calls about some kind of gunfight on an isolated corner of the airport. It would sound like a small scale war, hundreds of shots, full auto, and now it was punctuated by a hundred-foot fireball.

The person in charge wouldn't be in a big hurry to go rushing in. That was a sure way to get his people killed. He'd set up a perimeter, try to keep things contained while more and more resources showed up: SWAT teams, fire trucks, more officers, and hopefully somebody higher up in the food chain to take over the whole mess.

I looked at my watch, had to do a double take and look at it again. A little over thirteen minutes had passed since we'd rolled through the front gate and Tased the guard. It felt like a lifetime.

The airport was a huge piece of ground to try to secure. They probably didn't have an effective perimeter set up yet, but I needed to move quickly.

I looked at the fence. It was maybe seven feet tall, with a couple of strands of barbed wire on top. I started scaling. My left hand was still weak. When I reached up and took hold of the fence, a big dollop of blood ran off my wrist and landed on my goggles. I did my best to ignore it and kept climbing.

At the top, I wrapped my left arm around one of the supports holding the barbed wire up and pulled out my multi-tool. The barbed wire was really too thick for the wire cutters on the inside of the plier's jaws, but I had strong hands and I was motivated. I managed to cut both strands and slither over the fence.

I made it to the ground in the shadows of a tree on the other side. I realized I was dizzy. I decided to risk a little light and look at my arm.

I pulled the tactical vest off and immediately felt a ton lighter. I pulled my coveralls down to my waist and shined the light on my arm. I immediately wished I hadn't.

The top of my forearm was laid open from wrist to elbow. The deep end of the cut was near my elbow. I realized I was looking several inches into my arm, leaned forward, and vomited.

I squatted there for a minute, bent over and smelling my own puke. I felt cold and shivery all over. Shock.

"I don't think so," I said out loud. "I ain't dying this way."

I pulled the first aid kit off the front of the vest. I wrapped both battle dressings around my arm. It was awkward as hell doing it one handed. I had to tie the knots in the tails of the bandage with my teeth. The dressings turned dark with blood almost immediately, and the two of them together weren't even enough to cover the whole cut. The shallow end near my wrist was still open, but I hoped it would be enough to slow the bleeding down until I could figure something else out.

I skinned out of the coveralls and transferred a few items into my pockets: knife, flashlight, extra pistol mags. I shoved the Glock into my waistband and left the rest. I stood and started walking. Now instead of being dressed in a black tactical Ninja suit, I was wearing a T-shirt, jeans, partially melted boots, and had trauma dressings over a knife wound in my arm. I wasn't sure I was really much more inconspicuous, but it felt good not to be carrying all the weight.

I took a second to get my bearings. I was in a big field on the east side of the airport. Perfect. I forced myself to jog out to the road. I could hear plenty of sirens in the distance, but nothing close.

It was foggy and way too cold for just a sweat-soaked t-shirt. I wound my way through the light industrial area around the airport, hoping the map I'd committed to memory wasn't faulty. I felt woozy. It was hard to concentrate. I had to keep bringing myself back into focus.

Just when I had myself convinced that I was lost, that I'd been walking way too long and must have taken a wrong turn somewhere, or that Mandy's dad had let me down, there it was: my car.

I came around a corner and there was the white rental sedan. Or at least I hoped it was mine. Mandy's dad had texted the location and license plate to my phone. I couldn't remember the plate.

I walked up to the rear bumper, meant to squat, but halfway fell down instead. I took a second to collect myself and felt under the bumper. I pulled the strip of duct tape away and the key hit the pavement with a little metallic ting! that echoed up and down the streets. It was funny how sound traveled in the fog.

I managed to get the door unlocked. I leaned against the car and breathed deeply for a minute.

I realized I'd left a big bloody smear on the door. That wasn't going to help me be inconspicuous.

I sat down sideways in the driver's seat, my feet still on the pavement outside.

My vision started to get fuzzy around the edges. I leaned forward and it seemed to help. I guess because it brought more blood to my head. I had a vague idea that that suggested that maybe there wasn't enough blood in me to go around so everything could have its fair share.

I leaned sideways against the seat. Maybe if I just took a little nap, some kind of solution would occur to me. That sounded like a good idea and I thought about just letting my eyelids close.

Running footsteps echoed down the street and I sat up straight, listening. It was hard to tell how far away they were, or even what direction they were coming from. The fog again. The smart money was on starting the car and driving away. If it was a cop, I was screwed. If it was some citizen out jogging, he or she would see me, bloody and disheveled. Everybody carried a cell phone these days. My life had taken some directions I'd never expected lately, but I wasn't ready to take out some innocent jogger.

But I just sat there, listening, and there she was. Alex, jogging down the middle of the street with her EMT kit slung over her back. She ran up the car and stopped. She didn't even look all that out of breath.

"Dent?" She was standing there with her hands on her hips. I realized it was stupid for me to sit like that. I should hug her. Or something.

I stood up, just about pitched forward onto the concrete. She reached out and steadied me.

"Are you ok? What happened? Where's my dad?"

I focused on each question individually. "I'm not ok. I got stabbed and the plane blew up. I don't know where your dad is. We all ran out of the plane and got separated."

That had to be true, right? I made it out of the plane. Al would have only been a half a dozen steps behind me at most. Surely he was ok. He must have just been going in a different direction.

She lifted up my left hand, looked at my arm.

She hissed when she saw the wound. "You need to go to the hospital."

I shook my head. Big mistake. It made the world spin.

"No hospital. Cops." My words were slurred and my tongue felt thick.

She put her medical kit on the hood of the car and started to unzip it. "Here, at least let me…"

I cut her off, grabbed her arm. "No. We gotta go. Get a few miles away, then you can go to work."

I managed to stand, stagger around to passenger side, where I opened the door and fell into the seat.

"I think you should drive," I said.

She threw the medical kit in the back seat and climbed in.

As she started the car and pulled away from the curb, I cranked the heater all the way up. I was so cold. It was wonderful when the engine finally warmed up. I held my left hand up in front of one of the vents, trying to get some feeling back. I leaned my head against the glass of the window and passed out.

When I woke up we were somewhere dark. Alex was half straddling me.

"I really don't think this is the time Alex," I said and giggled.

"Shut up, Dent." Her voice was muffled and I realized she had a penlight in her mouth. She wrapped a rubber band around my right biceps. I felt the sharp poke of a needle.

"Ow!"

"Quit your complaining. Most of the people I do this to are dead."

One of her breasts was pressed against my cheek and she smelled good, so I just shut up. I tried to remember why I hadn't gone to bed with her that night.

Alex tied an IV bag to the headrest of my seat and plugged it into the needle in my arm. She shifted back into her seat and I sighed as she moved away. She wrapped my arm up in gauze.

"This is a poor way to treat a wound like that. You need a hospital."

I shook my head again. "Uh-uh. Not going back to jail."

"Dammit, Dent…"

"No. We gotta keep a low profile. Lay low for a few days." She swore and started the car. I realized we were in a dark parking lot behind a feed store. I managed to stay awake until we got on the freeway, then the drone of the tires and the hypnotic passing of the highway markers lulled me back to sleep again.

I woke up for little snippets of time: once as we pulled off the interstate and onto another road; again when Alex pulled off somewhere to change the IV bag; a third time when the car was braking hard and Alex swerved to avoid a pair of green glowing eyes bounding across the road. I got an impression of trees pressing in all around us.

Finally, we stopped. When I woke up we were in a garage somewhere. I could smell that musty garage smell but underneath it was the smell of the sea. It was still dark and she helped me out of the car. I remember thinking about how strong she was, then everything was black again.

CHAPTER THIRTY-FIVE

I came to in a bed, stripped to the waist. It was bright outside and Alex was hanging another IV bag off the headboard of the bed. Only this time the bag was a deep, rich red color and Alex had a piece of gauze wrapped around her arm.

"Good thing I'm a universal donor," Alex said.

"Huh?" My throat felt incredibly dry.

"Never mind."

"Where are we?" I asked.

"The beach house." She slid a needle into the IV line and I fell asleep again.

This time I must have been really asleep, instead of just passed out, because I dreamed, over and over again, about the dead girl I'd pulled out of the van at the airport. I'd pull her out and see Heather Swanson's face. I'd turn around and it was always somebody different, sometimes it was my mom, sometimes my dad. But there was always somebody there. They never said anything but they looked at me, and I could tell they thought I should have done better.

When I woke up, it was to a watery, rose-tinted light. I realized the sun was setting. I could smell the sea and hear the ocean faintly. The room was dim, the only light from the window. Alex sat in a chair, looking out the window with her long legs drawn up under her. A pump shotgun sat in a corner and her H&K and my Glock sat on the dresser.

I shifted and tried to speak. My throat was dry.

She stood and walked over to the bed, sat down on the edge. She had changed clothes. Now she wore a faded pair of jeans and an old thin t-shirt that had once had some sort of logo on it but was now lost to oblivion. She smelled clean, like soap.

She picked up a glass of water, held it to my lips. "Here. You're dehydrated from the blood loss."

I drank it greedily. It tasted wonderful. "Are we clean?" I managed to croak.

She set the glass on the nightstand and nodded. "Yeah. We're clean. I've got the car parked in the garage. I turned my cell phone off so nobody can track it. We got in after dark last night. The houses on both sides are empty. The Lindemans are usually in Florida this time of year. The other house is a rental and no one is there."

I looked at my arm. It was bandaged with fresh gauze and I could see the end of a row of neat stitches.

"You do good work," I said.

"Yeah. It's been a while since I had a live person to practice on."

She filled up the glass from a pitcher and popped a pill in my mouth. "Here, antibiotics. I've got a couple of days' worth stashed away, then we'll have to find you some more."

I swallowed the pill and drained the rest of the water. I propped myself up on the pillow and stared at her. The t-shirt was thin and it was obvious she wore nothing underneath. I caught myself staring, managed to make myself stop for a couple of seconds, then caught myself doing it again. She laughed.

"You seem to be feeling better."

I felt myself blush in a way I hadn't since I'd been a teenager. I tried to think of something smart to say. Should I apologize? The frank stare she was giving me back seemed to say no.

Stare or no stare, it took me at least a little by surprise when she swung a leg over me and straddled me with a long, denim covered thigh on either side of me. She leaned over and kissed me. Her hair cascaded down over both of us. It was still damp from the shower. I kissed her back with both eagerness and nervousness I hadn't felt since I was in high school.

It seemed natural for my hands to fall on her hips, and from there to slide up over the soft skin of her stomach. I could feel muscles rippling underneath. I slid my hands up her sides, just to the point where I could feel her ribs under my hands and she pulled up abruptly. I thought for half a second that I'd somehow gone too far, but she pulled the shirt over her head and flung it in a corner.

I let out a breath at the sight of her, and then she leaned over and started kissing me again. I couldn't remember the last time I'd gotten this turned on this quickly. My jeans were getting uncomfortable. I shifted to relieve some of the pressure.

Alex gave a wicked laugh, reached down to stroke me through my jeans.

"You seem to be feeling much better."

I was trying to make some kind of witty comment about her bedside manner but forgot all about it as she undid my pants. I forgot about saying anything, forgot about the bad dreams and destruction. I just buried my fingers in her hair and shut my eyes.

Later, I lay on my back with my left arm propped up on a pillow and Alex wrapped around my right side. I couldn't quit running my hands over her. It was almost like I couldn't believe she was really there and had to keep touching her to make sure she hadn't disappeared. She didn't seem to mind.

"I'm worried about my dad," she whispered.

"Me too," I said. I kept replaying those last few seconds in the plane. I hadn't seen Al get out. I'd been too busy getting clear. But he couldn't have been more than a few steps behind me. Al had been through so much, surely he wasn't going to go like that.

"What are we going to do next?" she asked.

"Lay low. Figure out some kind of contingency plan in case Todd's people find us here. Wait for your dad to figure out where we must have gone. He's going to figure out that we're here sooner or later."

Al and Alex ran the beach house as a rental, so it was registered to a limited liability corporation, not to them personally. It wasn't bulletproof, but Todd's people wouldn't find it unless they knew to look for it.

"What if we don't hear from him?"

"Let's give it a couple of days, then we'll see what happens."

"Ok."

She wasn't happy with that answer. I didn't blame her. I wasn't either. But she curled up closer to me and held me a little tighter. I just lay there and held her back, wishing that moment could go on forever.

The next two days passed like they were a dream, a good dream for a change. The house was stocked with food, and in a metal cabinet down in the basement was a shotgun, a couple of pistols and several grand in cash.

I slept. The blood loss from the arm wound left me feeling wiped out. My feet had some minor burns. It was a good thing I'd been wearing heavy leather boots, or I'd be walking around on stumps. I was also sore from head to toe from the van crash, and having Mickey land on me.

When I was awake, Alex was always near. I lost track of the number of times we made love. It was like we were both making up for lost time, and reminding ourselves that we were alive.

"We should have done this a long time ago," she said after one time.

"Yeah," I said.

She rolled over on her elbows to look at me. "Why didn't we?"

"Well… There was Audrey."

She blew hair out of her face. "Yeah. But what about before Audrey."

I shrugged. "I dunno. I guess it was hard for me in a way because you were Al's daughter."

She laughed. "Dad always wanted us to get together. He was glad you left the night you took me home when I was drunk though."

"You told him about that?"

"Of course. He's my dad."

I thought about my dad. I hadn't even been able to tell him I wanted to play electric guitar, much less about any of my girlfriends. I resolved that if I ever had a daughter, I wanted to be the same kind of father as Al.

She snuggled over close to me. "I'm just glad we're together now."

"Yeah."

Early in the evening of the second day, I was dozing on the couch when Alex woke me up. The house didn't have a TV, but it did have a radio.

"Hey, wake up. You have to hear this." She put the little portable radio on the glass coffee table and I stared at the speaker the way people always do when they are concentrating on a radio, like that will help them hear better.

"… statement from Portland Area FBI Office, Special Agent In Charge Brock Wheedon."

There was a moment of silence as the broadcast cut over, then a rustling sound and some murmurs. It made me think of a big room full of reporters with a microphone on a podium.

I didn't have much use for most Feds. Brock Wheedon was no exception. He'd gone to some big school back East. Harvard? Yale? Something like that. I'd always gotten the impression he was in the Bureau to punch his ticket before he started a political career or went into some kind of big business, not because he liked to put criminals in jail.

He had one hell of a speaking voice though.

"Good evening, ladies and gentlemen of the press," he began in polished, dulcet tones. Yeah, I could see him running for Senate or something. "I'd like to make a brief statement about our investigation into the terrorist attack at the Albany Oregon airport two days ago. After that, I'll take questions, but I have to caution you that the investigation is still developing."

"Early in the morning on the 23rd, local law enforcement agencies responded to a report of heavy automatic gunfire coming from the Cascade Aviation terminal at the Albany airport. As you know, Cascade Aviation is a civilian aviation contractor that provides various services to the United States government in support of the Global War on Terror. As the officers were arriving, they witnessed a massive explosion, caused by a fuel tank fire onboard one of Cascade's C-130 Hercules Transport planes."

"Our multi-agency investigation began as soon as the scene was safe, with the Federal Bureau of Investigation taking the role of the lead agency. We discovered that eight members of Cascade Aviation had been killed. Five were crew members on the airplane. Two were employees on the ground crew. The eighth was a young woman who was working as a temporary overseas worker for another civilian contractor who was killed in the crossfire."

I pictured the girl I'd hauled out of the van. They were saying she was working some kind of overseas job and was just being transported by Cascade. By their warped point of view, it was even true, sort of.

"Additionally, we recovered six other bodies, all of which were burned. Through forensic analysis, we've managed to identify two of them. The first is Ibrim Al Mohammad. The second is Fayed Bin Mussalli. Both men are known to the intelligence services of the United States to be members of Islamofascist groups dedicated to committing acts of violence against American interests. We are still working to identify the other subjects."

"The inevitable conclusion is that these men were engaged in a terrorist attack on American soil. Why they chose Cascade Aviation, in particular, is part of our ongoing investigation."

There was a whine in my ears that I recognized as my blood pressure heading for the stratosphere. My hands were clenched so hard I was in danger of popping a stitch in my arm. I tried to make myself relax.

The press conference continued. The reporters asked the predictable questions. Wheedon gave the usual answers, doing an excellent job of saying nothing with the maximum number of words possible.

Alex looked at me, wide-eyed. "What the hell is going on?"

"Todd and his friends at Cascade aviation were exporting American women to the Middle East and bringing Middle Eastern men to the United States, maybe so the CIA could interrogate them, maybe for... what? Who the hell knows? Anyway, we blew the lid off their little operation, but somebody has enough clout to screw with the investigation enough to get it declared a terrorist attack. It wouldn't be the first time an FBI investigation has turned up exactly what somebody wanted it to."

She chewed on that for a minute. The press conference ended and after a few minutes of vapid analysis, the radio station went back to its regular programming.

Alex shut it off. "How many prisoners were there on the plane?" She asked.

"Five, six. I'm not sure." We had discussed the raid.

I'd left out some of the details, but she'd hammered me pretty hard to pin down facts about where her dad had been when I'd last seen him, where everybody had been positioned. She didn't seem to blame me for not knowing whether Al had made it out or not. I wanted that to make it easier not to blame myself, but it wasn't working out that way.

She nodded, satisfied by that. "Then that accounts for all the unidentified bodies." She left unspoken that she was assuming that her father wasn't one of the burned corpses.

I wasn't so sure. The report said five members of the aircrew had been killed. I counted in my head: the guy on the ramp; the two guys trying to break out the side door; the guy getting his ass kicked by the prisoners; and the guy on the flight deck stairs. That made five. The problem with that math was that the two guys trying to break out the side door had been alive the last time I'd seen them, and perfectly capable of making it out the door of the plane.

Or maybe they had made it out, and maybe they'd been killed to tie up loose ends. They could blow holes in the "Middle Eastern Terrorist Attack" theory. Maybe Al was in that group too. If they could screw with the reality of what happened, they could screw with the body count too.

But I didn't say anything to Alex about that. Either Al was alive or he wasn't. Time would tell.

That night Alex went shopping. She managed to find me some clothes, and another pair of shoes to replace my melted boots. She walked up to a restaurant in town and called a cab from there. We'd taken one look at the inside of the rental car and nixed the idea of driving it. The inside was covered with blood, more than we could hope to clean up or cover up. So in addition to our other problem, we needed wheels.

I sat on the couch the whole time she was gone, shotgun on my lap. I kept telling myself that everything was fine, that there was no way Todd's people could have tracked us down to Lincoln City. They were probably still reeling and doing damage control.

But I was still relieved when she walked back in the door, carrying my clothes, fresh groceries and some takeout from a restaurant in town. She hadn't been able to find one thing I'd really wanted: a pair of pay as you go cellular phones. The beach house had a landline and Alex still had her cell phone but I didn't want to use those if we didn't have to.

We ate dinner that night, and I knew things had changed. The last day and a half had been almost like a little vacation. Alex and I had been hanging out, enjoying each other, making love, playing board games, reading next to each other on the couch, trying to keep our worries at arm's length. That wasn't going to last much longer.

After dinner, we went for a short walk on the beach. I made it about a hundred yards and had to sit down. I was still weak and my feet hurt from the burns. As I hobbled back to the house, I tried not to think about what would happen if Todd's people found us and we had to fight.

We were both quiet and subdued when we went to bed that night.

"We need to figure something out tomorrow," she said.

"I know."

I stared at the ceiling for most of the night, trying to figure out what that might be.

I cooked breakfast the next morning. This was going to be our last day of domestic bliss, and I intended to make the most of it. I was just sliding the scrambled eggs out of the skillet when the doorbell rang.

I turned the stove off and grabbed the shotgun from where I had leaned it in the corner by the china hutch. My Glock was stuffed in the back of my pants. Alex came out of the bathroom, her H&K in her hand.

I handed her the shotgun. My left hand was still too week for me to trust it with racking the shotgun. I looked out the window beside the door. A bored-looking kid in a Fed-Ex outfit stood on the porch, holding a package and cracking his gum.

A Fed-Ex guy. That was about the most common ruse to get somebody you wanted to come to the door. I'd used it myself more than a few times, although my real favorite was a mini-van with a "Lottery Prize Committee" magnetic sign and a bunch of balloons.

Alex stood in the corner of the living room with the shotgun. I stood to one side of the door.

"How can I help you?" I said through the door.

"Delivery for Pace." The kid sounded bored as hell. I replayed the image of him I'd seen. Maybe early twenties, if not younger, long stringy hair. Acne. If he'd been a guy in his early to mid-thirties with a high and tight hair cut I wouldn't have even answered, or I would have considered putting a round through the door.

"Who from?"

There was a pause as if he had to sound the words out for himself.

"Sez it's from an Al Pace. Look, can I get you to sign for this, I have some more deliveries to make before I go to class."

From Al. Maybe.

"Can I get you to leave it on the porch? I'm not dressed."

"You have to sign for all Fed-Ex packages." Asshole. The kid didn't say it but I could practically hear him thinking it.

"Ok. Hang on a sec, I'm not dressed." I gave that a second to sink in and create the impression that it would be a while before I would open the door, then immediately opened the door.

The kid jumped back in surprise. I looked at his hands first: a package and one of those electronic clipboard thingies they use these days. Then I looked around behind him. Nothing. Nobody moving. Nothing but a FedEx minivan.

The kid looked me up and down, saw that I was fully dressed and then looked at me like I was crazy. He thrust the clipboard forward.

I signed and he gave me the package, a cardboard mailer about the size of a hardcover book and not very heavy. The shipping label looked legit.

"Have a good 'un," he muttered and took off.

There was still a possibility that he was a legit Fed-Ex guy, but that the package wasn't. Alex started to walk forward and I motioned her back. I stepped in the kitchen, took a deep breath and opened the package.

Instead of an explosion, I got a TracPhone and a copy of Where the Wild Things Are.

I realized Alex was peeking around the corner. She walked in and grabbed the phone.

"That was my favorite book when I was a kid," she said. She turned the phone on.

"There's a number programmed in." She punched it. There were a few seconds of silence.

"Daddy?"

Then she started crying.

CHAPTER THIRTY-SIX

I listened to Alex talk to her dad for a couple of minutes. The conversation mostly consisted of her asking him over and over again if he was OK and alternately crying and laughing. It wasn't until she handed the phone to me that I realized I was crying a little too.

"Dent, are you taking good care of my daughter?" His voice sounded a little rough, but it was the same old Al.

That question stopped me cold for a second, as I reviewed some of the last two days' activities in my mind. I swallowed.

"Uh, yeah," I said.

"Good. I'm glad she was with you. Listen, have you heard any of the press on this?"

"Yeah. I caught Wheedon's press conference."

"I don't have to tell you this thing blew up in our faces, but the bottom line is, those girls are safe."

I breathed out a breath. At least it hadn't all been for nothing.

"Good. How's everybody else?"

"Bolle, Eddie and myself have some bumps and bruises, but we'll live."

"What about Todd? What about the cops?"

"Marshall has Todd on a tight leash and the FBI is doing what they are told. Everybody seems to find the story that this is a terrorist attack very convenient right now. There is no heat that I can tell. We're all clean of surveillance. I sent the phone to you that way because I figured you wouldn't use it unless it looked like I'd taken some basic precautions."

You got that right, I thought.

"So where do we go now?" I asked.

"This thing with Cascade is going to take time to develop. Bolle is flying cover for us. I'm actually a little worried about you personally."

"How's that?"

"The Bureau is having a review hearing for you at 1300 this afternoon. If you don't show up they're going to fire you," Al said.

"Al, I got framed up, tasered and arrested. I'm getting fired no matter what."

The thought of going back to my job at the Police Bureau seemed ludicrous right now. It seemed like it had been a lifetime since I had been a homicide detective. I guess if I did go back, I'd have a unique perspective on people who tried to cover up homicides.

"Look," Al said. "The word is that they are willing to settle with you, let you resign. The Bureau has been gun shy about this whole thing ever since Mandy woke up and fingered Marshall as the guy who attacked her. You're not going to be able to keep your job, but you don't have to walk out with your hat in your hand either. I've got a lawyer here standing by, he's a good guy. You need to come in."

I looked at my watch.

"The only car we've got is covered in blood." I looked down at myself. "And right now I'm wearing a pair of jeans and a sweatshirt with a cute little sea otter on it."

"Eddie is on his way already. He can get you to your house, get you changed and on your way to the meeting with time to spare. He'll be there in an hour and a half."

I couldn't argue with that. It was Al. "Ok."

"I'll meet you at your house." Al clicked off.

"Eddie will be here in about an hour and a half to take us back to Portland so I can be officially unemployed," I said to Alex.

"Well, come here then. I've got a job that will last you until he gets here." She grabbed my hand and dragged me towards the bedroom.

When Big Eddie showed up, he was as nattily attired as ever, this time in a dove gray double-breasted suit. The only thing ruining his image was the big bandage on the back of his neck.

"Got a little sunburn," was all he would say when I asked about it.

Sooner or later, we would all have to give our accounts of the aftermath of the disaster in the airplane. But not today. Eddie was driving the blandest looking late model minivan possible. I enjoyed sitting in the middle seat, holding Alex's hand and watching the scenery roll by.

The drive through the Coast Range was nice anytime. The mountains looked magical, otherworldly that day as they poked out of the fog. The forests looked like they had to hold some kind of secret. I realized it had been a long time since I'd been camping or hiking. Audrey had never liked to go much.

I looked over to Alex with new appreciation, thinking she'd probably be up for a little hiking and camping. Cool.

All too soon we were back in Portland, and pulling up to my house. Al's car was parked out front. He was the only other person that had a key to the place. Alex and I got out of the van. Eddie stayed behind the wheel. As we were getting out, he looked at his watch.

"Tick tock, man," he said.

"Yeah, I know." I was going to have to hurry.

Al was waiting by the door when we walked in. He wrapped Alex up in a big hug before letting go of her and shaking my hand. Then he did a sort of double take, looked from me to her, and somehow I knew that he knew. I felt myself blush again.

But he just grabbed her with one arm and me with another and hugged us both. I felt my eyes tear up again.

"It's good to see you two. Especially together." I didn't know what to say to that.

He looked at me. "You need to get ready, my friend."

I left them in my living room, such as it was. Alex was nice and didn't say anything about its barrenness. I made a mental note to buy some furniture.

As I shaved, I ran the numbers in my head. I'd checked all my accounts right before everything went to hell. I had enough money to live off of for a couple, three years, maybe more if I played it cool and stuck with bologna sandwiches. I could go back to school, open a bar, something like that.

I normally wasn't much of a clothes guy, but every year I went to one of those men's stores with a few hundred bucks and had them set me up with a pair of new suits, shirts and ties and such. I kept four suits around, and every time I bought something new, I'd retire the oldest pair to Goodwill. It kept me looking good for court. I had no fashion sense, but I knew that showing up to testify in last decade's lime green leisure suit wasn't a good way to build respect from a jury.

As I knotted my tie, I thought about how things had changed. A month ago the thought of being unemployed and having to burn through my life's savings would have given me heart palpitations. Now I was just looking forward to some time off. Maybe I could talk Alex into going camping with me. It was the rainy season, but that was what snuggling up in tents was for.

I checked myself in a mirror. I looked good. I had a bad moment when I realized I wouldn't be able to carry a weapon into the meeting, but I shoved it out of my mind. Al had shown every intention of coming, and Eddie would be driving. I knew they would both be packing heat.

There was another guy in the living room when I came out. Young guy, mid-thirties wearing a suit, with an expensive-looking haircut and an even more expensive looking briefcase. He looked pretty yuppie except for the long scar down one side of his face. Al introduced him.

"Hamilton Yost. Formerly of the US Navy, now of the Oregon Bar."

Interesting. Whatever Mr. Yost had done in the Navy, it probably wasn't chipping paint by the look of him. We walked out to the van. Al and Yost rode in the back.

Yost talked to me as we went, talking about evidence procedures, arbitration, union contracts. I listened, mostly. I nodded at the right places and tried to sound intelligent, but it was hard to focus. For one thing, I was still exhausted, more mentally than physically. I was looking forward to sleeping for a week. For another thing, I just wanted it done. I wanted to go home, buy furniture for my house, play my guitars, hang out with Alex.

It didn't seem to take very long to get to Central precinct, or maybe it was just because I'd zoned out for half the trip. Eddie pulled up into the loading zone in front and Yost, Al, Alex and I all got out.

Alex linked arms with her dad. "I'm going to take this old fart out for a cup of coffee. We'll meet you when you're done." She dropped the Tracphone into my hand, kissed me on the lips and walked off with her dad.

Yost stared at her a little as she walked away, but hell, I couldn't blame him. He caught himself and turned to me.

"You ready?"

"Let's do it." I motioned for him to go ahead.

I walked into Central Precinct for what I figured would be the last time. We had to spend 1% of all building costs for art in the city of Portland. The Central Precinct lobby's nod to the arts was some glass things that looked like upside-down mixing bowls. I saw the two deep cracks running along the marble floor where the records department had tried to save a couple of bucks by moving a giant, fireproof safe themselves.

I usually took the stairs, but this time we took the elevator to save some wear and tear on my feet. Lubbock, Winter, and the same HR guy from last time were all waiting for us in the conference room. They looked like they hadn't moved since the last time I'd been here.

Lubbock looked tired, and pale, almost like he was ill. Yost set his briefcase down on the table and Lubbock jumped. I wondered what the hell had gotten into him.

I sat down and we all just looked at each other for a minute. I was surprised to see Lubbock. Usually, if somebody was fired, it was done by at least a captain or commander, maybe even a deputy chief, maybe even more than one, if you were unpopular and everybody wanted to get in on the feeding frenzy.

I took the fact that it was just Lubbock as a sign that nobody above him wanted to be associated with this firing. Interesting.

Lubbock broke the silence first. "I know this is uncomfortable for all of us, so I'll cut right to it. In return for your release of all claims against the city, and an agreement that you will surrender your state certifications and never work as a police officer again, the city will accept your resignation, and drop all current criminal charges against you."

He slid a piece of paper across the table for me. There were little sticky notes helpfully placed near where I was to sign.

"So you want me to quit, get no severance pay, never work as a cop again, and not sue you?" I asked.

Lubbock nodded. He seemed relieved that I understood.

"Would you like a blow job too?"

Lubbock reddened. Winter's mouth compressed to a fine line. Yost leaned forward.

"What my client means is this," he said. "We are prepared to pursue wrongful prosecution, civil rights and excessive force issues with the city. Additionally, your threats of criminal proceedings are fantasies. The victim of the alleged assault has identified another suspect. You're going to have to do better than that."

It went back and forth from there. In the end, I walked out with more than I would have expected: almost a year's pay, no prosecution, and I didn't have to surrender my certifications.

I signed the forms. I stood up, put my copy in my suit pocket and headed for the door. Lubbock opened his mouth like he was going to say something, but I just kept going. I avoided the temptation to make some kind of parting shot, and anything he had to say wasn't important to me anymore.

So I just left. The door to the conference room swung shut behind me and I realized the precinct didn't feel like home to me anymore. It was just another building.

CHAPTER THIRTY-SEVEN

I shook Yost's hand in the elevator.

"Thanks." I meant it too. I had always figured if you got fired you were just out on your ear. I was actually walking away with something. Al had hooked me up again.

I picked up the phone, dialed Alex. She picked up on the first ring.

"Miss me?" I asked.

"Yes. Meet you out front?"

"Sure."

The sun was out when we stepped out. Al and Alex were waiting for me. Yost made his farewells, claiming he had to be at the courthouse. Alex put her hand around my waist and we walked down the sidewalk towards where Eddie waited by the curb with the van. Al was in the lead.

"So now what?" Alex asked.

"Rest," I said. "I'm tired."

She never got to reply. I stumbled then, my burned feet finally declaring that they had had enough. I almost pulled her over with me, steadied myself just in time.

Something whispered past my ear. Then the back of Al's head exploded.

I heard the sharp crack of the supersonic bullet passing us, but the sound of the rifle shot was oddly muffled and flat. We hit the ground and I covered Alex's body with my own. A second round hit the sidewalk beside us, throwing chips of concrete into my cheek and left eye. There was no cover anywhere. I just did my best to cover Alex up, hoped that whoever was doing the shooting would be satisfied with plugging me, and that the round wouldn't go through my body.

But the third shot never came. I realized Alex was screaming, trying to squirm out from under me to get to her dad.

I could barely see, but I could tell Al was dead. I'd seen it before: high velocity rifle to the head. I pulled Alex back and even more hell broke loose.

Big Eddie came running up, Glock in hand, and damn near got shot by the posse of cops that came boiling out of the front of Central Precinct. They had him cuffed and on the ground before I could protest that he wasn't the shooter. I hustled Alex inside, almost dragging her. I wanted her inside, under cover in case the sniper wasn't really gone.

Over the next few hours all the usual stuff happened. We told our stories a half a dozen times. I finally got it straightened out that Eddie hadn't shot anybody. They held him in a cell until somebody verified his Department of Justice credentials. I had my eye cleaned out by the EMTs.

Alex had skinned her knees and hands when I pushed her down. The EMTs cleaned her up and left. She was still shaking.

Al had been a legend in the Bureau. So now the command staff found itself in a real pickle. He had been assassinated in front of Police Headquarters in the company of his beloved daughter and a freshly fired rogue cop. They were doing their best to extend her every courtesy and pretend like I didn't exist.

Finally Alex had enough. She looked at the sea of Captains, Commanders, and Deputy Chiefs hovering around her and said, "Would you people just leave me the hell alone?" It worked. They were out in a heartbeat. One of the Deputy Chiefs shot me an evil look. I all but dared him to try to tell me to leave the room. I wanted very much to hit someone.

I walked over, held her. She leaned against me and didn't say anything for awhile.

"You going to be ok?" It was a stupid thing for me to ask.

"Just take me home," was all she said.

I found Eddie talking on the phone with one hand and trying to put his shoelaces back in his shoes with the other. He snapped the phone shut when we walked in.

"A guy will be here with a car for you two in a couple of minutes. There's some equipment you'll want in the trunk." Eddie's eyes looked different. There was no happy go lucky demeanor left in him. I felt myself go cold as I looked at him. I wondered if that look was the last thing some people saw.

"I need some people on Alex's house," I said. It would have felt good to be all macho and decide I would protect her myself, but I could barely walk and I was exhausted. A troop of girl scouts could have probably walked up on me just then and garroted me with their neckerchiefs.

He nodded. "They'll be there before you."

"Good people," I said, thinking of Mickey.

"I'd trust them with my sister. I'll be there myself later. But I have some stuff I gotta do."

"Ok."

We went out the back way. The second we stepped out the door, a Suburban pulled up and two hard asses got out. One of them handed me the keys before walking back to the identical Suburban idling behind it and getting in the back seat.

Alex got in. I ignored the honking traffic and looked in the back. I pulled a gym bag out and brought its comforting weight with me to the front seat.

Alex was silent all the way to her house. I didn't know what to say so I just kept my mouth shut. I counted four cars full of Eddie's hard asses on her street. They weren't even trying to be covert. Good.

I parked in front, started to turn the engine off.

"I really just would like to be alone right now, Dent," she said, staring straight ahead.

I put my hand on hers. "Ok. Give me a call when you want me to come over."

She pulled her hand away. "Dent, for right now, just stay away."

With that, she got out, strode to her front door, and vanished inside the house.

I didn't know what else to do, so I went home. I drove slow, dreading walking into my empty house. The sky was the color of lead.

I rolled up to my house, parked behind my pickup. I pulled a Glock out of the bag, checked the chamber before I stuffed it in my waistband. I had plenty of guns in the house, but right now I wanted one for the fifty foot walk to my front door.

The street was deserted and quiet. The loudest thing was my shuffling feet on the concrete as I walked up my sidewalk to the front door.

I put my key in the lock, pushed open the door, and my house exploded.

CHAPTER THIRTY-EIGHT

It's funny what can save your life sometimes.

Even as I was opening the door, I smelled gasoline. The smell hit me just as I was registering that it was harder to open the front door than it should have been.

I jerked back from the opening.

They did a sloppy job. They had it rigged to blow before the door opened all the way, so the door protected me from the jet of hot burning gas. I lost my eyebrows and the hair on my arm, but little else. If I'd taken a direct hit, it would have been different.

The front windows blew out, covering me with broken glass as I rolled across the front lawn. I came to my feet and checked myself. There were some superficial cuts, and the stitches on my arm were oozing blood, but there was nothing too bad. I couldn't believe it, so I checked myself again.

All I could see through the front windows was flames. I stood there for a few seconds watching my house burn, cataloging all the things inside.

I guessed putting off buying furniture was going to turn out to be a smart move after all. Then one thing popped to mind, and I started running to the back yard.

I knew it was stupid, but I wasn't going to let the bastards win completely. I made it to the back of the house and saw that the basement wasn't burning. The grade sloped back here, so the back door was on the basement level. I took one of my lawn chairs, busted out the window closest to the door.

I knocked out all the shards of glass with the Glock and stuck my head inside. The window wasn't big enough for me to crawl into, but it was big enough for me to stick my head inside and see that the basement wasn't rigged to blow the way the upstairs had been. I wasn't going through that again.

The basement door handle spun all the way around and the door opened without me using a key. That solved the mystery of how they'd gotten in. They'd punched out the lock. There were muddy footprints leading to the stairs. Bastards.

The air down here was clear still, but the smell of smoke was heavy. The fire above me was roaring like a beast and I could feel the air rushing in from the door I'd just opened to feed the flames above. I'd read once that fires double in size every thirty seconds.

I bypassed the gun safes and walked over to my guitar closet. My hands weren't even shaking as I undid the padlock on the door. My Strat was in its case, just inside the door. I picked it up and felt some small measure of victory. I dithered for a minute, trying to decide if I should grab another guitar or two, or maybe try to get in one of the gun safes.

There was an ominous cracking sound from above.

Quit while you're ahead.

I ran out of the house, and around to the front door. I never looked back as I put the guitar in my pickup, behind the seat. I pulled the duffel bag full of guns out of the Suburban. I figured it might come in handy.

I was proud that my pickup fired right up, the first time. I loved that old beast. Taking the Suburban had never even crossed my mind. As I pulled away from the curb my neighbors were coming out on their porches, staring at me as I drove past. I could hear the sirens in the background.

I left the city limits of Portland the same way I entered it the first time, all those years ago, on Interstate 5, with an old pickup and an even older guitar and very little else. I could see the plume of smoke from my burning house for quite a while, but finally, I lost it in the hills.

It was raining, so I settled into the right lane and went the speed limit. I flipped on the radio and spun the dial. Jimi Hendrix. All Along the Watchtower. An omen if I'd ever heard one.

I had a tank full of gas and a decent classic rock station, so I just drove. It had been way too long since I'd gone on a road trip, just driving for the sake of driving.

Every time it occurred to me that I had some deciding to do, I'd just decide to drive some more. Almost three hours later, I reached the point where I had to decide. The Junction City exit was a mile ahead. My feet were killing me, my arm hurt, I had to pee, and I had a quarter tank of gas, but that wasn't what was going to drive the decision.

The exit came up, and I drove on, perfectly balanced between taking it and not taking it for most of the exit lane. Finally, I swerved over, took the exit.

I got gas, took a leak, and bought a cup of bad coffee at a gas station just off the exit. The old geezer behind the counter looked askance at my torn and muddy suit but didn't hesitate to give me directions to the cemetery. Maybe he thought I was late for a funeral.

The cemetery was a pretty place, even with most of the trees bare. I had to hunt around for a while but eventually, I found her.

I knew I was getting close when a white sedan passed me on one of the cemetery roads. The woman behind the wheel paid me no mind. If she thought of it at all, she probably thought the truck belonged to one of the maintenance crews. But I damn near ran off the road. Heather had looked just like a younger version of the woman behind the wheel.

I pulled into the spot where the car had just left, got out and looked. There it was in the distance, a fresh grave, the ground still disturbed.

My feet hurt and I had to stop and rest twice before I got to Heather's grave, but that gave me a chance to find a good stone. It was round and smooth, white and shot through with blue veins. The sort of thing a girl younger than Heather might have gathered and kept in a drawer somewhere.

I stood over her grave and remembered.

I remembered finding her, remembered carrying her up the hill, how small she'd seemed.

I remembered pulling the trigger on Marshall, and no matter how hard I looked I couldn't find a shred of remorse inside myself.

But then I remembered Todd, and his crowd, all the people at Cascade Aviation, Marshall's father. Maybe I hadn't closed the case at all. Maybe there was still some work left.

Then I thought about Al.

I wondered who would put stones on his grave.

Al was dead, and in some ways, Alex was too. The old Alex died the second the sniper pulled the trigger and killed her dad right in front of her. The new Alex would always be a person who had seen her dad shot down and turned into a piece of meat on the pavement. I wondered who that person would be.

I gave Heather's grave one last look, put the rock on her headstone.

Maybe I'd be back with more.

I limped back to the truck, soaked to the bone. Right now all I owned was a pickup truck, a vintage guitar, and a bag full of guns and I liked it. I felt free for the first time in a long time.

I drove back through town, towards the interstate. Again I was just driving to be driving, seeing where my nose took me. I drifted towards the interstate, where I'd have to decide. North or South. Back towards Portland, or somewhere else.

I flipped on the radio, found a folk and bluegrass show. Bob Dylan's version of "Fixin To Die" rattled out of the old speakers in the truck. Originally by Bukka White, it had come to Bob via Ralph Stanley. It seemed as good a song as any right now.

Right or left. North or South. Portland or somewhere else.

I thought about Heather, with only one stone on her grave. I thought about Al, bleeding in front of the Police station where he'd spent so many years helping people.

I thought about Alex, screaming underneath me, just wanting to get to her father. I thought about Todd, huddling behind the scope of a sniper rifle.

I took the northbound lane. Back towards Portland.

Check out *Rose City Renegade, Dent Miller Thriller #2,* available now!

Did you enjoy *Rose City Free Fall*? Please leave a review.

Join the Dent Miller Army Mailing List and receive a free Dent Miller short story! Click here to join.

We promise not to spam your inbox. We'll email you a few times a year, when there is a new DL Barbur book release, or we have something interesting to say.

Get in touch via dlbarbur.com or on Facebook.

Made in the USA
Monee, IL
20 February 2021